BREAKING CHAOS

Praise for

THE CHASING GRAVES TRILOGY

"Galley's descriptive prose is simplistically beautiful."
—FANTASY FACTION

"To say that the concept of *Chasing Graves* is grimdark would be an understatement... The world building is fantastic and reminiscent of Michael Moorcock's Elric series."
—GRIMDARK MAGAZINE

"Dark, tense and surprisingly hilarious."
—LAURA M. HUGHES, AUTHOR OF *DANSE MACABRE*

"There's serious grounds here for building something spectacular."
—EMMA DAVIS, FANTASY BOOK REVIEW

"*Chasing Graves* might well be one of the best releases not only for December but for the entirety of 2018."
—BOOKNEST

"Galley's writing is both simple and elegant, with lovely turns of phrases and clever metaphors and puns... a great first book to a series I sincerely can't wait to complete."
—NOVEL NOTIONS

"The writing was smooth, fluid and beautiful at times. It never failed to create an awesome atmosphere. A solid book with a very interesting premise. 90/100."

—THE WEATHERWAX REPORT

"Galley has created a fascinating world that feels rife with stories that could be mined across multiple series. Its history is rich with detail and there're so many avenues to be explored."

—ADAM WELLER, FANTASY BOOK REVIEW

"*Chasing Graves* is a dark, compelling entry into a trilogy."

—ROCKSTARLIT BOOKASYLUM

"Unique, fantastic worldbuilding, interesting characters, and much more."

—THE FANTASY INN

"A heavy hitter, this follow-up to a gruesome, sometimes funny, and riveting tale, Grim Solace is a runaway winner."

—GRIMMEDIAN

BEN GALLEY

BREAKING CHAOS

THE CHASING GRAVES TRILOGY | 3

"This book is a work of fiction, but some works of fiction contain perhaps more truth than first intended, and therein lies the magic."
– Anonymous

BCHB1 First Edition 2022
ISBN: 978-1-8381625-9-7
Published by BenGalley.com

Edited by Andrew Lowe & Laura M. Hughes
Map Design by Ben Galley
Cover Illustration by Félix Ortiz
Cover Design & Interior Layout by STK·Kreations

For Lily

BREAKING CHAOS

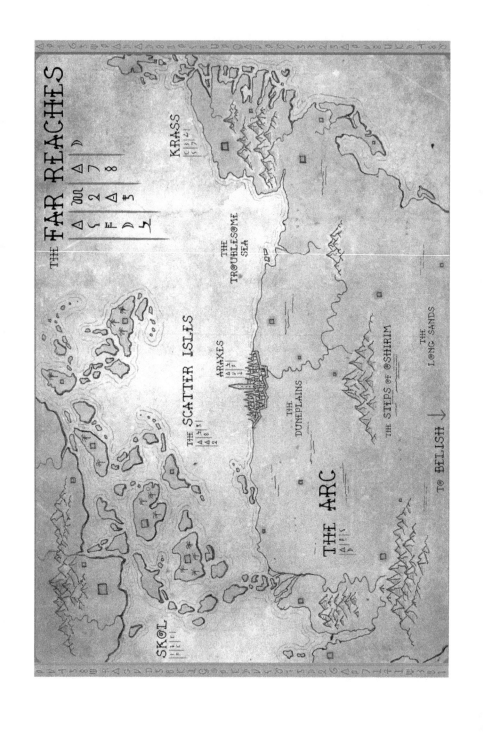

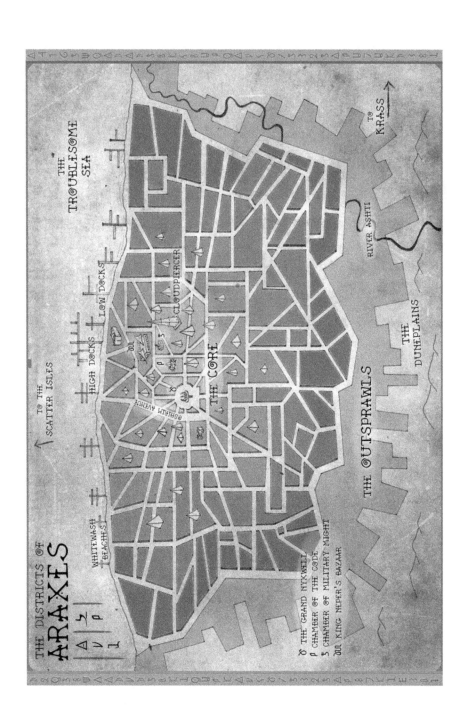

TENETS OF THE BOUND DEAD

They must die in turmoil.
They must be bound with copper half-coin and water of the Nyx.
They must be bound within forty days.
They shall be bound to whomever holds their coin.
They are slaved to their master's bidding.
They must bring their masters no harm.
They shall not express opinions nor own property.
They shall never know freedom unless it is gifted to them.

CHAPTER 1
THE SLATHERGHAST

What if the Nyx were to dry up? The question
has perplexed many a scholar and thinker since
the dawn of the Arctian Empire. You may as
well ask an Arctian, "What if the Duneplains
freeze over?" Nobody has ever needed to answer
such a preposterous question.

FROM 'A REACH HISTORY' BY GAERVIN JUBB

NILITH CAME AWAKE WITH A start so violent she slammed her head against the bars of the cage and knocked herself out afresh.

It was perhaps another hour before she woke again; groggy and head pounding. She kept her eyes shut and probed with her senses instead.

There had been many occasions on her quest where Nilith had awoken aching, bewildered, knowing some great evil was nearby. Far too many times, in fact, and here she was once more. She was growing rather exhausted with it. She would have sighed, but there was a quiet to her surroundings she did not want to shatter.

Nilith pieced together her situation.

She was on her back.

A rough wooden surface jiggled beneath her, hot with the sun every time her cheek rolled onto a fresh portion.

She was clothed, or so it seemed. Every brush of the fabric felt like the scuttling of insects.

Somebody whistled nearby, faintly and tunelessly.

There was a stench, too. Maybe hers.

And she ached. Oh, how she ached. This was no torn muscle or gaping wound. It was as if a poison burned through her veins.

Nilith racked her brains, trying to remember being cut with a blade. Trying to fathom the black void in her memory, the one between this painful moment and a man and a wagon. And a creature in a cage…

Her eyes snapped open, finding an eyeless slab of grey meat grinning at her through crisscross bars. Three fat tentacles flapped at the iron. Skeletal hands with claws of blue smoke groped for her, but the bars held them back.

Nilith wriggled as far away from the monster as she could. Which wasn't far, it turned out; her cage was pitifully meagre. She found more bars at her back, leaving an arm's reach between her and the beast's sickle-shaped claws. It whined, blubbering charcoal saliva from its lips and blue fangs, and Nilith kicked at the bars. The creature curled up on itself with a hissing laugh, its barbels waving at her from a coil of sweaty flesh. It tapped its vaporous talons idly against its arms, counting the moments she stared at it.

Movement beyond the monster caught her attention. Her head snapped up to a black shape stencilled against a bright sky. The shape wore a wide hat, and it was then she remembered a name. *Chaser Jobey.*

Whether it was rage or panic that forced Nilith upright, she didn't know, but she was soon thrashing around, trying to glimpse a horse and a falcon.

She was thankful to find Anoish behind her, tethered to the wagon and staring at her dolefully. He was leaving as much space between him and the vile creature as possible, his rope taut. Dried foam coated the horse's lips.

Bezel was nowhere to be seen, and the sky too bright to search for him properly. Nilith's eyes ached as if her pounding brain were trying to pop them from her skull. Instead, she hoped there was a dark speck somewhere high above, keeping watch. It was comforting to know hers was a situation shared, even if it was only with a horse and a foul-mouthed falcon.

'You!' she croaked, finding her voice once she'd hawked up enough sand. She had never thought her tongue could ache, but somehow it was managing it. 'You let me go this instant!'

Jobey sighed, not bothering to turn. 'I find that debtors always say that, as if being let go a moment later would be somehow inhumane.'

'How dare you! What did you… What did your *thing* do to me?'

'I did nothing but reclaim you in accordance with your debts. That "thing", as you call it, was merely the tool.'

Jobey had yet to look at her, and it inflamed Nilith's rage. 'Fucking let me go!'

As she brought up a leaden arm to strangle the bars, she felt it: a deathly cold, striking deep to the bones of her hand and wrist. She saw the colour in her peripheral vision, and somehow, she knew before her eyes could summon the courage to look down.

Where a live, dark-skinned hand should have been, a ghostly hand had taken its place. With wide eyes, Nilith traced the smoky sapphire lines of her knuckles and fingers, just visible in the parching sunlight. Where the shade gave the vapour more weight, she saw the faint glow light the wood. With her other, trembling hand, she dragged back her sleeve, where the apparition of a hand met her wrist, which was still very much alive. The border between life and death was as black as Nyxwater, and looked like a wound turned sour. It blistered in places, and blue shone through the cracked and pustulent skin. And on the back of her hand, a row of white stab-marks showed where the monster's fangs had punctured her skin.

'I… I…' she gasped. All her rage had withered like a shadow at dawn. Fear had swooped in to replace it, bringing its chums, panic and dread. All else was forgotten – Farazar, Araxes, Sisine, even Anoish and Bezel – as she stared down at her ghostly hand.

Nilith was petrified to move her hand and make the mirage real. She was afraid it would fall apart as dust, or evaporate into the sun in smoke. It took her an age to stomach flexing a single finger. She saw it move, but the sensation was absent, as if she'd lain on her arm for half the night and awoken with it numb. 'What foul curse is this?'

Chaser Jobey finally turned around, looking first at Nilith's hand, then at his pet. The creature seemed to sense it was the subject of conversation, and its greasy head poked out of its coil.

'I warned you,' the chaser said, no hint of remorse or guilt in his voice.

'What is this?!' Nilith screeched.

The man had the gall to sound proud. 'You sit beside a slatherghast, madam. A beast from the Far Scatter, on the outermost rim of the Reaches.'

'What did it do to me?'

'What I instructed it to do! They are quite loyal once trained, you know. The slatherghast bit you, plain and simple. Now its poison is at work. Fascinating creatures, and fabulous for chasing debtors. It's why the Consortium began to ship them in from the far north.'

Nilith would have given her whole arm to burst out of the cage and show the man exactly how much she disagreed. She could not tear her eyes from her hand. 'What poison? Answer me, Jobey. I have the right to know!'

'Slatherghasts, madam, live in wild Nyxwells, drinking their water from birth. It turns their teeth and claws to shade, making them half alive, half dead. Stuck somewhere between the two, or so the scribes say. A ghast doesn't savage you like any other wild beast would, but bites its prey only once. Then it waits, for slatherghasts are wonderfully patient, you see.'

Nilith hated to ask, but she found herself speaking involuntarily. 'Waits for what?'

Jobey withheld the answer for a moment, taking pleasure in watching her squirm. 'It waits for you to turn to shade before feasting on you.'

Nilith squinted at the man, longing for her stare to pierce his skin and gut him. '*That's* my fate? Slowly fading away?'

Jobey flashed a wide smile. 'You should be happy, madam. You can consider your debt to the Consortium paid once you're dead and working.'

'No! No!' Nilith had no other words. She yelled it over and over as reality sank in, as if arrowhead after arrowhead pierced her. Thoughts of Farazar and Sisine and Araxes filled her mind. Her mission had failed. 'NO!'

She seized the bars, and felt the copper in them sting her left hand. It was a pain like none she had experience before. Yet she endured the sensation as her vapours flared. 'How long? How long does it take?!'

'A week, perhaps more. Depends on the person.'

The bile churned in Nilith's gut. 'There must be a cure! An antidote!'

'A reversal?'

'Yes! Tell me!'

Jobey paused to suck his lip. 'No, I'm afraid not. And even if there were, the Consortium would not accept anything less than payment in full.'

'FUCK YOUR CONSORTIUM!' Nilith roared.

Jobey continued staring straight ahead, uncaring.

Defeated, Nilith slumped against the bars, her ghostly hand held in front of her face. She stared at it with abject hatred. It was a disease. A fungus, claiming her bit by bit. She could have sworn more of her wrist had disappeared since she had started yelling at Chaser Jobey. The Ghouls' clutches had been a circus compared to this man and his cage. His monster. Krona could not beat her, but Chaser Jobey had. Now Nilith was as good as dead. Worse, she would be a ghost slaving away in some hellish mine.

Chest as taut as harp strings, Nilith tried desperately to slow her breathing. The air came in quick and panicked gasps. She clawed at the skin of her forearm, finding it numb but still alive. She wondered if hacking it off would stop the poison's spread. She would have gladly given an arm – maybe both – to be rid of the slatherghast's curse and be on her way.

She stared at the creature again. It was still peeking at her over its folded arms. Even without eyes, with only slits for nostrils, and those grey, waving tentacles, she could feel it looking at her. Its claws had stopped tapping. Now they just shone a fierce blue, bright even in the harsh sunlight.

Nilith turned instead to the horizon, where streaks of clouds lay draped across a shining city. It was tantalisingly close; maybe thirty miles lay between them. She could even make out smaller buildings on the outskirts, and minor towers where the rooftops began to climb. She knew that from the edge of the Outsprawls, almost seventy miles of city remained between her and the Core Districts. Between her and the Grand Nyxwell. Many nights, she had dreamed of being this close, but the difference between dream and reality was like an icicle through the heart.

A week. Even if Nilith were free of that cage and on Anoish's back, it would still be a race to reach the well in time. An overwhelming feeling of failure washed through her, as if her blood had been replaced with river water. *So many miles. So much pain. So much work.* And all to end up like this.

Her heart started to drum again, and she tried to focus on what few positives remained. One small mercy was the fact Jobey was going north, not south, and that he was pushing his wagon at a fair trot. At least she didn't have to face lingering as well as a slatherghast's damning poison.

Nilith smacked her good hand against the bars, making the cage rattle. Jobey looked over his shoulder. 'What of the ghost? The shade I was with in your Consortium's so-called White Hell?'

'Kal Duat does not deserve such a name—'

She spat through the bars of the cage. 'Not been there, have you?' Jobey tutted. Nilith hoped she was beginning to nettle him.

'The shade will be found shortly. His tracks are heading north like you were, madam. Beetle tracks, if I'm not mistaken. Which I hardly ever am.'

'That's why you're not wasting any time.'

'It behooves one to be swift in all matters relating to business. His debt is still to be collected.'

At least that gave her time. At least Farazar would be back at her side, behind bars and far away from any Nyxwell. *Another small mercy.*

Nilith groaned and knocked her head against the bars, punishing herself for letting Chaser Jobey come anywhere near her. She should have learned from the brutality of the desert and shot him square between the eyes.

Many more times she pitted her head against the bars, and by the time afternoon was slipping into evening, she had quite the lump to nurse, and no brighter a mood for it. She had seen Bezel once, or so she thought, through her sun-blind eyes. Something dark and winged had fluttered low over a nearby dune, looking dishevelled but still alive.

Jobey pushed his wagon harder the closer the city loomed. He followed a rough road carved between the dunes that had begun to peter out and bow before Araxes' might. A handful of travellers had passed them by in wide berths, as was the custom, with wary eyes for the cage and its occupants.

When one horse tired, Jobey switched it for the other, and so maintained his pace. It was smart, and meant he could keep ploughing on through night and day, napping at the reins. Nilith had seen him do it once or twice, and took the opportunity to peer about the wagon for anything remotely useful for picking locks or hacking off poisoned arms. There was nothing in reach, and she was left to rattle the locks, infuriated. The slatherghast hissed at her noise, rearing up to face her. She gave it a foul gesture and told it to go fuck itself.

Jobey snuffled as he righted himself, and Nilith reassumed her moody slump, turning away from him. In the darkness, a few tears may have hurried down her cheek, eager not to be seen.

———————◆———————

THE BEETLE WAS BEHAVING AT last.

It could have even been said that Farazar was starting to enjoy the creature's lurching gait. It wasn't that he had learned to tolerate its unpredictability, but rather to work with its strange habits. All it had taken was perseverance.

It was this determination – this iron will – that had kept them moving and brought the city lights much closer. They filled his view, sunrise to sunset; myriad pinpricks of light set in a jagged mountain range of buildings, black against the purple dusk. For what must have been the hundredth time that day, he stared up at the mighty pillar of the Cloudpiercer – *his* Cloudpiercer – and grinned eagerly.

He kicked the beetle on, not that it did much to spur it. The throne awaited him, as did whatever his daughter or the torrid sereks had been plotting in his wife's absence. Nilith had jeopardised everything for her greed, and Farazar damned her for it. Damned her to the void. When he was on his throne again, he would keep her for forty days, and make her watch her body decay until she evaporated, banished forever. That would teach her. Grinning smugly, Farazar held his eyes on the city and let the beetle do the work beneath him.

It was when they rounded a dune that he saw the distant crack in the earth, black against the sand. It ran south from the edge of the Sprawls, lined by small candles hanging from rope railings. They stretched into the sands and gathered around a squat building. Bent over it was a bone-like structure: three huge black tusks upended so their points crossed. Several more buildings spread out in a line from there. They looked dilapidated, and those furthest out had been swallowed by the dunes. If Farazar squinted, he thought he could make out shapes moving across the maw of a bright square deeper into the Sprawls.

If he still had a heart, it would have been pounding against his ribs. Farazar leaned to the side, as he had learned to do, and slowly turned the beetle towards the Nyxwell. Even from a few miles away, there was no mistaking the dark river and the structure. The Nyxites had always marked their territory with flamboyance. Their version of it, anyway. Farazar thought it drab, macabre and outdated, just like the Nyxites. Perhaps Farazar would finally take control of the wells himself once he was back in the Cloudpiercer. Declare it a royal responsibility. This little trip through the desert had taught him a thing or two about seizing what a man wanted. He may not have been a man any more, but he knew what he wanted. He had spent long enough hiding in his sanctuaries, both north and south. He had grown soft, and though it had cost him his life, it would not cost him his rule.

He kicked at the beetle's armoured sides, and again, until the creature clicked in annoyance and finally put some speed into its gait. Farazar turned around to steady his body, and as he did he saw the dark mark on the face of a white dune, several miles behind him.

There was no moon tonight but stars aplenty, and in their light it looked like a wagon with three horses around it. He couldn't spy any people, but he recognised the shape of it enough to know he'd seen it before. The man in the gold and flat hat.

Farazar did not believe in coincidences. Once more he kicked the beetle, until it whined so much he feared it would stop moving altogether. It stumbled into a good trot, but so did the man behind them.

Farazar swore he heard the snap of a whip over the rushing breeze, and felt desperation descend. It made him lean forwards, urging his stupid insect on with what scant weight he had.

There was little time to fetch a half-coin from the Nyxites now. If they refused him, he could either race into the streets on the back of a beetle, or fuck the intentions of both this man and Nilith, and throw his body into the Nyx unbound. He had promised himself freedom, afterlife or the void, and though it disappointed him deeply not to have the freedom, he was a stubborn bastard. If it stopped Nilith, so be it.

With the beetle's stumbling canter, the Sprawls and the Nyxwell edged closer. Barely two miles to go, and they were agonising. Farazar spent them snatching looks over his shoulder, seeing the man and his wagon come closer every time. Now and again he would lose them between the dunes, and Farazar would tense in hope, glowing darker and moodier when they reappeared.

The chase drew so close that he could see a cage on the man's wagon, and something glowing faintly inside it. The two horses pulling the wagon were slathering and wide-eyed.

Farazar began to undo some of the ropes binding his body to the beetle's carapace, getting ready to push it into the first scrap of Nyxwater he could find. His corpse began to squelch, bouncing with the creature's canter. Even then, in that moment, hand hovering over the wrappings, Farazar wondered what his old self looked like after several weeks under the hot sun. He didn't dare to look.

He could see a handful of Nyxites now, milling between the buildings with candles in their hands. He could hear the music of some flute, wailing over the bustle of a nearby night bazaar. There was less than a quarter mile to go now. The rift was a stone's throw away, arcing towards him as though heading off the chase. He bit his lip as hard as his formless teeth allowed, straining to go faster.

'I need copper! Copper, Nyxites!' he bellowed.

None of the robed bastards moved, merely exchanging concerned looks. Farazar looked about for guards or sellswords, but there were none to be seen.

There came a hiss and a sudden thud, and the beetle came crashing to the earth. Farazar tumbled over its spiny head and into the dust with a cry. Without bones to break or a brain to stun, he wasted no time in sprinting back to the collapsed insect. A thick triggerbow bolt protruded from a gap in its carapace.

'Gah!' he grunted. 'It's your fault for not having a thicker shell!' The beetle burbled away woefully as Farazar dragged his body from its back and began to haul it towards the rift.

Farazar pushed all the strength he had into his hands and feet. The sand slipped beneath his bare soles, but the body moved, and quickly too. He heaved and he heaved, trying to ignore the approaching rumble of hooves and wheels.

'I need a copper coin! Help me!' he yelled again. A few Nyxites were coming forwards, tentatively. They were not looking at him, but at the wagon racing after him.

'Fuck you, then!' Farazar cursed, wild eyes turning to the Nyx and locking there. Only a score of yards remained. Sand scraped beneath the body; the strain was unbearable. *Ten yards.* His glow turned white as he screeched with the effort. *Now five.* The Nyxites began to scarper behind their building.

'So be it!' Farazar roared. 'So be it! No binding tonight, you fetid bastards!'

He slumped to a heap at the edge of the rift and threw everything he had behind his body. It teetered on the edge of the black-stained rock.

'YAH!' he cried, shoving once more as hooves and skidding wagon wheels sprayed him with sand. He felt the pull of the earth take his corpse as strong, inhuman arms grabbed him by the shoulders. He was dragged backward, but he did not care; his body would momentarily be in the Nyx, and he would soon be gone from this place.

Farazar looked around with a grin, trying to find Nilith before he was whisked into the ether. He wanted to see the shame and failure etched into her face.

Instead, he met a bulbous lump of grey skin with no eyes and a maw filled with glowing fangs. He realised then what held him in its grasp. The monster's jaws were already wide and poised to sink into his shoulder, which they did with relish.

He screamed as the pain ran through him. Black veins spread from where the fangs sank in. Glee turned to terror and Farazar began to thrash. It only made the pain worse, but somehow he found time to wonder whether he'd made a mistake in choosing the afterlife. It was turning out to be a severe disappointment.

'Desist!' somebody shouted. There came the snap of a switch. 'Not food!'

The monster let go, slithering back on a legless body and whining horribly. Farazar was left to sprawl on the sand and clutch at his shoulder and clench his ghostly teeth. The black veins receded, replaced with burning white lines. Some of his vapours were missing from a ragged patch around his shoulder, where bite marks still glowed.

Seething, he reached out towards the Nyx but only managed to claw at the sand. *What's wrong? Why am I not in the afterlife?*

'A fine attempt, shade, but you are out of luck,' said a voice, and Farazar looked up to find a resplendent-looking man in a wide-brimmed hat standing over him. He was pointing at the shallow rift. 'Go on, after you.'

Under the man's watchful eye, Farazar crawled forwards until he could peer into the Nyx. Instead of a pool or river of oily waters, he found only ink-stained rock. At the bottom of the rift, a dozen feet down, he spotted his body lying curled like a fat grub, dry as the stone around it. He understood now why the Nyxites were peeking out from behind their adobe walls. There had been no help to give.

Farazar's fist met the sand with a puff, and his forehead quickly followed. Disappointment was a sour draught. 'Where has it gone?' he mumbled against the earth as the man bound his hands with black rope. Judging by its weight, it had a copper core. 'It can't have just gone!'

'Haven't you heard, half-life? Nyx has all but dried up in the Sprawls.'

'Lies!'

'Truly. They say the city's not too far behind, despite the emperor increasing the price of Nyxwater. Shipments out from the city are too slow or too expensive for the folk in these parts.'

'Why?' came a familiar voice. Farazar looked up to see Nilith's face pressing against the thick bars of the cage atop the wagon. Still alive, which was a deep shame. One of her hands was hidden within her coat. He was irritated to see her healed, with new clothes on her back, and apart from the trace of worry in her eyes, fairly well rested. He inwardly cursed her.

'Why do they say the Nyx is drying up?' she asked.

The man shrugged. 'Unclear. The Nyxites are clueless. I believe the Cons—'

'One gods damned moment, peasant! Who the fuck are you to interfere with my dealings?' Farazar demanded as he was veritably carried to the wagon. The monster slithered alongside like a loyal snake, grey tongue lolling hungrily over its fangs. 'I have a right to my freedom!'

'I, shade, am Chaser Jobey of the Consortium—'

'And a right inconvenient shit,' muttered Nilith.

Jobey spared a moment to whack her fingers from the bars with his switch, but she was too quick. 'As I was saying, I am here to reclaim your debt.'

'What damn debt? Speak, man!'

Jobey looked a little put out by Farazar's regal tone. 'The toll to pass through the Kal Duat mine. Your debt has been set at your life. Seeing as that is already taken, your servitude will suffice. Freedom is no longer your right, I'm afraid.'

Farazar raised his chin, glaring fiercely as he was hitched by his bonds to Nilith's side of the cage. The creature was shepherded into the other side, behind the partition of bars. 'It was this woman's fault, not mine! Do you expect a shade to be responsible for his owner's actions?'

'You deplorable twat,' came the hiss from behind him.

Jobey moved to the rift with a hook attached to a rope. Within moments, he was hauling up the body and dragging it across the sand. 'Seeing as you fled this woman and this body is not yet bound, I can only assume you are nobody's property yet. Therefore you can be held responsible. You shall belong to the Consortium, and soon.'

'How dare you! I demand to know who this Consortium of yours thinks it is!'

Nilith had more words for them. 'A hive of inconvenient shits.'

Jobey whacked the bars again. He seemed a man short of temper. 'As I have already told your companion, shade, the Consortium are a group of businessmen, and exceptional ones at that. The Chamber of Trade thinks itself the power behind business in the Arc, but in fact that belongs to the Consortium. Hence you would do well to respect them.'

'That's why we have never heard of them, is it?' muttered Nilith.

The chaser occupied himself by dumping Farazar's body onto the wagon's rear. He craned his neck as far away from the bundle as possible, mouth at a severe downward angle. He clamped a scented napkin to his face as soon as a hand was free. 'It's the wise businessman who knows the benefits of confidentiality. Privacy. You have no right to know the Consortium's dealings.'

'And you have no right to levy spurious tolls! Only the emperor makes such rules, and he has not granted you any such permission!' Farazar barked at him.

Jobey gave him a sour yet smug look as he mounted the wagon's seat. 'Your woman said the same, and I shall tell you what I told her. The emperor has no care for this city. Only his wars. His own empress has fled, and his daughter has enough trouble with the city spiralling into havoc. That is why we save the royal family the trouble of passing decrees, and do as we please. And why not, when it was the last emperor who sold the Consortium the land in the first place, decades ago?

'We are not some measly market traders hawking yesterday's fish, shade. Why, where do you think the stone for the city's towers and high-roads comes from? Consortium quarries. Or the grain in Araxes' grain stores? Belish crops on Consortium wagons, sold to the Chamber of Trade. Or whose ships carry in furs and jewels for tors and tals? The Consortium's. If the emperor ever came out of his Sanctuary, he would learn that this empire consists of more than just the city of Araxes.' Jobey cocked his head then, as if trying to place a memory. 'I must say, you look rather familiar to me,' he said to Farazar.

Farazar narrowed his eyes. His bonds shook with the frustration and outrage running through him. His desires counted for nothing since his death. It was infuriating. A soul, at its heart, was nothing but desire. 'You'll get what's coming to you, Chaser Jobey. Both you and your Consortium!'

The wagon lurched forwards without care for Farazar's threats, heading parallel to the Outsprawl's edge and away from the curious looks of the Nyxites. No sooner had the wheels started moving than Nilith prodded him in the back and whispered in his ear.

'There's always comfort in knowing you were right, at least. You did tell me you'd see me in Araxes,' she snickered.

Farazar snarled as he hunched away from her, arms lashed and taut behind him. He stared at the empty Nyxwell until it was lost behind a dune, wishing death on this putrid man and his monster, on his Consortium, and on the wife who had brought all of this upon him. The wife sitting beside him in a cage, clutching her arm to her belly, looking sorrier than he had ever seen her.

At least that was some comfort.

CHAPTER 2
THE OUTSPRAWLS

How does the Arc control its borders? I'll tell
you how. Ghosts. A fucking million of them,
armed and armoured, spread between my
islands and Araxes' coast. They never need
food, water, rest, or medicine. That is why
nobody challenges Emperor Farazar's lands,
and why I cannot invade. My only tactic is
to outlast his ghostly hordes, let them smash
themselves against my copper gates, and wait
for the Arctian Empire to rot from within.

FROM SCATTER PRINCE PHYLAR'S DIARY,
DATED YEAR 999

RIT CRUNCHED BETWEEN HER TEETH and in the cracks of her dried tongue. She tried to pull more air into her lungs, but her jaw seemed locked in place. Her swollen eyes were cemented shut by sand and sun-baked blood.

Heles couldn't feel the rest of her body at all.

Panic forced her eyes open. Such a small and simple movement, and yet it took all she had. Bright sunlight surged into her throbbing eyes, and she retched.

Only then did she feel her body: afire in a hundred places as she convulsed, spewing up nothing but bloody water, and fuck all of it. It still threatened to drown her if she didn't move or tilt her head. Heles rolled herself between hurls, and chewed sand to keep her stomach still. If ribs could speak, hers would have been screeching in agony. Her legs were still numb, and she listened for a kick of sand as she tried muscles she had known for decades. To her relief, there was a gentle scuff; barely more than a twitch, but enough to know her spine wasn't broken, and that something bound her knees.

Though the sun blinded her, it was having a warming effect. Her pain had been so vicious she had not noticed she was cold. Freezing cold, in fact. She lay there for a moment, wondering how a single body could ache so much and not be dead.

Heles looked around, noting the sand's rosy glow and the dew on a nearby spur of butchered cactus. Its maroon, finger-like branches and scattered pale fruit, not dissimilar to eyeballs, shone with it. Somebody had wanted it out of their path. She knew how it felt.

No.

Only palms and flowers sprouted in Araxes. Crimson *rhipsa* usually grew where desert met city. Heles twitched at the realisation.

Breathing heavily, and ingesting copious handfuls of grit into her lungs, she forced her head up so she could survey her blurry surroundings.

Closing one eye showed her an adobe wall with a barred window. With a painful twist of her head, Heles saw a white cottage half-swallowed by a small dune. Between her and it lay another body. Just a dark lump, but somehow she knew it. Her heart began to stir some more.

Heles angled her head to see rippling sand leading off into the endless desert. Too pained to move, she put her ears to use. There was a ringing in one of them, and a persistent thumping in her head, but besides that, she heard the buzzing of insects, the sizzling of dew and the rumble of a distant city.

The Outsprawls. *They've dumped me in the fucking Sprawls.*

She attempted to move, but something bound her arms as well as her legs. Heles looked down, eyes bulging at the sackcloth that was wrapped around her. She began to writhe. Spittle foaming at her mouth, she heaved herself into a roll. She screamed when she turned over, feeling broken bones crunch in her wrist and smacking her split forehead against the sand.

Twice more she rolled, until the sackcloth had loosened enough for her bruised fingers to claw at the earth. Spitting what grit and vomit she could scrape from her mouth with her swollen tongue, Heles sprawled beneath the sky and let the sun warm her, perchance even heal her. She needed to feel something other than pain, and the roasting heat was in abundance. It let her know she was alive.

Despite her agony, she drifted in and out of consciousness until the sun scaled to its zenith. When Heles could stoke herself into action, she pushed herself from the sand with her good arm. Her skin was hot, burned in the places that were split or not used to sun. New wounds announced themselves with shocks of pain or vicious twinges. She poked at them, taking note of each.

Her right wrist was broken, and the skin around the suspicious-looking lump was a blue bordering on black. Purple and red patches covered the rest of her body. At least three ribs were broken. Her left knee was aflame. One eye was almost swollen shut, and at some point in the fight, her lips had clashed with her teeth and come off the worse. Two of the aforementioned teeth were absent. There was a gash on her forehead, and Heles couldn't decide whether it was grit or skull fragments she could feel in the wound. In any case, it had finished its bleeding, but not before painting her face crimson. She could feel it flaking under her fingertips, and they came away dark. It was probably why they had assumed her dead, but why she hadn't been bound and sold already was beyond her.

It took far too much time, but Heles got to her knees. Her scrutiniser's robes had been ripped and torn to the point of shreds, but the black cloth and silver lining were still recognisable. Scrutinisers were not loved any more in the Sprawls than they were in the city's core. With a grimace, she pulled at the threads of her uniform until it had fallen to the sand, then she heaved up the sackcloth and wore it as a makeshift cloak.

In a shambling crawl, she reached the nearby body. Her suspicions were proven true once the ragged black cloak had been torn away. It was Jym, jaw and nose caved in and teeth all gone, but Heles still recognised his eyes, all wide and wild. They were a snapshot of his emotions the moment of his death: dread and panic.

She thumped his chest several times, cursing him breathlessly until her aching throat formed a word out of spit and sand. 'Stupid!'

Heles fell back onto her arse, panting while she regained enough strength for standing. She had no doubt in her mind what task lay before her: return to the city. That was the only logical thing to do. Chamberlain Rebene had to be informed precisely what Horix had done. What she had under her garden. The scrutiniser in Heles could already see the links forming between Horix and Temsa. *Their ruthlessness, secrecy, and plotting…*

She stood, but kept her eyes on Jym as she rose. Horix had made a mistake in killing a proctor of the Chamber, but she had made a bigger mistake leaving a scrutiniser alive. She should have had the guards kick Heles' face in, too.

Using her good hand, Heles seized his heavy foot and, with much stumbling and lung-burning effort, dragged Jym's corpse towards a nearby drift of sand. With a shard of pottery she found in the shade, she gave him the best burial she could offer, dragging the sand over the broken body until it was hidden. At least there, on the very edge of the city, Jym's shade would have a better chance of hiding out until the Tenets dragged him to the afterlife.

Heles stumbled in the direction of the distant towers, eying every nook and cranny of the tumbledown buildings about her, flinching every time the hot breeze moaned over curved rooftops. A few empty shacks of palm-wood and broken crates sat in gaps between houses. These were the hovels of those almost at the very bottom of Araxes' social pyramid. It was still better than indenturement.

Few belongings remained inside the shells of buildings. Only gaudy graffiti and poles decorated with ceramic skulls. Crossed bones had been painted over door frames; a macabre welcome for any visitor. A few houses even had steps supported by clay skulls that grinned at the street.

Death held a mighty sway out on the edges of Araxes. Pickings were fewer, but the profits were huge. Binding had become more than a commerce to those of the Outsprawls. It had become a definition of life, something almost to be worshipped.

Heles kept her blurry, throbbing gaze fixed on the soaring core of the city, many miles north. The distance made her legs want to crumble, but she chastised them and dragged them on regardless. Weakness was a product of fear, and she refused to be afraid.

A lone yellow tower watched over the local sprawl of adobe and sand. It was a circular construction, decorated with rings of red stone. She heard a clanging emanating from its walls, and began to tread, or rather shuffle, quietly. She was in no mood nor shape to deal with any soulstealers or would-be chancers. Her soul was her own, and needed in the city.

Hobbling between the houses and shacks as fast as she could manage, Heles caught glimpses of a small leather-clad band gathered around an anvil. Beneath the sweat and forge-soot their arms and bare chests had been ringed with crimson-painted scars. The bigger the man, the more scars and rings he owned. Heles had rounded up enough soulstealer gangs to know their type. No doubt whatever sharp implements they were forging were not meant for good, and she hobbled on, eager to be gone. No eye caught her and no shouts followed. She kept her head up and her ears sharp, despite the piercing ringing in one of them.

In an alley she found a discarded crutch, left atop some sackcloth. It was as close to a grave as Araxes got these days, and clearly belonged to some beggar whisked away in the night by knife and greed. Heles gritted her teeth at the injustice, but as she tucked the crutch's splintered handle into her armpit, she guiltily thanked the stealers for their single-mindedness. All they cared for were souls. Countless times she had found coin-purses and rings discarded beside bloody clothes, as if they were as worthless as wood or papyrus. She wondered what the ancient days had been like, when bandits had taken either coin or lives, but never both. Now it was purely the latter.

A society that puts no price on murder is no society at all.

Pushing her anger down into her legs, Heles adopted a faster pace. She stuck to the shadows, half for shade, half for secrecy. Her crutch thudded softly on the sand. The bustle that had been so distant was growing louder, though to her eyes the towers had come no closer.

If the busyness of Araxes' core was a raging fire, then the Outsprawls were its scattered embers. In some places, like her current surroundings, they were char and ash; coals flung too eagerly in the desert. In others, they smouldered on, trying their best to burn like the core of the city did. Heles was glad for it; crowded spaces and broad daylight meant for safer passage than dark and empty streets. Even in Araxes.

Heles pressed a shoulder up against a corner and poked her head around it. There was a rainbow-coloured crowd at the far end of the deserted street. A few beggars dotted the doorways between her and the press of bright cloths and chattering voices. The beggars sat with their heads down, arms propped up on drawn knees, empty hands or upturned hats out for alms. A few sported cuts and bruises like she did, though none so gratuitous or numerous. A few were painted with white ash, a sign of complete poverty in the Sprawls. Beggars like these normally didn't last long. Either the soulstealers found them in the night, or the beggars sold themselves into indenturement just for a release from the mortal struggles of age, hunger or disease. Heles saw one man with his hat on the sand, his ashen hands busy twisting string and slathering it with dark yellow grease. A tallow candle, to light come nightfall. To let the stealers know he wouldn't put up a fight.

Heles pulled her ragged body forwards, leaning heavily on the crutch. It groaned in protest. The first beggar, the one busy with a candle, gave her a glancing look. His eyes soon swivelled back to her, wider now they had clocked the blood and bruises between the sackcloth. He gave her a sympathetic look, then turned to the candle in his hands and calmly set it to one side, unfinished. It was still there by the time she reached the busy street.

The commotion dizzied her after the sneaking and the silence of the abandoned streets. She took a moment to catch her breath against a column of a building and watched the stream of people rush past her. Half the street flowed one way, half flowed the other, and at the sides it was undecided, eddying around bright stalls and shopfronts. The chatter of voices combined into one incoherent drone, broken at times by merchants ringing bells every time a deal was struck. Heles didn't know if it was her aching eyes or the squat buildings allowing more sunlight into the streets, but the crowds seemed more colourful, more vibrant here than in the city proper.

Signs proclaimed their goods in Old Arctian as well as the Commontongue, and some glyphs Heles had never seen before: nomad scrawl, older than the empire itself. There were fewer shades mingling with the living, revealing the poorer nature of the Sprawlers, but plenty of beasts. Scarab beetles, cows, centipedes, donkeys and their riders plied their way through the radiant crowds. Some tugged along carts with merchants perched on top, yelling offers while waving bowls of nuts and silks in their hands. Desert crows and finches and parrots flitted back and forth between the stalls, carrying messages and trades between vendors. Heles took a breath, feeling overwhelmed, and spices stung her sore nose. She winced. There were scents on the breeze she did not recognise, and for the first time in decades, she felt foreign in her own city.

Heles' eyes followed a long-legged insect as it plodded through the crowds, towering over nine feet tall. A mere child sat atop it, a girl with a narrow gaze and a high chin. She was wrapped in shimmering silk, and held the reins aloofly, off to one side. Her beast's carapace was bright green. It had a tall domed head, and its legs were sharply arched and pointed. The insect trilled away to itself as it serenely picked its path. Heles had never seen the like of it.

She followed its movements until she spotted a trough in the gap between two stalls. Her thirst overrode all other thoughts, and before she knew it, she was limping over to it, tongue already lolling from her mouth.

For a brief moment, as she gazed down at the murky water, with its film of oil and slobber and scattered straw, her breeding stalled her. The spiny, mustard-yellow boar slurping away at the far end of the trough eyed her suspiciously, but all she could see was its lapping tongue between its sharp tusks. Thirst won her over, and she plunged her face into the trough.

The water was warm and tasted of animals, but she drank anyway, half-drowning before coming up for air. Her split lips and forehead stung anew, but she forced herself to cup the water and wash them as much as she could bear.

'Oi!' a voice yelled from behind her. 'That's for beasts, not beggars!'

Heles spared a moment to face the speaker, making sure her eyes carried heavy measures of dangerous and displeased. He was a pale-skinned man in a turban. In his hands he held a rope, the other end of which was looped about the boar's neck. The man caught the venom in her eyes and pouted.

'Who says I'm a beggar?' she croaked.

'Just look at yer! And yer filth is getting in all the drinkin' water. Who knows what diseases you lot carry?' His point made, he tugged at his spiny boar, who seemed irritated his drinking had been disturbed, and the two of them walked away.

Heles drank until her stomach ached before pushing herself back to her feet and crutch. Her antics and the man's shouts had drawn looks. Several of the nearby traders watched her, faces wrinkled in distaste. A few mercenary guards on the other side of the street were pointing at her. It was time to move on.

She walked for an hour, perhaps more. The guards followed her for a time, but they were only paid enough to guard so much of the street, and before long she had become somebody else's business.

The Outsprawls had not changed, growing no taller nor closer to the ever-present shadow of the city. The crowds ebbed and flowed between the compact districts. Some had been friendlier than others. Heles had seen a few figures huddled at the edges of streets, eyes flitting about the crowd. They had lingered on her for longer than was comfortable. They had the look of hawks watching a procession of rabbits, noting the injured, the lame, the young, the old.

Here and there, along broader streets, trouble stirred around warehouses of white stone propped up by black marble pillars. Brown-clad hooded figures stood behind rows of hired men, while queues of angry folk with buckets and barrels cried out and berated them. The shouts were too many, too emotional to glean much sense from them, but Heles knew Nyxites when she saw them. Queues at Nyxwells or warehouses were not uncommon in the outer districts, but these commotions seemed more serious. Heles also knew the beginnings of a riot when she saw one.

She wandered closer to the nearest warehouses, trying to pick complaints out of the barrage of noise and cursing. There must have been forty people clamouring at the broad steps of the warehouse, pressing against the sellswords' shield wall. The protestors were of all cuts and colours, from servants and workers to businessmen and soultraders. Halfway between their guards and the doorway, two Nyxites repeatedly waved their hands for peace and understanding, and were repeatedly denied.

'How can it have "dried up"?' came the bellow of one man in a shit-brown coat. He threw his papyrus pail to the dust and stamped on it, over and over. 'I don't have time for this!' he cried out between wild grunts of effort.

'Please! Calm! We are as concerned as you are!'

'What are we to do?' yelled a woman, reaching forward over the shields only to be barged back into the arms of another.

'I have souls to bind!' called yet another.

One of the Nyxites wore a shaky smile. 'Shipments are coming from the Core Districts, we assure you! And two of the Nyxwells in the next district over also have water!'

'Outrageous!' shouted the man in the turd-coloured coat. Leaving his pail in the dust, he threw up his hands and marched away, leading most of the mob north to the next well, like a blustering wind dragging a squall along with it. The two Nyxites blew sighs of relief as they hurried back into the safety of their warehouse. Heles loitered a moment by the building's edge, watching the sellswords and those who remained to wait and mutter angrily to themselves. With a humph, Heles slipped away to a quieter street, wondering what in the Reaches would cause the ever-present Nyxwell to dry up like a common desert spring.

Passing under the cool shadow of a crooked tower, she found a secluded doorway by a bustling junction and awkwardly collapsed into it. Her limbs were afire and several cuts had reopened during her stubborn shuffle north. The feet of the crowds trod inches from her own but she did not care, despite the tuts and curses aimed her way.

Breathing a deep sigh, Heles stared down at the awl she had swiped from a leatherman's table while he had been distracted screaming at a customer. It was a short, rusty thing, but it had a big enough spike for jamming into eyes or ribs or groins. She tried to grip it in her right fist, but pain lanced up her arm. Left arm, it would have to be. She secreted the weapon inside her makeshift sleeve. Once more, she lost herself in the crowd's noises; the gentle tapping of an artist's hammer; something sizzling in iron pans; the braying laughter after a crude joke; hooves and feet scuffing in the sand.

'There is but one god who still lives, friends. Neither dead nor lost, is he!'

Heles' eyes snapped open. Through the forest of legs and feet, she spotted a shade standing on a small wooden pedestal. He glowed even in the bright sunlight. His face beamed as he delivered his words, and his robes were the colour of blood. A small crowd had gathered around him. Many of them were free shades, with white feathers splayed across their breasts. The rest were fine-dressed dawdlers, as alive as Heles was.

The shade continued his speech. 'It is he who gave us the gift of binding, stolen from jealous gods who would seek to keep man and woman slave to their promise of afterlife. Who would ask us to devote our lives to giving them prayer. We were promised a paradise, friends, but it is an empty void. Nothing more. Nothing like the second life we owe to Sesh today!'

Although a shout of, 'Fuck off!' came from the crowd, the gathering at the preacher's pedestal grew in number. Heles heard their curious murmurs over the bustle.

With great difficulty, and a lot of grunting, she made it to her feet and set about navigating the flow of the junction. Despite the shoves and much, much stumbling, she reached the edges of the group, and hovered near to a wall. No doubt the day's sweat – not to mention being wrapped up in a sack for gods knew how long – had made her smell riper than an old chamberpot. She could not be bothered with attracting more attention.

As the shade waxed on about Sesh's gifts and endless love for both living and dead, Heles' eyes toured the gathered. When not intrigued, most faces were blank. A few nodded along to the words.

Heles caught sight of other hooded figures loitering on the far side of the pedestal. They too were clad in deep red, hooded and as still as the column she leaned against. They had the bulk of armour beneath their cloaks, and she noticed the glint of silver at their collars and cuffs. If they moved, she would no doubt see the shapes of swords at their hips.

Heles felt sweat on her injured brow; the sting of salt as well as cold.

The Cult were allowed no weapons. It was royal decree. Emperor Milizan himself had given that speech, many years ago, before retreating into his Sanctuary. Heles had been but a proctor then. A volunteer, just like Jym.

She knuckled her brow and winced, her hand coming away bloody from a reopened cut. Some of the blood began to drip into her swollen eye, and she turned around. The speaker's words caught her.

'We preach not what old religions demanded of you, such as tithe or prayer. We preach only understanding, friends. Fairness for all, and an end to the miserableness of the lie the Arc has told itself for centuries. An end to crime, to poverty such as this.'

Heles found the eyes of the gathering on her as the shade pointed her out, sackcloth bruises and all.

'Charity, friends. An old idea, long forgotten. Such as it is, the Church of Sesh has decided upon a momentous change. We are no longer a brotherhood of the dead, but of the living too. The light of Sesh should be for all, especially in times of such chaos and shortage.'

Heles spat blood in the sand and shuffled away. She already disliked the Cult – or *Church,* as they had haughtily rebranded themselves – but now she found new hatred for them, and for those who were stupid enough to believe their wily words. Although her feet pointed north, the exhausted, angry part of her wanted to drive that awl into every gullible face in that group. The Cult only served itself.

Worry plagued her as the walk took her anger away in scant increments. Horix and Temsa were the criminals that occupied her mind, but now the Cult's agenda had reared its head, and refused to leave. Heles felt the burden of duty weigh heavy on her, and her back bowed under its weight. She certainly fit the bill of beggar as she tottered towards the city, as fast as the pain would allow. The City of Countless Souls needed a saviour now more than ever. If it had to be her, so be it. It was her job, after all.

CHAPTER 3
DECISIONS

The Arctian Empire is obsessed with two
liquids. The first is Nyxwater. The second is
beer. And I can see why. The Skol have their
firewine, the Krass their medea. Even the
Scatter Isles can ferment sugar and palm nuts.
But they pale in comparison to the care and
passion of the brewhouses of Araxes. It is no
wonder they say an Arctian is the only man who
will drink himself to death and keep drinking.

EXCERPT FROM 'REACH AROUND - A
TRAVELLER'S GUIDE TO THE FAR REACHES'

I CAN'T BELIEVE YOU'VE DONE IT *again.*'

'What? This might be the last pint that ever passes my lips.' And fuck me, was I savouring every sip. The beer was as cold as spring snow off the Krass steppes and just as refreshing. The bubbles stung my tongue as they rushed down my throat. I swilled it against the roof of my borrowed mouth to taste the hops, and sighed.

'They aren't your lips.'

I looked again at the beaten bronze that clad the wall behind the bar. Statues of old emperors and empresses lined it, all skinny and regal with mighty crowns and crooked sceptres. Between their heads, I could see my goggled-eyed expression, and the way my face seemed to hang off my cheeks like wet linen.

It was probably due to the fact I'd knocked the man senseless with a brick. The unconscious body was almost as heavy as the dead one I'd worn to the last tavern. At least this one didn't reek as much and was roughly the same shape as the body I'd once inhabited. I patted my round belly for good measure, feeling the ripples reverberate around my ribs. It was strangely comforting.

Staring again at my bronze reflection, I examined my black and braided locks, light Scatter Isle skin, and teeth whiter than any Krassman could hope for. Though I was missing a few. I probed the gaps with my tongue. The ache at the back of my head had faded to a dull throbbing, and from what Pointy said, the blood was hardly noticeable. Not that the sight of a bleeding man would raise any eyebrows in this city.

My clothes were not rich, but neither were they poor. One of my fingers had a ring on. There had been another on the other hand, but that had gone to buying the beer. It wasn't my fault the man I'd borrowed hadn't been carrying any silver. I guessed he was some Scatterfolk merchant, and wondered what nearby stall or room he had left unattended. Shrugging, I downed my pint to its mealy dregs and signalled the barkeep for another.

'Okay,' I said to myself and the sword at my belt. 'This might be the last pint.'

'You're procrastinating. You still haven't decided, have you?'

'No, I have not.'

'I thought we were past this, after last time.'

I thought of a guard's body floating in the harbour, and flicked my nail against the blade of the sword to shut him up.

A ghost in a conical felt hat shuffled over. She was missing half her skull and had a canyon-like cut in her collarbone. I was curious how far it reached below the hem of her cotton gown.

'Another?' she asked, her voice hollow. I wondered if mine sounded like that when I was not stealing others' bodies. As it was, I spoke with a high-pitched voice, cracked at the edges with pipe-smoke.

'Please.'

'Fine blade,' she said, nodding to Pointy as she reached beneath the bar to work some spigots.

I tried a smile. Well… I contorted my limp face into something resembling one, and she blinked owlishly.

'What are you doing now, for dead gods' sake?'

'Drownin' sorrows or celebrating summin?' she asked.

I shrugged. 'Bit of both, I think.'

'Mm.' The ghost nodded sagely as she produced another clay tankard of foaming beer. 'Not a soul in this city that don't have a sorrow or two. More so now, what with all these attacks. Nyx dyin' out, too, or so they say. Streets are worse than they ever been, and that's sayin' summin.'

I looked to the doorway, hearing the muted splash of rain behind the shivering curtains. I pondered what waited for me beyond.

'Ahem.'

I offered up the other ring when I realised she was staring at me with her palm out, eyebrow raised. The shade rolled her eyes at my payment but still snatched it away in any case. There was a brief white glow in her fingers as they grazed my skin. She flashed me a curious look.

'What's your sorrow?' she asked. Whether she was genuinely interested or simply fulfilling the age-old role of a conversational barkeep, I didn't know. All the best ones know beer tastes sweeter when swilled alongside words.

'I had a difficult decision to make.' I found solace in the fact I'd found another ear to bend. Such is the way of lonely people sitting at bars, and nothing is better for teasing out problems than the blank judgement of a stranger. It made me feel alive again for a moment. I clung to it.

'Tough one, was it?'

'It was.' I nodded, though my thoughts turned inwards, my mind too busy to focus. I lost myself in the bronze, and those goggle eyes.

Several hours earlier

THE RAIN CAME LIKE A pirate invasion. It crept into Araxes from the sea and stormed the city street by street, darkening the sand and adobe walls with spots and streaks. I thought I imagined it at first, as the first drops hit Pointy's blade with musical chimes. But what started as tentative drizzle became fat, heavy dribbles, born of desert dust meeting cold ocean air. I had wondered why the night held no stars for me. No moon. Now I knew.

The city streets between me and the Core Districts were quiet and empty save for a few drunkards and shades still running errands. Arctians, even the dead ones, are no fans of rain. They scarpered as the downpour descended, leaving me alone with the sizzling lanterns and dying torches. The golden streetlight faded, leaving my glow to light my way. Raindrops flashed blue around me, seeming unearthly. The sand was bleached to grey as the rain drummed it into mud.

My stolen rags became sodden and unbearably heavy, slipping from my frame unless I concentrated. With Pointy hanging at my hip from a scrap of twine, I raised my hands and face to the dark sky, trying to drown myself in the soaring roar of rainfall.

I felt the fat drops fall through me, warm to my cold. Here and there, one would treat me with kindness, catching and rolling down my vapours for a moment. One hovered on my lip, but as I opened my mouth it was lost to the ground.

For somebody who had always found peace and quiet in the patter and kiss of rain, warm or cold, this was a tragic disappointment. I savoured what little I could before I trudged on, moodier than I had been before. There was no bird. No carriage. No wagon. Just my legs, and tonight they were feeling more jellied than usual after the haunting.

'We'll be lucky if we reach the widow by next nightfall,' I muttered to Pointy. 'This city is far too big for its own damn good.'

The sword's tone was wistful. 'I don't mind. This is the furthest I've been out of the Core Districts in decades.'

I hauled him from the makeshift belt and stared at the face on the pommel stone. Pointy's eyes were closed to the rain. I watched the drops bounce from the metal. 'You sound like you're enjoying this,' I accused him.

'It almost tastes like freedom. Almost.'

'Hmph.' I had to agree. I had escaped, after all. I was lost to Temsa, vanished in the honeycomb of Araxes' streets, and was headed to Horix to claim my coin at last, and yet even with all my good fortune, I still felt emptier than even a ghost should feel.

I threw a look over my shoulder, finding the streets behind me just as empty. I had run for hours, and still there was no sign of pursuit. 'Do you have a half-coin? I've never thought to ask,' I said to Pointy, trying to distract myself.

When I turned to look at the sword, the eyes were open and staring at me. 'My builders made it so that every soulblade is its own half-coin,' he said.

'How many of you are there?'

Pointy whistled, though gods knew how. 'No way to tell now. Deadbinding was quite the craze, and it carried on for years after I was bound. Many soulblades were destroyed or broken once the practice was banned. I was part of five made as a set for a Skol duke. Our names were Ortan, Larili, Renester, and Pereceph, and all of them were mute except me, Absia. That was my name. I was a mistake, really, which is perhaps why I survived the cull. Why I was passed from master to master over decades. Whoever keeps hold of a soulblade owns it, you see. In all my years, I've never figured out whether that is a blessing or a weakness.'

That seemed easy to me. 'Blessing, I'd say. At least you can't lose yourself.'

'I would say I've already lost most of me, wouldn't you agree? You forget, Caltro, that some dead lose more than others. You're lucky only your neck is slashed, and that you've only got a few holes in your belly.'

I thought of the ghost in Horix's tower, Kon, and his zigzag body, crippled even in death. There it was again: that guilty comfort in knowing your own situation could be worse.

'Look at me, Caltro. I feel like fair Faerina, trapped in her eternal chrysalis, aching to escape the foul clutches of Gar Rel—.'

'Pointy.'

The sword huffed. 'Don't you realise that after centuries like this, I would give anything to be other than what I am?'

His was a simple question, but it echoed my own pain and shamed it all at once. 'No. And yes.' I pursed my lips. 'I do now. I guess I was distracted with my own… you know.' I swore I saw the pommel blink.

'If that's what they call an apology in Krass, I'll accept it.'

Pointy had wormed it out of me, but I let him have it and said no more. The sword did have it worse than me, as did many others.

I saw one such creature at that very moment as I glanced idly down a side alley. The ghost was busy trying – and failing – to haul a body through the mud. It wasn't in my nature to gawk, but there was something sorry about this scene that made me pause and stare.

The ghost must have been fresh. For one, he was stark naked. Secondly, his grip didn't look strong enough. Only by wrapping his arms around a leg could he gain any sort of traction. The mud tripped him instantly. Again and again the sorry dance was repeated. An old saying floated through my head, half-remembered. Something about the connection between repetition, failure and madness. I could have scorned the ghost and walked away, but I understood what a half-life was. It was not life after death, but perpetual death after death. That breeds a special kind of desperation.

'What are you doing, Caltro?' whispered Pointy.

I took a few steps forwards, noting the vicious wound on the back of the ghost's head. I looked down at the body and found the same wound drawn in black blood and white skull. Something grey and fleshy lay within.

With a polite cough, I announced my presence. The ghost immediately fell over the body, snarling and thrashing at the air between us. He was an Arctian man. His slurred accent was noble. Judging by the silver-trimmed clothes on the corpse, so was the man.

'You stay away, shade!' he cried, ignorant to the irony.

I held up my empty hands, only to realise one still had a sword in it. I flashed a smile and quickly sheathed it. 'I don't have a white feather on my chest, see? I'm bound and have no interest in you. Or... *you.*' I gestured to the corpse.

The man futilely tried to spit at me. 'Get the fuck away!'

Pointy had some wisdom for me. *'He's got bats in his head, as the great Bastiga would say.'*

I began to tread backwards. 'I was only trying to help—'

'Go awa—'

The ghost went rigid as if he had been stung by something poisonous. Pointy was swiftly in my hand again. The ghost retched, his mists convulsing, twisting about him. With a crackle of white sparks, a flash of green polluted his cobalt glow. Like ink blooming in water, the putrid green quickly consumed his legs, then his torso, and finally his head. Within moments, he had gone from a bright sapphire to a duller emerald. When the ghost found his muscles again and began to rear up, his face had lengthened, his nose was a tall column and dark swirls underlined his eyes. They were piercing lights, and already they were fixed on me.

'Oh, not now. Not fucking now,' I muttered. I didn't need another visit from the dead gods. I'd already made up my mind.

'What is it with you and dead things rising around you?'

I waved Pointy at the ghost, wondering why I couldn't be left alone and unbothered for more than a few hours in this city.

'Caltro,' he wheezed, in a voice that sounded like an echo from a hundred miles away. It was almost lost in the drone of rain.

'That's me. And who might you be?' I challenged him.

The ghost stretched tall and I saw he'd found an extra few feet in height. His sickly glow bathed me, and although it was faint, it somehow drowned mine out, like cupping a hand around a candle. If I stared hard enough, I caught his vapours drawing the edges of a breastplate, gauntlets, and greaves. On his head there was the shadow of a tall crown.

'You have called me Oshirim for millennia. You may use that name.'

'What in the blasted fucking Reaches is going on?' Pointy blurted, forgetting to whisper in my head. 'Did you say "Oshirim"? As in the dead god Oshirim?'

I knuckled my brow. 'I apparently have a habit of attracting deities. This isn't the first time one has paid me a visit.'

'I...' Pointy was speechless. I looked to the pommel stone, half-expecting to catch his mouth flapping.

The ghost was also looking down at the sword. 'A soulblade, you call it? Such waste. So crude,' he intoned.

For an inanimate object, Pointy sounded rather out of breath. 'See, Caltro? He understands me.' To the ghost, he said, 'You should know that I would be bowing, my lord, if I could. I am honoured by your presence. However strange and unexpected.'

Oshirim inclined his head and then looked questioningly to me. I bit my lip and begrudgingly bent a knee. It was shallow, swift, and about all I owed to a foreign dead god.

'I thought there wasn't enough power left to come visit me again. Or did you gods lie about that too?' I asked bluntly.

'Caltro! Have some respect,' Pointy hissed.

Oshirim looked to the centre of the city, where the lights became a wash of orange behind the curtains of rain. 'Our great enemy became too curious. He took a chance that set him back, and it shared some of his power with us. I hope we are not wasting it once again. Come.'

Before leaving, he knelt to touch the corpse. Where his ghostly fingers met the robes, black liquid bubbled. The body deliquesced before my eyes, collapsing into the sand. Oshirim arose with a shiver, breathing long and slow, leaving me to stare with raised eyebrows at a simmering puddle of ink-stained robes.

'Er...' I began.

The god crooked a finger at me. 'Come.'

'Do as he says, Caltro, for gods' sa—I mean, just follow him.'

'You stay out of this, Pointy. You don't know what I know,' I snarled at the sword before stuffing him into my belt. It was my own fault, but the blade nicked my calf, and twisted my lips at the flash of pain. I could feel the cold creeping up my leg.

I jogged awkwardly to catch Oshirim's longer strides. Walking side by side, we bathed the mud and rain-slick walls with our green-blue glow.

The god wasted no time in speaking. 'You still dawdle while our enemy grows ever stronger.'

Perhaps it was Oshirim's calm, his expressionless face, or the ancientness pouring from him, but I felt like a student to a master again, one that I hadn't asked for. 'I am not dawdling. I have had my own problems to deal with, thank you. It's not easy being dead, you know. Besides, I have found the Cult, and I've spoken to them. Well, they spoke to me. They know what I can do. The so-called gift you gave me.'

The dead god growled, and for a moment I thought it was the sound of clouds grinding together. 'And now? What is in your mind?'

I crossed my arms. 'I want my half-coin back. That's all that matters to me. Not your flood, not Temsa's greed, not the Cult's games, not Horix's writ of freedom, nor any other empty promise I've heard since being dead. My freedom is what matters, and I trust nobody but myself to claim it. Doubt and desperation made me forget that, but I know my worth now. My power. And with it, I will win Araxes' game.'

The god sighed. 'How selfish.'

'It's what I'm owed!' I snapped.

Oshirim paused mid-stride, casting a withering look down on me. I wondered if all the gods had worn the same look, just hidden behind broken faces.

'You toy with the fate of countless millions, Caltro.'

'Just as you toy with countless more! That's right, Haphor told me what we are to you.'

'*Caltro...*'

I snarled at the whisper in my head. He knew nothing. 'We're nothing but sustenance to the gods, Pointy. Fuel. Slaves, just as we are here. They just want my help to survive, but they have given me no reason to help besides riddles and threats. Even the Cult were kind enough to promise me freedom.'

Oshirim towered over me, stepping close and looming like a cliff face. It seemed as though the weight of a building pressed down upon me. My vapours flapped as if a great wind sought to drag me away. Instead of a ghost before me, I saw a figure burning white, with a mitre of fire upon his head.

It lasted only a moment before he withered to my own height. His glow faded, growing sicklier. When he spoke, it was in the voice of an old man, tired of life and struggle. It was faint, and I had to strain to hear him over the rain.

'If you truly require an explanation, you shall have one. You were our ancestors' greatest creation. Despite your follies, we gave you sanctuary and haven amongst the stars, away from the trials this world has known for thousands upon thousands of years. We gave you life beyond death. *Duat*. Paradise, as you called it once, and a paradise it still is. All we asked was a copper coin for the boatman, to cross the river you know as the Nyx into *duat*.'

I kept my mouth shut, even though my questions and quips clamoured to be free.

'We may be gods, but we are not immortal. We are born. We die. Generations of us have watched over the passage of the living and the dead. And yes, Caltro, for every soul that passes our gates, our forms are sustained. You say it as though you are farm beasts. Meat. That is not so. It is kinship. Trade.'

Oshirim was talking faster now, his words coming like a waterfall. I struggled to understand them. The spell must have been fading, and fast, like his glow.

'You call us "dead" gods, and although that is not true, it shall be soon. Sesh killed the boatman and closed the gates to *duat*. Souls have waited a thousand years at those gates. Where the Nyx once flowed, it trickles. It is blocked, and the pressure grows... the world behind this one shakes in ways you cannot understand. Sesh's bonds fray. The god of death has no love for life. He sees it as a plague. Given a chance, he will rid the world of it. Do you wish for that to happen, Caltro?'

Oshirim staggered then, putting a hand to a wall and almost passing straight through it. I instinctively moved to catch him, and as my vapours brushed his, I saw that vast cavern stretched before me again. I felt the cold water seeping between my feet. I heard laughter echoing in the endless darkness.

'The wolf at the zoo,' I whispered, remembering the same darkness in its eyes.

'He made a mistake... wanted to see you for himself. See... who we'd chosen. Now the Cult know of you, time is shorter.'

'But why did you choose me?' It wasn't the most pertinent question. Haphor had already given me her verdict and it hadn't been a kind one. Perhaps I shallowly sought for more recognition, another reason besides randomness.

The ghost collapsed to his knees, splashing murky water. He looked up at me, and I saw a broken man poking through his regal emerald features. 'You crave freedom and justice more than most. As do we. There will be none if Sesh is not stopped. You can run. Fly, even. Flee as fast as you can. His flood will find you too.' He choked on something before pressing his hands together, palms flat. 'It is not in the nature of gods to beg...'

Those were his last words. I let him fall to the mud, knowing there was little I could do for him.

'Caltro!' Pointy called to me, but I was still lost in that great cavern, my gaze roaming over the countless millions of dead. Waiting. Pointless.

Oshirim's last words cut into me like a blade. 'Save yourself, if that is all you care about. Perhaps Haphor was right: in doing so, you might just save this world. The gods. The dead. That is our only hope. This is the last you shall hear from... us.'

No sooner had he finished speaking did his form lose its hold. He evaporated into the rain-soaked air, formless as the wafting smoke of a dead candle. Gone, his stolen ghost with him.

I rose from the mud without a word. Pointy was wise enough to hold his tongue, though no doubt he had plenty to say. Plenty of his own so-called wisdom to lacquer Oshirim's challenge with.

With a soft squelching, I resumed my march for the city. I knew one thing for certain after this visit from the god of gods: I needed a beer.

———◆———

I WATCHED THE BUBBLES POPPING in the foam, melting like the dead body had. The shade cleared her throat, and I realised her question was still waiting for an answer.

'Life or death all over again,' I said.

She looked at me skewed. Try as she might, she couldn't rid her face of contempt. 'You don't know what you're talking about.' With a snort, she left me with my beer and stalked back down the bar.

'*What a charmer you are.*'

'Shut up,' I said. The barkeep heard me, and before I could explain dumbly that I was talking to my sword, she narrowed her eyes over her shoulder and pointedly told me to go fuck myself.

Guessing two beers was probably my limit, I took a moment to swill the last of my brew down, rather unsatisfactorily. I left the tankard on the bar with a loud clank and made for the door. I almost forgot the skin wrapped around me and stumbled against a table on my way out, much to the grumbling of a hooded and sour-looking man. He flashed me a dangerous look, and I swiftly exited.

The rain had not slowed its onslaught, instead carrying on through the day and into the afternoon. I raised my face to the broody sky as I emerged into the largely empty street. Most citizens had been driven indoors. Only ghosts and drunks were left to walk through the down-pour. In my borrowed body, I could feel every pit and patter. To this warm skin, the drops were cold, smelling of salt and desert dust, a homely scent. Steam hovered faintly over the warm ground and churned mud. I drank it all in as deeply as I could before the sword cut through it all.

'Well?' he asked. 'Decided what you're going to do yet?'

'Stop hounding me. You're no better than a god.'

'You must be the only soul in the Arc, maybe the Reaches, who would resent being the chosen hero of the gods.'

'I'm no hero,' I grumbled. 'One of them said exactly that. I just died at the right time.'

'He said it was your stubbornness they needed. That I can believe. You say they've been visiting you ever since you died, correct? I'm sure they didn't choose the second-best locksmith in the Reaches by mere coincidence.'

My answer was a mutter. 'The *best* locksmith,' I told him. 'At the very least, I'm the best dead locksmith in this shit-smeared world.'

I held my tongue as I walked past a squad of ghosts in red cloth and black mail. They were carrying short swords and round shields, and for a moment they seemed like any other hire-swords patrolling the streets. It was then that I recognised their colours. I stared, brow furrowed, as they jogged around a corner.

Leaving Finel's zoo, I had been so set on my path. One visit from a god, and I was already questioning myself. Entangling my fingers in my soaking locks, I tugged at my hair, as if I could pull the answers from the garble of conflicting opinions and ideas, all clamouring for attention. My mind had been noisy in life. In death, the voices seemed to have developed a passion for volume.

My strangled grunt made a passerby flinch away, but I didn't care. I took the nearest alley and curved back in the direction of the city core. I was on its edge now, close.

The Enlightened Sisters had shown me the error of my insular ways, and so I decided to do something I had avoided like the plague in life: ask for advice.

'What would you do, Pointy? If you were me?' I asked, feeling cowardly seeking the answer in somebody else. 'Who would you trust?'

'Me? Truly?'

'You.'

The sword took a moment to think. 'None of them. I would run, if only to test my legs.' He sighed. 'And yes, I would probably drink a beer.'

I threw up my hands, about to curse his hypocrisy, but he was not finished.

'But I would feel wrong,' he added. 'Though I can hardly believe it, that was clearly one of the dead gods. Oshirim, no less. And to have him practically beg you...'

That made me raise my chin.

'Caltro, if their words are true, what would be the point in trusting any of the others? Just for a few more days of so-called freedom? I would do as they ask. I can't believe you've ignored them this long.'

'I bet I could make those days count,' I said, but I knew it was a lie even as the words were falling out of my mouth.

'You kid yourself.'

'I do. I always have.' I took a moment against a wooden beam, opening my mouth to taste the run-off from a crimson awning. It tasted sweet to me, earthy. Staring at the soaking cotton, I sighed. Sesh himself, this so-called dark lord of dark lords, had come to look at me. Oshirim had said Sesh had made a mistake in doing so, and perhaps he had. I had seen the evil in those eyes. The hunger. The animal rage. There had been nothing like that in the eyes of Basht, or Haphor.

'Perhaps this threat of a flood is real,' I admitted.

'Do you want to wait to find out?'

I took another gulp and spat into the street. I was determined to fit in as many old and trivial habits as possible before I lost this body. Tiredness was already seeping into me. 'Why's there always got to be some great evil? Hmm? That shit should be kept in fairy tales and bedtime fancies. Why can't people just be happy being fed and alive and fucking their days away? Why is it not enough? Why do people like Temsa and Horix and the Cult need more? Why does some dark lord always want to come and destroy life?'

'Where do you think those stories come from, Caltro? All the way through history, this has happened. Again and again. Peace and war. Back and forth. In fact, Bemia Timsule, the great second-century playwright who—'

'Pointy,' I warned him again, in as low a voice as I could manage.

'Fine. Timsule said we can't help it. Humans, that is. We're all bound to compete with each other so long as the concepts of "more" and "less" exist. Doomed to measure ourselves against one another. Food, silver, half-coins. Wherever there is something we don't have, we want it, and will do a great many things to get it. Better. More. Comparison is our great downfall, the mother of both envy and pride. Perhaps it's the same for the gods.'

I had been doing that all my years, only I had compared myself against what I thought I should be. Richer. Thinner. Freer. Better. I realised then the amount of angst that practice had brought me, and it had caused me to run for my entire life. I ran from my parents and their simple calling. I ran across half the Reaches to stay alive. I even ran to Araxes to escape penury in Taymar. I ran from that ship and had not stopped running since, even though I'd died in the process. I'd only wanted my half-coin so I could keep running. And why? My thirst for better and more.

I dwelled on that for a time, listening to the unique music of the rain, ever-changing. Its instruments were the puddles, the awnings, the clay chimney pots. I could lose myself in such moments, but this was not a time for retreat and insulation, which was what I normally would have chosen. This was a time for action. For change.

'Fuck it all.' I laughed as I spoke. 'I swore I'd get my freedom, and that's what I intend to do. If it means I have to save the rest of the world to do it, so be it. The gods can just count themselves lucky.'

With a flourish, I drew Pointy and raised him to the downpour before slamming him into the ground. I shrugged off my robes, and after a stumble, I was running headlong at the nearest wall: the bluff of some mighty tower above us. Angling down, I began to pry myself from the man's mind, muscle, and skin. With a wrench, I was free, skidding through the mud on my heels. The man careened forwards, arms at his side, angled at the wall like a billy goat.

There came a thud and the man went limp at the base of the wall, splayed and naked. I had the decency to drag him into an alley and cover him with discarded sackcloth. It may have been wrong to start a virtuous path by robbing a man and leaving him to the rain, but I guessed he would have thanked me, if he knew what I'd decided. Nobody liked a cataclysm. If they did then they were an idiot, and probably deserved to perish anyway.

Tugging Pointy from the mud, I thrust him into my new robes, and strode into the rain with the most purpose than I'd had since dying.

CHAPTER 4
A WIDOW'S WHIMS

Ironjaw, they called him, a warlord of few
words and untold bloodshed. Betrayed by
his fellow lords of Belish and left for dead,
Ironjaw returned to the city with nothing
but his armour and his sword. For weeks, he
waged war on the Belish lords, drawing out
and defeating every hero they chose, or scaling
the walls at night to murder them one by one
in their beds. So terrified of Ironjaw were
the remaining lords that they raised a mighty
army to stand against him. And so they did,
on the first day of a new year, Ironjaw with
nothing but his armour and a sword. They say
that when he finally died, every last lord lay
butchered at his feet, and his ghost arose from
his body to continue fighting.

OLD SOUTHERN FABLE

WIDOW HORIX WAS BORED.

She jousted with a cold slip of camel meat, pushing it around the gold circle of her plate with her knife. She barged aside a radish, sending it bouncing across the onyx tabletop.

All was silent except for the hissing of rain beyond the balcony, and the hum of a pair of hummingbirds dancing around a potted palm. Horix's chamber-shades hovered nearby at the edges of the dining hall, as silent as the dead should be.

Days had passed since Meleber Crale had reported, and far too many for Horix's patience. She had spent enough time counting the half-coins in her vaults, or watching the army in the basements hammering and sawing. She had barely eaten. Her nights had been more restless than usual. And all the while, no locksmith.

Horix hooked her fingers under the lip of the plate and hurled it against the nearest wall. The gold-painted porcelain shattered. Radishes and meat scraps flew in all directions. Both the hummingbirds and the chamber-shades made a swift exit, all save one half-life, who crawled around trying to gather scattered vegetables.

'Out!' the widow shrieked.

When she was alone, she slammed the butt of her knife against the onyx and fixed her eyes on the doorway at the end of the hall.

Once more, she struck the black stone, making the steel knife ring. The fist that held it trembled with frustration.

Horix was raising her hand for another blow when the thudding of monstrous boots announced Kalid's arrival at the door. 'Enter, Colonel!' Horix barked before his knuckles touched the wood.

'Intuitive as always, Mistress,' Kalid said, voice hoarse and deep from dust. He closed the door and strode along the impressive stretch of the onyx dining table.

'What news from the basement?' Horix asked. 'Is our new Master Builder Poldrew on schedule?'

'Yamak assures me he is. Perhaps even ahead of schedule.'

'Hmm.' Her trust in anything Yamak said had died several weeks ago. Horix looked up at her colonel as he came to attention. His forehead was furrowed in a frown. Puffy bags sat under his eyes, as black as his unkempt beard. 'You look tired, Kalid.'

'"pologies, Mistress. I've been up all night looking into this ruckus that happened over in Menkare District.'

Widow Horix placed her knife flat and reclined against the arch of her chair. 'And?'

Kalid reported as though she were a general. It was possible to take a man out of the military, but the military never left the man, staining him a soldier for the rest of time.

'I took ten of my men and we found nothing but a battlefield. A bloody mess. Seems Serek Finel was fond of keeping beasts, and they were let loose during the fighting. Someone told us the brawl was still raging between survivors in the nearby streets, but we found nothing of it except a few bodies, already being hauled away by beggars to be bound. I'm sorry to say the Cult were there, also, clearing up the mess and taking care of the wounded. They were wearing armour, but Chamber of Code scrutinisers and proctors stood right by them and didn't bat an eyelid. Some even helped them.'

'Sisine has gone too far. Where's Serek Finel?'

'He's missing, presumed dead.'

'Naturally. And who attacked him? Was it Temsa?'

Kalid bowed his head, as if he was personally responsible for the bad news. 'As per usual, nobody knows. Not a survivor amongst Finel's guards was worth talking to. The attackers wore no seals at all and only simple black armour. Sellswords and mercenaries, by the looks of them.'

Horix's long, ruby-painted fingernails drummed on the stone. 'The man is impetuous, and he grows far too bold. No doubt he has his eyes set on me,' she said. 'Any news from that half-life Crale? Or Caltro?'

Kalid's head stayed bowed. 'None, Mistress.'

The knife joined the shattered porcelain as Horix flung it angrily. 'I grow tired of waiting for that spook,' she snarled. 'Time is running out.'

It was then that she caught herself, fist raised and teeth bared. Her game was not one of emotion, but of cold, calculating precision. She took a deep breath, placed her palms flat on the onyx, and rose from the chair.

The doorway to the balcony had been left open. White cotton curtains were draped across it. They were still and unmoving in the absence of wind, looking like veils of frost on a windowpane. Horix batted them aside, shattering the illusion, and strode onto the rain-spattered balcony. She stopped a few inches from where the rain fell. There, she could avoid the wet and stare into the soaking streets, watching tiny figures hurry through the downpour. It had lessened throughout the morning, but it was still far wetter than an Arctian was used to. Already she could see the lighter cracks in the low clouds, where the sun was trying to burn through. The wet clay smell of rain churning the streets filled her nostrils.

Horix looked to the Cloudpiercer, pale against the dark skies. Its upper third was lost to the cloud, and she found herself narrowing her eyes at where its lofty peak would have been. The widow had plenty of practice. Many hours she had spent gazing up at the Cloud Court and the emperor's Sanctuary, grinding her teeth.

'Colonel!'

Kalid was at her side in moments.

'Gather your men. I believe it's market day, isn't that right?'

'I… every day is market day, Mistress.'

Horix sucked a morsel of camel meat from between her teeth, plucked it free and flicked it over the balcony's edge. 'Precisely,' she said.

———◆———

THE DOWNPOUR HAD CALMED TO a drizzle: a light, musical pattering on helmets, pauldrons and umbrellas. The calming of the foul weather had stirred some more life back into the streets of Araxes. Half-lives were out in their droves once more, smocks of all colours spattered with fresh mud. There seemed a hurry in their step, as if there was lost time to be made up for. They hauled sacks and bundles, carted scrolls by the dozen under their arms, or jogged between what few stalls and shops had stayed open on that rainy day.

A few minor nobles clung to the dryer edges of the streets, huddled with their guards or acquaintances. They stared out from under awnings and pulled faces at the granite sky. Beetles and spiders strode through the mucky streets with ease, their riders sitting high in saddles and dry under wide pyramidal umbrellas of cotton or woven and waxed palm fronds. Brawny centipedes carrying packs and barrels gleefully churned up the mud, naturally fond of the wet. Their human drivers were far from charmed by the antics of the insects. Their voices were dulled by the rainfall and sloshing of feet through mud, but Horix could hear their cursing and the cracking of whips.

The more Horix's gaze roamed the streets and avenues, the more she sensed the dangerous edge to the city's mood. A threatening atmosphere was commonplace, as ever-present in Araxes as the droves of dead, the smoke from the dockland chimneys, or the dust from the Duneplains. Today it had been honed to a razor. She saw it in the gangs of house-guards standing in every doorway, the empty high-roads, and the extra boards nailed across every window.

Beneath her umbrella of gold filigree and black satin, Widow Horix marched through the mud with haste and without care. The widow held a faint fondness for the rain. It reminded her of time spent in the far, far north, where no buildings scraped the sky, where the dead stayed in the Nyx, and where the deserts were of ice, not sand. Her travels there had been brief, but she had found a kindred spirit in the harsh mercilessness of the northern wastes. Where the desert sun was brash and forceful, cold seeped. Cold crept. It wasn't like Horix to reminisce, but her only pastime in the last few days had been waiting, and that tended to turn a mind backwards to days gone by.

Behind her, two chamber-shades scrabbled to keep up with Horix while holding her black frills aloft. Around them, Kalid and twenty of his men formed a diamond of gold armour, shields and short spears. The colonel marched at its head, using his sword to move aside any dawdling half-lives or living. The few nobles that crossed their path gave them a wide berth, using the whole stretch of the wide streets in their efforts to stay safe and separate. Suspicion was rifer than ever with all the gossip surrounding Serek Finel. The house-guards would glare at each other, spears would waggle, but that was all. Horix almost wished for some action, even if only to alleviate her boredom.

The soulmarket plaza looked like a dinner plate hastily scraped of its contents. It was so empty, Horix initially thought the market was closed for the day, but the gold rope ringing the platform at the centre signified otherwise. The sandy stone around it was awash with ochre mud. The edges of the plaza glowed blue where groups of shades stood about in shackles. Several sorry-looking soultraders huddled under covered wagons. Their wares were scant today. Normally there were two or three times the number of shades. None of the merchants had opened their stalls bar one: a grumpy-looking tea vendor in a driftwood chair. Horix was curious whether it was the rain or the Nyxwater shortage that had resulted in such a poor offering.

A handful of buyers and nobles stood about, each an isolated island with a reef of guards. They all seemed to be waiting on a man who had clearly made an error in choosing a cream cotton suit for his day's wear. Not only was it bespattered with mud, but it clashed with his thinning lemon-yellow hair, which had been plastered across his brown scalp like too little butter over too much toast. He was busy pacing back and forth between the traders, arguing in hushed tones about something that was apparently highly inconvenient to him and his business. Upon seeing Horix and her entourage emerge onto the plaza and join his threadbare crowd, the official tugged at his wet locks in frustration.

'Fine!' Horix heard him say, spraying rainwater as he spoke. He gestured to the soultraders, and with a complete lack of alacrity, they handed him their scrolls and began to stir their shades into action with copper rods and switches. The official stamped up the stairs to his wooden platform, shooing away a flock of scabious pigeons.

As the nobles began to gather before the stage, Horix's guards formed two concentric rings about her. Kalid stood close, sword-tip resting in the mud. Over the shields of his men, he eyed the other nobles and the seals on their house-guards' shields. 'Dire pickings, Mistress,' he growled.

'That may be, but I care little, Colonel. Time is wasting. We need workers.'

The guards parted so Horix could watch the first batch of shades take to the platform. They were indeed a sorry-looking lot. They were the quality of shade one might find in a desert mine, or the dockyards, or a Sprawl beetle farm. Out of the ten now slouched or shivering on the platform, one was missing an arm from the shoulder; another's face had been partially ripped off, leaving nothing but skull beneath; and another still had taken a knee to avoid trying to stand on a smashed foot.

'A fine morning to you all, and to you all a fine morning!' began the balding official, raising his fistfuls of scrolls to the dark skies in welcome. He was trying to keep a warm smile on his face. It was already cracking at the edges, like old papyrus.

Not a word came from the gathered nobles and buyers, maybe half a dozen at the most. One young man with an umbrella of peacock feathers left almost immediately, his guards sloshing around him. Undeterred, at least outwardly, the official bowed low and gestured to the half-lives on the stage. The soultrader standing behind his wares, a pale northerner, looked interminably bored.

With an officious clearing of his throat, the official started the proceedings.

'Might I present Boss Ubecht's lot. Ten souls. Mostly fresh shades…' He paused briefly to glance at Boss Ubecht. '…good condition and genuine kills as per the Code. Two skilled workers. Others good for garden or warehouse labour.'

'Lies!' proclaimed one buyer, barely waiting for the official's words to leave his mouth. He wore a wide-brimmed hat to keep the rain away. 'These are scrapings!'

Undeterred, the official forced his smile wider. 'We will start with twenty silvers—'

Ubecht stamped his boot.

'*Thirty* silvers.' The official corrected himself. 'Thirty silvers for the first shade. Answers to the name Jeena, a young chamber-shade. Ten years of experience.'

Again, the buyer scoffed. 'Outrageous!'

'Now, Master Feen. Due to the current shortage of Nyxwater, we unfortunately… er… have had to, erm—'

The buyer was undeterred by the man's stammering. 'I wouldn't give you ten silvers for one of these damaged souls, never mind thirty!'

'Fuck off!' Ubecht growled. 'What do you expect? You're lucky I ain't charging forty!'

The official attempted a casual laugh. 'So then, do I have thirty?' He looked to the remaining buyers with desperate hope glowing in his eyes, as if he were a condemned man about to be hanged and longed for mercy.

The official's determined smile was on the verge of collapse when Horix spoke up.

'One hundred fifty for the whole lot,' she called, drawing a glance from Kalid.

Despite the muttering and sniggers from the tiny crowd, Ubecht shrugged, threw a leather pouch to the official, and clomped down the platform stairs.

'Sold, to Widow Horix!'

Beneath her cowl, Horix met the stares of the other buyers. Some were perplexed, she could see that, while others clearly considered her an old fool of a woman, buying worthless half-lives.

The next batch of shades came lumbering through the mud and up the steps of the stage, poked and prodded by men in blue masks and a seal Horix could not have cared less for. They were a finer group, but only slightly. A few clean kills, others butchered in restrained ways. Horix saw a few of the other buyers cupping hands around their mouths, whispering to confidants.

A young girl in a waterfall of blue silks, barely out of childhood, swaggered across the platform, tapping a copper cane in an annoying rhythm. Glyphs adorned her face like rampant freckles.

'Our next lot comes from Boss Helios, comprised of twenty-six souls—'

'Five hundred.'

The official's mouth gaped like a cod out of water. 'P...pardon, Tal Horix?'

'Five hundred,' said the widow. 'For all of them.'

'I...'

Boss Helios banged her cane against the wood with a resounding thud. 'Fine with me!' she cheered, striding promptly from the stage.

The stares had become scowls. Horix felt Kalid bend down, closer to her. 'The basements are crowded as they are, Mis—'

'I told you I am done being patient, Colonel,' Horix replied, waggling a finger. 'Poldrew will find a use for them.'

The official slicked his hair over his scalp and blew rain as he checked the next listing on his scroll. Fifteen shades, bound in copper shackles, lined up awkwardly. These were an ugly-looking bunch, also, missing eyes, noses and other important pieces. They looked like old stock from the fight-pits. A hunched old man, his silver hair in braids, stood guard, along with a series of identical blond men, the only difference between them their age.

'Boss Rapeen and Sons present their next l—'

'Two hundred!' Horix yelled. The other buyers threw up their hands in displeasure.

'How dare you be so greedy, Tal?' one of them shouted, some puffed-up man with a wig of arrow-straight black hair.

'Leave some for us!' called another.

They both received the full force of Horix's withering gaze.

'Four hundred,' croaked old Boss Rapeen.

Horix shook her head. 'Two hundred fifty.'

'Mistress, the coffers.'

Horix turned on Kalid, lips puckered disapprovingly. 'And what will they matter when I get my vengeance? Do not get skittish now,

Colonel, not when we are so close,' she hissed.

Rapeen gave his final offer. 'Three hundred even!'

Horix nodded.

'Erm…' The official paused for a moment while he thought, dripping with rainwater. 'Sold?'

Rapeen and his sons were already herding their shades back to the mud.

The official checked his scroll and grimaced. He looked behind him to make sure, and when he turned around, he wore a practiced smile, one as hollow as a dead tree. 'And I believe we have come to the end of our lots for now. Please do return tomorrow!' And with that, the man shuffled away with much speed, seeking refuge in the crowd of traders and glowing shades.

'This is outrageous!' yelled the wig. 'I came from two districts over to find soultraders with Nyxwater.'

'I advise you to keep searching, then,' Horix called out. She could see the man desperately trying to place her seal of hanging corpses, and where she ranked in society. Horix imagined the amount of silver she'd just spent would give him a clue, but the guessing clearly infuriated him; she didn't see him stamp his foot, but she heard it, and his smattering of house-guards came sloppily to attention. Between the grilles in their gold helms, Horix could see they were befuddled as to why their tor was taking on this woman's glittering phalanx of ex-soldiers. The Nyx shortage was evidently causing more desperation than usual in Araxes.

Kalid's men didn't even need an order. They collapsed their circle into a tight bunch, spear-points pointing outwards like a sea urchin, its black centre the smug widow under her umbrella.

'You can't just buy them all!' argued the wig, clearly flustered.

'Can I not? Show to me in the Code or soulmarket rules where it says I cannot, and I will happily rescind my offers. If not, I bid you a good day.'

The man spluttered, but produced no argument she had an interest in, and Horix left him standing there, strangling the empty air with his painted nails.

After half an hour of scratching signatures, stamping seals on papyrus, and handing over bags of silver coins, a long train of shades was escorted from the market square by six of Kalid's soldiers.

Horix remained behind, finding the cold, wet air too refreshing to retreat to her tower just yet. Watching her new wares disappear around a corner, she spun her umbrella, spraying drips in a spiral. Kalid stood behind her, and she gazed up at him from beneath her cowl. The wet had caused the plume on his helmet to droop. Rainwater gave his golden armour a beaded texture. His usual stoic face had harder edges, and his gaze were lost in the streets. She prodded his breastplate with a fingernail.

'You doubt me, Colonel?'

Kalid shook his head emphatically. 'Never, Mistress. Not in twenty years. I would not dare.'

'Then speak your mind. Something troubles you.'

'We have visitors, Mistress,' he replied, drawing his sword with a flash of silver and a scraping whine.

Horix followed his gaze and observed two great, armour-bound hulks sloshing through the mud towards them. Her teeth crunched as she tensed her jaw.

Danib and Ani Jexebel.

A wall of shields was built in moments, making buyers and traders alike turn around to see what the commotion was. Spears were thrust out, their long steel points shedding raindrops. Kalid stood tall, holding his curved Arctian blade flat and in front of the widow as a barrier.

'Easy, now,' he muttered to his men.

Danib and Jexebel's weapons remained at their sides or strapped across their shoulders. All they carried with them was a small mahogany box, edged with brass.

'That's close enough,' warned Kalid, and the two brutes came to a halt a dozen paces away.

'As you wish,' sighed Jexebel in a resigned tone. Her pale face was even more impassive than Kalid's. Her leather-and-mail armour was soaked through, and she looked as though she had been a victim of a speeding carriage and a muddy puddle, but Horix got the impression that wasn't the sole root of her mood. The shade behind her shoulder was impossible to read, given the ghastly steel helmet that covered his face. Blue vapours curled out of its gaps like hot breath.

'My master Tor Temsa wishes to give you a gift,' said Jexebel.

'I only want one thing from him,' Horix snapped.

Jexebel extended the box anyway. One of Horix's guards stepped forwards, edging slowly through the muck until he grabbed the box. Danib twitched and the man came scurrying back in haste. Horix could see Kalid tense as the shade chuckled.

Behind the shield wall, the box was put in the mud, and carefully opened with the point of a spear.

The pink velvet innards of the box held nothing apart from some shards of copper. Horix looked closer, and pieced them together enough to make out the glyph for "Crale".

Horix's head snapped up, eyes switching rapidly between Jexebel and Danib. 'Temsa's point?'

'He wishes to let you know that he is willing to compensate you handsomely for Caltro Basalt's coin.' Jexebel said. Jexebel made it look like saying those words was as arduous as pushing a horse up stairs.

Horix was trembling with anger. Her hand wrapped around the

hilt of the knife under her silks and squeezed it so hard she almost drew blood. *The cheek of it. The audacity.* She was so insulted her lips stayed pursed, white as clay and speechless.

Jexebel continued. 'He wants it, and will have it. Whether it's the hard way or the easy way. His words.'

Without any ceremony or etiquette whatsoever, Jexebel turned and left, her shoulder clanking against Danib's as she clomped away. The steel-clad brute did not move, instead fixing his white eyes on Colonel Kalid for a long and uncomfortable moment. Horix watched the two of them – shade and man – measure each other silently. The leather of Kalid's gauntlets squeaked as he tightened his grip around his sword handle.

Just as the tension became unbearable, it was shattered. Not with the drawing of a sword and a thunderclap of steel, as Horix had half-expected, but with an unimpressed grunt. Danib swivelled on his heel and trailed after Jexebel, his vapours leaving a sapphire trail behind him. Mud and sand sprayed from his heavy steps.

Colonel Kalid only relaxed his stance when Danib had vanished from view, turning into the busier thoroughfare adjoining the market.

'The time may come, Colonel, when you will have to fight that monster,' Horix growled.

Kalid's tone gave no emotion away. 'Aye, Mistress. I suspected it might.'

Horix kicked the wooden box shut. 'Temsa becomes intolerable! Who does that soulstealer think he is?'

'What will you do, Mistress?'

'Destroy him, is what I will do, Colonel! He wishes to play games with me? I will—'

'Tal!' came an irate shout from behind her. It was the tor in the wig, striding towards her with a finger raised in the air and plenty of rehearsed words on his tongue. His house-guards struggled to keep up with his eager pace. A few of the other buyers huddled behind him. 'I am not satisfied!'

Horix's house-guards bristled, but she left them behind, walking out to meet the tor with her umbrella in one hand, the other hand open and empty.

'Mistress!' Kalid called after her.

'I demand you sell me some of your shades!' ordered the wig.

There must have been ten paces between them now. She closed them quickly. He had yet to realise his mistake, blinded by his indignity. All he saw was a rich but frail old woman.

They always do.

'It is outrageous for you to... I say, stop there—!'

In a blink, the blade lurched from her silk folds and plunged under the tor's ribs. It was so fast, his house-guards didn't quite register it had happened. The widow withdrew the knife, and stabbed again. And again, driving the blade into his stomach repeatedly. The wig coughed blood, eyes watering with disbelief. It took a yell from one of the onlooking soultraders to make the house-guards and other buyers realise, and by this time, Kalid and his guards had already formed up around their mistress and her victim. All present looked on aghast as Horix kept stabbing, working her way up to his throat. When the dagger became too slippery and escaped her fingers, she upended her umbrella and drove its point deep into the bloody mess of the man's stomach. She pressed down on it with all her weight, and the tor's eyes bulged. He croaked and spluttered, but could not manage any words.

'I told you to keep searching,' breathed Horix, before the tor fell limp.

With a snarl, the widow stepped away, leaving her filigree and satin umbrella upright in the man's chest, wobbling slightly. Horix looked around at the onlookers, her wild eyes and a blood-flecked face challenging them to speak. None did. Not the market officials, not the soultraders, not the scattered buyers. Not even the dead tor's house-guards, who had abruptly found themselves rather unemployed. The only sound was the squelching of feet as normality resumed. Nobody looked down at the bleeding corpse in the mud.

Waving to her house-guards, Horix strode purposefully towards the nearest avenue. Her guards clustered around her, leaving some of the more shameless house-guards to fight over their unbound master.

Horix popped each of her bloody knuckles in slow succession. Kalid waited patiently while she wiped them dry with a silk kerchief.

'I have one more job for you, Colonel, before you can rest,' she said, after some time.

There was a metallic thud as his heels came together. 'Whatever you command, Mistress.'

She said nothing more until their journey took them past a rookery. It consisted of a spindly tower, an angular effigy of a tree made from the detritus of the street: broken crates, discarded scaffolding poles, and twine. Bundles and bundles of twine. A wizened, bespectacled man stood at its base behind a battered table, strings tied to his wrist. The strings led up the tree to the legs of a dozen rooks. A large tarpaulin had been spread over the makeshift branches.

'Sending a scroll, Tal?' asked the man.

'Indeed. Fetch me papyrus and reed.'

He did so, and while Horix scratched out a message on the wobbly, pockmarked table, he pulled down a rook from the tree with much flapping and squawking, rolling the string around his wrist like a winch.

Horix pressed the papyrus into Kalid's hand. 'Dispatch this scroll for me, Colonel. Then I want you to station yourself and your soldiers near Temsa's new tower. Magistrate Ghoor's place. Keep watch there, and wait,' she ordered, speaking quietly over the raucous rook. The old man seemed too preoccupied to be eavesdropping.

Kalid eyed the glyphs. 'This is a bold play, Mistress, if you don't mind me saying.'

Horix placed her hands on her hips. 'And why not, Kalid? After the debacle at Finel's, it is a fine time to meddle in Tor Temsa's business. He has disposed of my spook, after all. If I am correct, he's already taken on a magistrate. Now a serek. He is overreaching. Most likely hurting from such a messy soulsteal. All the while, he draws more attention to himself,' she said. 'As I still have time, I have decided to take new steps, and skewer two birds with one bolt.' Much to the squawking of the birds above, Horix jabbed a hand at the Cloudpiercer, just a dark column to the west. 'I will do my civic duty, Colonel, and relay my concerns about a certain Tor Temsa to our good empress-in-waiting. As such, we will pry her out of that grand tower, bring her down into the streets. The gutters. Why not remove her now, and save ourselves the inconvenience later?'

Kalid's jaw bunched. His voice was low. 'I hope you don't mind me being honest, Mistress. I wouldn't be doing my duty if I wasn't. That sounds like a risky step. Why don't you let me gather my best soldiers and go solve this matter with Temsa once and for all instead of playing such games with the royalty?'

'I thought you would be pleased at the chance to wet your sword, Colonel, as you have been pining to for months. And you should know better when it comes to tactics! Divide and conquer, isn't that correct? Your worry has got the better of you, Kalid. Your only duty is to get me my locksmith back. That is all.' Her questioning look got a bow out of him, and he folded the papyrus in half. 'Let Temsa make the bloodbaths for now, and let me play my games. Besides, you think you can take on that Scatter woman, or Temsa's huge shade, and win? Let Sisine and Etane and the Royal Guard take care of them. You and your men are worth plenty of silver. Silver I do not want to waste.' There was a pause as she once again levelled a finger and prodded his breastplate. 'You especially, Colonel. You have served me well. Now is not the time to break that habit.'

Kalid's throat bobbed as he swallowed his pride. 'Yes, Mistress. We will be ready and waiting.'

'You had better,' she croaked. Before he turned away, she caught him with a crooked finger. 'And Kalid?'

'Yes, Mistress?'

'Make sure the empress-in-waiting stays breathing, if you can. I would like a word with her.'

CHAPTER 5
A DAY FOR BETRAYAL

Watch he who is without shades throw
the first stone.

OLD ARCTIAN PROVERB

THE LATE MORNING SUNLIGHT FELL in streaks across Sisine's face, tanned red by the painted glass. It must have been a fitting hue. The storm may have passed, but its fury lived on in the empress-in-waiting.

'How *dare* he! Who in Araxes does that half-life think he is? Offering me a *proposal*, like some common trader!' Sisine stabbed a yellow plum with her dagger, driving the point to the marble of the bowl beneath. She stared again at the gold-rimmed papyrus note that lay on the table beside it. Etane had delivered it barely an hour ago; already she had read its glyphs fifty times, and still the message refused to change. Boon had called a meeting of the Cloud Court without her approval. The message was a polite invite. *The pure cheek of it.*

'Maybe he wants to discuss something,' offered Etane, still unmoving from his spot by the door to her bedchamber. Irritatingly, his eyes were fixed on a point somewhere above her head. 'Like a truce.'

Boon had been a constant thorn in Sisine's side since Magistrate Ghoor had been killed. Not only had the Cult put shades on the streets of the outer districts despite her – or the emperor's – decrees, but the serek challenged every word that came from her mouth. Boon was not a shade. He was a huge, pompous mosquito, constantly buzzing around her.

Vexed, Sisine flung the plum at Etane's face. Ochre juice spattered his robes though the fruit flew straight through him. It burst apart on the far wall, redecorating a mosaic.

'A truce? Boon would not have spent so long berating me only to fold like bed linens! No, more likely he and his allies in the Court are planning to overthrow me. To get to Father. Did you think of that?'

Another plum lost its life, skewered by her silver blade. 'It has something to do with the fucking Cult. I know it. My spies see more and more of them all the time. Cult priests preaching on street corners, and some swear they have seen Cult soldiers. Rebene should be keeping them under control, not allowing them to spread like the crimson fungus they are!'

'With all due respect, Your Wonderfulness, I think Rebene's got enough on his plate without chasing after the Cult. I reckon he's one more murder away from slicing his own throat open. You wanted chaos. You seem to have it.'

She launched another plum at him. 'Do not tell me what I want!' Sisine shrieked, breathing hard. 'If Rebene dares to take the coward's way out, I'll have him bound and put to work in a quarry. Let's see how the chamberlain likes that. Time!'

Etane moved to an hourglass, marking the notches where the sand reached. 'Almost there, Princess.'

Sisine screeched, squashing another of the fruits in her bare hand. Its juice stained the papyrus an amber yellow. 'How dare he call the court to gather! This is *my* Cloudpiercer. *My* city! Nobody but my father holds more coins than I do! My father saw to it for this very purpose.'

'I—'

'The very cheek of it! Does he think me some lowly tal to be bartered with? It is *my* Cloud Court. *I* call the gatherings. *I* give the decrees. He does not dictate to me!' Sisine hissed, her voice cold with venom. One last plum succumbed to her wrath before she rose from her chair and clicked her fingers. 'Robe!'

Etane disappeared into another chamber and came back with a purple satin robe, trimmed with sable fur and gold tassels. Sisine wiped the plum juice from the dagger and thrust it into her belt, making sure it was front and centre for all to see.

'Sword!' she ordered. 'You may need it.'

Etane vanished again, eagerly rubbing his hands. This time he returned wearing a fine suit of mail. His massive sword, Pereceph, rested against his shoulder. Faint wisps of grey smoke emanated from its steel edge.

'Door!'

Fifty Royal Guards waited in the polished hallway, all lined up like statues against the grand walls. As Etane and the empress-in-waiting passed, they peeled away one by one and formed a double column that marched in perfect unison.

Sisine held her tongue, building up all manner of menacing words behind it, ready to unleash them on Boon and the rest of the recalcitrant sereks.

Temsa had been hard at work. So far – quite infuriatingly – he had ignored her list, but he was still inducing the same amount of panic she had hoped for. However, instead of gathering to support her, the sereks had begun looking to other places for solutions. Boon's suggestion of assistance from the Cult, for instance. Or calls for her father's army to be called back from the Scatter Isles. After all Sisine had done to distance the sereks from the nonsense of her father's babbling decrees, they still had no trust in her. No respect.

It made her blood boil daily. Sleep evaded her. She had almost worn a rut in her chambers from incessant pacing. Makeup and swirling dye tattoos covered it, but she had worn her fingertips to callouses by wringing her hands. Where once confidence had clad her will in iron, doubt now rusted it.

As the shade-drawn lift came to a halt, she realised she had spent the short journey cursing under her breath.

'Did you say something, Majesty?' Etane whispered, leaning in.

Sisine waved him aside irritably. 'Nothing, shade.'

When the great gold doors of the Cloud Court were pulled open and she emerged under the wide arch, she was deeply surprised to see the gilded benches of the court empty. The sky was streaked with clouds, and the sunlight fell in ever-moving patches. They moved lazily across the marble, like adventurous smears of mould. Silence hung in the room. Every footstep or clink of armour echoed brazenly. She stared at the empty throne, half-caught in a sunbeam, one side turquoise, one side a deep ocean blue.

'Boon!' Sisine screeched. 'What is the meaning of this?'

A young, finely-dressed shade waited on the far side of the hall, peeking out from a door that led to feasting chambers. When he saw Sisine, he quickly disappeared behind the jamb. The sound of marching rang out as soldiers appeared in his place. They were shades, clad in silver armour polished to a mirror state. Their blue glow shone through at the joints and narrow face-guards. The shades held no spears but their hands were firmly clasped on their sword handles.

Sisine could have spat when she saw Boon, draped in gold and silver finery. A necklace of carnelian glyphs hung around his neck. His dark, once-charred face held a smile for her. He looked less like a serek and more like a gaudy merchant in a bazaar. She longed to don a copper glove and smack that smile clean off.

Her guards bristled as Boon's entourage met them at the centre of the hall. Spears and broad shields formed two opposing walls. A good distance was kept between them, as was customary for such meetings between rival tors, tals or sereks. It was simply not the kind of meeting she had been expecting.

Sisine stepped forwards so she could look the blue bastard in the face, making sure she was the one to speak first. *This was her Cloud Court.*

'You think too much of yourself, Serek Boon, to treat your empress-in-waiting so disrespectfully as to summon her to a gathering, and then leave her waiting. What, might I ask, have you done with my Cloud Court? Is this some guise to get an audience with me? One might assume foul intentions.' She could feel her guards tensing around her.

Boon shook his head sadly, as if he was the bearer of bad news. 'I mean no disrespect, Your Majesty, and my intentions are pure. I am but a messenger. The sereks would like me to inform you that they are unwilling to leave their towers for fear of their lives. The attack on Serek Finel – one of our own – has sealed their doors. As such, they will not be gathering for court. Not today, nor any time soon.'

Sisine flashed a murderous glance at Etane. 'What attack?'

The serek had the gall to looked surprised. 'Why, Majesty, I thought you were the beating heart of this city, aware of its every move! Is that not the case?'

'Speak, half-life!'

She saw the flicker of hatred in the corner of Boon's scabbed mouth. Such a term was reserved for the bound dead, not a free shade, and especially not a serek.

Boon paced along his wall of guards, speaking between the gaps in armour. 'Serek Finel's home was attacked last night in a brazen assault, the like of which this city has not seen for five centuries. The attack then spilled into the streets and raged for almost an hour before Finel's guards and some intrepid independent keepers of the peace turned the tide. Unfortunately, the Chamber's proctors and scrutinisers arrived too late. As did your soldiers – the shades you so graciously donated. They were too thinly spread over the districts to be of any help. I'm afraid Serek Finel has been murdered and his body stolen.'

'Your point, Boon?'

'The city is in disarray, Majesty. There is bedlam in the streets. To add to the situation, your mother has still not returned, and your father still refuses to come out of his Sanctuary. In their stead you seem unable to protect us, and we have grown tired of living in fear.'

Sisine bubbled with anger, but she tried to keep it contained. 'We? Who is "we"?'

'The sereks, and several influential nobles.'

'And you, Serek Boon, have decided this for the entire city, have you? When you have no right of coin to make such decisions? I wonder how much silver you spent poisoning so many minds against me.'

Boon spread his hands wide. She saw the tortured whorls of vapour there, where his palms had melted before he died. 'I have been nominated merely as a spokesperson. This is the sereks' decision and therefore the city's. As a result, we have decided to take matters into our own hands. Time is a river, Empress-in-Waiting. We must move with it to avoid drowning.'

'This is treason!' Sisine yelled, her restraint dissolved by the shade's audacity. 'Utterly against the Code!' The word was like a command. Her guards snapped into an attack position, ready to spring forwards. Etane took his sword from his shoulder and spun it in his hand. His blue vapour began to wrap around its grip and crossguard.

Boon's guards made no countermove. Instead, the serek raised hands, scarred palms flat and empty, as though Sisine had a triggerbow and copper bolts trained on him. Oh, how she wished she did.

'This is nothing so dire as treason, Majesty.' A smug look came over his face. 'As you have been acting for the good of the emperor, we believe we can too.'

'You have no right! You do not outrank my father, or me! Those who rule make the rules, as we always have.'

Boon winked. 'Perhaps individually, we do not. Together, however, we just might. Did you ever think of that? Perhaps these are times for change.'

'That is not how the Code works!' Sisine wrapped a hand around her dagger.

'Be that as it may, we have simply accepted an offer of assistance on your father's behalf.'

'What offer of assistance? What have you done?'

Boon knitted his fingers together. 'Why, the offer from the Church of Sesh, of course.'

'The *Cult!*' Sisine corrected him. Again, she saw that flicker of anger.

'You'll find that the Church is not what it used to be, Majesty. They can patrol the streets alongside the Chamber and your soldier shades, help to bring peace to our chaotic streets. They have the ability, the willingness and the resources to help hunt down this wanton murderer.'

Sisine felt the cavernous chamber tilting on its side, felt her grip slipping. The doubt had grown into something with teeth and claws and was now sizing her up for a meal. 'I do not accept!' she bellowed.

'It is not for you to worry yourself with, Majesty. As I said, the offer has already been accepted on the emperor's behalf,' said the shade.

'I will have you all stoned for treason! You will find scrutinisers at your doors by sundown!' Sisine had half a mind to order Boon arrested that very moment.

'I think not.' The serek's smile was sickly. 'Rebene is busy enough. And with all the murders, imagine how it would look if the emperor and his daughter turned upon their own? The nobles might lose faith in you altogether. The districts will follow. The Code won't matter, not a button. Neither will your tower, and you can add riots to your list of problems. Instead, let me make Your Majesty an offer.'

'Speak quickly, Boon, or I'll make sure you never speak again.'

He stepped forwards, soldiers wrapping tighter around him, so that he looked like a sapphire stuck in a silver hedgehog. 'Don't stand in the way of this. Accept this change. The murderer will be found, and the Cloud Court will reconvene. You can play the magnanimous victor and normality will resume. At least, what counts for normal in this city.' Boon's voice held a simpering tone. 'Busy yourself with matters that are within your grasp, Majesty. Leave this murderer to the Court, the Church and the Chamber. There are trade issues to worry about. Your father's wars in the Scatter Isles, perhaps. And let's not forget the dire supplies of Nyxwater, which I imagine hasn't entered your mind in days, Majesty. I hear of riots in the Outsprawls. Why not accept the Church's help? You can carry on playing empress while your mother is away and your father is in hiding.'

Sisine drew her lips back into a snarl. Her words were guttural, fierce. She wished her gaze was a spear on which to impale Boon. The order to have him arrested hovered on her tongue.

Etane moved closer to her, his whisper almost indiscernible. 'Not here, Princess. Not now. You're smarter than that.'

The shade gestured with his eyes, and she saw Boon's guards as still as when they had first halted. Their blades remained in their scabbards. It was almost as if the serek wanted her to attack.

Etane lifted his blade onto his shoulder once more. Sisine managed to unclench her fists. She distracted the serek with a compromise.

'You tread on quicksand, Boon, and too heavily at that,' she said. 'The Cult are not allowed in the Core Districts. That decree remains final. Understand?'

Boon raised an eyebrow. 'I will relay your message—'

'UNDERSTAND?'

Boon let the echoes of her screech die before continuing, '—to the rest of the Cloud Court.'

With a loud chorus of clanging metal, his guards stepped backwards until their master had reached the door. The Royal Guard moved forwards to ensure their exit. Sisine waited until she heard the slam of the doors.

Etane was opening his mouth to speak when Sisine filled it with a fist. Her copper and gold rings gave her enough weight to strike him, and he reeled backwards. He was hardly ever caught off-guard, and Sisine saw the indignation in his eyes as he looked up.

'That's for not telling me about the attack on Serek Finel,' she spat, before sweeping from the chamber. Her guards jogged to keep up with her. Etane was left standing, rubbing his chin and muttering something to himself.

Sisine turned at a violent angle, making her guards slide on the marble. Once again they corralled her, spears out like an urchin's spines. When she came to her father's Sanctuary door, Sisine threw open the unlocked doors and slammed them behind her with an echoing bang. Lip curled, she took a measured walk around the bench and saw the pile of scrolls lying at the door's foot. She counted them. Seven lay there, and one rolled halfway under the bench.

She chose that one to look at and unfurled it snippily. It was the same old shit. Rambling orders with nothing to do with the murders, the failing Nyx, nor the fact this city was slowly slipping into chaos, and not quite the kind Sisine had planned on. She hadn't predicted the most self-centred people in the city banding together against her. That was a failing, but it would not be her failure.

Turning a shaking hand on the door, she made it a promise. 'I will pry you out, Father. I will pry you out of there if it's the last thing I do.'

The empress-in-waiting dropped the scroll at her feet, and crushed it with her sole.

———————◆———————

'BAD NEWS NEVER ARRIVES ALONE,' so they said, and it was certainly true that day. Sisine had barely reached her balcony and taken a moment to breathe in the cool air when the message arrived.

This scroll came by a ragged old rook. The decrepit thing wheezed as it struggled to reach the marble railing. The bird looked like it had been trying to reach the peak of the Piercer for some time. As she snatched the papyrus from its leg, it sprawled on the stone to catch its breath. It was so tired it didn't protest as Sisine's trembling hand closed around its neck. The snap of its spine came at the same time she finished the message, and read its scrawled anonymous "X".

Letting the black carcass tumble down to the city, Sisine scrunched up the papyrus in her fists and stood there with shoulders quivering, watching the clouds tumble across the blue sky.

First Boon, and now this. The betrayals were mounting, and with it the pressure in her skull. The inklings of another headache were starting. They had grown more frequent in the past weeks, pulsing behind her eyes for hours at a time. She winced as pain lanced through her head. With a growl, she threw open the balcony curtains.

Etane sat on a chair of antelope horn, his head down, clearly hoping her scorching gaze wouldn't find him. Pereceph was lying flat on his lap.

Sisine's eyes bored into his bald, scarred pate.

'Did you know of this?'

The scroll went flying at him, landing at his feet. He took a moment to flatten it out and read it.

'No, Princess,' said Etane. He tossed the scroll on the nearest couch, but his eyes remained firmly on the plush carpet.

'Look at me.'

He did so begrudgingly.

'Did you know of this?' Sisine asked again, louder and slower. The cotton curtains billowed around her.

'*No*, Princess. I did not.' Etane's expression was firm but blank, and she stared into his white eyes to try and see the lies hidden there. It was useless. Whether he was well-practised or innocent, he had now let her down twice.

'How am I supposed to claim the throne if I don't stay ahead?'

'With difficulty, Your Magnificentness.'

'Or not at all!' Sisine snatched up the scroll and strangled it, crushing its spindle. She wrenched the papyrus from it and stared at it once more against the light of the window.

'"Your locksmith is dead and in the company of Tor Boran Temsa. Faithfully, a Concerned Party. X."' She read it aloud. 'The gall of it! The impudence! The deceit!'

'If I may—'

'You may not!' Sisine screeched. 'You're the one who told Temsa about Caltro Basalt in the first place.'

Silence fell and hung between them like a bad smell. When Etane felt brave enough, he continued.

'Temsa has been using him well. And now we know where he is. He is ours again when we want him, and we're back to your original plan. Just in time.'

Sisine cursed him under her breath. Etane's most infuriating quality was being right more often than not. Deny it as vociferously as she might, he had the wisdom of almost a century behind him. He had watched these games play out a hundred times before. She cursed his age, and his smart tongue, and stared out of the window at the shades and peasants trundling about like sheep. She cursed them too, the fickle creatures.

'Fetch my carriage. Guards. Soldiers. And I want the fastest horses.'

Etane got to his feet, but hesitated. Sisine cut him off before he could say a word.

'NOW!'

SISINE WAS SO FIXATED ON the outside, her nose might as well have been pushed against the glass. She watched the passage of the city with an almost childlike avidity. Her eyes darted between the awnings and avenues, hunting for signs of red robes. Between the shade riders on black horses accompanying her carriage, all she glimpsed were mud-smeared citizens. Here and there, queues of people curved around the buttresses of spires, toting empty handcarts and wagons. They stretched to the steps and doors of grand warehouses. Over the rattle of the carriage wheels, Sisine swore she heard shouting, perhaps chanting. The scenes were snatched away from her before any sense could be made of them.

Etane remained silent. He had donned his armour, a relic as old as he was: an ornate cuirass with matching pauldrons, faulds and greaves, forged in layers of black and copper plates. Decorative glyphs ran along their sharp edges, seeming to dance as his vapours escaped from the gaps in the metal. Pereceph was strapped to his shoulders. Etane sat rigid, silent as marble, swaying with the motion of the hurried journey. He looked as if he had plenty to say, but Sisine had little desire to hear the shade speak. Instead she engrossed herself in trying to catch a glimpse of the Cult. Though it would be like drawing the point of a dagger down her arm, she needed to prove her spies and suspicions true. Her day was already lying in the gutter, she might as well kick it while it was down there.

Sisine was still staring out of the window when there came startled cries from outside the carriage. She saw her shade soldiers lower their spears, but there was no danger; just a pink pelican croaking loudly to itself as it swung low over the streets, a washing line and several scarves trailing from its rubbery foot. A few Chamber proctors were chasing it, trying and failing miserably to snatch the rope.

Sisine narrowed her eyes at it.

'We're here,' announced Etane as the carriage halted moments later. 'Temsa's new abode.'

The empress-in-waiting looked up at the sandstone spire as she emerged into the hot sun, her chainmail armour all a-glitter with polished steel and inlaid gems.

'Magistrate Ghoor's tower, indeed. Audacious bastard.'

'Better than a shit-smeared tavern in Bes District, Your Splendidness.'

'Hmph.'

Sisine waited for the soldiers and her Royal Guard to form a sharp arrowhead for wading through the streets. Already she heard the low murmur of onlookers. The golden, armoured carriage was enough to draw eyes, never mind the flash of royal colours and the steel of a hundred soldiers. The flow of the streets ground to a halt, and the gathered crowds were promptly cleared aside by General Hasheti's mute shades. The general himself walked at the head of the arrow, ordering bystanders out of the way with his sword raised.

Sisine pulled her silk veil over her head and face. She snuck glances through its shimmer. This was no poor district, but to the daughter of Emperor Farazar they were all poor compared. No silk shone so brightly as hers. No armour was as fine. No dyes matched the depths of her colours. No jewellery boasted such intricacy.

She noticed a few small children perched on shoulders to get a peek at her. Street artists madly sketched her entourage, bits of charcoal flying over their papyrus and parchment canvases. Beggars pushed through the finer crowds, hoping a mere glance of a princess would enrich their melancholic lives. Those at the edges, facing the soldier's spears, bowed or sank to their knees.

Such was the secluded nature of the royals, and the danger of Araxes' streets, that they were as myths come to life when they walked amongst the towers. Hers was a richness completely unattainable, mythic to most, and that made her a spectacle. Godly, even. As always, it also made her a target, hence her entire phalanx of soldiers. In the many eyes she passed over, she caught the glimpses of jealousy, that animalistic hunger, and the accompanying lick of the lips.

Sisine caught the look of a free shade, standing with his arm around a wife who was very much alive. Their eyes met briefly before she turned away, but it was enough for Sisine to recognise hatred.

'Etane, have them raise the shields. I don't want their filthy eyes on me,' Sisine ordered.

The shade called to Hasheti and waved his arm. Moments later, the soldiers and guards changed position to make a barricade of shields that was two rows high and angled to hide her from even the tallest gawper, including those on beetle and horseback.

With the pounding rhythm of boots, they came to Temsa's gates – or rather, old Ghoor's gates. To Sisine's surprise, they found no resistance at all. The lines of guards waiting in the walled-off courtyard did not challenge them. They merely kneeled awkwardly, as if they'd never tried it before. General Hasheti had his soldier shades march slowly, wary of an ambush.

'Looks like he's expecting us,' Etane remarked in a hushed voice.

Sisine flexed her gloved fingers and raised her chin to a regal angle. 'Good. Maybe he's realised his shame.'

When they approached the large, half-moon doorway, clad in varnished wood and black iron, it parted with barely a whine. The two monstrous shapes of Temsa's shade and bodyguard beckoned them inwards. Hasheti led the soldiers forwards, bunching into a column. They regained their triangle shape as they entered an expansive but austere atrium. The formation's points rotated slowly to the jingle of mail and plate. Etane spent the wait staring at the giant armoured shade, Danib, who in turn had his white, burning eyes fixed on Etane and his mighty sword. Sisine tried to gauge the shades' expressions. It was difficult through the narrow slits of their helms.

'Welcome, Your Majesty!' hollered a voice, interrupting her thoughts.

Sisine looked up to find Tor Temsa coming down the lavish, curving staircase, making a racket in the process with his cane and golden claws.

'I imagined it might be time for a visit, now that I have new lodgings. More appropriate and less suspicious when an empress-in-waiting feels like calling. Though, I must say, you've brought rather a lot of soldiers.'

'One must, when dealing with those known for lying, cheating and murdering,' Sisine called to him through a gap in her shield walls.

Temsa had made it to the marble floor. Now that he was close, he extended her a bow as deep as he could manage. Despite his striped silks of gold and sage, agate jewellery and abundance of rings on his fingers, he seemed more haggard than when last they had met. Powder and makeup had done nothing for him. Stress sat beneath his eyes and there were plenty of strays in his uncombed hair and sharp beard. There was a deep gash on his forehead, curved like a sickle, and his knuckles were dark with scrapes and bruises.

'You describe me well, Your Majesty. But you seem perturbed by this,' he replied. 'To what do I owe this imperial pleasure?'

She shook her head. 'Privacy, Tor. Then we will speak.'

Etane and forty soldiers peeled from the formation, leaving the rest behind in the atrium. Temsa led them up the stairs at a slow pace, but it gave Sisine time to shape her words. The carriage ride had not been enough.

As it turned out, 'privacy' was almost fifty bodies crammed into a red-velvet dining hall. A huge marble table ran its length. Sisine and her large majority occupied one end of it, while at the other end sat Temsa, his looming colleagues, and a smattering of black-clad guards. Temsa didn't seem perturbed by the fact that the emperor's daughter had come knocking unannounced, and wore a face as threatening as a battle-line.

Sisine decided she needed answers first if she were going to corner him. It had been a day of surprises, and she was not enthused at the prospect of more.

'Why Serek Finel?' she snapped. She spoke openly, knowing the soldiers around her were tongueless. Hasheti had remained downstairs to watch Temsa's black-armoured cronies lounge about the pillars.

Temsa drummed his ringed fingers on the table. 'Finel was richer than most and far out of the core.'

'And yet you failed, from what I've been told.'

'Failed, Majesty?' Temsa looked confused. 'I think not.'

'You set his zoo loose on the streets and brought the Chamber crashing in. The whole city is in uproar. The Cloud Court has refused to gather.'

Temsa thumbed his nose, looking between Danib and the woman. *Something Jexebel.* Jexebel simply shrugged, looking distinctly bored, while the shade only had eyes for Etane. They were still locked in a duel of stares.

'Well?' demanded Sisine.

With a sigh, Temsa reached for something beneath his chair.

The bloody head came to rest on the marble tabletop with a squelch. Sisine was no stranger to death – she saw it every day in Araxes, frozen in the blue wounds of the half-lives – but this made her gorge rise. Perhaps it was because the last time she had seen this head, it had been attached to a living serek, leering down at her from the galleries of the Cloud Court.

One of Finel's eyes was missing. A ruined hole remained, showing her brain and skull. The other eye was turned to the gold-leaf ceiling.

The serek's jaw hung open in a broken smile, and judging by the carnage around his neck, it looked as though Finel's head had been ripped off, not cut. Sisine's eyes slipped from the grotesque sight to the huge shade covering it in shadow.

'Serek Finel's body is far below us, already bound. His half-coins are being transferred as we speak.'

'And the banks don't grow suspicious?'

Temsa nodded, looking weary. 'My bank is no doubt getting fat and handsome off the profits from my half-coins. Even if they weren't, I've given the directors enough reasons to keep their lips shut too. Another Weighing and I might just make serek.'

Sisine didn't relish the thought of this gargoyle sat on the Cloud Court, if it ever convened again. 'What success you have had, Tor Temsa,' she said, catching Jexebel rolling her eyes, 'despite only seeing to one target on my carefully constructed list. Even then, you couldn't crack her vault, so instead you burned her tower to ashes.'

The little man stretched in his chair, entwining his fingers behind his head as if he were ready for a nap. 'Got the job done though, right? You wanted chaos. I've delivered it.'

Sisine pushed her way forwards, scattering soldiers so she could spread her palms on the long table. They quickly reassembled around her, flowing like autumn leaves chasing hurried steps. She felt their cold sweep through the gaps in her chainmail.

'Do not dare toy with me, man! You are lucky I haven't ordered my soldiers to make you look like Serek Finel there,' she hissed, pulling at the tension in the room like it was a bowstring. Danib stood taller. Jexebel patted her axe. Etane rested his huge sword on the edge of the table. There was silence.

'And yet,' Sisine continued, looking around the velvet walls, 'you managed Ghoor easily enough.'

Again, Temsa looked confused, though this time it looked genuine. It was time to pounce. She reached inside her folds of silk and threw a scrap of papyrus at him. He watched it skitter across the tabletop and nudged it with a bloody knuckle.

'What's this?'

'The secret to your recent success, it seems.'

Curiosity got the better of him and he gingerly opened the ball of papyrus. The empress-in-waiting sneered. Everybody knew the old tricks of hiding powders and poisons in messages. She was not that cheap. She liked to stare her enemies in the face. That way she could watch that delicious moment where they realised they had failed.

Temsa must have read the glyphs several times, but no inkling of failure or any similar emotion crossed his face. Only vexation. When he was done, he re-crumpled the papyrus and ground his thumb into his forehead. He remembered his wound and flinched.

His next word was a snarl. 'Horix.'

'Excuse me?'

'The bitch who sent this message. Widow Horix.'

'I do not give a golden fuck who sent it, Temsa. I want to know if it is true! Do you have Caltro Basalt in your possession?'

'No!' he snapped. 'Though it was true. That Krass bastard escaped me during the raid on Serek Finel.'

Sisine threw her hands to the ceiling. 'What a disappointment you are turning out to be, Boran Temsa! I should have you stoned and pulled apart by horses for your insolence and betrayal—'

The putrid little man burst from his chair and slammed his palms on the table. 'I know where he is!'

Sisine listened to the creaking of gauntlets gripping spear-shafts around her. Etane's sword grated against the marble, like a fiddler preparing his strings.

Temsa continued, calmer now. His hands left streaks of sweat on the marble as they withdrew. 'In fact, Empress-in-Waiting, I was just planning how to reclaim him before you arrived so unexpectedly.'

'Were you indeed? And at which point were going to tell me, your empress-in-waiting, about any of this? My shade explicitly ordered you to keep me informed!'

Temsa flashed her a glance under heavy brows, childlike, as if he had just been told off for guzzling too many sweets. 'When I had him back, obviously,' he growled. 'Caltro Basalt's half-coin belongs to a tal by the name of Widow Horix. She's an old crone that appears at the soulmarkets occasionally. I sold her Caltro not knowing who or what he was, and after Tor Busk stole him from her, I happened across the shade in the streets. Naturally I put him to good use, for our mutual benefit. But Horix is a meddling bitch, and she sent a spook by the name of Crale to come oust him. That failed, thanks to Danib, but Caltro got big ideas and slipped away during the attack on Finel, sneaking back to his mistress Horix, I'd wager. Before his escape, my intentions were to reclaim his coin. For you, Majesty, of course. I ask you, what use was it delivering you a shade that wasn't mine to give? A half-life that could be snuffed at any moment by a widow's whim? Now, I am a position to both claim Caltro's coin and stop Horix from interfering. I intend to do so promptly. Tomorrow night, in fact.' Temsa forced a polite smile. 'With your permission, of course, Majesty.'

'I see,' Sisine replied. It was an irritatingly sound argument, even if it did sound like Temsa had just yanked it out of his arsehole. The man had lied to her once already. That was not to be forgotten, nor forgiven. She stared deep into his bloodshot eyes, searching them for sign of deeper lies. 'What else are you keeping from me, I wonder? Is there anything beyond your own carelessness that may affect our arrangement?'

Temsa answered quickly and firmly. 'No, Empress-in-Waiting. There is not.'

'Then consider our business concluded, for now. You may deal with this Widow Horix, but I wish to be there.' With some satisfaction, Sisine watched Temsa's jaw clench. 'To add some royal supervision and ensure you don't fail me again. And after I have Caltro's coin, you will remove another serek from his tower.'

'Who might that be?'

'Serek Boon. I want him turned to smoke. And soon.'

Temsa nodded sagely. 'Right you are, Majesty. He'll be taken care of sure enough, after Horix.'

'Until tomorrow.'

Silks flailing, mail ringing, Sisine withdrew, though her eyes stuck fast to Temsa's even as her soldiers swarmed about her. It was only when the door slammed that the stare was broken.

Before the echoes had died, and before she was treading the stairs, Sisine had already made up her mind. She decided to tell Etane. *Decisions grow flesh when spoken aloud.*

'That man's time in this city is growing rather short.'

———◆———

TEMSA PUSHED HIMSELF BACK FROM the table, eyeing Finel's matted and bloodied hair. He distracted himself with ripping chunks of calloused skin from his fingertips.

As he pondered, Ani began to walk away, muttering to herself. Confused, a few guards trailed in her wake.

'And where do you think you are going, m'dear?' Temsa called after her.

She didn't bother to turn around. 'To see to the spoils. The binders have been grumbling about running out of Nyxwater.'

Temsa was on his feet in an instant, nails scraping at the marble. 'You face me when you speak to me, Ani!'

Ani turned, though her feet didn't skip a step. 'I warned you about playing a cult and an empress against each other,' she said in a strained voice. 'I remember a time when you answered to nobody. Now you've got two bosses to keep happy. Guess it's true what you Arctians say: the higher you climb up the mountain, the more treacherous it becomes.'

'You stop there!' Temsa's screech fell on deaf ears, and before he could barge his way clear of his seat, she had vanished into a stairwell.

An awkward silence came on the tail of his shouts. A few guards cleared their throats while Temsa stared, red-faced and shaking, at the doorway. It took some time before he realised Danib's gaze rested upon him.

'Don't you dare agree with her,' he warned the shade as he stamped away, sparks flying from his talons. 'Don't you fucking dare!'

Temsa limped his way along the breadth of the table, leaving his guards to blow sighs and shake their heads.

———◆———

'WHAT DO YOU MEAN "LEAVING"?'

'She's leaving! Have a look, Colonel.' The spyglass had been glued to the soldier's face for so long it had left a deep red ring around the man's eye.

Kalid snatched it to see for himself, grunting as he crouched down beside the chimney stack. From the low rooftop, he could see down the street and into Magistrate Ghoor's old courtyard. Sure enough, as the soldier had said, Sisine's entourage was filing out of the doorway.

Colonel Kalid tensed. He saw no bloodied weapons through the misted view. No wounds. Temsa's men even bowed accordingly as the empress-in-waiting departed.

'Fuck!' Kalid dashed the spyglass against the edge of the roof, watching the cracked lenses skitter over the whitewashed stone.

Two hours he and his best fighters had waited there, watching. Two hours his soldiers had spent crammed into alleyways and rooms below, poised to wet their blades. The brewing storm had petered out and left a limp wind in its place. That weasel Temsa must have talked himself out of his fate, or struck a deal, perhaps. Kalid felt unsettled. Not just anyone avoided the royal rage so deftly. It was almost – dare he think it – impressive.

Working his teeth around the inside of his lips, the colonel listened to the faint clanking on the air as he watched the glittering procession head back to its armoured carriage.

'Back to the tower!' he barked irascibly.

'But…why?'

'Ain't nothing happening here! Silver tongues win over steel today,' Colonel Kalid shouted as he followed his men down the stairs. His heels punished the steps as he grumbled privately.

The widow was going to be far from pleased.

CHAPTER 6
A POOR WELCOME

Araxes wasn't always the mighty city it is
today. In ancient times it was a scattered
collection of towns spread between the
Duneplains and the Troublesome Sea.
Farmers to fishermen, disparate faras – or
lords – fought for control. It was only when
Emperor Phaera's grandfather Narmenes
united the lords to fight the Scatter Isle pirates
that the Arctian Empire was born. How sad,
that it takes an enemy much greater than
ourselves to unite us.

FROM WRITINGS OF THE PHILOSOPHER
THEMETH

IT WAS A GLOOMY DAY that greeted Nilith when she finally gathered the energy to crack her eyes open. One of those rare squalls off the Troublesome Sea had come to wash the city of its blood. The dark clouds had finished with the Core Districts, and were now moving on to the Outsprawls. Blue sky had been replaced with a slate ceiling, and scattered patches of drizzle were already beginning to turn the sand to silt and mud.

Beyond the gloom and spatter of rain, there were other differences to frown at, and each of them were no cheerier than the approaching downpour. Since their veer into the Sprawls a day or more ago, the adobe huts and squalor had picked themselves up, brushed themselves off, and gathered some semblance of order. The streets and thoroughfares had begun to come alive.

Nilith's minder – the loathsome Chaser Jobey – had stuck to minor routes, steering clear of markets, and more often than not, covering the slatherghast with a sheet to keep it from prying eyes. The only attention they received was due to the wafting stench of Farazar's body, which had taken on a fresh reek given the added moisture. Farazar's ghost had spent half a day berating Jobey for his insolence, coming close to yelling his true name and identity once or twice. He would have done so had Nilith not kicked his bars and caused the slatherghast to gnash at him. Farazar was getting desperate, and that made him more dangerous than ever.

Sleep had been forgotten. Nilith blamed the wet and the freezing cold seeping up her left arm, making her shoulder ache as if she lay in ice. Instead, she busied herself by watching the slow passage of the streets. Nilith had spent so many desert nights longing to be within the city's boundaries once more. Now she was here, she wanted to drink it all in, despite the dire nature of her situation, despite the city's foulness.

If there was an air of danger and threat in the centre of Araxes, in the Sprawls it was a thick smog.

Groups of hooded figures lingered in doorways to avoid the rain, some emblazoned with tattoos, others covered head to toe in coats of leather or mail. Clubs and daggers hung from their belts, and even some of the sellswords gave them a wide berth. Smart-dressed fellows loitered under the eaves of smoky taverns and brothels, waiting for drunken fools to collapse into the gutter, or for bodies pushed from the higher windows, their throats already cut. Card dens and snuff houses employed young men and women with bare chests and faces caked with sparkling dust to stand at their doorways, beckoning people into small, dark, and questionable basements beneath the streets. A few whistled to the silk-wrapped Jobey, high on his cart, but the chaser didn't bat an eyelid.

Where merchants lined the wider streets, thieves went to work. For every two yells of a bargain, there was one of, 'Stop him!' or, 'Cutpurse!' Mercenary street guards seemed to ply their trades only when it suited them, content to slouch near the taverns or merchants that lined their pockets and watch the detritus pass by from under leather and duck-feather umbrellas.

Half the crowds were travellers, the other half an equal mix between dishevelled living and cheap-looking dead. Most of the shades Nilith saw were horrifically wounded, barely worth a few silvers at a soulmarket. Here and there, bellies were sliced to show glowing entrails. Others lacked jaws or eyes, or showed the viciousness of mutilation. One or two dragged themselves through the wet sand, legless, their deliveries strapped to their backs. Nilith caught Farazar staring at them too, and hoped he realised how kind her knife had been. It made her think of her own fate, lingering beneath the rags wrapped around her left forearm, and she had to look away. She refused to acknowledge the slatherghast's poison.

Nilith had thought she knew the depths of the city's depravity, but on seeing these streets, and what the Tenets and Code had driven their denizens to, she realised now that depravity was fathomless. Not for the first time in the last few days, she wondered why she had even started this quest in the first place. The benefits – the cause – were being drowned by the cost of struggle and loss.

That stoked a deep and righteous outrage in her, one that caused her to briefly consider ramming Farazar's head against the bars a dozen times, as fruitless a task as that would have been. Instead, she held the anger within her, nurtured it, and tried to turn it into something useful. Something to stoke her spirits and reassure her this path had not become a fruitless one.

A brief commotion broke out as a bald man came tearing from the mouth of an alley, rolling a fat barrel alongside him, one with black-stained staves. Spit streaming from his mouth, eyes wild, he narrowly dodged a beetle bearing a sack of wool before careening down an opposite alleyway. Before Nilith could wonder what was going on, a small mob of men and women appeared, hot on the man's tail and clamouring at the top of their voices. Several passersby joined their chase. Not for civic duty, of course, for this was Araxes. No, Nilith wagered the barrel was full of Nyxwater.

'There really is a shortage, isn't there?' she asked the chaser.

Jobey said little except to order them to be silent. He had grown tired of their conspiratorial whispering. They had planned nothing, but muttered small talk in an effort to distract the man. Anoish had done his part, even unknowingly. There were many things in a city capable of spooking a desert horse. The swarms of the dead, giant centipedes and scarabs, the clanging of a blacksmith, the frequent screams. More than once, Jobey had to halt the wagon to calm him. Fortunately for Anoish, the horse's stout legs and frame were worth the hassle, and Jobey's triggerbow stayed on his seat.

Bezel had shown his face twice so far, and each appearance had been overwhelmingly comforting. Once hovering over the face of the moon the night before, and again that very morning, perched and shrieking on a washing line, scaring away parrots and pigeons. If Jobey had noticed, Nilith hadn't seen it in his face. She wagered Bezel wasn't the only falcon in the mighty city of Araxes. Just the one with the foulest mouth.

Nilith looked around for the bird, but instead found the avid eyes of a cluster of young, skinny lads, a spectrum of ages from snot-nosed to sprouting his first chin hairs. Beneath their rags, they had the pale skin of Ede cave-folk, but had blistered in the Arctian heat so many times they looked pox-scarred. They clustered so tightly together in a dark culvert of stone that they looked like the face of an albino spider, many eyes blinking independently. Seeing Jobey's cream silks and gold chains, the boys emerged into the street and began to trail after the wagon, gaunt legs shifting quickly. Nilith watched them weave like hungry cats through the handcarts and travellers.

Before they could come closer, a sharp whistle from above stopped them dead. Back to the culvert they went, heads down, shoulders hunched. Nilith looked up to a balcony three stories above the street, where an obese woman, pale as milk and swaddled in blankets, sat with a spyglass balanced over one arm.

'What is it about you, Chaser Jobey, that keeps you from being robbed like every other poor bastard wearing gold and silks in the Sprawls?'

It took Jobey a moment to take the bait, but any chance to bray about his accomplishments and his Consortium was too juicy a worm to pass up. With a thumb, he raised one of the chains about his neck and showed Nilith a glyph carved in gold.

'Promises. Favours. Call them what you like, the Consortium have many connections in the Outsprawls.'

'Is that so?' Nilith mused. 'You make it sound as if the Consortium are like the Nyxites or the Chamber of the Code.'

'To many, they are. The royals think the city ends at the edge of the central districts. Out in the Sprawls, the Chamber and their scrutinisers might as well be a myth. The Consortium, however, are well known to those who matter, and it pays not to get on their bad side. Therefore, this glyph affords me some respect and safer travels,' he said, turning over his shoulder to face Nilith. 'Only fools or the uninitiated dare to attack an agent of the Consortium.'

'In all honesty, I'm surprised the Consortium would care so much for a lowly errand boy like you. If I was a waylayer or soulstealer, I personally wouldn't hesitate to drive a knife through your spine.'

'As I said: fools,' Jobey replied. 'Though it does not surprise me. You seem educated, noble, and yet you are clearly no more moralistic than any of the other people in these streets.'

'What are you implying?'

'That you're a murderer,' Jobey said, nodding to the silent and brooding Farazar. 'No? Is that not correct? I am not often interested in the details of those I chase and catch, but you, madam, have piqued my curiosity. What is he to you? Your half-life? How did you come by him?'

'None of your business, is how,' Nilith answered. 'He got what he deserved. Like any that insist on standing in my way.'

Jobey snorted. He was about to speak when another panicked whinny came from behind the wagon, distracting him. Nilith quickly flicked Farazar's arm, and he flinched away, looking disgusted at her touch. *Help me*, she mouthed.

'Blasted horse!' Jobey yelled. He pulled his own steeds to a halt and jumped down to the mud. Though Nilith's heart beat hurriedly, the bow stayed put on the seat once more. Jobey blew rainwater from his lips as he stalked past, eying his prisoners warily.

'We need to get out of here soon. This Consortium of Jobey's could be right around the corner,' Nilith whispered.

Farazar pretended she hadn't spoken, lifting his chin aloofly.

'You can't fool me, husband. I know you want out of this cage as much as I do. For different reasons, perhaps, but the same prick stands in our way. Let's work together. Just like in Abatwe.' She nodded towards the chaser, still trying to manhandle Anoish into calm. 'Farazar—'

'No!' the ghost snapped angrily, turning further away from her. 'I refuse to help you any longer. You started this. You can finish it.'

'I see you found some testicles in the dunes, husband.' Nilith dug her nails into the deck of the wagon in frustration, accidentally prising free a thick splinter. She clasped it in her palm, turning her back to the slatherghast. Somehow, she knew it was watching. Always watching. She shuffled to the side so the creature wouldn't see her grasping the lock of the cage. The splinter was stout, and she heard the click of tumblers as she waggled it about in the keyhole.

'You can't be serious,' Farazar muttered.

No, Nilith realised, she was not. The lock was a bulky cube of wrought iron, and she felt all sorts of teeth in its keyhole. 'Know any good locksmiths?'

'Ugh,' he sighed.

Without looking, Nilith couldn't see what the splinter was doing, if anything. Farazar watched her efforts avidly, growing more contemptuous by the moment. Anoish couldn't have known what they were up to, but he helped nonetheless, making a great fuss over the clatter of a nearby stonemasons. A few nearby street guards looked on, unamused by the racket.

'Easy, horse!' cried Jobey, wrapping Anoish's halter around his forearm to wrangle the animal.

Nilith swore as the splinter snapped and the sharp wood bit into her fingertip. 'This is hopeless.'

Farazar snickered. 'All that struggle. All those days and weeks spent traipsing the desert. And for what? To end up in some cage, doomed to work in some mine for eternity. I'm glad I will be there to see your face when you finally realise you've failed. And judging by that arm, I don't have long to wait.'

Nilith clenched her jaw, refusing to let him goad her. Her resolve already hung by a thread. Her eyes betrayed her, however, sneaking down to the ragged end of her tunic. The faint glow shone from rips in its rain-dark fabric, like a hooded lantern. The light reached all the way up to her elbow. Nilith shivered as if a cold hand had just run across her chest. She heard a wet slither, and out of her peripheries, she saw the slatherghast licking its fangs. She gave the creature the finger.

'And what of you, Farazar?' she asked. 'What will be your eternity, hmm? Working the same mine, no doubt. I fail, you fail, or have you forgotten?

'Gah!' Reminded that their fates were firmly entwined, the ghost lost his nerve. He tried to spit at her, still forgetful of his half-life limitations. 'I wouldn't even be in this cage if you had just left me in peace!'

Nilith's outrage got the better of her. 'There it is again! The famous Talin Renala self-obsession. You've never given a fuck about this city or its inhabitants, and even now, when it's staring you right in that ugly face of yours, you're still as blind as a newborn to it. Just look around! Look at what your negligence has given rise to. A Nyxwater shortage. Businessmen like the Consortium. Who knows how many souls they've dragged off like this for spurious debts? How many other such empires grow unchecked under your nose? Give that some thought for once, instead of your own vapours. This is all your fault, and when I'm out of this cage, I'll show you what it means to have a ruler, instead of just a monarch,' she seethed. 'Something the Krass learnt long ago.'

Farazar's eyes were glowing white slits. 'Ah, yes! The grand, righteous lesson that you crossed half the Reaches to teach me. How could I possibly forget? Well, I'm still waiting, wife, and yet no revelation has come.'

Nilith smiled with no trace of humour. 'The lesson is not over yet.' She clenched her jaw. That threat felt emptier than she would have liked.

'You're pathetic, wife!' he scoffed loudly, forgetting himself.

'I agree,' said Jobey's voice, hoarse and unexpectedly close by. The chaser had slipped back to the wagon and was now standing beside the bars, thumb and finger on his chin. 'All this whispering and bickering *is* quite pathetic. Husband and wife? Hmm.' He cocked his head. 'A surprise. I do not see the attraction between you two.'

At Nilith and Farazar's withering expressions, Jobey tugged at his collar. 'Not too far now, lady and shade.'

Nilith was following the chaser with her most acidic scowl when she noticed the bundle of soaking rags behind him, sitting in the gutter. It took a moment of staring to realise it was a person. It was hard to tell with all the rubbish strewn about the makeshift gutters. The shape was slumped up against the bricks of a dilapidated building, legs and arms hidden under dirty cloths. Two blackened eyes peered through a gap in the wrappings, blinking between the drips falling from the broken tiles above. They were fixed on Nilith and the ghost chained next to her with an avidity that was unusual for a beggar. Though that could have been explained by the glowing set of fangs hovering behind Nilith, grinning wide, the beggar's eyes held intrigue, not fear or the cross-eyed gaze of a drunkard.

As Chaser Jobey retook his seat and the wagon jolted onwards, the eyes followed Nilith, sticking to her until they rounded the next corner. Nilith eyed each crooked building as though it might be their final destination. She looked back, but could no longer see the beggar.

Farazar gripped the bars, letting his vapours turn white where they touched the metal. 'You're a liar,' he hissed at her. 'I know this whole quest of yours has just been to claim my half-coins and the throne. I will hear you say it before they put you out of your misery.'

Nilith held her tongue while another torturous hour passed, with every street holding the possibility of a destination. The rain fell heavier in all its pounding glory. Jobey hoisted a small umbrella and sat as stoic as a statue to pass the miles. Nilith raised her face to the sky and drank from the clouds. The chaser hadn't seen fit to give her any water that day, but now he had no choice. Rainclouds only came a few times a year to Araxes, and when it did, it rained ardently. Rain dripped from the bars in torrents. It gathered in the bottom of the cage in a thick puddle. Nilith felt the carriage skew as the streets completed their transition to mud. It slowed their going, and for that, she was grateful.

It didn't last long. As they turned into a narrow street, another man on a wagon passed them by, going in the opposite direction. He had a muscular bull pulling his load: an empty cage very much like the one Nilith currently had her face pressed against. She eyed the man's necklaces of gold and his sodden silks. Jobey angled his umbrella to the man and they nodded curtly to each other. No words passed between them, but Nilith knew.

'We're close,' Nilith breathed. 'Last chance, husband.'

Farazar just grunted, still brooding, though she saw the trepidation in his glowing face.

'I hope they make it slow and painful for you,' Farazar replied, his tone cold even for a ghost.

Nilith began to shake. She was tired. Oh, so incredibly tired. Tired of fighting. Tired of walking. Tired of this tumultuous existence she had built for herself. Nilith felt the words gather in her mouth, all spite and venom. Instead, she let them die on her tongue, and grabbed the bars with both hands, blue and tanned, letting the pain and cold run through her. She found a smile curling her lips. 'I should really thank you, Farazar.'

'What?'

'I should thank you,' Nilith said. 'I was on the cusp of giving up. Of forgetting why I first set out from Araxes all those weeks ago. But you, husband, have kindly reminded me what I've been fighting for.' A laugh broke from her, causing Chaser Jobey to look over his shoulder.

'Quiet down back there!' called the chaser.

'I've been fighting for *this*,' Nilith said loudly, waving her hand across the city before them, wrapped in rain and cloud.

'I said QUIET!'

'For anything but *this*! AAGH!' Nilith drove her shoulder against her bars with a yell akin to a war-cry. Once, twice, three times, she threw herself, before the chaser came striding through the mud, umbrella in one hand and switch in his other.

'You could not wait just a few more moments, could you?' he snapped, clearly devoid of patience with his prisoners.

Despite the growing pain in her shoulder, Nilith pushed again. This time she was rewarded with a scrape of iron against wood. Not a lock, or a hinge, but the cage itself.

'Stop it!' Jobey lashed at her with the switch, but it glanced off her skull and the bars. Instead, he began to whip Farazar, who yelped like a donkey.

'Hit *her*, not me!' he roared.

Another scrape, and Farazar was nudged from the edge of the wagon, momentarily occupying Jobey as he strived to catch his flailing legs. Mud sprayed in all directions.

The slatherghast sensed its prey making an exit and began to throw itself at its own bars, hungry for Nilith. The stupid creature actually helped, and before Nilith knew it, the cage was teetering over the side of the wagon.

Jobey threw himself against it, but the slatherghast was too frenzied. Nilith pressed herself to the bars, willing all her weight into the mud. Amid the clanging of iron and the snapping of jaws, she heard Jobey start to whistle, blowing at a golden shape on one of his necklaces. The noise was piercing, and it momentarily halted the slatherghast and the flailing Farazar.

In the pause, filled by the rattle of rain, Nilith heard something whistle in reply. It was half lost behind the downpour, but she knew it wasn't a good sign.

With a roar, she hurled herself at the bars one last time. With her hair trailing in the slatherghast's grip, she met the iron, and her world began to tip. A heartbeat passed, and then a crunch came as the cage met the sodden ground. Mud and sand flew into her face, half-choking her. She pressed herself to it as she saw the blue jaws gnashing through a crack in the bars.

There came a screech, and something tore through the rain. At first Nilith thought it was an arrow, and cursed every god she could think of for her poor fortune. But she heard Jobey's cry over her fierce muttering, and knuckled the mud from her eyes. She couldn't help but shudder at the freezing cold and emptiness of her left hand.

Another blur came out of the rain, and she saw blood flow from a cut above Jobey's eye. He began to thrash about with his switch, desperately trying to reach his triggerbow on the seat.

Birds.

Nilith realised it as the third shape appeared, wings flared and claws raking the chaser's back. The crow flapped into the rain, vanishing before Jobey's switch could catch it. She heard the keening wail of a falcon somewhere in the rainstorm and smiled.

Nilith began to kick at the buckled bars, hoping one would crack for her too. Farazar was busy yanking at his ropes. She watched him with one eye, praying he didn't get loose before she did.

Thunk!

The explosion of the triggerbow interrupted her, and a gull landed in the muck near the wagon. A bolt had run it through.

Another cry pierced the scene, and a roar rose up to compete with the noise of rain. Wings flapped, beaks chattered, and crying and mewing filled the air. Forgetting to reload, Jobey sprinted to the cage, keys jangling in his free hand.

'I've never lost a repayment, and I shan't today!' he yelled in Nilith's face.

Jobey yanked the buckled door open and hauled Nilith free by the legs. Mud filled her mouth. She felt grit under her eyelids. She began to kick for all her worth, catching Jobey in the knee, twisting it sideways. He stumbled clear of her, just as a dozen finches descended on him. They swarmed his face like bees, chirruping as they pecked holes in his hands.

The chaser's whistle was clamped in his mouth now, blowing with every shriek of pain. Crows, pigeons, parrots, even a falcon or two – they swooped down to harry the man. Blood and feathers began to join the rain in the churned puddles.

Nilith sprang up, pulling at Farazar's bindings. The fucker had the gall to aim a punch at her, a vicious splinter clasped between his blue knuckles. She let it pierce her shoulder before she batted his arm away with her ghostly hand and threw him against the wagon's wheel.

'No! Not ever again. You are mine until the end of this!' Nilith growled fiercely in his cold ear. She set her hands to the complicated knots binding him, ripping more than untying. While she tackled them, she heard more whistles coming to greet them. Maybe running boots, if her numb ears weren't lying to her.

Jobey had produced a knife, and was busy cutting birds from the air between frantic yells. One grazed his skull with its claws before barrelling into the mud beside Nilith's hands. Blood flowed from its breast. It was the falcon.

Bezel looked up at her, showing pain in his eyes. 'Now you owe me even more, Your Majesty.' He pointed a bloodied wing to the swarming birds. 'See? Don't fuck with birds.'

'I'll remember that!'

Wrenching the rope free, Nilith wrapped one end around Farazar's neck and the other around his body. She draped both around Anoish's neck before seeing to his tether. Bezel flapped awkwardly behind her, watching the chaos. Jobey had realised their escape and was desperately trying to run after them. Birds flapping around his head like some bizarre crown, he scrambled through the mud, knife waving.

'Men coming!'

Nilith saw them: long-robed men in green and silver armour, plumes on their ridged helmets, holding longswords out in front of them. They had a distinctly unfriendly look. Something about the lavishness of their armour screamed *Consortium*.

'Stay where you are!' yelled Jobey, barely a spear-thrust away from seizing them.

At that moment, a figure draped in soaking rags burst from the rain and cannoned into the chaser. Jobey was thrown against his cage, where the slatherghast still writhed in a hungry panic. Its claws sank into the man's shoulder, and he howled with pain.

'Move! Now!' hissed the bundle of muddy rags. A woman. She jabbed a hand towards the mouth of an alleyway.

'Not without these!' Nilith asserted, trying and failing to tackle the second knot with only one hand. The woman produced a broken shard of glass and slashed the tether with a snap. Anoish reared up, hooves beating the air. Nilith grabbed the rope and hauled him with her, racing after the bundle of rags.

———————◆——————

'JUST WHO THE FUCK IN the Reaches are you?' Nilith spat, bringing the horse and its macabre cargo to a halt. The ghost of Farazar picked himself up, his rags and vapours smeared in reddish brown mud. He muttered something foul to himself.

The bundle of rags shook her head, indicating the Cloudpiercer.

'No,' Nilith said, glancing over her shoulder to see if she could afford such stubbornness. Rain, only rain, and stark, square buildings lay behind her. Light from their windows cast golden pools for the rain to play in. A few ghosts made their way back and forth across the quiet street, their smocks sodden and dragging in the muck. 'We go no further until I know who you are. I've learnt the downfalls of trust.'

The woman stopped, shoulders rising and falling with a sigh. She turned, slowly, dragging down the strips around her face with a crooked finger. Nilith saw the green and purple rings around her eyes and the bend in her nose, still sporting deep cuts thick with scab. Nilith had seen her own face just as beaten not so long ago.

'Chamber Scrutiniser Heles, madam. I suppose it would be a pleasure under any other circumstances.'

The woman certainly didn't look like any scrutiniser Nilith had ever seen, though she could spy the curves of black tattoos creeping onto her neck and cheek. 'I had no idea scrutinisers were dispatched this far out in the Sprawls.'

'We aren't.'

'Where's your uniform?'

Heles didn't answer. Nilith watched her, noting how the woman's eyes were looking past her cheek. At Farazar. Nilith stepped in her line of sight, wishing she had a weapon. A cold, heavy weight clutched her heart. Another vermin, come to stand in her way.

Heles pushed back more of her rags, letting the steam rise from her forehead and shaved, bruised scalp. 'Aren't you going to introduce yourself?' she asked, letting the question hang in the sodden air.

'Sula,' Nilith said, plucking her mother's name from some recess of her mind. She could see more of the woman's tattooed spirals now. By the looks of their complexity, Heles had earned a high rank in the Chamber, and if these were real, this Heles was a seasoned professional. Nilith wondered whose bad side she had wandered onto.

Heles chuckled, managing to do it without a trace of mirth. 'I see. And your shade?'

'None of your business,' Nilith snapped. Behind her, Anoish whinnied, as bored with interlopers as Nilith was. Bezel lay on the horse's back, and clacked his beak fiercely.

The so-called scrutiniser held her bandaged hands and took a moment to lean up against a sandstone column, carved in the shape of a desert cat. 'I've spent the last few days working my way through these gods damned Sprawls. Soulstealers, pickpockets, madmen. And these businessmen you pissed off. If one doesn't catch you, the others will. I thought it was bad in the city, but—'

'Is there a point to this? I haven't the luxury of time and chatter,' Nilith grumbled.

Heles sucked her swollen lip noisily. 'Few people know the meaning of kindness out here, fewer than in the city. Imagine my surprise when a man dropped a silver at my feet earlier today, while I was catching sleep. He was drunk, by the look of him, but even then, he could have fallen upon me with fists instead of charity.'

Heles pulled a silver coin from the folds of her mucky rags and held it up, showing the skyline of Araxes stamped into the metal. 'Imagine how much greater my surprise was when, just a few hours later, I looked up from that coin, and found the same face bumbling past on the side of a wagon. Arguing with his wife, no less,' she said, turning to Farazar. 'A face that's supposed to be at the top of the Cloudpiercer in his armoured sanctuary at this very moment. How is that possible, I wonder?'

Heles turned the coin, showing the other side: a regal profile of Nilith's loathsome husband. She had always detested how young he insisted they make him look, and she detested it all the more now.

'Correct me if I'm wrong, Your Majesties,' Heles said, calm as sunrise. 'I see this is where you've been, my Empress Nilith. Not "Sula". Not in the east like they said.'

Nilith took a step backwards, longing for a weapon. She would pounce on the horse and run this woman down. She said nothing, simply sharing a stare with her. Heles did not show any reverence, but there was no glint of greed or murder in those bloodshot eyes.

Farazar had been listening in, and had loosened his noose enough to talk. 'Scrutiniser! Arrest this woman! She has murdered your emperor!'

Nilith slapped him hard, though her lack of copper meant her hand merely fondled his cheek. 'You stay back, Scrutiniser. This is none of your business.'

Heles stepped forwards. 'You're both wrong, I'm afraid. As a servant of the Code, it's my responsibility to see to the interests of the ruler and family. As you've been slain, Emperor Farazar – and I don't want to know how – I must defer to the living empress.'

Nilith and Farazar swapped a glance, one scowling deeply, the other smiling.

'How dare you—'

'Whatever complaints you have, Emperor, I frankly couldn't care less. And whatever game you're playing, Empress, this city has enough problems at the moment. But... it's my duty to protect you now, and so I shall.'

Farazar wasn't best pleased by the scrutiniser's ambivalence. 'This is outrageous! I'll have the chamberlain flog you to death when—'

Nilith was struggling to buy what Heles was selling. 'You're telling me you know the emperor's body is right there, unclaimed, and you're not considering becoming the next empress of Araxes? Ruler of an empire?'

Heles' eyes betrayed her for a moment, shifting to the muddied bundle of stench that hung at an angle from the horse's side. There wasn't a person in the world that wouldn't have spent a moment in wonder, thinking what it would be like to sit at the pinnacle of the Cloudpiercer, to rule the vastest civilisation the world had ever seen.

That was all it was for Heles. A moment. Her gaze came straight back to Nilith. She brushed rainwater from her face and shook her head. 'Greater people than me have tried to rule this city and failed. Araxes is unruly by nature. You do what you wish with the body. If you had the power to shove the whole city into the sea and start afresh, however, you'd already be lying dead in a puddle.'

It was fierce and blunt talk, but Nilith was grateful for it. She was fed up of cryptic answers and slippery lies. Plain talk was what she wanted, and the scrutiniser's opinions were music to her aching ears.

She turned to face Anoish and the falcon on his back. Bezel had his wing held flat, leaking blood down the horse's flank. As Nilith raised a hand to flick a raindrop from her nose, she felt the sting of cold and snatched the ghostly hand away.

'Do we trust her?' Nilith asked. It was the first time she had asked for advice since striking out to claim her husband. She was like a beggar, asking for alms.

'Do we have a choice?' Bezel replied, voice hoarse.

Nilith endured the ache in her bones as she turned back around. Heles had not moved.

'Fine, but first we need rest. And food.'

Heles wrinkled a lip, but nodded as she squelched away. 'Just hope there's some city left to claim when we get back to it.'

CHAPTER 7
THE HALF-COIN

It was interesting that copper, not silver or gold, became the most precious metal in all the lands. It was a stroke of luck for a small group of desert mines to the west of the Arc, where seams of copper stretch for miles. Their group – or their consortium, as history recalls them – became richer in silver than any emperor to sit on the throne of the empire.

FROM A TREATISE ON ARCTIAN
ECONOMIC THEORY

THE SUN ROSE FURIOUSLY, AS though it felt cheated by being ousted by the rain. The dawn hauled a fog from the ground. It skulked around the buttresses of buildings, thick enough to lose one's legs in, and marred the blue sky above with indifferent streaks of low cloud and mist. Wherever there was a gap in the murk, the sunlight fell eagerly, draping the city and its mountainous spires in hazy bars of shadow and gold.

One such lance of light found a slit in the shutters and fell upon the face of a sleeping Boran Temsa. His dreams were shallow, filled with half-coins tumbling like sandstorms, and it didn't take long for the light to rouse him. With a snarl, Temsa opened his eyes, was immediately blinded and rolled over to escape the glare.

Thunk.

'Fucking bastard bed!' he hissed to the terracotta tile against which his face was now pressed.

He waited for the throbbing in his head to subside before he put his palms to the floor. Pain lanced through his wrist, and he bit his lip. The injuries from the raid on Finel's were refusing to heal. A twinge in his ribs had also spoken up. He lay still once more, seething while he waited for the pain to die.

Dead gods, I need to piss.

Propping himself up on his shoulder, he shuffled his good leg underneath him and pushed. He experienced a good number of clicks and cracks before he made it to kneeling. Time and toil had taken their toll on his body. The mornings were becoming more and more painful. Temsa was glad it didn't rain often; the moisture always made the stump of his leg ache. He winced as he tested its tortured, scarred end on the floor. The pain raced up his spine, and as always, he was left cursing the Butcher who had taken his limb from him.

Clutching one arm to his side, he hooked the chamberpot from beneath the bed and sat the gold-plated thing in front of him. His bladder was insistent, and the unbuttoning of his breeches was frantic, and he almost sprayed his legs before pointing at the pot.

Relieved at long last, Temsa shifted his knee to stand, and in doing so, kicked the chamberpot flying. He would have cursed to the rafters if hot piss hadn't been dripping down his thighs.

With a strangled roar he ripped the rest of his tunic open and dabbed at his face and neck. The rest was spattered down his front. Temsa bared his teeth as he thrust himself to his foot.

As he did so, the door to his chamber creaked open and a shade peered around the jamb.

'Tor? We heard a noise—' The shade's voice drifted off as he saw the wet, half-naked Temsa and the chamberpot lying upended on the floor.

'Get the fuck out!' Temsa bellowed. 'And fetch some water!'

While trying to avoid breathing in through his nose, Temsa reached for his golden leg, lying on a table next to the bed. He set it to the floor with a loud clang, thrust his thigh into it, and set about tying the straps.

By the time he was done, the shade had returned with a jug of water. He opened the door a crack and timidly poked it into the room. The tor thumped his way over and snatched it from him.

'Fresh tunic and breeches!' Temsa yelled.

The shade bumbled into the room, bowing so low he was practically doubled over. He scuttled to a vast set of doors along the wall. With the tug of a rope, they parted to reveal a rainbow of robes and tunics, cloaks and silks. Meanwhile, Temsa doused himself in water, and when the shade returned with a purple and green affair, he used it as a towel.

'Gold.'

'Of course, Tor.'

The shade produced a gold robe with jade beads and Temsa allowed him to dress him in it. At least Ghoor had trained his house-shades well. The half-life's cold fingers did not touch him once.

There came a booming knock and Danib strode into the room. He raised his chin at the sight of the puddle and overturned chamberpot.

'What?' Temsa challenged him.

Danib blinked.

'Already? It's barely an hour past dawn. Eager, for a dead bitch,' Temsa growled. He saw Danib's blue gaze narrowing. 'Don't you give me that look. Fine. I'm ready.'

As Temsa was handed his cane, he jabbed a thumb at the house-shade. 'See this one has his tongue cut out.'

'What? No! I—' the half-life stammered.

The shade was silenced as Danib clasped his head in both enormous hands and dragged him from the room. Temsa followed, watching his legs thrash, vapours curling in his wake. The morning could go fuck itself for all he cared. It was the evening that occupied his mind.

Several floors below, in a great hall no doubt designed with orgies in mind, Enlightened Sister Yaridin – or perhaps Liria, Temsa could never tell – was waiting for him on a humongous couch. It dwarfed her, and its regal purple clashed with her glow and crimson robe. Temsa had taken Ani's surly advice and involved the Cult. Too many corners were being cut, too many threads fraying. The old Temsa would never have moved so fast; he realised that after Finel's. What irked him about the old Temsa was that he had been poor.

When he entered, armoured men in his wake, the sister arose and offered him a smile. It was Yaridin after all. 'We are surprised to see you well, Tor. The rumours say Finel's was a bloodbath.'

Temsa chose a nearby armchair, one with manacles suspiciously attached to its arms. He kept his hands on his cane, silently vowing to invest in different furniture. 'That it was, but you will have your shades, Sister. No need to fret. The good serek was kind enough to die.'

'At quite a cost and rather noisily, or so we understand. We hear the Cloud Court is suspended because of your actions.'

If she was looking for an explanation, or an excuse, or an apology, she was sorely disappointed on all fronts. Temsa shrugged.

'What have you done with him?' asked the shade.

'The same as I have all the others. Gained their scrawl, made sure they can't be identified, and then sent them south. To Kal Duat, if you must know.'

If Temsa didn't know better, he could have sworn Yaridin hid a wrinkling of her nose. 'The White Hell. We know of it, and the Consortium that owns it.'

Temsa waved his hands. 'Businessmen. They don't care where their shades come from, and neither should you. Takes a special conscience.'

'Or lack thereof,' Yaridin replied, managing to sound sweet. She sat and crossed her hands on her scarlet lap. 'You wished to discuss something?'

The tor sucked his teeth. 'Discuss is a strong word. "Inform" is more to my liking.'

Yaridin stiffened, if that was possible for a half-life. 'And?'

'The final name on your list will have to wait. Somebody else is more deserving of my time for now.'

The sister's face was blank, patient. 'Who is this lucky citizen?

'Tal Horix. An old widow I've done business with in the past. I sold her something I want. *Need*. Now I want it back.'

'What?'

'A locksmith. She has his half-coin and I want it.'

'Ah, we see.'

Temsa got up from his chair, showing he thought the matter final. 'If you wish me to take on Serek Boon successfully, I suggest you agree with me. Otherwise, you shall have another bloodbath.'

Wrapped up in thought, Yaridin's eyes toured the gilded statues and tapestries that lined the wall. 'We acquiesce. You may remove Horix,' she said, 'but our agreement still stands.'

'Fair enough,' Temsa said, already half turned around. He made for the door. 'You know,' he said, 'they might be wrong about you Cult types.'

'Oh yes?'

Temsa hovered in the doorway, swirling his cane around as if divining the right words. 'Indeed. You're not completely worthless.' He slammed the door before he could see the scowl on Yaridin's vapours.

Danib had finished with his chores, and was waiting outside the hall. Temsa didn't stop walking, giving his orders as he marched.

'Get Ani up. Get everybody up! I want every blade sharp enough to cut a cloud! Every bit of armour black as night! Horix better enjoy her last day in the Arc!'

Temsa was coming for her.

———————◆———————

THE LUMP OF GREEN PHLEGM arced over the balcony and plummeted down to the streets below. Horix listened, knowingly kidding herself she could hear the splat. She heard nothing but the banging of carpenters far below, and she blamed them instead of the height and her old ears.

A day had passed since Horix had sent Kalid and his soldiers back to the rooftop, and there was still no news. Nothing. No blood painting the sand red outside Ghoor's tower. No Temsa being hauled off to the

Chamber of the Code. No public mutilation and burning announced. No parading of the charred corpse.

What has this city come to? Horix wondered. Grey knuckles resting on the stone railing, she looked over it all, surveying the myriad rooftops and tiles spread out below her. The sun was high now, and the mists had been burned away.

She looked west, to where the uppity spike of Magistrate Ghoor's tower rose into the blue sky. It was distant, but detailed enough for her to curse its features, and the man who sat behind its orange walls, scheming and plotting.

There came the sound of heavy breathing. The stink of sweat soured the breeze. Horix turned around to find Yamak standing in the balcony doorway. He had a silk scarf scrunched up between his sausage-like fingers, and his hair was plastered sideways with the sweat.

'What?' she hissed.

'It's almost done, Widow. With your new workers, the construction sped along.'

Horix felt the prickles climbing slowly from her arms to her shoulders and neck. It had been an age since she had felt anything besides anger, and that smouldered away inside her. But this feeling she remembered: excitement. She could have gone as far as pleasure. Like a child saving the last slice of cake, she had starved herself of such things for two decades, knowing they would taste all the sweeter once she was finished. Watching. Waiting.

'What is "almost"?'

'Poldrew assures me it will be finished by this evening. The mixture is ready to be prepared. All the scaffolding has been cleared, but I don't know if I trust him—'

'It is not your place to trust, Master Yamak. You are no builder. It seems the shade is.'

Yamak turned his eyes floorwards. Horix saw the resentment in the darker flush of his cheeks.

'It is a sorry state of affairs when the dead show up the living, isn't it?' she sighed, moving past him and throwing up a cavernous hood. 'You may return to your duties.'

Once in the corridor, she sniffed again, eager to smell something other than Yamak's pungent odour. In its place, she tasted brick and sawdust on her tongue. Horix smiled a rare smile, reserved only for her and the burnished gold of her mirrors. Her vengeance was finally close at hand.

As she descended the steps, she fished inside her ruffles and produced a half-coin affixed to a chain. Staring at it was enough to crack her smile, but just slightly.

She would give Caltro Basalt the day.

WHILE THE SUN HAD DONE its best to dry Araxes out and eradicate any trace of rain, some shadows in the City of Countless Souls were never touched by sunlight. The thick fog that rose at dawn had covered the Core Districts in its blanket for the entire day. Now it seemed set on claiming the night, too.

Colonel Kalid rubbed the dew from his grizzled chin and shook his hand to warm it up. He shifted his armoured leg, hearing his hip pop, and cursed the wear of age and damp nights. The new spyglass was cold against his eye. Droplets smeared its lenses, and after a good cleaning, he tried again, peering through the dark.

The misty streets glowed blue in patches where shades went about their masters' business. A few brave living plied the haze, trying not to collide. Or fall again, as their sand-caked clothes suggested. Their caution wasn't just for fashion; the rain had flooded the ancient sewers, or washed the gutters into the road. Kalid could smell the effluence on the air. That, and his soldiers' stink. Maybe his own.

Two nights they'd spent on the rooftop and crouched in the rooms below, waiting to pounce. Horix had yet to send a messenger telling them to do otherwise, and so Kalid had kept up his watch.

Temsa's tower was silent save for a few shades dangling from ropes two thirds of the way up. They had hammer and chisels in hand, and were still attacking the same balcony they'd been working on since midday. Kalid had sneered when they started, and he sneered now; the one-legged bastard was getting comfy in his new abode. Comfy meant careless.

Wagons had come and gone all day, using various entrances and always under the cover of umbrellas or tarpaulins. It had been an hour since the flow stopped. Guards still patrolled the courtyard and the tower's base in regular rounds. Kalid eyed their black figures now, cloaked and fuzzy in the mists. He tried counting, but whenever he finished, one more always appeared or vanished.

Another snap and cry rang out across the streets, and Kalid watched the streak of blue falling from the tower's side. There was a dull *whump* as the shade disappeared behind the courtyard walls. A puff of sand drifted into the air. Moments later, he watched the same shade approaching the main doorway, brushing himself off while the guards laughed at him.

Kalid reached for his stub of charcoal and scratched another mark on the wall. He counted. *Eleven.* Temsa needed to invest in some better ropes.

'Casimi.' He had to say it twice; the first attempt came out as an unintelligible grunt. It had been a while since he had spoken. 'Casimi!'

A bearded soldier nearby came awake with a start, bald head snapping up and eyelids fluttering. 'Hmm?' He stared at the black marks on the wall. 'Four more,' he said.

'Aye, and not a peep from the man himself.'

'You remember the trenches at Scatterpeak? How we waited for days, thinking Prince Phylar's army had given up? And all the while building catapults and armour. I'm telling you, Temsa's up to—'

Something caught Casimi's eye. He stared past the colonel. Kalid followed the man's pointing finger, whipping the spyglass up so fast he bruised his eye socket.

Light was spilling into the courtyard. The circular door of the tower was peeling back. Black figures filled the pool of gold. *Ten, twenty, fifty, one hundred, two...* Kalid soon lost count.

'Casimi?'

'Aye, Colonel.'

'Get running. Tell the widow she'll soon have company. Temsa's bringing the fight to us.'

The man didn't spare a moment of thought. He scrambled up and bolted for the stairs.

———————◆———————

'CALTRO?'

The voice broke me from my reverie. 'What?' I asked irately. The peace and quiet had been glorious.

Pointy huffed. 'We've been here for over an hour, and you haven't said a word.'

'I'm still thinking.'

'About what?'

I pointed to the widow's tower as if it were the only structure around for miles. Thanks to the thick fog, it practically was: a dark void in the grey, half swallowed by the haze. Its sharp angles were softened and blurred, but it was no less ominous than before.

'You wouldn't understand. My old master called it "visualising".'

'Sounds made-up to me, and I know my fiction.'

I pinched my forehead between two fingers. It was impossible for me to be tired, but I felt thinner, like a bubbling pot that had boiled off some of my vapours with all the stress and effort. The last haunting had taken much from me. Crossing the districts back to Horix had been a thankfully uneventful affair. The rain and mists had given the sword and me quieter streets and a distinct lack of scrutiny. But it had been a frantic, non-stop journey. If I'd flesh and bone still, my neck would be aching from so much time looking over my shoulder. Through it all, Pointy had been there, eager as always to fill any silence with wise words, irritating poetry, or general prattle. Like any kind of company, there were times when it was comforting, and times when it was irritating. In this moment, it was the latter.

'Well, I know my eyes and they can't see through walls,' I told him. 'I've got to imagine it instead. Plot the ways out if… damn it! Why am I explaining this to you? You're wasting my time.'

Silence, at least for a moment. I had just affixed the top floor in my mind when—

'Are you always this nervous when you pick locks?' asked the sword.

I smothered Pointy's pommel with my hand and went back to my staring. 'I've never had to burgle my own freedom back before, all right? Fuck's sake, sword.'

Pointy resorted to humming while I looked back to Horix's tower. On a gloomy and foggy night such as this, its windows and slits should have been glowing with light, like most of the other spires in the vicinity. Only one light broke the blackness of the obelisk, and that was near its lofty point: the widow's chambers.

A smattering of guards hung around the central courtyard. The mist was thicker than it had been in the morning, but I could see the guards were clad in full armour, with silver helmets sporting black horse-tails. From my vantage point atop the roof of a small bazaar squished between two spires, I could watch them idly patrolling the shadows around the gate.

'So what's your plan, then? The suspense is going to kill me a second time.'

I took a moment. I liked to think of myself as a master of my craft, and that was why it stung me to admit it: there was only one way in and to my half-coin, and that was giving myself up. It felt like cheating. A liar's way, not a thief's. I had built map after map in my head, dreamed up a hundred different places where my coin might be stashed, and even had time for fantasising about finding another bird or two, but it was no use. The guards clumped in groups, sticking to the door. The old bat was sealed up tight.

I pretended to clear my throat, ready to reveal my grand idea. 'We're going in the front door. We play prodigal locksmith, grateful to be back and safe, find out where Horix has my coin kept, haunt somebody, and vanish.' I said this proudly, though hearing it aloud, I realised how boneless my plan seemed. Shaky, at best.

'Is... is that it?' said the sword, ever my conscience.

'Yes. Yes, it is.'

'That took you an hour?'

'Well—'

'And what of me, Caltro? I told you before, Horix isn't going to let you have a sword. Especially a damn soulblade. From what you've told me, she's a smart, shrewd woman. A veritable Ignoble Hernea.'

'I don't know who that is. I don't know any of these people you constantly mention. I don't even know if they're real. Just... just... fuck!' I hung my head, more annoyed at Horix than I was at the sword, though that didn't mean he wasn't being irksome.

'Hmph.'

The time for contemplation was over. I got to my feet and levelled the sword at the tower. 'You forget, Pointy, that you're in the company of the finest locksmith in all the Reaches. Burgling and thieving are what I was born to do. I can haunt who and what I want. There isn't a tor or tal in this city who can keep me out of their tower. Even Widow Horix. What I'm saying, Pointy, is you needn't worry. You're in excellent hands.'

'Well, this is a new Caltro I see before me,' said the sword as I thrust him into my belt.

'I was getting bored of the old one. Perhaps it has something to do with the god of gods begging me for help.'

'You're letting it go to your head, I see.'

As I began to work my way down the bazaar's scaffolding, I showed Pointy my attempt at a cheery face. 'Or maybe I just know I can cut my way to my coin with you, if I need to.'

'How enjoyable for me. Do you realise what it's like, Caltro, to pass through somebody's guts? I see it all flash by me. Bone and bile and shit—'

'Why are you so sharp, anyway?' I distracted him, and myself for that matter. I walked perhaps slower than I had to, but at least I was walking. It felt wrong to knock on a door, rather than pick its lock.

'They hone the soul as well as the steel. First with stone, then with copper. The soul gives a finer edge than any metal can. I cut into the spaces between things,' Pointy explained.

'That makes sense,' I said. The pommel wore a squint. 'I'm serious. Look at me, I'm dead. I can apparently haunt things. I get it. I also should have called you Sharpy instead of Pointy.'

'Or you could use one of my actual names,' he replied snippily. 'The Black Death? Absia?'

I merely chuckled. 'Black Death.'

The sword gave a metallic sigh. 'If it comes to that – to fighting – what kind of swordsman are you?'

I thought about that for a moment. I'd held a weapon before, here and there. Even wore armour once as a disguise for sneaking into a palace, but never had I swung a sword or gone toe to toe in a duel. I'd never understood doing something so moronic. I preferred better odds than fifty-fifty.

'The kind that has no idea what he's doing.'

'Then fear not, Caltro. It's you who's in excellent hands.'

'Erm. You don't have hands?' I stared at his pommel, examining his smug face, and in that moment my vapours seemed to pour over the crossguard and blade. In turn, grey vapour crept up my wrist. I tried to shake them off, but my arm stayed rigid.

I heard a chuckle deep in my head, though Pointy spoke aloud. He changed the subject. 'So, your plan for me?'

'I keep you close. Hide you,' I suggested.

'No. Last time that was tried, I spent thirty years in a duke's lock-box in Belish.'

'Then I give you as a gift to Horix, then steal you back.'

'No! She sounds as bad as Temsa.'

'What's she going to do, melt you?'

'Most likely.'

Grumbling, I waved him about as I thought. These were some of my best ideas he was shrugging aside. 'What if I—'

My words were stolen from me as a man in gold armour came sprinting past, knocking me aside. I got an, 'Excuse me!' for my troubles, but that was only because of my stolen robe, and the white feather I'd drawn onto it with stolen chalk.

Something in the man's face made me watch him run. It looked a lot like panic. That, and anyone bolting through a city street looks suspicious, even more so in Araxes. I looked around, but saw no chase. The soldier ran straight for Horix's tower, disappearing behind its surrounding walls like a rat into a hole.

'That doesn't look good,' said Pointy.

'Not good at all.' I turned around again, poking my head into an adjoining street. The mist had deadened most of the city noise, and it made me wary. I strained my poor ears, listening for the dull music of boots and armour. A name surfaced in my head and stuck there: *Temsa*. Horix had been his next victim after Finel's and already several days had passed. No doubt losing me had spurred his plans.

As I started walking again, faster this time, I heard the squeak of a wagon wheel. A dark shadow passed in front of a distant brazier, just a faint patch of light in the mist. My feet trod quicker, scuffing sand. The faint rhythm of marching feet reached my ears over the slam and clang of gates. I broke into a jog. The marching grew louder still.

The widow's tower loomed above me, dark and ominous, growing in detail with every long and hurried stride. As I drew nearer to its gates, the marching sound stopped abruptly. Like orange lightning coursing through clouds, an army of torches sparked into life in the street before me. Jagged silhouettes were cast on the mist, armed with spears and blades. Startled, I threw myself against some nearby stonework and hugged the lip of a wall.

'Caltro? What's happening?' Pointy's voice was low and tense.

'I don't know!' I whispered. 'But it's fucking inconveniently timed!'

I crept closer, peering into the mist. Two rough columns of soldiers filled the street in front of the widow's tower, clothed in shining tabards. They were enough to make my mouth hang open. Tropical turquoise shone between threads of gold. Elegant glyphs lined their edges. The seal of the royal family was sewn in copper thread on their breasts and backs.

'Horix is in trouble with the emperor?' I asked aloud. 'Surely not...'

'Open in the name of the emperor and the Code!' came a shout from the ranks, sounding a fraction slurred. Not a sound followed it. No retort, no insult. The widow's tower remained as silent as an oak tree.

Coming as close as I dared while the soldiers began to approach the gates, I watched them closely. It was then that I saw how awkwardly the tabards were being worn, hitched up in places, showing charcoal-black armour hiding beneath. What faces I could see were stern or smug.

'It's a ruse,' I said.

'What?'

'We're too late!' I snapped, cursing my procrastination on the roof-top. 'He's come for her. For my half-coin.'

'Who?'

'Who do you think? Temsa!'

The soldiers had begun to pound on the gates, repeating their claims of the emperor and Code. It was a fine ruse, if Horix had any respect for anybody but herself. It was a slim sliver of hope in this abruptly grim situation: Temsa didn't know what he was up against.

'That stunted bastard has got bigger balls than I thought, pretend-ing to be royal soldiers.'

'Or he's got friends in high places, remember?' whispered the sword. 'I know a thing or two about tactics, and this is what they call pincered, Caltro.'

The gates were so firmly locked they didn't even rattle. I watched the soldiers shrug to each other until somebody screeched for a ram to be brought up the lines.

'This is not good.' Pointy voiced my thoughts.

'Not good at all.'

Hearing a cry, the kind that dying things make, I threw a look over my shoulder.

'Wait.'

THE IMPATIENT CLANG OF TALONS on flagstones made Ani and Danib flinch instinctively.

'Where are the rest of them?' Temsa yelled, arching his neck to peer over the heads of his soldiers. The confounded mist curtained off the streets, crafting a small, grey-walled arena around Horix's walls and tower.

Danib said nothing, focused on a dent in his battle armour. Ani seemed to share his impatience. She'd been injured at Serek Finel's. One of the bear-like creatures had given her a cut that split her cheek almost to the teeth. It had been crudely sewn: bristles of spare thread poked out of her skin like a lost sideburn. It had put her in a foul mood; her first major injury in over a decade. Temsa could see the urge for violence brewing in her.

'It's the fucking mist. They should be here. They left first,' she grunted, jaw barely moving.

'Maybe it's your doltish sergeants, m'dear. These soldiers are sorely lacking in training. You can roll a turd in gold dust, but it's still a turd. No matter what tabards we put them in, they're no army!' Temsa growled. 'Now get that gate open.'

'Fine.'

Ani strode forwards, battle-axes quivering at her sides, showing her frustration. She deserved to share a portion of his tension. Temsa carried enough problems for everybody in the street to have one. Maybe two. Why should he shoulder them all? He raised the large metal speaking-cone to his lips once again.

'Open up in the name of the emperor and the Code!' he bellowed. 'Or suffer the consequences!'

The battering ram had just reached the gates when a heavy thud came from above. Halfway up the tower, just below where the mist swallowed it, a column of light broke the sheer darkness of its walls.

Temsa peered up at the black knife of a figure that came to stand at the balcony's edge. Though she was a good distance away, he recognised the cowl, the crooked posture, and the glint in the charcoal eyes, catching the torchlight at her gates.

'Boran Temsa!' came her shrill voice, cracked at the edges like old papyrus. 'Your royal colours don't fool me. What a pitiful ruse indeed!'

Casting one last sour look over his shoulder into the darkness of the alleyway, Temsa walked forwards into the light, one arm held out and palm open. 'You'll find it's *Tor* Boran Temsa now, you old hag!'

'You should look at the crags in your own face, Temsa. And these are dire times indeed, if soulstealers like you can call themselves tor.'

Temsa ignored the cheap jibe, and showed her the white of his teeth instead. 'I have a feeling it might even be *Serek* Temsa by tomorrow morning, Widow.'

'Finally come to add my coins to your collection, have you?' she cried out.

'A happy bonus. I'm here for only one coin, in fact, Horix. And one shade.'

'And I told your lump of a bodyguard. I will not give up the locksmith's coin.'

Temsa waited to be heard over the first bash of the ram.

Bang! The gates barely shivered.

Ani returned to his side, her eyes trained on the widow. 'Told you she was stubborn.'

'Seeing as I'm here, I'll make you one last offer. Send Caltro out with his coin and we'll be on our way.'

Temsa watched the widow duck into the light momentarily, and then emerge with her hands on her hips.

'What game are you playing now, you weasel?' she yelled.

Temsa was confused by that, he had to admit. 'Game? Why don't you tell me?'

'We both know Caltro Basalt is your prisoner, Temsa. Don't lie to me.'

Bang!

Still no budge came from the gates. He suppressed a scowl. The widow had paid good silver for her fortress. 'What did you say to her, Ani?' he said to the woman by his side.

'Exactly what you told me to say. That you want his coin, and she can give it up easy, or the hard way.'

Temsa turned back to Horix. 'I think you're the game-player here, Widow! We'll play it the hard way after all,' he yelled, spittle flying alongside his words. The woman's gall stung him. 'Surrender now, or—'

A regal voice soared over the ugly proceedings. 'Or in the name of the emperor and the Code, we will see justice executed.'

From the shadows of the alley, clanging steel emerged into the street, silver tanned yellow by torchlight. Shields and wide, forward-curved blades formed a fan around a striking figure of gold mail and turquoise silks. Etane walked beside the empress-in-waiting, his mighty sword across his back.

'Bow!' he yelled, and any soldier not manhandling the ram got to their knees.

Temsa stayed leaning on his cane. He caught Sisine's gaze, and hoped she could see the anger and irritation in his eyes. She was ruining his evening, his retribution. She was like a vulture swooping in on a dunewyrm's carcass.

'My, my,' called Horix. No wit or insult came tumbling down from the balcony. The battering ram thudded once more in the silence. A lonely hinge squeaked, but there was no splintering.

Sisine cleared her throat. 'You were not known to me, Tal Horix, until you stood in my way. That was a mistake. Thankfully, this good servant of the emperor…' She gestured broadly to Temsa, who wore a frown. '…was kind enough to inform me of your theft of royal property. One Caltro Basalt.'

Horix's voice was fainter now, coarser. 'This is the sort of servant you consort with, Sisine?'

Temsa stamped his talons on the ground once more. 'Can we all stop saying "servant"? Open the fucking gates, Widow! Your stubbornness bores me!'

Horix shook her head. 'You speak of mistakes, Sisine. You have made a great one by coming here.'

The empress-in-waiting bristled while Etane crept forwards through the soldiers, eyes narrowed at the balcony.

'You dare to speak to me with such familiarity, old woman?'

All that followed was a cackle as Horix vanished from the railings and the light was extinguished.

'Break those gates!' Temsa roared.

The tempo of the ram increased. Five more times it was driven against the stout wood and iron, and on the sixth, even with little sign of give, the gates parted with a crunch.

Under snarling orders from Ani, Temsa's soldiers rammed their shoulders against the gates, rabid as winter-starved wolves. Within moments, they were sprawling in the dust, the two halves of the gate flying open easily. The gold and turquoise crowd surged inwards, carelessly trampling the fallen in their eagerness to spill blood.

The courtyard disappointed them immensely. A long space lined with columns, it held nothing but dark shadows. A lone brazier stood at the top of the square steps, beside the tower's door. Its light was hazy. The soldiers' war-cries faded as they hesitated.

Temsa was about to tell the idlers to get moving when he heard a strange crackle, like an abrupt gust of wind. It took him moment to recognise the sound of bows being loosed. Before he could flinch, screams filled the night sky. Body after body crumpled into heaps, pincushions for arrows.

Men scrambled to be free of the courtyard, but Ani pushed them back in. 'Get those fucking bowmen!' she screeched. Danib waded through them all, broadsword held high. He cared little for the arrows, which stuck in his armour or lodged in his vapours. No amount of them seemed to slow him. Soldiers in silver armour broke from the shadows, charging the great shade with spears and blades and brave shouts. Danib parried, hacked, and bludgeoned, commencing the slaughter by himself. Wherever he moved, piles of dead were left behind him.

Seeing the maelstrom that was on their side, Temsa's soldiers regained their courage and began to flood into the courtyard once more, re-trampling those who had just peeled themselves out of the mud, dazed and bloody. Triggermen duelled with bowmen up in the towers' higher balconies or shooting through tiny slits in the stone. Rocks came crashing down intermittently, crushing helmets and bones.

It was a bloody half hour, but by the end of it, Temsa's men had won the courtyard. The tor swaggered to the gateway, where the ram was being picked up, ready to tackle the door. The soldiers hoisting it up decided to give the weapon some momentum, and ran at the doorway full pelt. With an almighty crack, the ram bounced from the door, sending men sprawling on the steps. With a groan, Temsa clicked his fingers, and a nearby soldier with a forest of facial hair disappeared into the mist.

Danib plodded closer, each footstep a resounding thud and clank. His broadsword was notched like the toothy edge of a saw. Temsa knew he was missing the soulblade Caltro had pilfered. 'Hold this courtyard for as long as you must. Get grapples on the lower balconies if you can.

Ah, here we are.'

The hairy soldier had returned, now with a skinny figure struggling in his arms.

'Ready, Tooth?' asked Temsa. 'It's on you now. Find me a way in.'

The locksmith pushed some matted hair out of her face and mumbled something, lips moving but no real words coming forth.

'Good! You'd better!' he said.

Temsa pushed her forwards, making her whimper, and the soldier hauled her towards the tower. With his hulking bodyguards at his side, Temsa joined the royal entourage, who were working their way back into the alley, out of range of any other bows Horix might be hiding. Temsa caught Sisine's eye through the raised shields of her guards

'Enjoying the show, eh, Your Majesty?'

The look Sisine threw him was so cold Temsa was surprised he didn't see his breath in the air. 'I will enjoy it when I have Caltro's half-coin in my hand, Tor!' she called.

'Fair enough,' he muttered as his own guards folded around him. His aching wounds had reminded him of the value of leading from behind. If it was good enough for a princess, it was good enough for him.

That lesson was immediately reinforced when he heard a rising roar coming from a side street. For a moment, he wore a beaming grin; the rest of his soldiers had finally found their way. But it was a short-lived thing, and it withered when he saw the large shape of a man clad in silver battle armour leading a hundred-strong charge of bellowing soldiers into their misty arena.

'What the fuck is this, Tor?' Sisine snarled at him.

Temsa wished he knew.

'WE NEED TO GO!'

'Don't you think I know that?' I snapped as the flood of silver armour filled the street. The arrival of the empress-in-waiting had been enough to make my jaw drop. I had wished for a distraction, not a war.

'Now, Caltro!'

I caught sight of the muscular figure at their head. 'It's Colonel Kalid. Horix's man!'

'Move!'

'No…' I watched the men rush past me, recognising the seal emblazoned on their breastplates. They ignored the ghost curled in the gutter, focused only on their tower.

'Now!'

'Shut up!' I hissed, waiting a fraction before bounding from my hiding place. Sand flew as I sprinted after the last rank of soldiers. 'Now!'

Being dead, I was naturally breathless, but I still felt the panic riling against my efforts to dim my glow. I ran with my lips clamped shut, an effigy of strain. Pointy bobbed frantically by my side, the face on his pommel as uneasy as my own.

I must have been obvious, a streak of blue amongst a mass of flesh and bone, but none of Kalid's soldiers seemed to notice or care once the blades began to clash, and what a thunderous collision it was. Skidding to a halt beside the gate's ornate hinges, I watched the shining crowds roil about the courtyard. Ranks heaved against each other, what little space remained between them turned into areas of fierce butchery. Blood spurted in black arcs above the sea of helmets. The madness of it momentarily stunned me.

'Dead gods, don't just stand there!' Pointy shouted at me.

My eyes darted left and right as I ducked into the shadows, stepping over corpses littered with broken triggerbows. A soldier flew into the wall ahead of me, his unprotected skull painting the stone all kinds of colours. I flitted past him before his corpse could fall. A spear nicked me as it hurtled past. Its owner was too busy dying to use it. The snaggle-toothed woman's blood sprayed my smock as her neck was split by a sword. Her dying moan somehow lodged in my ears, giving an eerie echo to the crash and roar of the courtyard.

Somehow, I ducked and dodged my way around the edges of the fighting, which was already turning in Colonel Kalid's favour. His soldiers were on home ground now, and they were military types, ex-soldiers, honed in the emperor's wars in the Scatter; not scrawny sells-words hauled out of taverns and slapped in armour.

By the time Kalid had reclaimed the doorway of the tower, there were more corpses in the courtyard than fighters. Temsa's soldiers fled or fought their way back through the gates. I was now crouched close to the steps, busy hugging a column. Kalid and his soldiers now stood between me and the door. I considered rushing around to the rear of the tower, but large stones blocked the way.

There came another roar, this time beyond the walls. I heard Kalid bellow frantically for formations. A few of his soldiers began to pound on the great tower door. It seemed Temsa had learnt a trick from old Finel: he had more men waiting in the streets, waiting to pounce.

'The colonel has sprung his trap too early!' Pointy yelled to me. I was not listening. I was staring at the gate, where the twin lumps of Danib and Jexebel had appeared. Men in sooty armour flowed around them like a black tide.

I ran too, driving myself up the steps. I poured all my concentration into the nearest of Kalid's men, and hurled myself at his chest. With a muted *whump* I bounced straight off him, and sprawled awkwardly across the steps.

Fucking copper! I cursed.

He slashed at me and I rolled away, waving Pointy madly. By luck,

I sheared the point from his blade, and he staggered, yelling for the colonel.

Kalid saw me then, standing in my blood-stained smock, fake white feather on my breast, rubbing confusion from my eyes. 'Caltro!' he shouted. He saw me look up, dazed, and knew then it was me. 'Seize that shade! Get him into the tower!'

Three soldiers tore themselves from the ranks to grab me. I let them, seeing as I wanted very much to be inside, and away from all this chaos. I clasped Pointy to my chest, and perhaps the white feather was the reason they didn't take him. Perhaps they believed I was a free shade. Their grip was lighter than I had become accustomed to.

Kalid's shout had reached the ears of Danib. The great armoured ghost scythed his way through Horix's soldiers with his broadsword. No living man or woman in that courtyard was a match for his brute strength and massive blade. Blows fell upon him in their dozens but they did nothing to halt his ferocious momentum. Those who escaped his lunging swings fell to Jexebel's axes instead. Her arms windmilled, chopping at anything that moved like an unhinged lumberjack.

I too began to pound on the door. I felt the shudder of locks unwinding between strikes. Horix had locked herself in too tight. 'Colonel!' I shouted. 'Hurry the fuck up!'

I watched Kalid's gaze sweep around the courtyard, taking in every corpse, every black-clad attacker, and every sweep of Danib's sword. It took him barely a moment to decide. With a wordless roar, he beat his sword against his chest and marched to meet Danib. I craned my neck, hand hovering over the steel of the door. This, I had to see.

'Get into the tower! All of you!' he bellowed.

The colonel was huge in his own right, but the ghost had maybe a foot or more on him. Danib's vapours curled from the grille in his new visor. I wished there was some great horned and furious beast around so I could teach the ghost another lesson.

Danib waved Jexebel back with a grunt, and she went about her hacking. Kalid struck first, sliding under the ghost's arm and driving his sword at a gap in his armour. Red sparks flew as the hardened copper found its mark.

The ghost made no sound, though I saw white smoke curling over the thrashing crowds. His giant sword came slashing in great arcs, forcing Kalid to weave. He jabbed where he could, but the blade came closer every time; Danib was getting the measure of him. I wondered how many decades the ghost had on his opponent. How many hundreds he had killed.

With a screech of steel, Kalid's pauldron was ripped from his shoulder. He rolled to avoid being split in half by the next swing. He was spry, for a big man. Cunning, too, as he went for Danib's heel. Like most men who strive for muscle, he was top-heavy. With a crunch, the colonel cut deep enough to make the ghost kneel.

Kalid spun full circle, almost acrobatic. His sword slammed into Danib's breastplate, bludgeoning him to the ground. I stared on, shocked and strangely still while the fight raged around them. I heard the last clicks of locks, but I strained on my tiptoes to watch the colonel drive a sword through the ghost's shoulder. I could almost hear the sizzle of vapour against copper-lined steel. Kalid pressed down on the blade with all his weight, trying to sever the limb.

Hands grabbed me, but not before I saw Danib reach up and knit his gauntlets behind Kalid's head. The colonel tried to wrench free, but somehow the ghost held him. I yelled as I was ushered into the blazing light of the tower. The last thing I glimpsed was the colonel's face being driven into the pommel of his own sword, again and again, until the man's face was a horrid cavern of crimson and white bone.

I felt sorry for his ghost, but that didn't halt my guilty elation that I was in the tower and he was not.

CHAPTER 8
VENGEANCE IS A VIRTUE

Revenge is a dish best served while your
enemy isn't looking.

OLD SKOL SAYING

FROM THE SAFETY OF HER balcony's railing, the widow glared down into her courtyard and watched the silver-plated body slump to the blood-churned earth. The giant ghost extricated himself from the sword; the corpse rolled to face the misty skies, and there Horix saw the ruin of Colonel Kalid's face.

A snarl rose in her throat, building to a roar. Not one of anguish, or sorrow, but anger. Kalid had failed her in his final moments. In twenty seconds, he had undone twenty years of fine service, and she was now minus one fine colonel. A dull ache spread through her chest.

With the torches quenched, her high balcony was kept in shadow, far out of range of any triggerbows, and Horix lingered for a moment more. The fighting was down to blades and fists now. Nails and teeth, in some cases. If she leaned out, Horix saw her men pressed against the door, being yanked through one by one. The tide had turned once more, and not in her favour. Hungry waves of Temsa's black-clad soldiers continued to flow through the gates. The weasel himself was standing in the gateway now. Sisine waited not far behind, guarded by Etane. Horix found it hard to tear her eyes away from them. *The uppity little curs.*

Horix spat over the railing into the battle below, wrenching herself away from the cold, foggy air. It made her bones ache. Clasping a pearl cane in one hand, she pressed the other to her chest, feeling the blunt edges of the half-coin she'd hung on a chain around her neck.

'Yamak!' she cried once she'd entered the light in the corridor. A single torch held back the shadows. The sweaty man came bumbling out of the darkness, his borrowed shirt of mail clinking musically.

'Mistress?'

'Your cutters.'

Yamak fiddled under his shirt for a moment before producing a pair of steel shears. They were small but stocky, and perfect for reducing a half-coin to shreds.

'Widow?' Yamak asked.

'If Caltro's not in Temsa's possession, and he's not in mine, then he has clearly fled. I cannot have that, not when the empress-in-waiting is loitering outside my gates, winkled from her Cloudpiercer! The time is now! I cannot wait any longer.'

'But they—'

Horix set the cutters to the half-coin, aiming to snick its corner. She took a moment before she pressed, gently at first, watching the steel bite into the softer copper.

A piteous wail rose up from the stairwell, slicing through the clangs and echoes of dying. Horix yanked coin and cutters apart, shoving the latter into Yamak's podgy stomach. He spluttered, moving promptly out of her way as she strode to the nearest balustrade. Torches wheeled below her in the spiralling darkness, like some poorly-timed theatre act.

'CALTRO BASALT!' she screeched.

MY HEAD WHEELED FROM THE pain. I shook as white fire sprinted back and forth down my arm. My name rang out above me. I knew that voice's hoarse edges. Its bitter core. *The widow*. In that moment I had not a scrap of love for her, only hatred that she was about to snuff me so cleanly. Effortlessly.

'The fuck was that?!' I yelled up at the staircase, feeling dizzy as I eyed its spirals, trying to find her. I saw a black notch between its railings. It was working its way swiftly down towards me. A fat man bobbed behind her.

I clutched Pointy to my side, using him as a prop as I struggled to stay upright. The soldiers had left me sprawled on the marble. They were too busy helping their comrades close the door on those too slow or too injured to drag themselves from the fighting. Gauntlets and sword pommels thumped frantically on the steel as the bolts were rammed into place and the cogs turned.

As the grim music faded, drummer by drummer, an eerie silence fell over the atrium. All was quiet save for feet and skirts brushing against steps. Then there came a scraping, as armoured corpses were cleared from the steps. Not a single order was given on the other side of the door.

'Caltro Basalt!' the widow said again, this time a hiss. Perhaps she imagined ears pressed against the door.

'Widow Horix,' I replied, noting the half-coin dangling from a gold chain in her hand. 'It's been too long. Apparently almost too long to bear, seeing as you were about to snuff me.'

I was greeted with a sharp slap around the face. Her copper rings carried the weight of it, and I reeled. The soldiers bunched up around me, realising I might not be as harmless as they originally thought.

'That is for taking your time coming back to me. And what is that?' She jabbed a finger at the sword, now held fast in my grip.

'My sword.'

I think I recognise this woman…' the sword mused inside my head. I had no time for half-memories, only assurances.

Horix cackled. Her eyes bored into mine. 'A bound shade owns no possessions. Especially not as ornate as this.'

The door shuddered as a ram collided with it. I let the echoes of the boom die before I spoke. 'I doubt you have the time to argue.'

'Relieve him of it,' the widow growled. I felt gauntlets snaking between my ribs and arms. I had just been considering running at her, seeing what haunting that leathery old skin was like.

'I need it,' I asserted. 'For whatever job you want me so badly for. So badly you would kill me to stop Temsa or the empress-in-waiting from getting hold of me. Looks like I must be the best locksmith in the Reaches after all.'

She stepped closer. I watched the flicker of torches play amongst the crags of her face. 'And here I was, hoping Temsa or Busk had cut out your tongue for your cheek. Keep the sword. But you will be watched closely.'

The gauntlets stayed on my wrists and shoulders, and I was marched after the widow. Instead of up, Horix made for the basement door, the one I remembered sneaking through not so long ago. The terror of the courtyard was fading quickly, abruptly replaced by excitement. After enduring the company of Busk and Temsa, I had completely forgotten Horix's secrets, and my own desperation to know them. That burning curiosity hooked me afresh. Better yet, all was about to be revealed. I would have done a quick jig if I hadn't been held tight.

'Well, that was easier than I expected,' said the sword.

'Mhm,' I agreed. It looked as though luck could throw you a bone in death as well as life. I was glad for it.

A soldier with stripes on his armour and a tattoo of a scarab on his bald head rushed past me. He stood to attention at the widow's side. I heard his rushed whisper.

'Shouldn't we barricade the door, Mistress?'

Horix sized him up, prodding him in the breastplate with her pearl-topped cane. 'You are Kalid's replacement?'

'Yes, Widow! Capt—Colonel Omshin.'

'Well, Omshin, we only need to keep them out for a short while, don't we?'

'Well… yes, Mistress.'

'Good. Then stop wasting my time with ridiculous questions and get your men aboard.'

Aboard. My excitement grew.

'Forwards!' Omshin immediately cried, leading his soldiers tramping down the stairs. Two stayed to hold me. Yamak wheezed behind the widow.

Dozens of torches blazed in sconces, adding smoke to the dust that filled the air. We passed through the cave I remembered, where tools and rubble had been piled. That pile was a mountain now, touching the ceiling. Scrapings on the floor suggested many more carts had been taken elsewhere. We skirted the mound and crept around a corner, where we were painted in a bright green glow; a hue born of competing ghost and torch light. They kept the fire to the entranceway, as if it were forbidden to take it any further.

My eyes took their time taking in the cavern Horix had hidden for so long. Several hundred dead stood around the mighty cavern; in crowds in the pit below us, or lining ramparts and scaffolding. All of them stood silently, waiting. These were the diggers, the builders, the architects of the great void my gaze had somehow missed on my first visit. I bucked in the grip of the guards, wanting to stop so I could put all my concentration into staring. They muscled me on.

I have witnessed many great feats of human architecture in my life. There were those that aimed for size, such as the Bonebridge at Urul Gorge. The Cloudpiercer. Even Araxes itself. Or there were feats of beauty, like the Coralossus in the Scatter. What Horix had achieved was one of sheer ingenuity and boldness.

'So this… this is what you've been hiding from the world…' I whispered.

The widow flashed me a look of pure delight. Her brand of it, at least. It was a mad, wolfish thing.

The contraption was huge, filling the cavern to the roof. At its base was a ship's hull, its silvery planks full of uneven portholes and gaps that showed metal ribs beneath. Spikes of iron bristled on the hull's prow, like an adolescent's beard. A word was splayed across it in black paint: *VENGEANCE*. Spars poked downwards like insectile protrusions, holding the construction steady against its scaffolding. Leather-wrapped palms on poles clung to its sides. They looked suspiciously like oars to me. Bulging from the top of the hull was a great patchwork balloon of writhing fabric; red, gold and blue. It had a waxed sheen to it, full of heavy stitching and daubs of pitch. It looked like the bulged neck of a humongous – and very ill – toad.

I heard bubbling and hissing somewhere in the wavering shadows of the cavern. I looked up to see wooden rafters, where more ghosts perched like roosting pigeons. Thick cogs spoke of something mechanical, but I couldn't tell what. One ghost was dangling from a rope, patching a section of the balloon where a thin trail of steam or smoke escaped. The ghost-light caught the gleam of a ceiling made of iron bars and wooden planks.

'What the fuck is it, Horix?' I asked, finally finding my voice.

A soldier's shout stole my chance for an answer.

'They're trying to reach the rear of the tower!' came the holler.

Horix shrugged as she led us up a ramp, perhaps the same one I had cowered under before Kalid had seized me and dragged me to the sarcophagus. Who knew this monstrous creation had been lingering above me?

A line of ghosts occupied one side of the ramp. Several looked expectantly at the widow as she walked past, but were ignored completely. One ghost I recognised very well indeed. He was unmistakeable.

'Kon,' I whispered as I walked past.

At first the crumpled ghost looked pleased to see me, and then he saw the false white feather on my breast, and his eyes fell to my feet. I had nothing to say, and no time to say it. It was a poor goodbye.

The ramp walked us up to a doorway in the hull of the colossal machine. I watched with horror as its rough floor seemed to sag beneath the weight of Yamak, and the gap between it and the ramp widened marginally. I flinched away from it.

'Is it… floating?' Pointy asked, as aghast as I was. His pommel was open-mouthed.

'What is this sorcery?' I asked again, louder this time. I knew I sounded like a dullard peasant. I gawped like one too. Even in this world of bound ghosts and talking swords, this still had the capacity to shock me.

'The Chamber of Thinking call it "science", Caltro. I wouldn't have expected you to be so skittish,' said Horix as she marched inwards and took her place on a chair overlooking a wide porthole in the bow.

I thought I had a right to be skittish, when asked to board a floating ship. And yet, I had no choice in the matter. I had elected to follow my coin, and besides, the guards muscled me through its doorway before I could make a complaint.

I felt the craft wavering below me as I stared about at its boat-like interior, made of planks or crisscross panels. Its iron ribs were supported by skinny wooden beams. There seemed to be a deck above, accessed by a ladder. Some sort of commotion was going on up there, but I couldn't tell what kind. Shadow pervaded where my glow couldn't reach.

I threw up my hands. 'Now what?'

My answer came in the form of a soldier pushing me into a corner. I waited in silence while the rest of the soldiers filed aboard, taking their places about the hull, treading the stairs, and thumping on the boards over my head. Through the many gaps, I could see them slumping against the beams, breathing quiet sighs of relief. I wasn't convinced enough of our safety to share their emotion.

Light came in the form of fifty shades, marched in through the door by the last soldiers. The innards of the hull shone blue. They spared me a sour glance as they passed me, heading to grasp the palm-wood oars on the deck above. I vaguely recognised one or two but that was all. No Kon in sight. Horix was abandoning him, and all her other shades besides. Her vaults. Even many of her soldiers. She was sacrificing everything for this machine.

There came shouts for more of something I didn't recognise the name of – something with gift or lift in it – and there was a strange sensation as the craft pushed at my heels. There was another cry of warning from high above us. A shudder coursed through the machine.

'Release her!' came the widow's shrill order, and I heard the great cogs above us begin to turn with ponderous clanks. I realised then what the machinery in the roof had been for. It was pointless, but I tried to hold a breath anyway.

***

'CHARGE, YOU FUCKING HOUNDS!' TEMSA bellowed at his soldiers, spit plastering his face as he followed their charge over the bricks they'd battered out of the way. This was not how he had predicted this night turning out, but he was determined to right it. An empress-in-waiting was watching.

Temsa's cane stabbed at the rubble. His leg ached, prickling his hips and back with needles, but he pressed on, turning the pain into anger. He thought of Horix's white-haired head and its scowling face, dangling from his bloody grip. Perhaps he'd fashion it into a tankard, something to remind guests of the price of trying to beat him.

Horix's gardens were paltry, and the soldiers found just a patch of earth between them and a stout but small door. No brave and foolish guards stood ready in defence. They were alone against the tower.

'Bring up the ram!' Temsa ordered. He stood by the walls, wary of the shadows between the scattered palms and shrubs to his left. Danib stood nearby, glowing white through the gaping rent in his breastplate. One arm hung limper than the other. His huge sword dragged in the mist-wreathed dust.

Something grumbled in the earth beneath them. Temsa felt it running through his talons. Ani seemed to feel it too. She looked to him, and they shared a blank look.

A puff of dust raced across the ground, splitting the garden with a dark line. Sand fell away, as if pouring down a giant hourglass. The ground was edging apart in two halves, creating a rectangular pit. Several soldiers lost their footing to the gap, crying out as the space opened beneath their feet. They clawed at the sand as they slipped.

'Back! Back!' Ani roared at the others.

The men were slow, heavy with confusion. As the gap yawned wider, showing a black void beneath the earth, half a dozen lost their grip and tumbled inwards with piteous cries. They were short-lived, and Temsa's confusion grew. He whirled around to stare at the royal entourage, waiting back in the courtyard. He could see the ice in Sisine's eyes even from a distance, as damning as a falling icicle.

'Horix! What is this farce?' Temsa cried. 'Triggermen! Fire into that pit!'

A few bodies came forward, bows waggling at the darkness. But the shifting ground made their feet skittish. Arrows sailed high and wide. A few of Horix's soldiers had appeared on balconies, and were taking pot-shots at them with short bows. Soldiers were soon scattering for cover.

There came a resounding *bang* as the pit found its boundaries, taking up practically all of the dusty space between the garden walls.

Temsa heard the cries rise from below, cut off suddenly. Then it appeared. An arc of red and gold cloth, swollen and puffed, rose up above the dust without a sound. One of his men was clinging to it, whimpering as he slowly slid from its curves and landed with a bang somewhere far below.

The patchwork cloth bulged into a huge, misshapen balloon, rising further and further until it forced Temsa's head back, making his neck crunch. Clinging to the balloon's underside was the bottom half of a small wooden ship, clinker-built and complete with keel and rudder. Silence fell across the garden as the soldiers gawped at the bizarre contraption.

No sooner had it come into view did Temsa see a porthole, and the triggerbow poking from it. He spared not a shout, throwing himself behind Danib as the bolt was loosed. Stone chips sprayed as it met the wall behind him.

Another flurry of bolts followed, peppering his men. More bodies tumbled into the pit, their wails now prolonged and each ending in a crash.

'Do something, Temsa!' shrieked Sisine, now standing beside them, mouth agape in horror at the sight of the machine effortlessly plying the air, defying the gods themselves. Palm frond and feather oars made the craft spin as it climbed into the mist.

Temsa cursed as a bolt clanged off his talons. He shoved Danib in the back. 'You heard her. Fucking do something!' he cursed.

With a grunt, Danib hefted his sword. Holding it over his shoulder, he took a step, stretched backwards, and then threw the blade like an axe. Torchlight ran along its steel, making it seem almost liquid. Mist spiralled in the weapon's path. A panicked shout came from behind one of the portholes, only to be silenced as the sword struck the ship's hull, just below where the wood met canvas. With an almighty crack, it was buried up to the hilt.

Temsa watched Horix's craft list to the right and veer madly around the pillar of a building. Over the strangled sounds of pain and confusion, he heard a faint reptilian hiss coming from the craft, and the cries of, "Leak!" behind the silver wood hull.

Before the craft was swallowed by the haze, Temsa saw a flash of blue standing at a dark doorway in its side. A figure stood by him: shorter, more crooked, cowl thrown back and face frozen in a victorious smile. He could see it clearly in the cold glow of the shade at her side. Even at that distance, Temsa could tell that smile was not for him. Though Caltro's gaze bored into him, Horix's did not. Her gaze ran past him, reserved for the empress-in-waiting who stood shaking with rage nearby.

As resoundingly as a door shutting, the flying contraption vanished into the night. The awkward silence soured quickly. Temsa looked to Sisine. Her face was flushed with blood. With a bark of an order, Sisine and her entourage about-faced and made for the broken gates. She had no words for Temsa but a strangled, 'Tomorrow.'

Temsa watched her leave, analysing her sour expression. As a man who prided himself on reducing people to blubbering, bleeding wrecks, he liked to think he could recognise fear when he saw it. He witnessed it then, in the empress-in-waiting's face.

Sisine looked as though she had seen a ghost.

———◆———

SISINE WAS A HURRICANE OF gold and turquoise. The soldiers struggled to keep up with her, wincing at the vehemence of her cursing. As she snatched her silk train from the blood-soaked stones, Sisine glared at the street beyond, where gawkers had gathered, and chancers already tugged at the fresh bodies in the hope of claiming a soul. Some saw her and prostrated themselves in the damp sand. Others were too occupied with trying to raise their social status.

Before the soldiers guided her back to her armoured carriage, Sisine spied a glimpse of red standing amongst the crowd. She saw one of the Cult sisters standing in the same alleyway she had lurked in, watching, waiting. The sister had a group of cloaked and armoured shades at her back; Sisine could see their muted glow painting the mist blue. There were living standing with them, too, wearing proctors' and scrutinisers' garb. Chamber and Cult, standing side by side, and both against her. They wore confused expressions upon seeing all the royal tabards lying blood-stained and punctured, and the empress-in-waiting wading through a street full of corpses.

Sisine locked eyes with the dead sister. Unlike the others around her, the shade's face was unreadable. Sisine clenched her jaw, raised her chin to the appropriate royal height, and gave her a silent promise of another death.

As she walked, her golden sandal slipped upon something that looked suspiciously like stray entrails, and her ankle betrayed her. She flopped sideways, but was saved from falling by a cold grip on her arm. Etane righted her, and she immediately swatted him away, cutting a white mark across his cheek with her ring.

Sisine snarled, the pain in her ankle lending her viciousness. 'How dare you touch me, shade?' Sisine looked around as she tried not to hobble, daring her soldiers to look at her. Through their golden shields, she saw some bow their heads in muted chuckles.

'Back to the Piercer!' Sisine barked, her mind bursting with flying contraptions and old faces.

CHAPTER 9
THE HUNTED

Soulblades were a short-lived intersection
between Nyxite binding magic and
blacksmithing. Interminably difficult to
accomplish, and vexingly inconsistent, the
practice of binding souls into weapons of war
was a step too far for deadbinding. Madness
seemed to follow most blades like a stench.
Very few were worth their silver, or the risks of
keeping one, and so they were shunned, and
fell from fashion, forgotten to all but collectors
of antiques and master swordsmen.

FROM 'THE GENERAL'S HANDBOOK', A
CHAMBER OF MILITARY MIGHT PUBLICATION

I *TELL YOU, I RECOGNISE THIS woman,'* Pointy said again.

'So you keep saying,' I muttered from one side of my mouth. 'Saying it over and over doesn't make it any more useful to our situation.'

Our situation was poor, that was for certain. There was a frantic racket above me as soldiers tried to mend the holes and keep the fabric from sputtering open. An "envelope", I'd heard them call it. With its red paint, I imagined it more of a ruptured heart, pissing away lifeblood over the city.

I leaned forwards, peeking at the city below us through the dark doorway. The mist was merciful; it kept our real height above the ground a mystery, obscuring much of the streets. The occasional black rooftop rushed beneath. They were getting more common now, and not just towers threatening to scrape us from the sky. I felt the craft veer at an order, and saw the spiky tower of a pyramid sail past the hull.

Horix's screeching could be heard over all the sounds of panic. 'Height, curse it! We need height! Turn her around!'

Respect and formality had the tendency to dwindle under situations of pressure. This was no different. The men working the levers and wheels in the craft's nose yelled back at her.

'We're trying!'

'We need more of the gas!'

I wondered if I too should be afraid, but I knew unless I fell into a copper mangle, height posed no threat to me, or any ghost aboard. They still rowed the air as if it should have, though. I heard the *whoosh, whoosh* of their palm and feather oars, making the craft lurch up and down, or yaw to the side. More than one living soul aboard had decorated the boards with vomit during our short flight.

I was just impressed they'd managed to keep the *Vengeance* in the air so long. An hour, I guessed; maybe more, since Danib had speared us like a floeshark. I was just happy to be ignored, and wonder how long this strange journey would last.

That didn't stop me watching the widow like an eagle watches a nest of rabbits. I couldn't see my coin but I could almost feel its presence, tugging at me. Perhaps that was just my lust for it, but in any case, I had found myself creeping from my spot, only to squat down again as the soldiers rushed about. Nobody stood guard. I looked out of the doorway again, and contemplated falling.

'Now?' Pointy asked, sensing my thoughts.

'Higher, damn it!' Horix yelled. 'And turn around! The Piercer is behind us!'

There it was. The depth of Horix's madness. Or genius. I had yet to decide. I realised her ambition, at least. It seemed Temsa and Sisine weren't the only one with the emperor's Sanctuary in their sights. Horix had simply decided on taking a far, far different route to the throne. Part of me was impressed. The other parts were shocked.

Once more, my numb backside left my seat. Sliding the sword through the belt of the smock, I shuffled forwards, looking anywhere but the widow to belie my intentions. Her cowl was turned away from me, fixed on the window in the inverted bow. I looked too, and saw the early morning spread before me: just a blurry canvas of dark mists and shapes below, speckled with yellow and blue. Spires poked through the mist like needles through a blanket of wool. Dawn was still some time away, but its light had begun to rise and paint the night with pipe-smoke grey.

The stocky tower of a storage house loomed ahead, and all eyes had turned upon it. Shouts drowned out my uneven stumbling and unbidden yelp as the *Vengeance* lurched again. A clang sounded as one of the spars struck a minaret.

'More height!' Horix yelled.

'It won't climb, Tal!' replied one of the men at the controls.

I crept forwards until I hovered behind the widow, craning my neck to see hers, and my coin on her breast. My thief's hands already twitched with anticipation, fingers gracing thumbs.

There. My half-coin. I saw the tantalising glint of copper dangling from a chain. Horix yelled another order as I reached, too clumsy in my eagerness. I had never been a good pickpocket. The craft swung to the left and my hand thwacked her cowl. I cursed myself as she turned, lightning fast for her age, so much so that I thought her neck might snap there and then, and save me the trouble.

But no. I was met with eyes like two flint daggers, and a resounding backhand from the new colonel. I was sent spinning to the floor, my cheek shivering with white fire. Horix was already standing over me when I raised my head. I saw my coin then, free of her hand, and a desperate rage took me. I ripped Pointy from my belt, slicing it in two in the process, and swung for the widow's neck. It was the most murderous action I had ever taken, and I even had time to gawp in surprise as I watched the obsidian blade cut through the air.

Air was all the blade touched. Reverberations ran though my hand as Omshin kicked the flat of the blade, just above the hilt, and sent Pointy clattering from my grasp. Another kick came to my face, and knocked my skull back against the wood.

'Treachery from all sides,' Horix was muttering, picking her way over me, ensuring her skirts came nowhere near my cold blue skin. She bent to pick up Pointy between two fingers and held him over me. I wondered how she had the time for such torture while her precious *Ven-*

geance looked to be moments from crashing. As it turned out, she didn't. The widow was simply reading the hieroglyphs along the soulblade.

'I know this sword,' she told me, reading the faint glyphs in the obsidian. 'Absia. I have seen this blade before. It was my grandfather's sword.'

'*I was bloody right!*' Pointy whispered, strangely elated for his precarious position. '*Wait, that means she is—*'

'An ugly thing then, and an ugly thing now. How you came by it is none of my concern. What does worry me is that you think it is yours.' She paused to chuckle, like gravel being sifted. Her eyes fell upon my smudged white feather. 'Even if you were free.'

With a toss so casual I thought she was playing a trick, Horix threw Pointy from the *Vengeance*'s doorway. I watched the sword pirouette into the night, the face on his pommel as aghast as the look on mine.

'No!' I would have thrown myself over too had Omshin and another soldier not hauled me back into the corner.

'*Caltro!*' I heard Pointy's cry fade as he disappeared into the mist and the endless city below. I desperately looked to the spires, trying to remember where he fell.

'No!'

'There,' said the widow, wiping her hands. 'The matter is solved. If you'll excuse me…'

'You fucking bitch!' I cared little for my freedom in that moment, wanting only to see her punished for her cruelty. Horix ignored my cursing, which only served to infuriate me further. Instead, she turned back to the men battling the cogs and levers and took a breath to bellow.

'Dead gods damn it! Land her!'

'You said more height!' they chorused.

'Land her, I said! If she won't fly, slow it down and put her there!'

Between the steel-clad arms and fluttering cobalt glow, I couldn't see what she pointed to, but I hoped it was sharp and deadly. Like a spear factory, or a warehouse of stalagmites. Anything to teach the widow a lesson, to see her sneering face dashed open. I wondered at the fury running through my vapours.

Each of us wears a veil. It is one of decorum and civilisation, and we drape it over the animal skin we wore for millennia before towers and cobbles. Even in a city such as Araxes, such veils are worn by all. Some veils are thicker, taking something drastic to tear or wrench them away. A knife against a lover's throat, perhaps. Others only need a little fraying to show the beast beneath. Sometimes all it takes is the sun going down.

I had thought my veil long since in tatters, but now I knew I had been wearing its shreds for some time. My lips drew back to show my teeth, and my chest heaved without breath. I looked down at where my fists clenched against armour, and saw my glow had turned a darker shade.

Though others around me bit their lips and undoubtedly clenched their arseholes, I kept my eyes open every moment of that descent, watching the *Vengeance* falling to the earth, praying death on all those around me. I would pluck my half-coin from amongst the corpses.

———————◆————

AS IT TURNED OUT, THE art of conversation had died in Araxes during Nilith's absence. Even being hauled along like meat in Krona's caravan, there had been taunts and jibes. Talk of some sort, at least.

This scrutiniser offered as much chat as a plaster wall.

Nilith understood the need for silence. During their night of creeping she had heard far too many shouts and screams floating through the mist. It was a fine night for soulstealing, it seemed, and the denizens of the sprawls were well aware of it.

As usual, only ghosts, idiots, and their little group dared to ply the murky darkness. Though, to be fair, their group could have fallen into the idiot category. They certainly looked like a plump target for soulstealers, or thieves of any kind, for that matter. Farazar had been draped over Anoish, next to his body, gagged and bound. Bezel hid within the covers, keeping watch on him. Nilith and Heles walked out front, boots testing the sand quietly as they listened for trouble.

Hours they had travelled this way: silent and wary. Straight lines were foreign to them. They frequently took detours to avoid noises or bright patches of light. More than once they'd had to duck into an alley or side street to let some poor unfortunate sprint past, a pack of stealers on their heels. They even avoided ghosts; Heles knew they often worked as trackers for soulstealing gangs. Those had been the last words she had uttered, just after freeing them from Jobey and the Consortium, of whom there had been no sign since.

Nilith hung back a few paces to run her hand along Anoish's snout. The desert horse was not a fan of the streets and night-noises. She could see the tension in his haunches and flanks, sitting right alongside tiredness. She didn't blame him. It seemed as if they had been running for years, not just a handful of weeks. Every fibre in her cried out for rest, even if it meant slumping into a gutter for half an hour. She was cold too, and aching, as if her blood carried seawater in it.

Making sure Heles was watching the streets and not her, Nilith dug her fingers under the hem of her cloak so she could look at her arm. Patchwork wrappings betrayed the cold glow underneath them. The light reached up to her elbow now. The numbness had spread further, making her shoulder tingle. Pain spasmed across her chest. Nilith prodded gingerly, and found her finger pressing deep into her sleeve, far more than flesh and bone would allow. She felt the cold and wrenched her hand away, catching some of the cloak with it. A lance of blue fell across the street.

Heles froze, eyes darting about. She raised her makeshift club; a rusty piece of gate. 'What was that?'

'Nothing,' Nilith replied, voice hoarse. As luck would have it, Farazar poked his head from his coverings, and the scrutiniser looked at him accusingly.

'Better stay hidden,' she said. 'Majesty.'

Farazar muttered something foul and irritably pulled the sackcloth back over him.

Satisfied, Heles moved onwards, face moody in the darkness. It had been some time since they had heard the last scream. It seemed even murderers had a bedtime. Nilith looked again at the shadows of bruises under the scrutiniser's eyes. She had wanted to ask for hours, and now the question bubbled up. 'What happened to you, to bring you out here? You have no uniform. You're clearly injured.'

'Long story, Empress.'

'Nilith.'

'What?'

'Call me Nilith. It's my name, after all.'

Heles frowned. 'Still a long story.'

'I think we have the time. I can make it a royal order if you like, Scrutiniser.' It was strange to utter such words and see another person's will crumble before hers. It had been some time since Nilith had played empress, and it was a bitterer taste than she remembered.

Heles frown deepened, but duty held sway. 'I was investigating the murders of several tors and tals.'

'What murders?'

'You have been away for a long time, Majesty. Several citizens have grown rather bold in your absence. The empress-in-waiting has taken steps, but tors and tals keep dying. Merlec. Askeu. Yeera. Kanus. Urma. Busk. Probably more since I've been gone.'

Nilith knew a few of those names. 'And what did my daughter's "steps" look like?'

'Well... she put soldier-shades from the Scatter in the streets to help Chamberlain Rebene. Her own stock, apparently. Not much else, aside from enjoying your disappearance.'

And issuing royal decrees, Nilith thought.

'Soldiers, taken away from my wars?' Blue light bathed the sand as Farazar reared his head once more.

'Stay hidden, you dolt.' Nilith reached to thwack him.

'No love lost between you two, if you'll forgive me for saying so, Empress.'

'Nilith. And you haven't answered the question.'

Heles pursed her split lips. 'I am here because Tal Horix deemed it fit to put me here. I was investigating her property. Somewhat... spontaneously. I had assumed she was involved with a soulstealer named Boran Temsa, the man I think is behind the murders. Instead, I found she was hiding something under her tower. She was building something. I was caught before I could find out what.'

'And this Tal Horix did this?' Nilith pointed a finger to Heles' bruised face as they walked.

'Horix ordered it done. Killed a proctor, too. Jym. A good young man from these very Sprawls. She was foolish enough to leave me alive, however. As such, I will bring her to justice.' Her tone was cold and sharp as knapped flint.

'Sounds more like revenge to me.'

Heles shrugged. 'Revenge and justice are not too different. In the end, somebody still has to pay.'

Nilith couldn't argue with that. In fact, she rather agreed. She shook off a shiver, hating the cold ache in her arm. 'Tal Horix. Boran Temsa. I don't know these names.'

'I have a feeling you will, soon enough.'

'And they still believe the emperor to be in his Sanctuary?'

'They did before I was dragged out to the Sprawls.'

Nilith sensed some of the weight lying on her shoulders dissolve, but not as much as she would have liked. The slatherghast's poison filled her with a dull pain, and a weariness she hadn't felt since Krona's clutches.

'How exactly did you pry His Imperial Majesty from his Sanctuary, then?' Heles asked. She didn't look at all apologetic for her boldness.

A shout stole the moment, and they both froze in their steps. Another shout answered, somewhere closer, and Heles nodded into a side street. Nilith tugged the horse after them. Bezel momentarily awoke with a yawn, and she caught his bleary gaze. He looked exhausted. Death's door had swung ajar for him, but he was healing, just as he'd promised.

They hovered between houses with barred iron doors and boarded windows. Here and there, where a few people still practised the desert charms, woven palm wreaths and glyphs drawn in sand offered protection where locks and deadbolts could not. No lights shone.

'Is it always like this? In the Sprawls?' Nilith whispered, and Heles offered another shrug.

'Did you expect better? If I am honest, the whole city has gone from bad to worse ever since your husband locked himself away and forgot his city. People like Temsa don't flourish on good deeds.'

Nilith fought not to smile. Weeks – months – she had been trawling the desert, repeating her reasons privately to herself almost as often as she'd put boot to sand. Doubt had plagued her more than any other villainy the desert had offered. Secrecy had kept her silent, and when an idea was solely kept in one mind, it was no firmer than a ghost's vapour. To hear it whispered by another gave it skin and flesh. Vindication was a sweet and heady liquor.

Nilith thought she heard a whooshing noise in the air, faint and muffled by the stubborn fog. She was about to crane her neck when a black figure flitted across the entrance to their street. Without a word, they pressed themselves to the walls of a grand-looking bakery. Even Anoish tucked himself into the shadows, his big backside nudging the orange shutters.

'What now?' Nilith muttered.

Heles made fists, cracking knuckles. 'Trouble, is what. With any luck they won't—'

A whistle split the air, sharp and damning. Others joined in, sounding out from nearby streets. A head poked around the edge of the building, scraggy-haired and featureless in the darkness.

A set of shoulders followed the head, then a scrawny body of a young man, barely more than a boy. The curve of a dagger lurked at his side. He walked without pause or fear, coming straight at them. Another shout rang out, closer now, sounding higher than the streets. The strange whooshing was growing louder, closer. Even in that moment, as tense and full of hammering heartbeats as it was, Nilith looked up. High above, the mists swirled suspiciously, but no shape accompanied the strange sounds. Nilith swore she could hear harsh and frantic voices. Arguing.

Fists raised, Heles limped forwards to meet the boy. He was lifting his fingers to whistle again, drawing his fellow soulstealers closer. The scrutiniser limped faster. There came a whistle, but not from the boy's lips. It was short-lived, and culminated in a loud crunch.

Something black and silver plummeted out of the dark fog. It struck the boy on the crown of his shaggy head, and drove him to the sand with a speed that would have snapped his neck had it not already been full of steel. The momentum impaled him against the earth, a dark blade bursting from his collar before burying itself in the ground.

The boy's head, tongue lolling and eyes crossed, was pinched between crossbar and sand.

Missing her swing, Heles stumbled over the body, and ended up on her arse. Nilith was too shocked to move. Her eyes switched from the bleeding corpse to the sky, hearing the whooshing and arguing diminish somewhere to the south.

'That was fucking lucky,' Heles wheezed, clearly hiding some more injuries beneath her rags.

Nilith didn't dare comment, as if admitting it would break whatever fortune the desert had left with her. She thought of the beldam, and the visit she had dismissed so easily as a dream.

The scrutiniser wrenched the sword from the boy's brain and quickly tucked it into her rags. 'There's an Arctian saying—'

'Whatever falls from the sky in a desert is a bounty. You forget how long I've spent in the empire.'

'Hmph,' Heles grunted. She tucked herself into the shadows and scuttled past like a scarab beetle. 'This way.'

Nilith joined her, and with the horse and his sorry baggage trailing behind her, they continued to weave their zig-zag path from street to street, avoiding the cat-calls and whistles that rose up like ugly birdsong behind them. At least they had left the soulstealers with a corpse as a distraction. They travelled silently, hurriedly, and with their hearts in their mouths.

'You need to rest, Majesty,' said Heles when they had breath spare for talk. She had slowed to a hobble. Her eyes had been roaming over Nilith for some time now, taking sidelong peeks.

'Speak for yourself. Neither of us are in prime condition at the moment.'

'Fine. *I* need rest. And you can afford to spare an hour. Maybe two. The shittier stealers get more desperate the closer it gets to dawn. We'll hole up somewhere.'

Nilith saw what the scrutiniser was trying to do. Heles was trying to save her the shame of needing to sit down for a spell. It wasn't shame that kept her from halting, but rather the need to keep moving.

'It would be a shame, to go through all you've undoubtedly been through, only to die here, in the Sprawls. Be sold off like some houseshade.'

Nilith narrowed her eyes. Heles was clever – coercive, even – but right. With a tut, Nilith relented and let the scrutiniser sniff out a place to hole up, as she had put it. It sounded contradictory to her.

It took a short while to find one: a broken door in the wall of a tiny abandoned house. The building clung to the base of a tall warehouse like a baby mouse to its mother. Its mudbrick walls were scorched and cracked by the sun, and the door was no more than a stolen table wedged into a hole. Somebody had kicked the original door out of its makeshift frame some time ago, and no doubt had their way with whatever poor souls had lain within at the time.

Nilith was surprised, and somewhat sickened, to be greeted by a severed head. It still lay where it had been dropped, its eyes swollen like raisins left too long in milk. It was a man of the north, a foreigner here, face as pale as porcelain even despite the rot.

The house was more of a hovel, bereft of furniture or wall-hangings. Just the faint smell of death. The rug was crispy with dried blood, the mattresses slashed to ribbons and straw, but two stools lay unbroken. Heles propped them up as Nilith tried to get Anoish to back into the hovel. The horse seemed as eager as she was to get off the hellish streets. By then, Heles had found a resting place for the head, and scattered sand across the gore. The horse still grumbled and ground his teeth at the new smells. It seemed Farazar's body, still strapped across his back, had finally stopped reeking. Perhaps whatever squelching parts of it were left had finally dried to leather.

Bezel reared his head as Nilith scooped him up and laid him down. Farazar waggled his hands expectantly at Heles, but she loosened none of the knots.

'What are you playing at, woman? One of you was bad enough!'

'Charming, isn't he?' said Nilith. To Farazar, she replied, 'This is what you get for trying to run away. I can't trust you any more. Not that I ever could. Now, are you going to be a good little candle for us and stay silent? Or will I have to cover you up?'

'Unleash me, fucking damn you!'

Nilith covered him with the sacking. He thrashed around before she gestured for the sword that had fallen from the sky. Heles gave it up immediately, and Nilith thwacked the ghost on the head with the flat of the blade with a musical chime. He cursed her viciously, but fell still.

'Good ghost.' She pulled back the sacking from his head so they had some light.

The empress held the sword up to him. In his paltry, wavering glow, she saw the copper veins running through its obsidian blade. It was a truly ornate sword, straight as a lance and vicious at its edges. Nilith tested it lightly and instantly found a crimson bead on her fingertip.

'Dead gods, that's sharp.' She glanced at its silver handle, twisted like tree roots and gripping a black pommel stone, where a sour, tight-lipped carving of a face stared back at her.

'If I can say so, Majesty,' ventured Heles, 'you haven't answered my question, and I have to know: how did you sneak him out of the Sanctuary?'

Farazar snarled at her. 'She didn't, Scrutiniser Heles. I did! Now remember your place, you useless worm of the Chamber! I'll have Chamberlain Reb—'

The blade sang as it cut the air, coming to rest against Farazar's cheek. His vapours sizzled softly.

'Please give me an excuse, husband. I'm in the mood for some drastic reshaping of your face,' Nilith warned coldly. The ghost muttered something about women and swords but stayed otherwise silent. The coward still resided in him, even after all his rebellion. She retreated to the other side of the hovel, letting Anoish lie down and crush Farazar's legs beneath his side. The ghost was distracted enough by that to stay out of their conversation.

Nilith rested upon the other stool, finding a position that didn't ache or stab her, and ran her fingers through her sandy, mud-clumped hair. 'As much as I detest admitting he's right, he is,' she said with a sigh. 'He pulled it off. Conned the whole city, the Cloud Court, even his wife and daughter. For years Farazar managed to convince us all he was safe and sound within his Sanctuary while he enjoyed the delights – and daughters – of Belish.

'I realised after far too many years of passing his decrees to the court. A loathsome job, with time. They became erratic. Sometimes odd. He refused to speak to me through the door or even emerge at all, as he used to. He ignored us all, and I was the one blamed for it, especially by Sisine. When I began to suspect something was different, I couldn't shake the inkling, as preposterous as it sounded. I started to track him down. It took a year of questions, asked as quietly as possible, but when I found out where he was, I left immediately. That was almost three months ago. I haven't stopped since.'

'The Court and Chamber thought you had run east to Krass, back to your father.'

Nilith nodded. 'And that was the story I let them believe while I went south. There were more than a few times on the road when I wished I had gone east, and seen my father, grey and sitting by his fireplace. It would have been a short-lived peace. Araxes' evil will spread in time.'

Heles worked her jaw while she thought. 'From here to Belish and back. A treacherous road.'

'You wouldn't believe.'

'How long has it been?'

There seemed to be no avoiding that question. It was a cloud that had followed her since raking the knife across Farazar's throat, and it had grown darker and stormier each day. *It's only when a person is running out of time that they curse not using it more wisely.* Perhaps that was the entire reason Nilith sat there, beaten and exhausted, with the ghost of her husband draped over her horse. She could remember staring at the intricate workings of the Sanctuary door and wondering how a decade had swallowed up her life in a blink. Minor trinkets had distracted her here and there: learning Arctian history; playing the Court's games; staying alive, of course, which was always an accomplishment in the City of Countless Souls. All petty things. No true deeds of wonder besides a daughter whom Nilith had been banned from raising. Nothing to etch into the base of her statue when they erected it beside Farazar's in time to come. No great imprint upon the world. Nilith could remember staring over the railing of her Piercer balcony, contemplating the streets far, far below, and letting her mind ponder them for too long.

Heles cleared her throat. 'Hard to count them?'

'Not at all.' Every day was lodged firmly and vividly in her mind. Even when she had spent them in bleary, swollen-eyed dazes, she had logged them.

'Thirty-five days.'

The scrutiniser tried to whistle, but a loose tooth proved problematic. 'Five left.'

In the corner, the ghost growled bitterly.

Heles looked stiffer than she had before, and Nilith found her eyes avoiding her. She began to replay her words, wondering what she had said, but the scrutiniser had enough confidence, or enough exhaustion, to challenge her empress. Perhaps murder lowered the need for respect.

'And so this is your great deed?' said Heles.

'What?' This echo of her thoughts threw Nilith.

'To claim the throne? Be the first empress in, what – three generations to forge a new family line?' Heles met Nilith's gaze then, and with accusation in her eyes. Her voice was a strained whisper. 'I told you duty bound me to your side. Well, that's a lie. My duty is to the city and its salvation. When I first saw you in that cage, arguing with the ghost, I heard you say something I don't think this empire has ever heard uttered. You said, "When I'm out of this cage, you'll know what it means to have a ruler, instead of a monarch". I never thought I would hear such words from a royal, not in twelve years fighting for justice in these bloody streets. I have worked for it, tortured and killed for it, and I have even prayed for it on more desperate nights. I had all but given up hope, about to take matters into my own hands for the last time, when your cage came past. Well, you're out of that cage, Majesty, but you're not sounding like any ruler I would want in the emperor's place.'

Nilith drew herself up, her royal blood and breeding kindled. *You forget yourself*, were the words poised on her tongue, but they sounded far too similar to Farazar's, and she bit her lip. 'You do not and cannot know what I have in mind, Scrutiniser Heles,' she replied, trying to restrain her regal tone. 'And if you did, you wouldn't doubt me. Your empress.'

'What, then? What have all these lies been for? All this struggle and hardship?'

'Yes, what, Nilith?' Farazar piped up. 'Do tell us. It would be about fucking time.'

'You must trust me, Heles.'

'And that's the problem. I don't trust anyone. If there's anything I've learnt in all my years in the Chamber, it's that people are fickle. People are liars. People are greedy. People change their minds.'

'And how am I to trust you?'

'You're the one with the sword, Empress,' Heles said coldly. 'And that's fortunate for you, seeing as I don't take kindly to people doubting my loyalty.'

Perhaps it was the anger in her heart. Perhaps it was how long she had held her secret, trusting nobody, and now, like a fermenting barrel lashed to her back, it threatened to burst. She was tired of carrying it alone. Maybe it was the fact Nilith wanted to hear whether it was madness after all. All such ideas were fragile in that way.

'I intend to release them,' Nilith said, her voice shaking, a tremble in her hands.

The silence was not comforting in the slightest.

The first question came from Heles. Farazar was too busy curling his lip.

'Release them? Who?'

'The bound dead. The ghosts. The shades.' Nilith felt the sword twitch in her hands. Its metal grew colder.

'Which ones?' the emperor snarled, eyes wild and glowing white. Spittle would have flown their way had he not been dead. Furrows were gouged in the sand around his fingers.

Nilith fought the urge to sag and got to her feet instead, staring down at his pathetic display of rage.

'All of them,' she said. 'Every single one of them.'

'You cannot be serious!'

'You thought this was all for you and your coins, Farazar. You think far, far too much of yourself. This is for Araxes. For Krass. For the Reaches.'

'I...' Heles stammered. 'How...' She blinked, eyes glazed in thought.

Nilith stood taller. 'That is the only cure for the city's sickness. End binding. Restore the balance. Accept nothing short of complete reversal.'

'You're mad! A fool! It will never be accepted!' Farazar was half-laughing, half-apoplectic with indignation. 'A thousand years, we have bound the dead, and you think you can simply take the throne and change it all? Ha! They'll destroy you!'

'They will try,' Nilith replied. Her blood rushed through her in a way she hadn't experienced since breaking out of the Cloudpiercer at night, heading south for Belish. 'They can try all they want, and they will see what a Krass empress can be made of.'

There was an awkward moment as Heles also struggled to her feet. Nilith's hand alighted on the pommel of the sword, but Heles took no action other than to bow, as low and as long as she could.

'Finally,' said the scrutiniser. 'I've heard the first words of sense ever spoken in this city.'

Nilith bowed back, their bruised and bloodshot eyes locked.

Farazar exploded with rage. 'They will kill you! You can't be seriou—'

A mound of cloth descended on him, snuffing out any further argument. Heles and Nilith shared a look before seeking their beds. 'Five days?' asked the scrutiniser.

Nilith nodded grimly. 'Five days.'

———◆———

IT WAS A GOLDEN AND dewy morning that awoke the city. The fog started to fade away, and dawn's fingers probed eagerly into the streets, sneaking into shutters until they forced them to open.

Chaser Jobey watched the night's shadows edge away from the toe of his black boot, replaced with yellow sunlight. The warmth didn't improve his mood. His tortured face remained in a scowl. His hands were firmly tucked into his armpits, lest the pain of itching of his face be forgotten and he scratch again. Instead, he picked at the scabs and dried blood under his nails.

The birds had wreaked havoc on his face. His left eye had been rent in two, blinded and useless. One ear was practically shredded. Claw-marks crisscrossed his face and neck. Both forearms were heavily bound in cloth. A mound of a bandage sat on his shoulder like a white tortoise.

The cage at his side rattled again, and the slithering hiss came to meet him in a cloud of breath. Jobey had been lucky the slatherghast had only clawed him during the fight, not bit him. It was still striving for the last flesh it had sank its fangs into: the debtor from the desert. *The escapee.*

'Shortly,' Jobey grunted. 'Have no fear.'

No sooner had he said it than a door whined behind him. The chaser did not move, instead waiting for the woman to stand by his shoulder.

'The directors will give you another chance,' said the overseer in a flat tone. No emotion was necessary in business.

'As well they should. You know my record. I have never lost a repayment before and I refuse to now. I will not disappoint them a second time.'

The overseer tutted. 'You had better not. You know the rules, Chaser Jobey: the first mistake is free. The rest cost. Remember that.'

Jobey nodded, itching to drag his nails over his face. 'Circumstances were out of my control.'

'Hmm, apparently so. Birds, was it? How strange.'

He slowly turned his face to her, and after much avoidance, she looked at the mess of gashes and scrapes. Her eyebrow raised ques-tioningly. Jobey knew better than to expect sympathy. 'Birds indeed. A dozen of them,' he said. 'And a beggar too.'

The overseer's disapproving look didn't wilt. 'I have seen chasers return their debts with limbs turned to stumps and still bleeding, Jobey.

If you want to be considered for promotion, I suggest you get back out there and change the directors' minds. And mine, while you're at it.'

With a parting tut, she left him to the morning and went inside. Jobey was left with his slatherghast and the rising heat of dawn. He looked down at the creature weaving back and forth, its eyeless gaze locked somewhere in the north. Its grin was wide; it had the scent of its prey. If Jobey wasn't mistaken, he thought he heard a grumble come from the ghast's bunched coils.

CHAPTER 10
TIME'S LANCE

The sky is just another ocean calling
to be sailed.

EXCERPT FROM A CONTROVERSIAL SPEECH BY
ADMIRAL NILO, CHAMPION OF TWARZA

F LYING IS NOT MEANT FOR those born without wings. That which dares to ply the skies in defiance of the dead gods' natural laws must invariably come crashing to the ground.

And so we did.

The *Vengeance* clipped the roof of a squat tower with a dire crunch. The whole craft bucked, sending half its occupants sprawling. Beneath me, I felt the hull being ripped away in chunks. I stared out of a porthole and saw ochre rubble and splinters spinning in our wake. As I watched, the ground abruptly turned from brick and adobe to undisturbed sand. We had left the city behind us and now the desert was rushing up to meet the craft and punish us for Widow Horix's audacity.

Although I was already dead, an odd horror run through me as I watched the gap close between earth and flying machine. The sand became a butter-yellow blur in the dawn's half-light. It rose and fell suddenly, grazing the splintered hull again as we passed over a sharp dune.

On the next wave of sand, there came an almighty bang as we struck again. Grit sprayed through the cracks in the hull. The window in the bow became a cloud of sand. The men handling the cogs and levers were smashed against it. One left a bloody streak and a spider's web of cracks in the glass before slumping over the controls. The soldiers surrounding Horix tried to drag his body out of the way before the next crash, but they were too slow, or the *Vengeance* too fast. I couldn't tell.

The rumpled peak of the next dune reared up before us. It broke our fall, and by the sound and judder of it, half the ship too. Yells and screams accompanied the crunching of wood and nails. With what little weight I possessed, I was tossed from my seat and thrown forward with the ship's momentum, my vapours trailing behind me. I met the gust of sand and wind that burst through the front window. I fell against a bulkhead, feeling no pain, only inordinate confusion.

The *Vengeance* begin to slide down the dune, like one of those Scatter Isle brats on their wooden wave-boards. I rolled across the deck, bodies falling with me. My fear grew as the ship skewed to the side, almost rolling onto the ballon-like envelope. Amongst the pile of bodies bunching up around Horix's chair, I heard my fear shared in the horrified silence of those around me.

In that elongated moment of terror, time seemed to slow, and every slip of sand beneath us was palpable. *Vengeance* teetered on her side during the slide, but thankfully she righted with a thud at the base of the dune.

The collective exhale was audible. Several soldiers slumped in relief, banging their helmets on the wood. The ghosts aboard began to extricate themselves from broken oar spars and the moaning living.

'Everybody out!' yelled a muffled voice. It sounded like the new colonel. As people began to pick themselves up, he was soon uncovered beneath splintered panels, sporting a bloody nose smeared across his cheek.

Horix had apparently strapped herself into her chair using some sort of belt across her shoulders and chest. Soldiers clung to handles on its base, or to each other. They were pale, for Arctians.

Judging by the way Horix rubbed the neck under her cowl, she hadn't escaped completely unscathed. I found myself disappointed. My guards had given up guarding me in the crash. One was in fact lying against the stairwell, his neck at an odd angle. I wondered whether I had time to snatch up one of the discarded spears around my feet and finish the job of taking my half-coin. I didn't. Horix was quickly upright and limping from her craft. I followed her, watching her as if she were an unattended chest of gold.

Dawn was still in the process of rising over the Arc. Halos of mist still wreathed some of the city's towers, but otherwise had faded with the morning's warmth. The sun was a dusty rose in the east, but the night still held sway on the other points of the compass. I could feel the heat rising in the air already.

A sheepish breeze stirred the sand at my feet, adding to the ripples etched there, as if a tide had recently receded. I idly traced the footsteps spreading out from the *Vengeance*, and found my gaze dragged to the vast horizons. The desert seemed an endless carpet of dunes and scorched earth, ending in hazy, dark peaks to the south. I still had never felt so dwarfed by a landscape. 'Barren' was a description it wore effortlessly. In Krass, there was always some snowy peak, gully, steppe or forest in the way. Here, there was just undulating sand, stretching for more miles than even the map-makers could accurately count.

I instantly loathed the fucking place.

Araxes occupied the north, and most of the east and west. Against the indigo sky of dawn, the buildings were a black mountain range speckled with lights. Only then did I realise the claims of Araxes as the largest city in the Reaches – perhaps the known world – were true. There was no arguing it, even if I could be bothered to do so. I had seen the breadth of it from the Troublesome Sea, but not the depth, the ocean of adobe that stretched from the Outsprawls to the core. And above it all, the Cloudpiercer: miles of stone rising up in a tall spike to scrape the heavens.

'Caltro!' came a hoarse yell. Horix had remembered me.

Soldiers came on the tail of my name, quickly grabbing me before I could wander off into the dunes. It had crossed my mind, but I suspected wandering aimlessly through an endless desert for the rest of eternity would have made me feel more like a ghost than I already did.

The widow met me with hands on hips, a brace of soldiers standing either side of her. They seized me by the shoulders immediately. A few spots of blood lingered on Horix's pursed lips, as if she'd bitten one in the crash. There was a quiver in her wrinkles, as if her temper raged beneath the surface, barely kept in check.

'What?' I asked brusquely.

Horix slapped me good and hard again, rings scratching white lines on my cheek. I set my jaw and waited for the pain to subside.

'If you are harbouring any ideas of wandering off, you can forget them immediately. I refuse to lose any more useful things today.' She patted my half-coin, still around her neck. I couldn't take my eyes off it as I answered her.

'There's no freedom for me out there in the desert,' I said.

'Good half-life.'

I was not finished. I was confident I now knew Horix's plans, but there was something missing. Reason, besides greed and games. This plan of hers must have been years in the making. Decades. Patience of that calibre was always driven by some deeper emotion: great hurt, sorrow, or anger, and I wanted to hear it from the widow's mouth. 'But I will take some answers,' I said.

I saw her jaw working, grinding old teeth together. I just smiled at her, and laid my logic bare. 'If you want me to work for you, I think I deserve to know what you have in mind for me. And why.'

'The dead deserve nothing. I gave you your writ of freedom—'

'I think we both know how worthless that writ was. A distraction. An empty promise.' Never mind it being trapped in Horix's tower, with everything else she'd abandoned.

She smiled knowingly. 'You are merely property. You will do as I say.'

'Not without answers. If not, you can break my coin right here and be done with me.' It was a bold bluff, but I suspected my worth was the only thing that mattered right now, with her precious flying machine nosing the sand behind us and Kalid still lying dead and broken in her courtyard. And since she had thrown Pointy from the *Vengeance*, I was in no mood to parry niceties. I cast a look over my shoulder at the peaks of the city and wondered how in the Reaches I would ever find the sword again.

Horix held up my half-coin then, and the soldiers' grips tightened as I involuntarily flinched. She pinched it, trying to crush it between finger and thumb. Fresh blood trickled from her lip as she bit it again.

'Bah!' she hissed, sweeping away from me. 'Colonel Kal—Omshin!'

An eager shout came from behind me. 'Yes, Mistress!'

Horix strode in a figure of eight, her black skirts making patterns in the sand. 'Have your men encircle the *Vengeance*. I will not tolerate the curiosity of any filthy Sprawlers or nomads. Nor any of the foul Cult. I saw their spies at my tower. Get the shades working! I want my ship ready by evening. We have no time to waste. Sisine knows our game now.'

'Yes, Widow!'

I watched her until she had completed her moody tour of the sands, waiting before I pressured her. 'And what exactly is that game?' I added a 'Mistress' for good measure.

Horix narrowed her eyes at me, ignoring my question once more. 'You have no right to ask anything of me, half-life,' she snarled.

I shrugged as much I could with my arms held tightly. I bared my ruined neck to her as I raised my chin. I had never been a gambler, preferring to make my own luck, but at that moment I was willing to gamble to know what the fuck this woman was planning. Knowledge is power, or so they said. I say knowledge is leverage.

'Fine. Then I won't help you. Torture me all you want, but something tells me you don't have the time or the inclination.'

Horix paused, measuring me with her sharp eyes. 'I see you have grown bolder in your absence, Caltro. What lies did Temsa feed you?'

I took a final stab at her, pushing my bluff to its extremities. 'None, aside from confirm my suspicions that I am indeed the best locksmith in the Reaches. You clearly are in need of me. Perhaps now more than ever, what with Kalid dead.' Judging by the fury in her eyes, I thought she would end me right there and then, but she abstained. As much as punching me in the face was abstaining. I smirked as I righted myself. 'If you know another thief better than I am, like I said: be done with me. Do me that favour. I'm too tired to care any longer.'

I could hear her teeth crunching now, almost musical to my ears. With a snarl, Horix waved away my guards, keeping only one by her side. I rubbed my arms as she began to climb the dune we had slid down. I followed, kicking at the ruts of sand. The grains barely slipped under my feet, and I traipsed in the widow's footprints. My glow stained the ochre sand an eerie green in the morning light.

At the rumpled peak of the dune, Horix took a stand, staring at the grand city before her. I joined her moments after, and spent a while staring over the Outsprawls I had heard so much about. They were the foothills to the mountainous city, and they fit their name perfectly. They were an endless wash of low, pale stone, broken by glittering veins of streets and the occasional intrepid tower. I wondered how many people lived there, outside the city core; how many dead and living, crammed into the muddle of adobe and sand. I spied a few people milling around the Sprawl's edges, where the desert fought with Araxes for space. Their black, hazy shapes tottered drunkenly, either early drinkers or late. In any case, they paid no heed to our distant silhouettes, despite my ghost-glow.

I looked up to the thick bar of the Cloudpiercer, stark against the lightening sky. It seemed obvious now I stood back and stared at it. The tower was the very definition of impenetrable, except to my locksmith's eyes. There was always a way in to everything. Every fortress, every spire, every soaring roadway was built with boots and hooves and wheels in mind. Not wings, nor bloated flying contraptions.

'The Piercer is why you built your machine, isn't it?' I asked the widow. I had heard her shout its name before the crash. Even if I hadn't, it was the only logical reason why anyone would build this monstrosity. To my thief's mind, trained to find all manner of ways of circumventing doors and guards, it was nothing short of genius.

'A fool's guess. I'm surprised it took you that long.'

'But correct nonetheless. Which means you're after the Sanctuary. Which means you want me to break into it for you, exactly as the empress-in-waiting wanted.'

'Yes. And thanks to you, Boran Temsa and the empress-in-waiting, the element of surprise has been shattered.' There was thick contempt in her voice, and it wasn't all for Temsa. She seemed to harbour a deep hatred for the royals, and I wondered why. 'All of you forced my hand. Years of planning ruined'

I chuckled quietly, confident in my position as her key weapon. 'You're just like all the rest. You want to claim the emperor's half-coins. Put a throne beneath your arse.'

Horix turned on me, fixing me with a look so sour my vapours quivered. I thought she would strike me again, but her hand remained clenched by her side. 'I am far from all the rest. Far and above. Tell me, *thief*, is it stealing if something is rightfully yours?'

'You and everybody else in that accursed city think the throne is yours for the taking. Your laws have bred a misplaced sense of entitlement. You, Widow, are no different. Fuck it, even I could lay claim to it if I had the time and inclination.'

Horix dangled my half-coin with her far hand, too distant to snatch. 'You? Ha! Not when you are my property, Caltro,' she reminded me. 'And as *my* property, you are still mine to do with as I please.'

I wagged a blue finger. 'But not to snuff out like a candle. Not if you want to reach the inside of Emperor Farazar's Sanctuary. And seeing as your soldiers are dwindling, and you tossed away a soulblade that could have cut at least to the mechanism – yes, that's right. Lost now, though, isn't he? – I appear to be your only hope.' I paused, watching her craggy face bunch and crinkle over and over with all different shades of anger. 'Face it. Your grand plan now rests on a broken machine and a dead man. Unless you think you can walk me into the Cloudpiercer with your handful of men, you're treading on thin ice.'

Horix cocked her head at me and I realised the Krass phrase had no bearing in the desert.

'Treading on quicksand…?' I tried.

'You Krassmen and your disgusting tongue. Yes, I want into that Sanctuary. And while you are still useful to me, Caltro Basalt, no, I will not snuff you. You are going to open up that vault for me.'

I looked around, watching a soldier gathering broken panels of wood. 'You're forgetting one huge problem, Mistress. Your machine is in pieces.'

'Nothing changes. We repair, we return to the sky, and we teach Temsa, the Cult, and Sisine Talin Renala a lesson.'

I caught the growl underpinning that name, and wondered what it was the empress-in-waiting had done to the widow to deserve such anger. She hadn't uttered Temsa's or the Cult's name in the same way, and to me, they were the villains of my tale. I wondered what I had missed.

'We teach them all a lesson,' the widow hissed, bitter as a winter's edge.

'What did the royals do to you that distresses you so much?' I asked. *What makes you so withered and curled around your spite like a tree root around a stone?*

Horix stiffened beneath her shawl like a crow flicking rain from its feathers. 'What did they do to me, Caltro? They took everything from me. A great debt is owed to me, and I intend to reclaim it. What better way to do that than exercising the right of law set in thousand-year-old stone, condoning Farazar's murder should I succeed in its execution?'

'Vengeance.'

'Precisely.'

It saddened me that I saw the logic in it; a cold and ruthless dagger, good for nothing but murder. I heard the guard to my right grunt with something I took to be pride. 'What a dim allegiance you Arctians owe to each other. Murderers, the lot of you. The only difference is you've legalised it. Made a mockery of decency and order.'

Horix laughed at me then. 'And the Krass are so different? Give it a decade or two, Caltro Basalt, and your king will be locked in his own vault, sitting on his own mountain of half-coins.'

I held my tongue, not trusting myself to speak. It pained me to think she could be right.

'There is no denying progress, Caltro. The dead are here to stay. Who do you think built that?' She waved her hand across the whole gargantuan stretch of city. I couldn't even see Araxes' boundaries, no matter how much I squinted. Like a weak star, the more I looked for them, the fainter they became.

'More ambitious minds than the one who now sits on its throne, that is for certain,' Horix continued, voice like boots on gravel. 'Grander, wiser minds than that pustulent coward who calls himself emperor. He is nothing but a selfish child, hoarding his toys.'

Her withered hand poked from her sleeve and grasped at the giant building in the distance, the pillar for the sky. For a moment, as she pretended to crush it with her fingers, I glimpsed behind that veil of spite. I saw the simplicity of a woman who had been deeply wronged and was fighting to make it right, just as I fought for my freedom. I longed to know how or why she had been slighted, but in any case it had turned Horix into the widow who now stood crookedly atop a dune: her face aglow with dawn, eyes narrowed, driven solely by vengeance. For a moment, it gave Horix a humanity I had previously been blind to, and made sense of her cruelty.

It was but a brief moment, and she snatched back her hand, realising I was watching.

'Farazar will see the error of his ways soon enough,' she assured me.

'And then what?' I asked.

Horix cocked her head, as if her plans ended with the slaying of the emperor, and she had never thought past the lesson she ached to teach. Her bitterness had blinkered her. 'I will rule this empire as it's meant to be ruled, of course. With an iron fist, not through a steel door. Rodents like Temsa and the Cult of Sesh will find themselves wishing they had never darkened my doorstep.'

I did a short and circuitous tour of the dune's edges, considering fishing for answers, maybe to distract myself from my uncomfortable mood. Something was bothering me about the widow's words, and the amount of venom in them. The guard shuffled with me, making sure I didn't run. Horix didn't seem to care.

'What has the Cult ever done to you?' I asked.

The widow's shoulders arched, vulturelike, and that grasping hand came to claw for me. 'They sought to break the very walls of society. Take the throne down altogether. They are a sisterhood of vipers, stuck in old ways of worshipping old gods of darkness. Deluded fucks and dangerous fools, Caltro Basalt. That is what they are.'

I arched my back to avoid her nails. I saw the copper in their chipped varnish. 'Fair point. Well made,' came my rapid reply. Horix turned from me, clearly done with our conversation, her patience worn thin.

'And what happens after, if I break the Sanctuary for you? Now that my writ means nothing?' I called after her. I hoped to snatch my half-coin before it got that far, but I needed to hear it. 'Will you honour our bargain and free me?'

'Break the Sanctuary, and our bargain will be honoured,' Horix said over her shoulder.

As she walked away, I realised I had one last question, and a challenging one at that. Not for the widow, but for me. 'And what if I can't?'

The widow whirled, hands on skinny hips, face puckered into a glower. 'Can't *what?*' she snapped, as if it was a question so pointless and rare it confused her.

'Not once have you thought to ask me whether I'm capable of opening the emperor's Sanctuary.'

'This? From the so-called best locksmith in the Reaches?'

I held my hands wide. 'Do you not remember our conversations, Widow? Of my failing the earl and his son? I may be the best, but there are some locks in the world even I can't break.'

'Then I will take my chances,' came the taut reply, and I believed her. I knew I wasn't important enough to halt her plans completely. Where a lock cannot be broken through skill, brute force can usually win it over. Horix's purchase of me at the soulmarket had been a fortunate happenstance for her, no matter how much importance she or I tried to daub on it.

I tried to hide my wince, but she saw it, and leered.

'And that is why you will test me no further, shade. You're fortunate I've tolerated your questions so far. I advise you not to keep trying, unless you wish to learn the true depths of death.'

'Fine. I'm done. But I won't forget your promise of freedom, Widow. That still stands.'

Horix chuckled as she walked away, feet leaving gouges in the silvery sand. Her guards clamoured around her like hens to a coop as they escorted her back to the downed *Vengeance*. I stayed atop the dune, alone but for my thoughts.

I tried to tease apart what little I knew of Araxes' web of lies and found myself only more tangled. Whys and what-ifs plague a soul throughout life and in death. It is human to mourn the past, and to curse the way time slips through our fingers like sand, impossible to catch or reclaim. But there comes a moment – in my experience, usually in old age, the gutters, or in last, painful minutes– where a soul must let go and surrender to time's nature. I had heard a scholar once call it "time's arrow". Judging by how it seemed to me since Kech's knife, I'd have called it time's dirty great big lance.

Trying to relax my churning mind, I gathered up what I knew for certain. I was in one piece. The half-coin was still around the widow's wattled neck. Pointy was lost to the Sprawls. But primarily, I knew I was the linchpin of several plots, all of which centred around Emperor Farazar's Sanctuary and the throne it led to. No surprise, really. Power was always the brightest diamond in the pile. Some believe it was money, or men in armour, or land, but all of those were tools to breed power. Not the other way around.

In the many jobs I'd taken on for others, their prize was almost always a means to more power. The thrill and challenge had been enough for me. Again, the immutable past taunted me, and in that moment, I asked myself whether I had aimed too low in life.

Thrusting the useless question away from me, I asked myself what else I knew. Clearly, I didn't trust Horix with my half-coin any more than I trusted Temsa, or Sisine, or any of the living I'd met in the accursed city. Trust was a long-lost concept. Liars and cheats surrounded me, and I was a thief. That was a life and world I was supposed to be used to. In truth, only the gods and a pair of enlightened sisters had offered me attention that didn't involve putting a bag over my head or forcing me to clean silverware.

That much was clear. *But what* don't *I know?* That was often the more dangerous of the two questions a person had to ask themselves from time to time.

I turned back to the Cloudpiercer. Its lofty height was now catching the first light of day. The summit glowed a liquid gold as the sun touched it, and I saw the shining glass at its peak. I watched, eyes half closed, as the dawn ascended its sheer flanks. I pondered the Sanctuary hidden within it: the locks, the mechanism, the strength of its bolts, the ingeniousness of its creators. Stories and rumours of its impregnability roamed far and wide through the underbelly of the Reaches, even as far as my remote part of Krass. I felt trepidation and intrigue in equal measure.

Farazar's Sanctuary was said to be the finest vault ever built by human hands. Unbeatable. Uncrackable. Uncircumventable, and a whole armada of other un-words that were bound to put the sweat on any thief's brow. Until now, the Sanctuary had stayed in a part of my brain reserved for things not even worth trying, such as wooing the Krass king's daughter, moving a wagon with my mind, or wrestling a fenrir with one arm tied behind my back. There was an apt word for such things, and that was "impossible". And now I was being asked to do the impossible.

I put my teeth against my lips, tasting nothing but cold and wondering what lock I'd broken that had got the attention of such people as an empress-in-waiting. I had never known such faith in me in life. What rumours of my work had crossed the sea, and how had they grown so swollen with distance and telling? It was irksome that only in death had I become the greatest locksmith in the Far Reaches. I considered whether I should hold out on claiming my coin; if it was worth trying my ghostly hands at the Sanctuary...

With a tut that belied the depth of my disappointment, I dismissed that nonsense. My opportunities to claim my coin were best taken now, while I could. I would stick to my promise to myself and the dead gods. My freedom came first.

'CALTRO! Heel!'

I wished dearly that I could have spat in the sand.

As I turned, I gave the city one last glower, and saw a faint glow on the edge of the Outsprawls. I was jealous of that ghost, whoever she or he may have been. For they were not me, and they had not the weight of the world on their shoulders, like the old myths. With a snort, I left them to it.

CHAPTER 11
A FOOL DOESN'T PREPARE

Talliers hold a sacred position in the banking institutions of Araxes. They are trained in arithmetic, record-keeping, and weights and measures for no less than seven years. Like Nyxites, or monks of the west, talliers are utterly devoted to the crafts, often spending their entire careers with just one bank.

FROM 'THE CITY OF COUNTLESS SOULS —
A KEEN-EYED GUIDE'

T HE HEAT FROM THE SMOKING sand made Liria want to cough, as if she had a throat once more. In all her centuries, she had never gotten used to it. Its crimson flashes stained her bare hands a deep purple. From the corner of her eye, she watched the dark grit rise and fall, building itself into brief yet broken and disfigured statues. One moment, the glare of a jackal. Another, a hunched man, missing limbs. The next attempt, a forked tail.

'Perfect is the enemy of done, dear sister,' Liria said, louder this time over the hiss and rumble of the forge. 'Had we not forced the Widow Horix's hand tonight, we would have been clueless.'

'And we do not like... cluelessness.' The voice was like a blade being dragged down the strings of an arghul, each vowel the shifting of dunes.

'No, Lord,' chorused the sisters.

Yaridin spoke up, less confident than Liria. 'I apologise. My sister is right. Better we know and have time to adjust our plans.'

Red veins ran through the dark pile of churning sand, puffing more acrid smoke. 'Adjust away. Adjust. Adjust,' replied the voice.

'We know where she is. A brother in the outermost southern Sprawls has spotted them,' said Yaridin.

'We will strike tonight, and rescue our brother Caltro. See he is delivered to the right hands,' added Liria.

Again, the dark pile of sand glowed crimson, hotter this time. Angrier.

'We draw closssse...' The sibilance was drawn out as the sand in the forge settled down, turning in circles as though something burrowed into the hot stone beneath it. No more shapes rose. The smoke began to settle in thick black dust, coating the edges of the stone altar. The coals beneath the slab cooled to a dim russet glow.

Liria pulled her eyes away from it and turned to her sister, who was glowing brighter now the light had diminished. Yaridin yanked up her hood and led the way out of the room.

The corridor beyond its low ceilings and tiles of polished stone was cooler, airier. They followed it up a set of intricately zigzagging stairs that hugged huge square pillars, touching the doorsteps of one room for just a moment before jutting up to the next. Always up, tracing the edges of great vaults and caverns. Shade-glow bruised them blue and purple. Red cloaks flowed like blood in living hearts, swelling in open chambers. Myriad feet made hardly any noise on the white stones.

On a level far above the forge's room they found a particularly swollen chamber of hewn rock, packed with blue and red forms. There were raised voices deeper into the press.

'Move aside,' spoke Yaridin, and the crowd of shades – and a large number of still-living brothers and sisters – parted eagerly.

'Away, all those with less than five decades under their feet,' Liria ordered, and almost all of the room departed with muted whispering. There remained half a dozen shades, standing stoically at a channel cut into the far side of the chamber. Its walls had been plastered and painted. Black, for the most part, but with crimson stars echoing the map of the heavens above.

Liria and Yaridin approached, gauging the looks of the other shades. Two living members of the church stood to the side, hooded heads bowed but hands firmly grasping the edges of stained barrels.

'The matter, fellow brothers and sisters?'

One of the living spoke, one of their own Nyxites for their private stream of Nyxwater. 'It has turned to a trickle, Enlightened Sister. Sesh's Vein is failing us.'

Another spoke up in a squirrelly voice. The pins beneath his white feather told them he was a scholar. 'For the first time in centuries.'

Liria went to rest her hands on the edge of the sandstone channel. Above it, on the wall, five stars had been painted. Four hung lower, simple dots, while the fifth that sat higher in the black sky was drawn in great flourishes of red. It held her eye for a moment before she looked down.

The channel ran across the back wall, from one side of the room to the other. Its sandstone had been smoothed but not eaten by the years the Nyx had flowed over it. The dark stain the waters had left on the channel was the evidence of its waning. Halfway down the channel, the sandstone turned ashen, then a dark grey, and at its base, a rivulet of inky water no thicker than a decent rope.

'But it still flows, yes?' she asked the small crowd.

One of the Nyxites spoke up. 'Yes... Sister, but—'

'And how many hekats have you stored in the cellars below us? Or the warehouses above? Or across the city?'

The two Nyxites looked at each other, lips quivering as they silently spoke numbers. A conversation of shrugging followed before one of them turned back and said. 'Tens of thousands, maybe hundreds of thousands, Sister.'

Liria waved her arm, dismissing the two men to continue their work. 'Then keep gathering.'

'Keep storing,' said Yaridin. 'And the rest of you should know better than to gawk and gossip. You especially, scholar. Do not let talk of this spread.'

The shade in question smiled at her. 'The time is near, Sisters,' he said, before hustling down a set of stairs.

'Almost, Brother.'

The two sisters paused for a moment, gazing out over the red and blue masses that teemed below them. There seemed to be more every day now. The preachers had been plying their trade across Araxes, journeying further all the time. Their sanctums across the city had swollen in size and number, but here, deep beneath the Avenue of Oshirim and the statue of the old god himself, the Great Vault could have been a city in itself.

Yaridin broke their silence first, sharing the same thought. 'City of Countless Souls indeed, Sister Liria.'

'You are not wrong, Sister Yaridin.' She sighed, somewhat wistfully. 'South, then?'

'South it is.'

———◆———

THE CITY HAD LOST ITS spine. In the baking heat of the sun, only hooded shades trod the dust or flagstones, and even they were decimated in number. The only living that dared to walk amongst them were either drunk, stupid, or paid to be there. Outside the Core Districts, soldiers in red cloaks were often found standing in clumps at crossroads, preachers at their back. Inside the Core were Royal Guards, proctors, scrutinisers, and soldiers from the Scatter Isle skirmishes. They crowded into guard posts and patrolled in great formations, trying to restore the peace – what little of it there was now crime had apparently become a war-game.

Despite the presence of armoured shade and flesh, the city had no taste for the bright and sunny morning. It could be wagered that almost every door in that vast city was locked, and locked tightly.

The usual clamour of the High and Low Docks had become a low whisper, and a surprising number of ships and dhows had wandered off in the night. The horizon was full of sails.

The Royal Markets were closed. Half the Fish District was barely trading; what few merchants there were sung their offers half-heartedly, timid as songbirds when a cat prowls close by. Also taking an avian stance were the few nervous clusters of nobles, seen peeking over the parapets of their high-roads and towers, owl-like in their hungry stares.

The Avenue of Oshirim, and the grand streets leading from it into the banking districts, were grimly silent. Even commerce didn't halt for war on the streets; a small smattering of the grander banks stayed open, trusting in their fortresses and small private armies of guards. But it seemed few had the heart for trading silver or half-coins today, and the patrons showed it in their absence. Those whose interests lay solely in riches always had a strong desire to stay rich, and that meant staying alive. It was why they always cowered over their glittering piles before they became corpses, and slaves to a half-life.

Temsa took another twirl around, waving his cane in a wide circle. A lack of crowds was a special thing in this city, especially here, in its beating heart of commerce. Even his soldiers had spread out, eager to be away from their sweaty comrades. Temsa was glad for it too. He had kept them working since last night for their idiocy and inability to do simple things like storm a tower. The breeze and the heat were doing nothing for the stench, but they would learn. And he was more stubborn than they would ever know.

'What a glorious day, wouldn't you say, m'dear? Danib?'

Two matching grunts came from behind him, where his two pets lumbered sullenly. They'd been in foul moods since the failure; since the escape of both Horix and Caltro. A shit-show, Ani had called it, and though Temsa was inclined to agree, he was beginning to hate every word out of her mouth. Danib at least had the decency to stay mute, hiding behind the thick steel of his horned helm. Only his white, burning eyes showed through its slits.

The tor pointed his cane at the bright blue sky, where the sun hung low and fresh in the east. 'I said a GLORIOUS DAY!' he roared. The echo bounced around the vast stone plaza between the banks that soared up into the sky. Ani and Danib listened to the question three times before it died.

'Fine day, Tor. Though I am still wondering if this is the right time,' Ani elaborated, though at Temsa's stare, she added, 'For your safety.'

His reply was taut, but genuine. 'I appreciate the concern,' he said, walking on towards Fenec's Coinery. The sweeping curves that softened its sheer sides reminded Temsa of leg bones, and where they met, sockets and knuckles. An elongated yawning skull could be made out of the patterned tiles surrounding the huge, inverted triangle of a doorway. Temsa's black-clad soldiers formed up once more, and he was reminded of their stench. Perhaps bringing fifty was too many. Not to mention the hundred he had manhandling the wagons of half-coins.

Inside, the mood was even more sombre. The impossibly tall desks were largely empty. The bank guards remained, but the clerks and sigils and coincounters had mostly disappeared. Those that remained sweated profusely even in the cool of the bank, hands flashing over scrolls and papyrus like they were being whipped. Stacks of documents fell in great heaps every now and again, down into the waiting hands of runners, who scampered off into a myriad of doors. A handful of customers stood tapping toes, each clutching something precious to them, their guards tightly pressed against the next in line's.

Temsa could have laughed as he and his entourage entered. Fifty soldiers probably was too many.

The sun shone behind them, casting many-fingered shadows across the elaborate marble. Gasps and clanks filled the grand chamber, but Temsa strode forwards with his spare hand high and empty.

'Just another customer, good people, fellow citizens. A fellow tor here for Fenec's trusty services,' he told them, worrying more about a fight than for their safety. He simply could not be bothered with another. He was scrapped out for the time being, even though Boon was high on his list of priorities. The "shit-show" at Horix's tower had soured his mood, the princess', and most likely the Cult's. Neither of them had tried to contact him as yet, and even as he strode past the frightened commoners straight towards the upper level, Temsa wondered if he was still under Sisine's protection, or meant for a sister's dagger.

The serek was last on both their lists. Killing Boon would set at least one of them straight, hopefully both. Not that Temsa cared about honour, or duty to either of them. He simply didn't want a cult on his back, nor his admittance to the Cloudpiercer revoked. Horix's bold grab for power had stirred a vigour inside him, as if he had finally found a match worthy of competition. The old bitch had made her first move, and it was a strong one. He had to catch up. What better way to kill a serek than to become a serek? Ani had called it vanity, much to his sour displeasure.

'Tor Fenec and son!'

Both Fenec the elder and younger had emerged from their grand office, and were clasping their hands the way people did when telling somebody of a death. Their eyes stretched even wider as they watched Temsa's soldiers begin to roam about the desks, flicking nods to the guards and generally making everybody present uncomfortable. There were a handful more clerks here, and they peered over their desks warily, drops of sweat falling from their arched noses.

'Tor Temsa. What a surprise,' Tor Fenec greeted him with a low bow. His son, Russun Fenec, bowed even lower. When he came up, his eyes seemed to have become glued to the marble.

'We missed you last night, Russun. And the night before.' Temsa used his shorter stature to creep into the sigil's eye-line. Russun met his stare only once, and then flinched away. 'Fortunately, our business had to be postponed, so no harm done.'

'Forgive me, I'm confused…' Tor Fenec's blood vacated his cheeks. Whether he knew of the hold Temsa had on his son and played along, or he had just figured it out, Temsa didn't care. It only mattered that the tor's face was taking on a pale hue,

'Not a good trait, for the director of a bank as proud as this, Tor. Now, I have come to be Weighed. Today.' Temsa waved his cane to the bangs and thuds from the lower level as his other men began to unload the barrows and boxes. 'Business has been going well. I believe a serekdom is at hand.'

'Yes. Today…' The tor wrung his hands. 'And a serek now, you say…'

'A problem, Fenec?' Temsa took a step, clanging his foot on the marble near the man's toes.

Tor Fenec sniffed. If the man had whiskers, they would have twitched. There was something rodent-like about the man. 'A slight issue, Tor Temsa. There is a new royal decree.'

'From whom?'

Fenec looked bamboozled. 'Why, the Cloudpiercer, of course.'

'Empress-in-waiting, or Emperor Farazar?'

'The… emperor? Who else, Tor Temsa?'

Temsa found himself letting that reply linger in his ear a little longer than necessary. The pause had dragged out too long. He found Ani staring sideways at him, eyes burrowing into him as if she read his thoughts.

'And what decree interferes with such simple business as a Weighing? It must happen forty times a day here.'

'It does, Tor, but a shift from tal or tor to serek *requires* a recommendation from a serek, and said serek to be present, and then a presenting to the Cloud Court. But now the Cloud Court has been disbanded – temporarily, we hope – the emperor has discounted all Weighings until this state of emergency is over.'

Fenec spoke as if he'd written the decree himself and memorised it in front of a mirror. Temsa considered violence, as he always did, but instead he pinched his forehead and sighed.

'Do it anyway.'

'But—'

'I said do it anyway.'

'Tor…' Ani muttered, but Temsa held up his hand.

'Is there a decree banning Weighings?'

'No, only… they don't count.' Fenec had realised the walls of his argument had crumbled.

'Then weigh my half-coins, add them to the contents of my vaults, add it to your scroll, and tell me where I stand in this fucking city,' Temsa said with a smile. 'That way, you'll be ahead when the decree is lifted, won't you, Tor Fenec?'

It took a moment for the man to further realise he was wasting precious time, and the faster he moved, the faster Temsa and his soldiers would be out of his bank.

'Fetch Tallier Nhun,' Fenec whispered to his son. Russun whispered something back behind a hand, and the tor snapped, 'Then wake him! It's the middle of the morning, dead gods curse it!'

Temsa had to smile. They had no idea what a relief it would be when he decided to leave them alone. Like a dunewyrm, it was not often Temsa let his prey go. Sometimes, though, enough torture was enough torture, and death was not needed. But not yet. Not until he found another bank to bend over.

The great doors slid open as before. The lamps were lit to make the copper of the scales burn. Ani and Danib saw to the opening of other, smaller doors that led securely from the street to the Weighing Room. The first time, Temsa had been making a point. This time, he could afford to follow the procedures, and watch how the shadows played on the stone as barrows and wagons full of his coins began to flood the room.

Tallier Nhun came sleepy-eyed from the adjoining office and nearly stumbled at the mere sight of the scene. It wasn't often, Temsa guessed, that a tallier got to preside over a tor rising to a serek. It usually made the rumour mill, and it hadn't for some time.

'Let it begin,' came Tor Fenec's hoarse shout, and as before, figures in white robes appeared from alcoves to grab the coins from Temsa's men.

Half-coins tumbled musically into the vast pan in initial trickles, but before long they flowed like a copper river. Though in Temsa's mind, this time the river was wider, and fiercer. He let his gaze get lost in the glittering.

He came to as Nhun shouted once more, ordering his helpers back from the sides of the scale, where they held coins in place with brushes. The pile was threatening to landslide.

Fenec had almost been fascinated by the tumble of half-coins. 'Sigil, fetch the Ledger of Bindings.' Russun went to fetch it from the office. When he returned, carting the trolley and enormous scroll, and when Nhun finished bending over by the measure, the tor cleared his throat ceremoniously.

'And the Weight is?'

Nhun moved over to Fenec's side to show him the numbers. 'Again,' said the tor, and the tallier repeated his counting. Only when Nhun had come back to show him undoubtedly the same numbers did Fenec relent, and start to stalk up and down the Ledger as Russun rolled it out. A dark line of glyphs lay across it near the top, where a thicker, grander golden line separated all but a few names. They were redacted for royal eyes only.

Temsa couldn't help but stand over them, casting as much shadow as he could while Russun and his father's fingers prodded at names and glyphs. To his annoyance, they kept dancing close to the line, but only once past it.

'Another problem, gentlemen?'

'Here... *Tor* Temsa.' Fenec placed his finger between two names he didn't recognise. They were a good handful of entries below the red line between tor and serek. The finger was shaking. 'I... if business continues at this rate, I am sure in a few weeks – days – you will be a—'

CLANG!

Temsa's talons pierced the thick scroll and dug into the rich marble beneath. The noise echoed around the Weighing Room.

'Tor Temsa, I must insist!' cried Fenec as he rose to his feet. He instantly withered, but it was good to know the man still had some spirit in him. His son, however, kept to his place on the floor.

'Insist what, Fenec?' Temsa challenged him. 'You've got your coins. You've added my considerable worth to your vaults. More leverage to your dealings. Stock and share, I believe you call it? The coin within coin.' Temsa leaned closer. 'And let us not forget your life. If that is of any worth to you.'

Fenec nodded, and withdrew so that Temsa could tug his talons from the papyrus. He wondered if he had by chance skewered any names he had skewered in life, but there was little time for whimsy or irony.

'I bid you a good day, gentlemen,' he said. 'Take care of my fortune.'

Ani and Danib swept in behind him like hulking wings as Temsa left with a brisker limp than usual. His soldiers formed a rough oval, knocking a few benches and barrows over as they did so.

Temsa walked in silence, letting his pace do the talking. Ani was as mute as Danib. The soldiers were silent too, just wafting their stench across him. That was enough reason for a swift pace, even if he didn't have things to do.

His new armoured carriage, pilfered from Horix's tower, waited where he'd left it on the edge of the plaza. The horses bucked in their harnesses, eager to move. Temsa knew that feeling.

With a hop and a clang, he was inside and ensconced in the velvet seats, individually curved for each passenger. The carriage fit six, but with Ani and Danib filling the space, it already felt far too full. Temsa put an elbow to his knee and propped his head to stare out of the window: two thick plates of glass, warped with age. It twisted the city into odd shapes as they jolted away; coloured it a dull green against the sun-baked ochre and gleaming blue sky.

'You heard what he said in there,' Temsa said when he was ready.

Ani had already been staring at him. Now her eyebrows raised. 'I know that look. You've got an idea in you. Somethin' tells me it's not a good one.'

'You, m'dear, are sorely mistaken.' Temsa paused to swallow the anger. It would sour the moment. '*Emperor* Temsa. It has a fine ring to it, don't you think? A fine ring indeed. The first of a new royal line.'

Danib bowed his head. Ani cupped a hand behind her ear.

'What?'

'The first of a new royal line.'

'I knew it wouldn't be a good 'un,' Ani whispered. She spared a moment to press her fists against her forehead. 'Are you... Have you... Have you fucking lost it, Boss?'

Temsa levelled his cane at her. 'I have told you time and time again—'

Ani had the nerve the interrupt him. 'Tor Temsa, Serek Temsa. Now *Emperor* Temsa? It sounds like madness, Boss. More than greed. You used to plan and scheme and bide your time, but now you're rushin' in like a headless shade. Finel's was a disaster. You've fuckin' lost Caltro. The widow is somewhere with an ungodly flying machine, and yet you're pretending as if nothing has happened! As if we're not stuck between the claws of the Cult and royal fangs. Or as if last night wasn't a failure. It's not like you at all, and I say that as your loyal guard of almost ten years! You pay me to worry about your safety, so I'm fucking worrying.'

Temsa fought the spit and vigour behind his teeth. He had plenty of it to give; for Ani's cheek, her insolence, her doubt. Her never-ending doubt. Not for the first time, the thought of firing her, or something more permanent, crossed Temsa's mind. He swallowed once more.

'Miss Jexebel, I must remind you of your position, and suggest that you hold your fucking tongue when it comes to who makes the plans. You wish for me to plateau? Now that I have come so far? Fine. I will find a bodyguard who wants to gaze down at Araxes from the Cloudpiercer. Someone who wants to be grand general, or whatever. Or even serek. You can go back to scratching a living in some tavern, dreamless and average.'

Ani somehow looked offended. 'Is that what you think this is about?'

'That is what this has always been about! What it is *all* about, Ani. What greater heist is there in this city other than the throne, hmm? Tell me that, and I will never step under the Piercer's arches again in my life. And while we're on the subject of pretending nothing has happened, I could hold you accountable for fucking up the entire attack on Horix, but I've done you the favour of ignoring it. I could easily punish you instead.'

Ani's words were strikes of flint on steel. 'For what?'

Temsa leaned closer to her. 'Did you not think to check if the widow still had Caltro? No, you didn't, embarrassing me in front of the Cult and the empress-in-waiting.'

He didn't know whether it was her lack of vocabulary, lack of confidence, or that she was too full of raging words to dare speak, but Ani held her tongue, and looked away to the other window. He saw how white her knuckles had turned, gripping the handle of her axe.

'And you, Danib?' Temsa turned to the hulking shade, challenging him. 'Want to complain about the way I do things?'

The shade shrugged, then shook his head, and Temsa took that to mean the usual no, or, "whatever". It was the best he ever got out of the dumb shade, but at least it was consistent. All Danib cared about was the simple matter of bloodshed. Unlike Ani. Who would have thought the big, battle-scarred Scatterwoman lacked backbone when it mattered?

'Just as I thought. You should learn to be more like Danib here, m'dear,' Temsa ordered. 'As for Caltro and Horix, I have eyes looking all over the main city. Danib wounded her machine. She can't hide for long now that the mists have faded. Now, if you're finished complaining...?'

Silence answered him, and Temsa turned back to the window with a sigh.

Emperor Temsa. It had a ring like a lunch bell on a summer's day. Where he had grown up in Belish, before a man had taken his leg, he had heard such a tolling from the riverbanks, and raced through meadows with the cackling of fellow children in his ears. Those were fine days. Fairy tale days. But all fairy tales hid an inner darkness, no matter how sparkly the prince, how determined the princess. There was always a witch. A wolf. A dragon. Temsa's had been a butcher. A man who made a job of removing limbs from those who hadn't the coin to save them. Boran Temsa had avoided debtors' prison, and the Nyx, but he'd paid all the same. And he'd paid more. In sweat, silver, and blood. Not his own, mind, but hired blood, from hired swords. Up and up and up he'd climbed, building businesses from the sand until a whole district was his. Now tordom. Shortly a serek. *Perhaps even an emperor.* And why not? It was owed to him. Just like every other Arctian. He had taken what was his. Dared to take steps no others had yet taken. Why shouldn't the throne be his, dead gods curse it?

Emperor Temsa. 'Emperor fucking Temsa,' he whispered under his breath to a distorted cityscape.

———————◆———————

A FAMILIAR FACE GREETED HIM at the gates of his tower: Etane, standing in gold armour and with a mask of mail pushed up onto his forehead. His inordinately large sword was strapped to his back.

'What?' Temsa greeted him coldly as he stepped from his carriage. His soldiers swarmed around him, but he waved most of them away. 'Hasn't the princess forgiven me yet?'

'For which failure?' Etane asked, smiling in a sickly way. 'For failing to stop Horix escaping? For losing her locksmith? Or for consorting with the Cult?'

Temsa was the picture of shocked innocence. 'I did no such things.'

'I will convey your rebuttal to Her Majesty.'

'You do that,' said Temsa, brushing past him on his way into his courtyard. To his dismay, Etane followed his entourage in. Danib did a poor job of keeping the shade separated from Temsa; he practically strolled alongside Etane, staring down at his sword.

'Did you have any other purpose here, besides loitering?' Temsa challenged him.

'Yes, indeed,' Etane replied, coming closer. Even Ani didn't bother to keep him out of reach, and Temsa had to keep Etane's distance with his cane.

'The empress-in-waiting wishes you to eliminate Serek Boon, as requested. And she gives not a fuck for whatever dealings you have in place with the Enlightened Fuckwits. She wishes you to know that you had better not fail a third time, or she'll cut you to pieces herself and throw them from the Cloud Court as morsels for the crows.'

Temsa tapped his claws. He was almost impressed. He had also never seen Ani's eyebrows lifted so high. 'Her words?'

Etane nodded. 'Her words.'

Stomping his cane, Temsa sighed dramatically. 'Fortunately for her, I am loyal to the throne and our good empress-in-waiting. Rest assured, shade. Preparations to put good Serek Boon to death for good are already underway.'

'Are they, now?' The shade looked far from convinced.

Temsa jabbed his cane at his second in command. 'Ani? M'dear?'

'Underway,' she growled, eyes hazed and firmly fixed on the skyline.

Temsa had barely let his sellswords sleep, never mind getting them ready for an assault. He could push them, though. He had enough men. That was one thing he'd learnt in all his years of letting others bleed for him. Most things can be accomplished if enough meat or vapour is thrust at it.

'How soon might Her Majesty expect the task done?'

'We will be paying Boon a visit imminently,' said Temsa. 'Tonight, in fact.'

Etane clapped his hands together, making barely a sound. 'Good news. It'll go some way to improving the empress-in-waiting's foul mood, I'm sure.'

Temsa performed a shallow yet elaborate bow. 'How glad I am to hear it.'

Etane turned, his eyes lingering on Danib as he spoke. 'I highly recommend you don't fail her again, Tor. It could spell the end of this business relationship,' he warned. With that, he strode away, pulling a white silk hood over his head to keep himself from the hot sun.

Temsa clanked his way towards the grand doorway, letting a clearly fuming Ani stomp alongside him.

'Tonight, Tor? *Tonight?*' she grumbled. 'We can't—'

'We have the men. Some of them have no doubt had a nap at their posts by now. Give them a good wash, a feed, new blades, and they'll be ready to do some sharp-work in no time.' Temsa tried to ignore the poorly-concealed groan from his soldiers.

'We have no time to waste!' he barked at them. 'No time at all!'

'You—'

Temsa whirled on her, heat prickling his cheeks. 'What, Ani? What is it now?'

The woman stared back at him, matching his glare for intensity. An awkward silence passed as scores of soldiers looked on, waiting, watching. Danib even stretched for his sword at one point, just before Ani relented with a great clearing of her throat.

'Inside, you reeking bastards. Have a fucking wash.'

Temsa smirked as he passed beneath the arch of the doorway. 'Better, m'dear. Much better.'

The look Ani chased him with could have speared him alive, but he was too busy muttering the word 'emperor' over and over to care.

CHAPTER 12
THE VENGEANCE

Announcing the annual centipede races,
covering twenty miles of Duneplain and
Outsprawl city street! Organised by Tor
Finel, a keen enthusiast of all things furred,
feathered, or shelled, the race will grant the
winner fifty shades! Price of entry = one
shade. Apply within.

FROM A TATTERED POSTER FOUND IN
FAR DISTRICT

MY MORNING HAD BEEN SPENT mostly staring at the sorry attempts of the shades to patch up the ship from bits that had been strewn about in the crash. It was an amusing entertainment, of sorts, and it passed the time easily enough. All I had to worry about was shifting about at regular intervals so I could stay in the shadow of the great, sagging envelope.

Envelope. The word peppered the shades' jumbled shouts. It didn't sound like a bloated, patchwork bag for whatever gas or smoke lifted it. *Envelope* sounded like something that had horns and bounded across the desert, but I wasn't going to argue. The crew seemed as tense as me, wondering where their half-coins were, whether Temsa had yet claimed them, and whether they still owed any allegiance to the widow.

After days apart from my coin, I sensed a strange pull towards her, it had to be said. I think it was only clearer when I tried to rail against it, like a reminder of the binding spell's leash. Why somebody would want to worship a god that invented binding a soul like this was beyond me.

Somewhere around noon, when the shadows were at their shortest, a call come from a lookout on the dune above us. I swear the thing had shifted somehow without me noticing, and I had done enough mindless sitting and staring that morning than most people do in a month. The ripple in its peak had changed and seemed further away from me, as if these dunes were waves stuck in slower time than us, breaking on the shores of the city. I had never seen the like of them, yet already my fascination with the vast reaches of sand and grit was wearing thin.

Horix came striding out from inside the ship, where she had been sitting all morning, bawling the occasional order at a hopeless lackey. Her soldiers had fanned out into a rough circle, with half of them roasting in the sun for hours on end. I had tried the sun, hoping it would stir some warmth into my cold vapours, but it had just reminded me of being staked down in the widow's garden, and I decided the shade was best.

'What is it?' she hissed at her new captain. A call was sent up and the lookout came sliding down the dune-face. Even with weight behind him, the sand still tired him, and he came running up breathless.

'Shapes moving between the outlying buildings, sir. Tal.'

'People, soldier?'

'Lots, Tal Horix. In groups, moving from spot to spot as if looking for something. Shades, mostly. Some living with them, too.'

Horix jabbed a finger into the man's chest. 'Red robes?'

'Well…' The soldier thought for a moment. 'Mostly grey with some red underneath.'

'Cult,' said Horix, spitting the word out like a melon seed. 'They want their piece of the *Vengeance*. Omshin! Get your soldiers ready. I want this ship defended. Shades! Have you fixed my ship yet?'

I let the shouts and hollering wash over me, as I wondered what the Cult would want with Horix and her machine, and how she fit into the Enlightened Sisters' plans. She likely didn't fit at all, and that was probably why they were so keen to hunt her down. I wondered how much of their plans Horix and her flying machine had jeopardised. And me, for that matter, and my escape from Temsa. Since my chat with the sisters, I had attacked one of their own and run from them twice. Part of me wondered if this was them coming to fetch me, as they had promised, or coming to end me.

Stay useful, Caltro Basalt.

It was shady – pardoning the pun – how the Cult had arrived in the Outsprawls so quickly. They either truly had a great reach, or ran like rats through tunnels. I couldn't help but admit I was intrigued by what these cultists were up to.

A score of Omshin's soldiers, copper- and silver-plated, spread out in a semicircle and slowly proceeded up the dune while the rest formed a tight ring around the *Vengeance*. I tucked myself behind their shields and watched between their heads.

I don't know how long I watched, but no matter how much I stared, no arrows swarmed the sky, no bodies came rolling down the dunes. It was one of those moments you can feel hovering like a buzzard, waiting to strike. Yet it never came. The soldiers began to spread out and hunker down to peer over the lip of sand.

Hushed whispers floated down on the breezes. Omshin had turned and was nodding deeply at the widow, confirming the lookout's warning. She saw him, and I could hear her foul muttering. Using the butt of his spear, Omshin scratched a glyph in the slope of the dune. It looked like twenty. Or thirty. The higher Arctian numbers got, the more they confused me.

The rough word for "cult" followed, and Horix's mind was made up.

'Don't let them get anywhere near the *Vengeance*!' the widow yelled across the bowl of sand she had claimed as her own. 'Kill on sight. No quarter for these shades, nor the living dolts that have fallen in with them!'

A clap of thunder sounded, making me jump before I realised it was the soldiers, thudding their gauntlets or spears against their shields in unison.

'And you shades! Get back to work!'

'Yes, Tal!' came the not so enthusiastic response from the dead. Even so, the hammering and shovelling rose to a new level of fervour. I turned back to the dune and watched the soldiers digging into the sand. Triggerbows and short, recurved bows were run up to them. The sandy peak soon bristled with bolts and arrows, waiting to be nocked.

And that was it. Nothing happened for several hours. I began those hours tense – as any person would be when they found themselves on the cusp of battle – but I ended them slumped in the envelope's shadow, rolling my eyes and trying to hold sand grains in my hands.

I poked my finger into the hot sand by my elbow, eliciting a hiss and reminding me it was almost time to move. I felt like one of the sabre-cats the Krass lords liked to keep lounging by their fires. Wherever it was cosiest, the tufted cats would sprawl. I favoured the cool instead, shifting where the breezes blew and the shade kept the sand at a respectable temperature. Beyond the shadow, I could have roasted ham and eggs on the sand.

The soldiers had tried to evade the sun as much as possible, but where the formations had to be maintained, the men and women had baked in their armour. Shields were held like umbrellas, holes dug in the sand, but still quite a few collapsed, and had to be swapped with soldiers from the ship. The Arctians were not immune to the sun, no more than I was immune to striding across a Krass ice-steppe naked with my bollocks swinging free.

Whatever the banging and tinkering was achieving, it wasn't making the widow happy. Hours had bought the workers only more anger from their mistress. I had no idea how close they were to fixing the *Vengeance*, but until the flying beast was sitting upright and straining at its tethers, Horix kept striding back and forth, screeching orders. I wondered if it would take another night, and if that was what the Cult bided their time for.

They were clearly out there. Omshin and his dune-dwellers had spotted them shifting about all day, sometimes striking far out east and west, as if to double back and surround them, or sometimes hammering some contraptions of their own together in ramshackle huts. There were more of them now, too. The captain didn't know where they were coming from but they trickled in one by one in irregular intervals. Frequent enough to be worrying.

Despite the Cult's charm and charity, nobody likes to be surrounded. As the sun began to lose some of its bright edge and slip to the west, I found myself up and wandering the formations of guards. I peered at the surrounding dunes, watching for a blur of red or blue in these accursed heat-waves. I was not a fan of them. If the air itself did not want to touch the sand, then why should I be forced to do it?

I pitied anyone that had need to walk across the whole fucking desert.

EVENING CAME TO WASH THE sky of its colours, and still the Cult had not reared their heads. My lookout duties had gone from idle wandering to intense staring into the greying desert. The sun had not long since disappeared below the jagged, distant reaches of the desert and Sprawls. When I found a moment, I looked upwards to watch the heavens fade from red to black.

The silence had become interminable. Torches had been lit, and their crackling was the only conversation. The shades were busy sewing patches from the inside of the huge balloon. Needles and glue made far less noise than hammers and nails, but I would have taken them back. Silence was too blank a canvas. Every desert noise was stark and strange, raising my hackles even though I was sure I had fewer worries than those around me.

Horix had ensconced herself in the prow, nestled into the controls, brooding and peering out through the doorway with a fierce glare. Her eyes glinted under her hood, and whenever I passed by on my circuits, I watched them follow me, like a haunted painting.

As night won over the sunset, Omshin called for more torches and spread his soldiers in a wide ring around the hollow between the dunes. Still nothing challenged them. I crouched, feeling useless and increasingly perturbed with every moment that dragged on. The Cult certainly knew how to make a person wait.

In my prickly brand of boredom, I took to climbing the western dune. I found it even harder than the soldiers made it look. My lack of weight only made the sand slip more, and it took me some time to wade up to the top. I was greeted by several furrowed brows on my arrival. One grizzled old soldier was mid-sip on a hip flask. The other was a woman, seemingly annoyed at how I'd spent so long reaching them.

'Slow night, huh?' I said, using whatever time they gave me to look out into the desert. I wanted to spy a gleam of blue. A puff of sand. Anything to give this lingering threat a face. The human mind was cursed with the idea that knowing what was coming for you somehow made it less fearsome. I felt the morbid urge, same as all, but I despised the logic. *Just because I can see that the beast charging at me is a twelve-foot, slavering bear doesn't change the fact my face is about to be gnawed off.* In fact, if that had been my death, I'd rather not know a fucking thing, and take my own blade to my throat instead. That wasn't cowardice. That was just good sense.

The soldiers knew their orders and had no words for me. They followed my gaze instead, and the three of us watched the desert in awkward silence. In my peripheries, I could see others watching us, uneasy that I wandered free. Half a dozen more wisecracks limped through my head before I decided that I didn't care any more, and began to slide back down the slope.

A dune must have been the only hill that could tire a person going down it. There was a strange weakness in my legs, and the difficulty of keeping my feet free from the cloying sand. Even on the flatter climes it shifted with every step.

The wind said my name. It was spoken so softly I could have dismissed it as my imagination. *Caltro*, it whispered, a breath that stirred my vapours into curls.

I stared out past the *Vengeance* and the weaving channel the dunes made. A low ripple of sand made a fine wall for the soldiers. There was a gap between two of them, no doubt on purpose to tempt the attackers in. I strolled towards it, and as I walked I heard the hiss of the envelope filling up, and of whatever alchemy the shades were brewing inside it. I had asked the workers all sorts of questions earlier in the day, but got few answers. I had seen powder in sacks being carted about, full of something like crushed crystal. Whatever magic it was, the rumpled balloon had begun to bloat again, and rise, tilting the craft slightly further upright.

My feet took me to the gap, where I was no doubt watched carefully for a few moments before the soldiers' eyes turned outward again. It was the cusp of twilight; the colour had been sapped from the day and eyes were still struggling to adjust. No moon shone tonight, just one lonesome star on the horizon.

I stared over the slight ridge, where a small, shadowy gully had collected wheels of dry, knotted bramble around a beetle carcass. They scraped against each other with every breath of wind. I hadn't heard my name again, neither in the breeze nor the skeletal rasping of what passed for plants in this desert. I came to the conclusion that my boredom was concocting intrigue for me.

Sand shifted to my right. I looked up to the soldier on that side, but he was lying with his chin on his hands, dazedly looking far out into the dunes. The soldier on the left was doing something similar.

'Caltro.'

This time there was no imagination at play. The whisper was quiet but clear as a chime. It came from where the sand was still slipping. A black mask appeared as it turned, no smile, no features, just two glowing blue eye-holes. It looked as if some mannequin had been buried for decades beneath the dunes, waiting to haunt me. I saw the rest of her shape, faint and half-hidden beneath the sand, but made up of a sand-coloured coat and trews. She was lying so motionless, I couldn't tell where she began and the desert ended.

'Liria or Yaridin?'

'Liria, as I die and glow.'

I was relieved, to be honest. 'This is a new look for you.'

'We are very resourceful. A gift from the old Tribes of Sesha that once walked the Duneplains. They used these garments to sneak up on their prey.'

My eyes switched between the soldiers as I took a casual step towards her, putting me between her and at least one of their views. I silently searched the sand for other black masks poking up, eyes gleaming at me like the ghouls of old stories.

'And am I prey?' I asked her. 'I take it you didn't come here to give me a lesson on Arctian society.'

Liria blinked slowly, and I wondered how she was holding back her glow. In the half-light, her eyes were like soft blue chalk, barely casting any light. Maybe that was why the guards had spent so long looking for the Cult. And here they were: poised on the edge of our camp. I looked for weapons on her indistinct form but found none. I was curious whether she was a fighter, as well as a sneak.

'That is for you to answer,' she told me plainly. 'How you act from here on in defines you. Run with Horix, or come with us.'

Finally, they were freely welcoming me in. I could have smiled. Reaching deeper into the Cult was easier than I had expected it to be, and that was why I clarified, 'To my freedom, or back to Temsa?'

Liria did not lie. 'Not to Temsa. To us.'

'Why do you insist on trusting that vile snake?' It probably wasn't the best time for questions, but I still wanted to know.

'Trust has nothing to do with it. Faith, more like, that he will continue grasping for the throne as expected. Fortunately, he does not need you in that quest any more. Your trial is over.'

I personally hated the word 'quest'. It gave grandeur to often droll or questionable tasks. Pomp to those with no excuse to call themselves heroes. Don't even get me started on what I thought about 'trial'. That was not a comfortable word for any thief to hear. I didn't like it when the sisters had first said it, but I didn't mind it now it was almost over.

'You wanted a rabid wolf for the job of taking the throne. Well, now you have two, and this particular wolf can fly. Why not let me open the Sanctuary for her instead of Temsa?' I didn't say it to protect Horix, but for myself. Selfishness is often hidden behind drapes of good intention and compassion. I had a chance at picking the greatest vault ever constructed. It was a jewel that now gleamed almost as brightly as my freedom.

'Chaos is an art, seeming random but made of small and subtle changes. Horix is a force too great, and must be curbed.'

'She's ruffling your feathers, isn't she?'

Liria looked at me as if she'd never seen a bird in her life. I tried another turn of phrase from my homeland.

'She's shitting on your bonfire.'

I didn't need the ghost to remove the mask to know she pouted with annoyance beneath it. It was the usual facial expression my wit received.

'She is unpredictable, yes,' she said. 'You want your freedom, Caltro, yet you continue to put your faith in the widow's false promises. You ran from Temsa when we asked you to stay. We offer you safety, and you talk of helping Horix to open the Sanctuary. Unlike her, we have your best interests at heart. We are your kin, if nothing else. Can you say that of anybody else you've dealt with in Araxes?'

I thought of lying, and pretending this whole thing had been a ruse to let the Cult have a shot at Horix, but I already felt weak just thinking of it.

'No,' I said instead, shaking my head. Not even of the dead gods. *Damn it if these sisters didn't make a huge amount of sense.* 'But she still has my coin. And that is final.'

'Join us, Caltro, and the morning may tell a different story. For her and for you.'

I knew whatever I decided would not save anybody's life tonight. Only my own interests, and they were largely self-preservative. And here I was, being invited into the Cult of Sesh, and having an army claim my half-coin while I was at it. I hoped Oshirim and his posse were happy, wherever they stared down from. I certainly was, though I played nonchalant.

'Fine. Try your luck with the widow. And if you get my half-coin off her, I will consider it.'

'Oh, it was never your choice to make, Caltro. The widow has made an enemy of us without you. Yours was to stand by or defy us. A final chance,' said Liria. I heard the smile in her voice, and it unsettled my nerves. 'Let's test your widow, Caltro.'

With a rustle of sand, I withdrew from the ridge and nodded politely to the soldiers. Part of me wanted to give them a fighting chance. I could have laughed. I'd never been given one; they didn't deserve it either.

It's an odd thing, deciding where to watch a slaughter from. You have to consider such matters as blood splatter, crossfire, and general getting in the way. I had no armour to speak of, only my ripped and borrowed smock. I decided on a spot halfway up a dune; far enough away from the ship, and with a rock as a pillow. I reclined against it and stared down at the battleground. My posture was so casual as to look foolish, and yet inside I was as tense as a ghost can be. It was as though I'd bet for both contenders in a fight, and somehow found myself down in the pit with them.

I saw the crooked form of Horix watching me from within the shadows of the *Vengeance*'s doorway. Her eyes had that glint to them again. There came a strange tug on me as she clutched the half-coin at her neck. I braced myself against it.

'Come here, Caltro!' she called me.

The despising look on my face said everything, as did my stillness. The only move I made was to entwine my hands behind my head. I had made my decision. Aligned my walls to a lord's castle, as the Krass peasants put it. It was reaping time.

'You continue to test my patience, shade!'

Three soldiers were already tramping towards me, the widow striding behind them like a gale hurrying leaves down a street. She had wrenched my coin from her neck and raised it high as if it was the severed head of some enemy she'd won a victory over. Horix waited as her men came to fetch me. It took them some time with the sloping sand, but when they did, they did so roughly. I was thrown back down the slopes, rolling to a stop at the widow's feet. Copper spear-points stopped me from getting up.

Horix stood over me, face drawn back in displeasure. 'You are a pestilent creature, Caltro, and I am past being tired of it. What is it you don't realise about your status in this world? You are lesser. Beneath. Half alive. And yet you roam about like some prize feline, refusing to come when I, your owner, call. You are bloated on your own confidence, shade. I thought we had come to an understanding on that matter, but it appears I will have to keep reminding you of it until your task is done. When I can finally be rid of you.'

I was about to give her a whole new perspective on understanding when three black arrows interrupted us. With a *snicker-snack*, they found a place in each of the soldiers' necks, where the armour was soft. Blood flecks spattered Horix's cheek as the nearest one gurgled around steel and wood.

The widow was fast on her feet for an old bag. She was already inside the *Vengeance* before the soldiers had head-butted the sand. I retreated to a nearby torch, eager to show myself off, being in the ring of soldiers and all.

'Inside, Caltro!'

I didn't move, knowing she was too cautious to fetch me. Arrows zipped past my shoulders, steel-tipped instead of copper. For flesh, not vapour. Another soldier pitched into the grit with an arrow in his face.

'To arms!' came the cry from Omshin, cut off as an arrow found his shoulder. I watched him half-run, half-fall down the dunes. The soldiers not cut down by arrows, those too burrowed in the sand to be easy targets, followed behind. Bolstering the others, shields clanked together in a firm circle around the airship. Dark figures began to rise from the gaps in their perimeter. Sand poured from their edges. Dark blades emerged from shadow. Screams came from the ridge I had lingered on.

More figures appeared on the dune's peak. Their black faces and glowing eyes would have set fear in the hearts of any traveller. But Horix's soldiers were worth every purse of silver she had paid for them. Old army fellows, well used to fighting the dead and the living.

Those still carrying bows fired a volley. Two of the Cult were turned to pincushions. Blue smoke puffed from sleeves and eye-holes and they collapsed in a bundle of cloth. Many wore arrows but kept on striding across the sand, and I wondered what it took to turn my kind permanently dead with a blade.

Another volley was launched and more garments littered the dune.

Omshin yelled something and every third member of their line strode outwards, spears balanced in a groove in their shields. They roamed like marauders, fighting each cultist as they came. They fought like scorpions, pinning their enemy with heavy strikes from their shields before stabbing them. When they tired, they retreated to be replaced by another soldier. It was a clever rotating mill of death. It kept the fighting as far away from the *Vengeance* as possible.

Frequent flashes of white showed colours in the grey sand. Blue bursts intermingled with occasional splashes of blood and filth. The only cries came from Horix's soldiers. The Cult worked silently, impassively, even the live ones. The other sounds were the frantic hissing of those working away inside the *Vengeance*, burning their precious powder to make gas.

They had no formation, no visible tactics besides numbers. Ever increasing numbers. Those in the camouflaged cloaks had been cut down, and now plain cultists in grey and red cloaks were wading down into the clamorous hollow. I spied some in armour waiting on the ridge, holding spears. I knew little of battle, but I knew if somebody had the balls – even ghostly blue ones – to stand so casually on the edge of a fight, it was a worrying sign.

Omshin was yelling out targets, striding from one side of his circle to the other. An arrow shaft still protruded from his arm. The formation contracted slightly with every soldier that fell. Two score still remained, however. Maybe more. I had already counted almost double that in piles of clothes. A few cultists had yet to die, and were squirming about in the sand, glowing brightly where stumps had replaced limbs.

And still they came.

Armoured shades came striding down the hill, swinging curved swords or wiggling spears. They took on the roaming soldiers head-on, moving fast and viciously. The number of cries and dead increased palpably.

The *Vengeance* groaned as it tilted almost upright. The bag of gas billowed in the places it had begun to sag. New patches strained. A pop of something inside the craft punched some more lift into the saggier places, and with another groan the *Vengeance* sat upright on its awkward hull.

'Caltro! Get inside now!' called Horix.

Arrows rained, seeking to puncture the thick leather hide of the envelope, but it was no use. Instead of lifting up, the craft listed sideways, carving a deep furrow in the sand.

'Now, Caltro!' the widow yelled.

I moved only towards the half-coin dangling around her neck, looser on its retied chain. More pops and hisses came from the inside of the envelope, and the *Vengeance* lurched into the sky. Ropes were dangled for the soldiers able to leave the fray. I held onto one, but did not climb it. I simply stared at Horix, holding her eyes while I waited to pounce.

Omshin and his soldiers moved with us, dragging the fight up the gully between the dunes. The cultists followed, bunching up into a mob that followed, but didn't exactly chase. A few raced forwards to keep the soldiers busy, while the rest climbed the sides of the dunes, firing down at the escapees.

'Climb, you useless shade. Here! Now!' Horix continued to snarl at me.

I looked back at the cultists and saw Enlightened Sister Liria standing in amongst the masked fray. She was hard to see in the dust cloud the fighting had kicked up, but I saw that she had removed her mask. Her face glowed now. She had eyes only for me.

I felt the rope slide through my grip along to the shout of, 'CLIMB!' from the widow. Above me, a red-faced Widow Horix, clawing at thin air for me. Her yellow teeth were bared in a fiercely desperate gurn.

'Come to me, Caltro!'

I saw the copper half-moon dangling around her neck, bright against the black of her cloth. And so I climbed, hand over slipping hand, until my legs dangled beneath me and once again I knew what it was like to fly.

Once I was near, Horix got to her knees, beckoning me ever closer, black silks flapping around her face. The wind blew hot and fresh through my vapours. I lunged for the edge of the *Vengeance*, fell short, but stayed dangling from the rope. I stared up at her wild eyes, her flowing stream of silver hair, and waited.

She reached for me, the stupid old woman. Even she, who was so loathsomely inclined towards ghosts, was so overcome by greed and necessity that she reached out for my cold, dead hand. And she grabbed it too, those copper-painted nails of hers drawing white lines in my wrist.

I could have cried out, but instead I smiled.

Widow Horix reached for the shoulder of my smock. She did not see my other hand clamping around my half-coin. It was cold and sharp, but if it stung my palm, I did not feel it.

It took all I had not to bellow with laughter at that moment, right in her face. I made a show of heaving up, but as she straightened with me, I pulled. Hard and quick. She sensed the snap of something around her wattled neck. The simple breaking of a gold chain, yet the shattering of all her hopes, and the pinnacle of mine. Her mad grin of success faltered in the space of a blink.

I stayed in her grasp just long enough to watch the realisation dawn. Long enough for her eyes to meet mine, and for her to see the wide grin on my face.

'I'd like to say it's been a pleasure,' I said.

It was then I let go, flinging myself backwards and watching her recede into the sky. A glorious wind rushed through me.

Her expression was worth more than all the jewels and auburn gold in all the Reaches. It was a sight that I knew I would take to my second grave, or the afterlife, or wherever I was destined. One that would help me smile in any dark places yet to befall me.

Whether it was my vapour, my weight, or my imagination, I did not know, but I seemed to fall slowly, like a blue feather. I descended past the queue of soldiers on the ropes, great targets for those with triggerbows. Several went limp and fell alongside me, blood trailing with them.

I looked over my shoulder. A dwindling ring of armour ushered yet more bodies up the ropes as the *Vengeance* gathered wind and height. It was blowing east, parallel to the Sprawls, but I was sure Horix would have cursed any direction right now. She shrieked untold streams of curses at me, leaning far out of the doorway, so far the soldiers tried to drag her back in.

Whump. The landing drove no breath from me, only cutting through my thoughts and leaving me dazed. There was no pain, and for that I was glad, for it would have ruined the elation.

Only then did I realise my own coin was not burning me, as other copper did. It sat calmly in my palm, not sizzling. No white lights shot up my arm. The only marks on me were the scratches left by the widow's claws.

Omshin made a grab for me, but the Cult chose that moment to swarm. They pushed the remaining soldiers to the ground, trampling those that weren't lucky enough to grab a rope. The rest dangled like odd fruit on a strange vine, swaying back and forth as they climbed frantically. I would have done no different, with arrows flying like disturbed hornets.

I clamped my hands around my coin, even going so far as to wrap the chain around my wrist, and got to my feet. My instincts told me to run. To leg it as far into the Sprawls or the sands as I could and see what my newfound freedom could fetch me. I'd come to the desert to find it, but my coin was finally my own. I looked down at the sand-encrusted breast of my smock, half-expecting a white feather to appear there magically.

'I am free,' I breathed.

'A fine moment for any shade,' came the silky tones of Sister Liria over my shoulder. 'Reclaiming your coin. I am pleased we could help.'

Sandy garb discarded, Liria stood now in a red cloak. For once she was hoodless, showing me her bald head and, for the first time, the scars beneath her ears, where she had been slain unknown decades ago.

'Well, technically you just provided a distraction,' I replied, not meaning to sound so dry. Involuntarily, I began to pace backwards.

'A fair point.'

Another red-cloaked shade emerged from the haze and stood beside her sister. 'Are you ready to travel?' Yaridin asked us. I'd known she couldn't have been far away.

'That is up to our friend Caltro, dear Sister.' Liria fixed me with a look.

'Where?'

'The safest place for our kind, Brother,' said Yaridin.

'What will it be? Keep running, or come with us? You can finally have the answers to your questions.'

'And some justice, perhaps.' Yaridin added a garnish. That pricked my ears.

I couldn't lie to myself: their offer sounded fantastic, and in my moment of elation, I almost accepted immediately. And yet if I looked closely, I realised how many shades were gathered around the hollow, just in case I should run. All I could think about was the evil I had seen in the eyes of a dead wolf at Finel's zoo.

I suppressed my shiver well, and lowered my head as if in thought. I had sworn to follow my own path, and it had brought me my freedom. I decided to follow my curiosity and the dead gods' wishes. After all, this was the best offer I'd received in all my time in Araxes. I deserved some peace and quiet, if only for an evening. Maybe some answers to the gods' claims. And if it were to end in fire or some fetid hole, at least I had gained my freedom, as I had promised. I was just irked I was so soon out of choices in my first few moments of freedom.

'Fine,' I said, playing the guest. 'Lead the way.'

The sisters turned without a word and led me back along the gully. I followed through the sand, enjoying the lingering warmth in the half-coin, thumbing the edges where the chisel had cut. Such a simple act, and yet it could bind a soul between worlds. Trap it.

As a locksmith, I prided myself on knowing a key when I saw one, and in my hand I knew I held the most important key in all the Reaches. At least to me.

A battlefield will draw even the most resistant eye. I gazed down at the corpses the Cult now picked through like sandy magpies. One man had been torn in two by the chop of a sword, shoulder to belt, and now he lay splayed in the sand. His head had lolled back, and his open eyes were frozen and clouded in death. I flinched as they blinked.

I held that gaze – ghost to corpse – for several strides. They followed me each step of the way. I looked away, seeking something brighter in the next slain soldier. A woman with a slit throat cracked her neck to stare at me. And another, lying in the crook of the woman's arm, face smashed but one dangling eye still managing to turn to watch my journey.

So it continued, to my growing horror. Every corpse I passed locked me with its dead gaze until I managed to turn my back on it. Then I would find another, and another, gawping at me from beyond the grave.

Despite the deep sense of unease with which it filled me, and strange as it may seem, I saw no malice in any of the stares. No hate or hunger. Only caution. I wondered which dead god hid behind which dead eye.

We mounted the ridge and were immediately bathed in the glow of Araxes. Though the sisters stared reverently for a moment, I had found one last corpse. This one had an arrow protruding from his throat, and lo and behold, a stare for me. I held this one while Liria and Yaridin waited for their guard to assemble around us.

'Everything all right, Caltro?' Liria's voice dragged me from my staring match with the dead man, and I nodded avidly. Yaridin was staring at the corpse now, eyebrow raised.

'Perfect,' I said. 'I'm just not one for battle.'

They hummed sympathetically and turned their backs. As they signalled for us to move off, I glanced back at the soldier. His eyes were back on me yet again, and before I looked away, he threw me a wink. Shaking my head, I turned away, and set my eyes on the city.

Even with my freedom finally clutched in my hands, it still felt as if I was strolling back into the dragon's lair.

CHAPTER 13
A DARKER SHADE

In the City of Countless Souls, it pays to keep
your friends as close as your enemies. They
might be one and the same.

COMMON ARAXES SAYING

I HAD EXPECTED FROM THE SISTER'S mention of 'travelling' that it would be an armoured carriage and procession affair. But after they had led me through a warren of streets, completely bamboozling me with an adobe maze, they showed me an empty courtyard and a well of stairs.

My next assumption had been a private tunnel, and something on rope and rails. But the candlelit room at the bottom of the winding stairs had only one entrance, and we had just come through it.

I should have guessed earlier: the sisters had got to the Sprawls unnaturally fast. And unnatural it was.

A bath, was what it was. An ornate contraption of brass and copper, cradled in a font of black rock in the centre of the room. It glowed in the flickering light. Papyrus tubes wrapped in wire sprouted from its sides and base. Holes drilled into the floor swallowed them. In the silence, I heard the pop of bubbles.

No other furniture greeted us besides the bathtub. A few scrolls hid in one corner, and racks of spare cloaks and smocks, but that was it.

Members of the Cult – though I suppose I should have called it the Church – spread out around the room, beginning to hang up their cloaks. Some were more ragged and stained than others. I spotted a few missing limbs hiding under the rents, glowing a fresh white. If that had been me, I would still be howling, but even the most wounded amongst them was as stoic as a brick wall.

Yaridin stepped forwards to the bath. She dipped a finger in it, as if testing its temperature. Liria hung at my side, watching her sister. 'You have no doubt wondered how we travelled to the Sprawls with such alacrity.'

I had.

'The great god Sesh gave us many gifts, Caltro. Healing, for example, and many that others have no knowledge of – even the Nyxites, who claim to be the shepherds of the Nyx. That is our task, not theirs.'

'And here I was thinking it was time to bathe.'

She smiled sweetly, though I suspected her thoughts were sour. I wondered how long they'd tolerate my cheek.

'Being a part of our Church has benefits, as we will show you. Bathing is not one of them. What you see before you is a Whorl. A Nyxwhorl, to be precise.'

'And what does it do?'

'The Nyx is a river for souls, yes? Then it must flow, surely?'

I nodded along.

'The Whorl makes it flow where a soul wants. Where we want, and in this case it is from Whorl to Whorl.'

It seemed like an untrustworthy kind of magic to me, but I wasn't about to be rude. Not too rude, at least. 'Bath portal. Got it,' I replied. I swore I got a snigger from one of the cultists. *Not infallible after all, then*, I guessed. Part of me waited expectantly for a dry chuckle or daring tut inside my head, and then I remembered Pointy no longer hung from my side.

'One question.' I held up my half-coin, still firmly wrapped in my hand, and it caught the light of the candles spread around the room. 'Won't that count as me throwing my coin into the Nyx, and send me to the afterlife?'

'It would, without the Whorl. They are complex machines that temper Sesh's spell, Caltro. How do you think we do it?'

As Liria spoke, Yaridin disrobed, dropping her road robe to the floor. She was naked beneath, devoid of wounds besides the twin scars at her neck. And there hung her own half-coin on a silver chain. Her serpentine form glowed brightly, and though I might have been a ghost, I was still a man, and some stirrings survive the grave. Beauty is the same, dead or alive.

I watched, perhaps too closely, as she stepped gracefully into the Whorl. It was deeper than it looked, and she seemed to sink into it with a hiss. Liria pointed the way for me.

'You will be fine, Caltro. Not many get the honour of Whorl-travel.'

'The honour, you say,' I replied, looking down at the rippled grey water. It was murky enough that I couldn't see an inch past its surface. Still, I shuffled out of my smock and stood awkwardly in the candle-light. I clutched my half-coin in front of my belly and… other parts.

'After you,' Liria prompted me.

I dipped a toe, not trusting this bath an inch, but knowing I hadn't any other choice. It was cold, even to a ghost, and I shivered as I stood upright on the slanted sides of the bath. I let go tentatively, but as soon as my fingertips parted with the copper, the Nyx sucked me down.

The rushing press of a river consumed me, as if I deliquesced and became water myself. It was bitingly cold, and loud. Alongside the constant roar of water and bubbles, I heard those countless voices again, calling from a cavern beyond the Nyx. They sounded angry, impatient. Trapped.

Before I could give them any serious thought, I was bursting into air again. Not gasping for breath, no, but just as desperate to be free of the cloying, black water. My hands clawed at nothing until they found the curving edges of metal under them. I grasped and hauled, and after much blinking, found myself in a very similar room to the one I'd just left.

At first, I thought it a trick, taking Yaridin's warm smile for mockery. But I saw the tunnel beyond the door, leading out into a cavernous space.

'Caltro Basalt, welcome to the Katra Rasaan. The Cathedral On Its Head. You may call it the Cathedral for ease,' said Yaridin, and as the Nyxwater cleared from my ears I heard the roar of voices and bustle far ahead.

Another splash came from behind me and I moved out of the way to let Liria, also naked except for her coin, step from the bathtub. The Whorl.

Yaridin held a robe out for her sister, identical to the one she had just left in the Sprawls, and handed me a grey version.

'I would have assumed red.'

'You are not one of us, Caltro,' said Liria with a slight chuckle. 'Not yet.'

'Good,' I replied, a little harsher than I had planned. 'Red's not my colour.'

Yaridin distracted me by tapping the white feather embroidered on the breast. I thumbed it, somewhat irritated I couldn't feel the detail of the silver thread. It felt good to put it on without forging it; to have it lingering in my peripheries, emblazoned where my heart should be. I realised I had been making a dent in the vapours of my palm with my half-coin, and instead wrapped it around my butchered neck. I paused for a moment, wishing I had their small scars and not this gaping knife-wound.

The sisters had an annoying knack of guessing my thoughts. Liria spoke them aloud. 'Be proud of your wounds, brother. It's what makes you dead.'

'Had we not been raised in the Church of Sesh, we would likely bear a wound like yours.'

'Or worse.'

'Come.'

If I was still alive, I wagered my neck would be sore from looking between the sisters all day. They spoke as if they batted a ball to one another, with me standing on the sidelines trying to keep score.

Letting them lead me on, we emerged from the tunnel into a huge cavern, walls carved straight from the stone and peppered with windows, doorways and paths. The walls came to a narrow point below my feet in concatenating steps, and I saw the meaning of Katra Rasaan, the Cathedral On Its Head. I tilted my head, and saw how the roof could have been the Cathedral floor. It must have been two hundred feet above us, tiled like flagstones. It even had huge transepts, reaching off into long chambers just beneath the streets. It seemed Horix wasn't the only one who had chosen to build down instead of up in a city full of sky-scraping buildings.

On the walkways of stone and dark wood, and below us in the crisscross of streets, rivers of shades and living ran red and shining blue. I saw ghosts of every shape and race, all proudly bearing the white feather. I saw preachers standing on corners, gathering flocks to them. I saw a market of sorts, selling wares only a cultist could need. Spare cloaks and scrolls on Sesh, no doubt. I saw food for the living members of the Cult too, hundreds compared to the thousands of dead filling the Cathedral. Most importantly, I saw I was not alone. Not just slit throats, but there were wounds in those crowds I couldn't begin to fathom the cause of. Some used crutches or canes; others, chairs with wheels.

I decided to cut straight to the obvious. I had planned to get answers while I was here; it was time to get some. 'How many people know this place exists? I take it the emperor and his daughter don't?'

The sisters answered in turn, standing either side of me. 'No. A few fortunate citizens. Most established members of the Church.'

'Which includes several sereks, many nobles, and a few within the Chamber of the Grand Builder.'

'And you, Caltro.'

'Most believe we skulk in basements or old crypts. And the Church did, for a time. We have been building the Katra Rasaan for a hundred years, long before we were banished from the Core.'

I was busy gazing up at the walkways and the tumble of buildings they connected. Perhaps it was the thief in me, but I realised it all the same. 'There are no guards,' I said.

'There are, but at the entrances and more sensitive areas reserved for the more enlightened.'

I pointed a finger between the pair of them. 'Like you two?'

Yaridin and Liria traded a proud look. The latter spoke. 'Caltro. We have been with the Church from birth until our thirtieth years, and for four hundred years since the knife.'

'There are few as enlightened as we are. We are honoured to lead the Church.'

Liria held up a finger before I could ask anything else. Every reply spawned two more questions, and my head was already bursting. The head of the Cult, standing right before me, with the nearest soldier back in the Whorl room, donning a cloak. It was her trust in me that would have stayed my hand, had I a weapon. That, and my burning curiosity.

'Later, Caltro. For now, come with us. We have arranged a welcome for you.'

'A gift, if you will.'

'For trusting us this far.'

'How kind,' I said, wondering what kind of gift they could possibly have for me. Surely not Pointy. Maybe it was a nice new scarf.

The sisters led me up a spiral staircase carved from a single block of limestone. We continued to climb, using the sloping paths that wound around the inside of the upturned spire. The crowds made space for us wherever we went, greeting the sisters with reverent nods, bows, and saying, 'Welcome! Welcome!' to me every chance they got. To the sisters, they said, 'Sesh be praised.' To which the apparent reply was, 'In life and death.' I was severely bored of all such words by the time we reached a thick, round doorway.

With the slightest of pushes, we entered a long hall with a low ceiling. There were guards here, clad in red cloth and plate mail. Four of them, standing behind the doorway and beyond the light of the bright lanterns. They were not lit by flame, but by something fluttering behind frosted glass and cages of black iron.

I had ended up in enough cells in my youth to know a prison when I saw one, and they never failed to make me itchy, apparently even when I was dead. Saraka's Dunrong Dungeon had been a particularly lengthy stay, due to breaking an arm shortly after being thrown into it. I'd heard the rule for surviving prison was to pick the biggest thug in the cell and break his jaw on day one. What they don't tell you is if you fail to accomplish that most sweat-inducing of tasks with the first punch, you rarely get a second. They also don't tell you what to do if the thug has friends. Not only did I fail to break his jaw, but the three of them succeeded in breaking my arm and several ribs for trying. And my pride, for that matter. But there isn't a cage in the Reaches that can hold me for long. I'm proud to say I let myself out of that cell two weeks later, and left them to rot.

This place beneath the streets was most certainly a place of locks and keys, albeit the cleanest prison I had ever seen. The milky light of the lanterns showed no vomit or shit or blood. Not a single twitch-nosed rat, hardly a mote of dust. The light fell on rows of thick copper bars, not clad but cast in the metal. They were set deep into the wall, floor, and ceiling. At the sound of the door and shuffling robes, I saw a few glowing hands come to clutch the bars.

'What is this place? A prison for ghosts that haven't said their prayers?' I asked.

Yaridin chuckled again, though it lacked any friendliness. 'You make your jokes, Caltro. Humour is a convenient shield for the new and the uninitiated.'

That cut through me like a hot knife. I muttered incoherently under my breath and followed behind like a hound until they brought me to a packed cell halfway down the row. Two more cultists stood by, unseen in alcoves until now. A number of ghosts were clustered in the large cell. I looked over their glowing faces, not recognising a single one. Half of them were naked. The rest were in rags. One had his belly opened like somebody grinning mid-chew. Another woman had been nearly split open shoulder to groin. Most still had their coins about their necks. Free, yet prisoners all the same. I imagined how infuriating that would be, and all too suddenly, the notion that I was about to join them sprang into my mind like a crocodile's gaping jaws bursting from the shallows.

I began to edge away from the door. 'Why am I here?'

'Fear not, Caltro. These cells are for those who would seek to hurt the Church. Intruders, thieves, soulstealers looking to take a sister's or brother's freedom,' Liria explained.

'Heretics, too, and those who do not align with our plans.'

'If they do not conform, we pass them to the Chamber of the Code for punishment.'

'Though with their backlog, it does take some time.' There was no hint of snide vindictiveness in her voice, as I might have heard in Horix's or Temsa's. Only a factual tone.

I was surprised at their honesty, but not at the darker underbelly of the Cult. That had already been made clear to me several times. It was why I was here to ask questions, why my eyes roved in every corner, why I was so taut I almost walked on tiptoes. And yet these cells were paltry compared to what I'd expected. If anything, they looked a world better than the basements beneath the *Rusty Slab*.

'Some, we deliver justice to ourselves, and therein lies your gift.'

My ears pricked. 'I don't understand.'

'Justice, Caltro. Brothers, if you please.'

Liria motioned a hand to the guards, and they wiggled stout, complex keys in the cell door. The ghosts inside moved back towards the walls, nervously muttering. I searched their faces again, wondering who it was amongst them that had wronged me in this life or before.

One by one, each shade was hauled out and pushed into a nearby cell. Twenty-two I counted before the flow stopped. I stared down at the huddled figure that remained. He must have been hiding behind the others, knelt down and head hung. With copper-core rope, the brothers hauled him up and dragged him to my feet.

The ghost glowed a darker blue. He had lank, greasy hair that reached to his shoulders. His nose had been broken, and one eye bulged as if he had been pummelled before he died. I stared down at his naked body, noting the deep wounds in his chest and stomach where something with prongs had impaled him. He stared back at my neck with a cold, uncaring smirk, and in that moment I knew him.

'You remember Kech, don't you, Caltro?' Liria asked in my ear.

'How could I forget?' I said, even though I had. A great many things had happened since his knife.

The guards forced him to his knees. Copper rings in their gauntlets wiped some of the smirk from his face. I moved into the cell to stand over the man who had taken my life. The man who had started all this. I almost asked to borrow their armour, so I could smack the rest of that grin off his face with a firm backhand.

The sisters stood behind me now, explaining.

'He came to us amongst a group of shades we reclaimed from Temsa.'

'A purchase of Tor Busk's, apparently. He was taken when our mutual friend invaded his tower.'

'I remember,' I interjected.

'When we tried to share our wisdom and ways with him, he became violent. He began to roam the streets, looking for one Caltro Basalt.'

'We had him put here, just in case.'

'And now you can have the justice you rightly deserve.'

I found something solid touching my elbow. I looked down to find a small triggerbow in one of Liria's hands, its stock facing towards me. A copper-tipped bolt sat already cocked and loaded. In Liria's other hand was a half-coin. Kech's half-coin, to be precise.

I met her eyes, and her soft tone turned firm. 'A punishment can be true and fair even outside the law. Or the Code.'

Yaridin stepped closer. 'Some punishments are well deserved.'

The triggerbow hovered there, untaken. I saw Kech's eyes search mine. His curling lips took a downward turn. He began to fidget.

'This ain't fair,' he complained. 'Cold blood is what it is!'

'There is no blood in either of us. And whose fault is that?' I asked him, taking the bow from Liria. I pointed it at the floor for the time being, trying to ignore the infectious reasoning of the sisters. They didn't press me further, instead keeping to a respectful silence. But their seeds had been sown. I fidgeted now, internally.

I am no murderer, I reminded myself. *At least not intentionally.* That moral line was the last thread between me and my old self. It had been a thin thread when I was alive, but it had kept me a thief, not a killer. It was why the death of the earl's boy had cut me so deeply, and driven me so far from home.

I had clung to that distinction in life and I clung to it now, even though somehow my aim had crept up to Kech's stomach. The darker side of me – the same that lurks inside all of us – pleaded to squeeze the trigger. This ghost had taken everything from me, put me on the cursed path that brought me here. The man deserved worse than a copper bolt and oblivion. I wanted him to suffer.

'Apologise,' I ordered him. It was the closest I could get to revenge without firing, and a much-needed distraction from the cries of, *Do it!* inside my head. 'Apologise, and I might spare you.'

'Apologise for what? Doing my job? You were the one who kicked me, fought back. Got me stabbed!'

'I fought back…?' I pressed the butt of the bow to his forehead. It was soft, gelatinous, and I was disappointed there was no hiss of copper. 'Apologise for taking my life.'

I wanted to see him crumble. I wanted to see a ghost sweat. I wanted to see him break and know he was a snivelling coward. But his sneer came right back, making me look like the coward.

With a snarl, I withdrew, pressing the triggerbow into Liria's grip. 'No,' I said, striding for the open air of the Cathedral.

It took a moment for the sisters to join me. They waited patiently for me to speak, which I did, after much staring and pouting over the sandstone and marble cavern beneath me.

'Better to let him rot as a half-life than give him the peace and quiet of nothingness.'

'Is that what you believe this is, Caltro? Half a life?'

I laughed in her face. 'Don't you? We are stuck between longing for our flesh back and a lie of an afterlife. A wailing waiting room the size of a cavern. I know you've been there, as I have. I even heard the screams in the Whorl. Don't start lying to me now.'

Liria bowed her head. 'Most shades never see that place, but we know of it, and how it has become worse over the decades. That is a half-life: waiting for a paradise that the gods promised us but never delivered. This, here.' She paused to show me her hands and clench them into fists. 'This is more than flesh can ever be. You know this, and yet you forget it so easily. Come. We will show you more.'

At my snorts of disbelief, they led me inexorably onwards. This time we wound down to the deeper levels, like a screw into a wine cork. We descended past the market, and the sights of the rainbow tables and steaming pots had me pining for a sense of smell once again. Beyond the market, our path led between vaulted arches and grand rooms filled with hooded cultists. They stood in silence before shrines to alabaster statues of a god. Sesh, or so I assumed, though each statue was different. Some were carved like a long-nosed wolf with a winding, forked tail. Others were simple, like a clenched fist, or a column with clusters of staring eyes.

'The many faces of Sesh,' Yaridin whispered to me. 'Everywhere, but nowhere. Death and chaos itself.'

I shook my head. 'Sounds positive.'

Yaridin smiled that honeyed smile of hers. 'What else would a shade worship, Caltro? Life? Or the turmoil and death that make us what we are?'

I cursed the sisters and their clever points, and let them lead me past their worshipping rooms to skinny halls crammed with storeys of shelves, scrolls, and networks of ladders. Further down, I saw rooms full of kneeling students, rapt before a teacher drawing glyphs on a black wall in chalk.

Deeper still we found cavernous forges, where multitudes of shades in red smocks worked great machines. Rivers of fiery, molten metal poured from the machines' charred spouts. Bundles of spears and swords lay stacked between arches. The hammering was raucous compared to the silence above, and I found myself wincing even with my muted senses.

In darker parts of the caverns, I saw half a dozen hulking shapes with arms and legs: statues carved like the proud gods and kings of old. They were bound with ropes like tangled puppets. Shades encrusted them, still chiselling away at their features. It reminded me of the ruined statue I had seen in the plaza of the Grand Nyxwell, running errands for Vex. I wondered what had become of him.

Past the forges, in the very pit of the Cathedral, I was shown to a balcony overlooking a long hall. Its walls were roughly hewn compared to the carved stone above us. I wondered if this part was newer. Below me, a multitude of naked shades and living toiled, not with metal or scripture or literature, but with weapons, or fists wrapped in copper gloves. There was hardly any panting, no yelling except from the shades in robes strolling between the ranks. Only the scuff of feet on sand and the *thwip* of blades slicing through warm, muggy air. No torches burned here either. Just the strange white lanterns, which to my ears sounded like they were full of moths.

Before I could ask any questions, Liria joined me at the balcony. To my surprise, Yaridin had vanished while I had been busy staring.

'I know you have heard the rumours of the Church, or the Cult, as we once were. Rumours that you may have taken to heart, which we understand. So before we continue, Caltro, allow us to tell you our history, and what we believe. Our side of the story, if you will.'

It was about time I heard another side. I'd always found hearing both sides of an argument useful. It either sated my curiosity or gave me a good laugh, and so I nodded for her to continue.

'In the time before the Tenets and the Code, when every woman or man worshipped whomever they wanted, and the only trade was with silver and gems, there was an argument between the gods. Though there are many minor gods, there were six that ruled the afterlife: the world beyond this one, called *duat*. There was Oshirim, the god of light and life. Anoish, god and shepherd of the dead. Horush, the god of the sky. Haphor, goddess of the earth. Basht, the goddess of protection, and Sesh, the god of chaos and death. Together they struck a balance, offering a lie of an afterlife in return for belief, which in turn sustained their forms. And so people prayed each day, and when death came knocking they knew it was not the end. This balance, called *ma'at* in Arctian, existed for centuries until Oshirim decided to proclaim himself the god of all gods. Sesh, however, knew his own domains were of greater importance, and disagreed. Life is not permanent, you see, Caltro, but all things are visited by death, and chaos is what gives light to order.

'The two gods argued until Oshirim became so angry that he struck Sesh down, mutilating him. No other gods or goddesses stood to defend him, and for fear of being murdered, he fled to our world. As penance for such an insult, Sesh took his justice on the gods by changing the flow of the Nyx – the river that ferried the dead to Anoish and onwards to *duat* – feeding it into our world instead. It was then that Sesh taught our ancestors how to bind the dead; to have an afterlife here in a world not controlled by self-indulgent gods. A second life, not a half-life, and one with a choice. *Duat* was still there, if one so chose to reach it, and stand waiting in that great cavern for untold centuries.

'When the gods realised their lifeblood had been halted, they fell upon Sesh in force and imprisoned him in a void beyond our world and the gods. It hurt them to do so, drained them, and since that day they have lurked behind their shut gates, feeding off what few souls already reached the afterlife.'

I was enjoying this story, primarily because of its contrast to Pointy's stories. And Oshirim's own words, for that matter. I decided to poke a hole. 'Then how did the Tenets come about?'

She shook her head solemnly, and I almost believed the act. 'Because of us, Caltro. Human greed overweighed Sesh's teachings. Without his guidance, and with so many of his church poisoned against him by other beliefs, our ancestors realised that binding the dead could be lucrative. Most lucrative, in fact. *Ma'at* was abandoned once Emperor Phaera decreed that whomsoever holds the most shades rules. Sesh's decrees formed only the first, second, and third of the Tenets; the rest were made by human hands. Much like the Code, which the Arc now follows or ignores blindly. Take the Nyxites, for example. They proclaimed themselves the authority over the Nyx almost a thousand years ago, and even now they still fulfil the role, when it should be a servant of Sesh.

'Centuries have passed since then. Sesh's prison still remains. But the treatment of his gifts has left the Nyx weak, drying up in places. If we do not act soon, the Nyx will stop, and we shades will suffer because of it. With binding, the games between the tors and tals will become more vicious. Temsa has set a trend, like it or not, Caltro.'

'And wasn't that your idea? Chaos is your thing, right? But for what?'

'It was, of sorts. We needed fear to unite Araxes behind a new ruler. Temsa was perfect for that. He is not suited to the throne. I see the frown in your face, but do not worry. That would be madness. No. We do not want war. Quite the opposite. That is why Sisine Talin Renala the Thirty-Seventh is our chosen successor to Emperor Farazar.'

I was as blunt as I was surprised. 'Doesn't she hate you?'

Liria looked almost proud. 'The Church will glow in her eyes, and soon. There are many ways in which we will be of use to her. We are already aiding the Chamber of the Code, and bolstering the scrutinisers' efforts in the city. Our stockpiling of Nyxwater has begun to stop the shortages, and we are negotiating with the Chamber of Trade to allow us to help the Nyxites. With the empress-in-waiting, we will be able to save the city, and instead of chaos, bring peace and balance once more. As we told you when we first met, Caltro, we are a charitable organisation. We want nothing but the best for our city. Our empire.'

'But in actual fact, you get to reclaim what's yours.' It was a statement, not a question, but she had an answer for me anyway.

She fixed me with a sharp look. 'Rightly so, Brother.'

Without another word Liria gestured down to the nearest stairs, and we descended into the pit of mechanical shades punching and hacking the air. Liria edged around them, seeking the back of the cavern, where already I heard strange noises.

An alcove hidden behind the rock welcomed us in with lantern-light and a crowd of red-robed trainers blocking the view. I could see flashes of white and blue between them and the rock walls. Liria clapped her hands and the trainers parted, tapping ivory canes on the floor. Beyond them lay strangeness of all shades and sizes.

A wooden target shaped like a soldier hung on a thick chain. It bucked and threw splinters as a muscular wolf, standing on two legs and as tall as I, savaged it with metal claws. Whatever robe it had been wearing was now taut and shredded across its chest. Its glowing fur was patchy, and between it I saw hairless blue skin.

Beyond the wolf, another shade, this one decidedly a human shape, attacked a straw mattress against the wall. Her fists moved in a cobalt blur, and her vapours left trails behind her as she ducked and weaved.

Elsewhere, I saw a shade clench until his vapours went thin as Aerenna glass, so faint that I saw the rock beyond him. I envied him immediately.

Behind him, three shades pressed their heads together, chanting and heaving until they consumed themselves, rippling into a swirling mass of vapour. Skeletal arms clawed at the air as they sought to coalesce into something else, but in the end the three shades collapsed on the floor with a white flash.

A dozen more, maybe a score, trained beyond them, but behind the flurry of activity I couldn't see much. Only a dark shape twice the height of a man, hunched and knuckles dragging. It was shaped in blocks and sharp angles, but shining blue at its joints. I heard a crunch, a short cheer, and then a mighty sigh. The light swelled, showing me a mighty chiselled breastplate and iron helmet.

I knew Liria was watching me. I saw it in my peripheries. Turning, I saw her smile, and I confessed my sense of marvel with one guilty look.

'The Strange Ranks,' she informed me. 'You are not the only one of power, gifted by some trick of the Nyx – or for the lucky ones, by Sesh.'

I decided to hold my tongue, lest the words of the gods slip out.

'As well as your attempt at fleeing Temsa's tavern, Danib told us of your escape at Finel's zoo. How you managed to haunt all manner of bodies and beasts. I don't think he has quite forgiven you for the elasmotherm. You're the only soul who's ever wounded him and walked away to tell the tale.'

Another reason not to go back to Temsa. 'The what?'

'The rather large creature with the horn for a nose. They are called coelo in the old dialects, and are from the far west of the Reaches, past Skol. They would call it the unicorn,' Liria educated me. 'The point is, what you see before you is another reason we brought you here. You can see that binding and the old experiments of the Nyxites have left many who are just as unique as you. You are gifted, Caltro. Special. Chosen by Sesh, and we would see you use and expand that gift. That is what these shades are free to do, and why we brought you here. To show you that you are not alone.'

I wondered whether this was for their agenda, or for my own, and I kept silent on that matter. 'I didn't think this was possible.' *I thought I was the only one.*

Liria smiled. 'And shades cannot be bound with other souls, no?' She waved a hand towards the wolf-man standing in the corner. He was now staring at me, eyes black as moonless nights.

'Or to fade to almost nothing, like the ghosts of ancient times? Or able to haunt, Caltro?'

'You make a fine point.' I threw up my hands, noticing more and more of the Ranks were halting to take a look at me. The crimson-clad trainers, too.

'You'll find a great deal of what you thought impossible is possible through Sesh, and his Church.'

I stepped closer, wary of the hush gradually falling over the cave. 'But why?' I asked, coming to the crux in a small voice. I had heard what I needed to hear. So far, at least. 'Why do you show me all this? Why trust me, a well-known locksmith, with it? What do you expect in return? I know this city and its greed, and "free" is a word only heard by those sitting atop mountains of half-coins. Something for everything, that's what I've heard it called, and I find it hard to believe that even you, as generous and charitable as you seem to be, want nothing from me.'

Liria's eyes had been searching my face, drinking in every tiny expression that I couldn't hide. Yaridin appeared over her shoulder amongst the other shades, watching just as keenly.

Liria stepped closer to me, her voice a whisper. 'You speak plainly. So shall I. You are not coveted by all without reason, locksmith. We want you to open the Sanctuary for the empress-in-waiting, and stand with us when she places her father into the Nyx with half a coin held tightly in her hand. We know she originally summoned you here.'

'You want my allegiance.'

'No, Caltro,' she said, softer still. 'We want your help. For you to share in our justice. To be a part of a new era for shades. Death as you've never known it. True freedom.'

I looked away in thought, but a cold hand on my chin pulled me back to face her.

'Aren't you angry, Caltro? Aren't you enraged by what you see in the streets above us? How even the free must fight to be heard? We are. We're angry at the limpness of the Chamber of the Code. At the very nature of life. Do you not feel rage in your mind, whenever a moment of silence can be found? Every day, when we look upon the injustice and crime that even daylight can't hold back, we feel it. When we see the downtrodden slitting their wrists just to be free of life, no matter how cruel their master will be in death. Or visitors, afraid of stepping onto land past sunset, who have to listen to the howls and screams of soulstealers. Don't you feel it, as we do? As we all will continue to feel until change comes?'

I knew the anger she spoke of extraordinarily well. It was ubiquitous, just like the Nyx, sprouting and bubbling here, but always just under the surface. Like it or not, Liria's words had kindled it in me. I felt it in the tautness of my jaw. Justification for my anger flashed through my mind, old moments of cruelty and torture. Of injustice. There was no finer word for it.

I was selfish in my anger. I thought of the greater evil, and how I could feel a greater pain for my fellow dead, but I thought only of me. My shattered dreams. My interrupted life. My trials and tribulations. My gruesome end at the sharp edge of a knife. My fight for my coin had blinded me until now.

Sweeping from the cave, I found the stairs, and then the corridor leading upwards. The good part of being a talented locksmith was that my mind drew maps in an instant, and fine ones at that. I followed my memory with long, determined strides. The cries of, 'Welcome!' and, 'Sesh be praised!' flowed over me. I clenched my fists harder around my coin. I didn't know if Liria and Yaridin trailed behind me; I just kept marching.

When I found the round door, I barged it aside and caused the guards to start. They followed me down the corridor, spears waggling in my face, until a shout to leave me be came echoing. The sisters had followed me after all.

I strode to the cell and took a stand a few inches from its bars. The shades had been put back inside, and they huddled together as before.

'Kech! You fetid fucker. Show your face!' I let the anger fly.

The shades parted eagerly, slowly revealing a familiar glaring set of eyes between lank tendrils of hair.

'Back again?' Kech rasped. 'Thought up some more big words to say?'

At a polite cough by my side, I looked at the sisters. Liria was holding the triggerbow as before. I snatched it from her, uncaring.

Kech snorted. 'You couldn't pull it before, you ain't—'

Thunk!

The copper bolt found his knee, driving straight through his vapours and lodging there. As he began to seethe from the white light lancing up his leg, I was already reloading.

The second bolt pinned his forearm against the wall. A lucky shot. I had been aiming for his other leg. The guards swung open the door for me, and I marched inwards, standing over the snarling Kech.

'You fucking bastard!'

I made no reply but the click of the triggerbow tightening.

Thunk!

The third bolt struck him in the groin. It was a cheap shot, and not as much of an insult to a dead man as to a live one, but it got the desired effect. I leaned over him, watching him squint and howl through the pain. I had endured my share of copper. It was time for his.

'You deserve every moment of this, Kech,' I found myself saying, as if another had taken control of my tongue. It felt as though I was haunting myself, and far from in control of the reins. 'To suffer as you made me suffer.'

Another bolt met his shoulder at almost point-blank range.

'Get it over with!' he yowled.

I threw the triggerbow aside, making the other shades scatter deeper into the corners of the cell. They watched on with horror, and rightly so.

'Do you still have that half-coin?' I turned to Liria, and her hand opened like a blue flower to show me a tarnished half-moon of copper.

'Even a half-life is too good for you,' I snarled at Kech, showing him his coin. I found the sister at my side now, holding a pair of sharp cutters.

'You don't even deserve to wait in that dark place, and know the pain of others you stole life from. Soulstealer. The void is what you deserve. Nothing.'

'No, please!'

Without a second thought, I snatched up the cutters and took one point from Kech's half-coin. It was tough work cutting with my weak strength, but the anger drove me on.

The vapours of his feet and hands began to lose their shapes like smoke on a breeze. I cut again, making a quarter of his coin, and he started to pull apart; blue knitting yanked by loose threads.

'I'm sorry!' Kech screeched.

It was too late. It took one more cut before he died a second death, and his form collapsed in a puff of blue smoke. Before they faded completely, his vapours turned to black under the white lanterns.

I let the last shard of his coin fall, and listened to it jump over the flagstones with a musical note. The other shades watched me as I exited their cell without a word.

'Do you feel better?'

I didn't know what I felt besides faint satisfaction. I had made him whimper, beg, even apologise in the end, and yet there was no great upwelling of relief, or release. I was still dead; colours and sounds were still muted, and the world was still mired with shit. It just had one less soul in it.

'When? When am I bound for Sisine?' I asked, distracting myself. There was no guilt, just confusion over who I had been with that bow and those cutters in my hands.

Both sisters smiled warmly. 'Soon. But for now, we have something else we think you might like to see,' Yaridin replied.

'Another gift?' I raised an eyebrow.

'Of sorts,' said Liria. 'More justice to be served.'

My promise to the dead gods was not forgotten, but for the moment, try to deny it as I might, my suspicions about the Cult had been chipped away.

I held up the cutters, finding my hands trembling with effort. 'Lead the way.'

CHAPTER 14
THE LAST HEIST

The wise businessman does not pay for loyalty.

CONSORTIUM CANON, CHAPTER 4

A SHAMBLES. THAT WAS WHAT IT was.

Ani Jexebel had known the mercenary life for over twenty years now, verging on thirty. In the earlier days she had been a bloodstained brawler, scourge of more than a dozen fighting pits. Then some wrinkled old bastard put an axe in one hand and a silver in the other, and a sellsword she had become. Since then, Ani had never known anything but. Coin and constant work had been her only goals. There was pleasure in it, of course: the satisfying snap of a neck, a vault of silver and a closet of sharp and pretty things, but those were extras. Pride in her work had kept her straight and flush. That, and never picking a fight she couldn't hack her way out of. There had been few of those across the stretch of years, but tonight, as she stared across the shambolic gathering of soldiers, she felt an old and familiar chill across her nape.

Half the soldiers were too busy yawning to put their armour on right. Spears clattered on the flagstones every now and again as clumsy fingers attempted too many things. A good chunk of the soldiers were late, still stumbling out of the door. Two dozen were missing completely. They had left their things and run to find kinder employment, and a boss who wasn't chasing maniacal dreams.

Suicidal dreams.

Ani watched Temsa stomp about, the occasional spark flying under his claws. He yelled this and that, half encouragement and promises of riches, the other half threats of skinning alive or boiling oil trickled into the ears. Most of it she had trouble hearing over the mutters and clanging.

Ani shook her head and thumbed her axe once more. It was infuriating to have so many years of loyalty slapped aside as if they'd never mattered. To invest so much in a boss, only to watch him become a fool.

'He's losing it, Danib. If he ain't already lost it,' she muttered.

The big shade standing by her side grunted noncommittally.

'Don't give me that. You see it plain as I do. Gone mad on his own success. I've seen it before in other bosses. Didn't take Temsa for the sort. Not at first.'

Danib sighed. *That's more like it.*

'Look at this fucking mess,' she said, pointing her axehead at the motley crew of soldiers. A hundred, maybe a hundred and a half. A sore number to take on a serek's tower and guard. 'We need another day at least, but he won't listen. His arrogance is going to get us all killed and bound. First bit's no trouble for you, of course, but who knows who'll buy you?' Ani grumbled. 'What are we to do about it, hmm?'

Danib looked down at her, and she saw blank eyes behind the sharp slits of his visor.

'Nothing? Well, he's not my master. Just my employer.'

The shade thunked the tip of his greatsword in the sand.

Ani growled. 'Fine. You just carry on ignoring it. Trustin' him. See if you don't have a different master by sunrise.'

Temsa was limping back towards them, a deep frown on his forehead and a displeased grimace on his mouth. Ani didn't even dare dwell on his new look. He was wearing a bright yellow suit with a golden sash across him, adorned with the fake medals some tors liked to wear. His eyes had been underlined with black and cobalt paints, as was the fashion of the rich, and she couldn't see the skin of his fingers for all the gold and silver rings on them.

'I thought they'd be ready by now, Miss Jexebel,' he snapped.

Ani cocked a hand behind her ear, and he huffed irritably before repeating himself.

'As did I,' she muttered in reply. 'Half of them 'aven't slept. Those who did still haven't had time for supper, or to even clean their armour or blades from last night.'

Temsa came closer. 'They're street thugs and sellswords. They wouldn't know a bath if they drowned in one. Who cares?'

Ani did, but only in the context of saving her own life. 'A crusty blade or stiff armour or a sleepy mind is no good in a fight,' she said. 'But fuck it, right, Tor? Dead bodies don't need paying.'

She strode away from him, barely resisting the urge to barge him with her elbow, and yelled at her gang of would-be soldiers. 'FORM UP, YOU MURDEROUS INGRATES!'

A DARK AND QUIET NIGHT had fallen over Araxes. The streets were even emptier than in the day. Barely any lamps or torches lit the way for Temsa's armoured carriage. Weak starlight found its way through the buildings, casting bands of faint shadow across the dust and flagstone. The hoofbeats of the four horses and clattering of the ironclad wheels behind them were the only noises, and they sounded deafening against the quiet of the fearful city.

Silence had been the topic of conversation during the journey deeper into the city's core. Not a word was said between the three gathered in the carriage. Ani had sharpened her axe with her whetstone, nothing else. Danib had gone into some sort of trance, suspiciously quiet even for a mute. Temsa watched the city as always, counting down the streets until they arrived at Boon's tower.

The Cult's notes had been very descriptive with Boon, far more so than any other mark on their list. Temsa had read their spidery glyphs so many times he had them memorised.

Three entrances. The rear is a shade and servant entrance.

Guard change at first morning bell.

Minor stairwell leads to main, guarded and locked at every second floor.

Boon resides on the twenty-first. Half his hoard is stored with him. Be–

neath his bed.

He saw the tower before they reached it. 'Phallic' was the word that came to mind upon viewing it. It was not as tall as some of the sereks' spires, but it was a strangely shaped thing. Too modern, for Temsa's tastes; bulbous at the top and sloping to a pyramid base. No roadways or bridges touched its sides. Lanterns shone from every other window down its pink sandstone flanks. Temsa hated the serek more just for building this cock-like monstrosity.

The tor knew little of Boon apart from the fact he was a free shade who sat on the Cloud Court. That was enough cause for affront in itself. Free shades did not deserve such seats of power. Boon was high-ranked amongst sereks – which meant filthy rich – and dead for enough years to think his own tower more secure than the banks. Oh, and hated enough by both the royals and the Cult to top both their lists.

Minutes passed, and with a lurch the carriage halted. Temsa was quick to escape its stilted atmosphere. He stood by its thick wheels and gestured for Ani to take charge. If she had complaints, she could see to their fixing.

Temsa waited with his hands folded over his new obsidian cane, golden and amethyst rings tapping on its stone while his underlings got the soldiers into some sort of order. They had stopped two streets away from Boon's tower. Temsa listened to the absence of noise around them. Just the occasional rattle of a heavy carriage, and none close enough to worry. No night-markets had dared to open with so much warring in the streets. Barely even a blue glow could be seen. And as for soldiers or scrutinisers, well, it looked as though they had been given the night off.

'See, m'dear? A fine night for a heist,' Temsa said to Ani as she loped up to him, her axe down by her side. He took a deep breath of city air in through his nostrils. It always smelled less foul in the Core.

'Hmph,' Ani replied. 'Conveniently quiet.'

Temsa chuckled, refusing to share in her dark mood. 'Nonsense. More like my reputation precedes me.'

'Hmph.'

'Onwards, Miss Jexebel. As we discussed.'

'Aye.'

With a wave, Ani took half the soldiers, Danib the other. They peeled apart at the junction, and crept along either side of the street. Temsa followed behind them in the deepest shadows, cane tapping, leg chiming. He felt that familiar excitement rise up; the one he'd developed a taste for in recent weeks. He ran his hands over his rings and his new silk, and grinned to himself in the darkness.

Serek Boon's walls were high and topped with curls of copper and glass. The gates on this side of his property relied on stoutness rather than grandeur. They were just taller than a man, but made of thick Krass oak and copper. The two columns of soldiers held back, twenty paces from the gate, sticking to the shadow of the adjoining street.

A ruse was called for, and a ruse Temsa had concocted. An old one, but a classic. Ani gestured again, and a shade emerged from the ranks, looking altogether bamboozled as she ripped his cloak from him. His blue glow lit the tired yet grim faces of the soldiers. Another wave, and Tooth appeared, wringing her hands but coming forwards sure enough.

Tooth led the other shade to the gate and knocked three times. No answer came, and so she tried again. Lanterns hanging high on the pink walls sparked into life with sharp clicks, dousing the street yellow. Temsa hugged his wall, watching hungrily past his crouching soldiers.

'Who goes there?' asked a voice. Blue light fell in shafts through grilles in the gates. *Trust a shade to trust in other shades*, Temsa thought.

Tooth mumbled something incoherent, gesturing to the shade, and then up to the tower. It was confusing enough to bring the house-guard closer, up to the grille.

'What are you saying?'

Tooth carried on blabbering, pointing and miming.

'One of ours? Is that what you're trying to say?'

The locksmith danced through all sorts of actions until the guard grew impatient.

'Shitting hell... all right! Stand back!'

Something behind the grille was flicked, and a stone block each side of the gate rotated to show a silver mirror. The guard peered earnestly into each one, looking up and down the walls until he was sure nothing sharp hid in wait. With a thud, the mirrors turned back around.

There was a squeak as the gate opened a few inches.

'Go,' Temsa hissed. Tooth began miming something about plumbing, by the looks of her waggling hand. At least she was buying time as the soldiers scuttled across the flagstones. It was only moments before they were spotted in the glow of the lanterns, but at that point Tooth pounced, throwing the shade into the door and jamming him into the gap. She ducked as Ani's axe came crashing inwards. The blade hammered through the grille and sent the gate reeling on its hinges. The guard flew backwards under the impact. Before he could get up, the axe had been wrenched clear and driven deep into his chest. With a burst of blue smoke, just his armour remained.

'Onwards!' Temsa ordered, following his soldiers into the small courtyard. A single door beckoned them into the tower. Tooth was up, already fiddling with lockpicks. When those only got her so far, chisels and iron bars did the rest, prising the door open.

Darkness welcomed them into a long storeroom, and forced them to light lamps. They crept on until they found a winding set of steps, reaching up into a high sandstone ceiling. Ani and Danib led them forward, Temsa at the back.

Not a peep of a house-guard was seen or heard. The hour was late, and though this was the house of a shade, it seemed to be sound asleep. They passed corridors of shades standing in spacious, ornate alcoves. Wide-eyed and worried, a few looked set to flee, but the hulking shape of Danib kept them still.

As per the Cult's instructions, they found the main stairwell, coiling upwards through a stark yet magnificent interior. The pink sandstone was grey wherever there wasn't a lantern to light it. Plush pallid carpets the colour of beaten eggs covered the stairs. No tapestries or paintings hung upon the walls, only glyphs in rough iron, copper, silver and gems.

A house-guard in ruby and gold armour waited for them on the next curve of stairs. A single shout managed to escape his throat before it was slit. It didn't bring the clamour Temsa was expecting, and though it was strange, he still grinned at his fortune. He thought of all those who had laughed in his face over the decades. The Butcher, as he was removing his leg. The soultraders of Neper's Bazaar, turning his first wares away. Horix, grinning down from her tower. Even Ani Jexebel and her doubts. Here he was, on the steps of a serek's tower, one Weighing away from claiming the same title. How he would laugh in those faces soon, and heartily.

Flat-barred cage doors kept each of the floors separate. They fell one by one under the combined force of Tooth's lockpicks, Ani's axes, and a brute of a shade in full armour. What few guards stood before them were quickly swarmed and put to either their first or second death. Their efforts seemed half-hearted, as if they had not been paid or promised enough for the job. Temsa quietly chastised Boon. He should have invested his silver better. It would turn out to be the second death of him.

The defence began to increase soon afterwards, with a line of Boon's guards forming up behind one of the next cage doors. They jabbed through the bars at Temsa's soldiers, making blood run down the stairs. Bodies were thrown aside, left to tumble and clatter back the way they had come.

To the beat of Temsa's cane striking the steps, the killing proceeded with all the inexorable ambivalence of a turning cog. Gradually the fighting turned against the guards, and when Danib had broken the bars, Temsa's soldiers trod over two-score corpses in their climb.

Finding the next set of cage doors open, and the next, the soldiers grew thirsty for more. They rushed up the steps, which had become steeper and taller now they reached the peak. They panted like war-dogs, trailing blood in their sandy footprints. Ani called for control, but she was ignored, and overruled by Temsa. The tor continued to stamp his cane on the floor until the soldiers picked up the rhythm, barking or hammering on their breastplates with him.

'Fetch, you hounds! Kill!' Temsa roared, a mad cackle escaping at the end.

No sooner had the words left his mouth than the clash of armour sounded from above. A dozen bodies fell screaming from the stairwell's edges before Temsa made it up to the next floor, where a grand landing offered respite from the climb. Ani was already there, doing her best to carve a flank out of the wall of shields and spears that blocked their way. These house-guards were all shades, and they glowed through the joints in their armour. Danib waded through them like a farmer threshing crops. Blue bodies scattered before him, but few collapsed to smoke.

'Boon, you dead swine! There's no use fighting the inevitable!' Temsa yelled. All secrecy had long since evaporated, and yet even as he uttered his challenge, he saw more shades coming to fill the gaps his fighters had cut. He wondered how many more shades were hiding between him and the next floor. He pulled a blade from his cane and stabbed here and there into the fray, or stamped on any half-lives that came stumbling through the shield-wall.

On and on their battle raged, fierce and loud. Temsa was down to thirty soldiers when his smile crumbled. Within him was a deep urge telling him to walk away, the voice of a younger, less ambitious Temsa. But then he saw Boon's guards breaking, scattering from behind their makeshift wall of shields. Thankfully, Temsa's soldiers took their time instead of rushing in, picking their way through their fallen sword-fellows and wiping entrails from their hands. They looked exhausted. Silence had fallen again in Serek Boon's tower. There came no shouts. No orders. No bells.

Temsa shooed his soldiers forwards, up the last set of stairs and into Boon's chambers. They were surprisingly expansive, given he lived in the slender part of the tower. The shaft, Temsa wanted to call it. He had thought it odd for the serek not to be at the peak, as most nobles chose, but the rich were known for their eccentricity.

Temsa was the first to stride into the empty chambers, his remaining attackers spread out behind him. While he stared up at the engraved columns and painted statues of some dog-like creature, he made a mental note to hire more mercenaries come the morning. Too many had failed him tonight. Plenty more bodies would be needed for his final push.

'Be ready,' he muttered to Ani as she lumbered beside him, breathing heavily. She stank of death and shit, and left a patter of crimson drips on the glasslike marble where she walked. Temsa was glad the air was scented with perfumes.

'I'm always ready,' Ani growled. 'But this is nonsense, Temsa. More than half our number are dead. You'd better hope we don't have to fight our way out.'

'I'd better hope? You forget yourself for the last time.' Temsa's voice was as sharp as a sandstorm's breath. They traded dark and troubled stares for a moment before he drew himself up to his full height and said, 'You, Miss Jexebel, have been treading a dangerous path. I warned you not to continue, but you didn't heed my words, and kept up your insolence. I won't tolerate it any more. Survive tonight, and consider your service ended. Go serve a noble of similar low ambition, and be happy.' Temsa tapped his cane-sword on the floor, making it sing. 'Oh, and I should wish you good luck, Miss Jexebel. I hear finding employment in this city can be murder.'

Before Ani could reply, before she could even wipe the look of half-shock, half-hatred off her face, a voice boomed through an ornately carved doorway at the end of the chambers.

'BORAN TEMSA!'

'Move. Do what I pay you to do,' Temsa snapped at the hulking woman, and Ani stomped forwards without a word. Temsa outwardly smirked, though trepidation grew inside him. This was the first heist in which he'd been announced into his prey's chambers.

'Serek Boon, I presume?' called Temsa, following his soldiers into a darkened chamber. There was a feel of reverence to it. Gems studded the walls in the shapes of stars. A marble lectern sat upon a dais. A handful of white lanterns, filled with fluttering somethings, sat at its base, casting a weak glow.

The only other light was Boon, standing with his elbow on the lectern, like a preacher about to deliver some wisdom. An animal sat at his side, a sharp-eared dog with a long snout. It was just as dead as Boon was, and its blue teeth were bared in a low growl.

'You have made it at last. Took you some time,' announced the serek in a charming tone.

'Get him,' Temsa whispered to Danib and Ani, but they did not move, and held the soldiers back with fierce glares. Not that they needed any encouragement. The word 'trap' was already spreading through the bloody ranks. Temsa felt sweat creep onto his forehead.

'I said get him!' he snapped. Nobody but Boon moved.

The serek strode around the dais, his phantom plodding along behind him. Boon wore a sheer silk robe that shone blue with his glow. Gold chains hung around his chest, the kind that would have drowned a man in seconds had he jumped from the docks. His skin had been burned and charred before he'd died; it held a fractured pattern, and in places was darker than the rest of him.

'Welcome to my home, Tor Temsa. I see you've already had the tour.'

Temsa may not have been a champion of armour and swords, but he did know how to duel with wit. 'You should have paid a prettier coin for your house-guards, half-life. They gave up easily enough.'

Boon visibly prickled at the insult. He forced a smile.

'I've heard a lot about you, Tor Temsa. Rumours, mostly, but every rumour has a root, does it not? One just has to weed it out. And here you are, in the flesh… and gold, apparently. You've climbed to quite the respectable height on the Ledger, I must say.'

'Almost a serek like you, Boon,' Temsa snapped.

'"Almost" being the operative word, *Tor*. There are no "almosts" or "maybes" in this game. You should know that. There are only numbers. Cold and simple as death itself.'

'It's high time you met yours. And this time, stay dead,' replied Temsa. 'You'll forgive me, but I am not one for talk and banter this evening. It has been a long and arduous week, killing people just like you; people who think themselves safe from the knives of people like me. You can hide behind all the locks and shields you want, but there will always be somebody just like me ready to take what you have, as long as you have more and the ambitious have less. And here we are, and you're stalling in the hopes you can evade the inevitable. Unfortunately for you, Serek Boon, I can't be bartered with or turned away. Even if I had an empathetic bone in my body, this is not personal. It's business. As I told the others, your name simply ended up on the wrong list. Yours ended up on two wrong lists, as it happens. Now, are you ready to get this over with?'

Temsa clicked his fingers, but only Danib stepped forwards. Ani was rooted to the spot, staring past Temsa at Boon. She only moved when the pause became unbearable, sauntering forward with no haste in her step.

Faced with these two bloodied champions – a pair who normally caused most opponents they met to wet their loincloths – the serek should have been quaking. Instead, he looked as if he were about to laugh. Boon seemed too confident, too calm for Temsa's liking. There was a glimmer in his eye that deeply perturbed the tor.

'Ah yes, the list. There were those who didn't expect you to make it to the end.'

Temsa took a moment to make sense of that. Ani threw him a fierce look over her shoulder. 'Excuse me?' he said, his voice hoarse.

'Some thought Finel would be the end of you. I am glad you made it. It would have been a shame otherwise.'

The beads of sweat that had been gathering on Temsa's forehead ran down into his eye, stinging him. When he blinked it away, cursing liberally, he became aware of a glow. Faint at first, grey in colour, but the brighter it became, the bluer it turned. Thick columns were carved out of the darkness. What Temsa had thought to be the edges of the room were thrown back, and what appeared to be a modest space was shown to be a large chamber. The gaps between the vaulted columns glowed fiercely now, and he caught the shape of hoods and spearheads.

'Ani!' Temsa yelled. The woman hefted her battle-axe, but although the soldiers took it as a sign to ready themselves, she stayed put. She had daggers in her eyes and they were aimed solely at Temsa. Danib also remained motionless, the point of his broadsword in the plush carpet.

It was immediately clear they were outnumbered and surrounded. A hundred shades – maybe two hundred – emerged from every part of the room, clad in crimson robes and plate mail. They didn't have the look of the house-guards, but the Cult instead. Though they kept their distance, it was no less menacing to be encircled by blades.

Two lithe and familiar figures in crimson had joined Boon on the dais. Other shades gathered around them, faces shrouded with hoods. One wore grey instead of the Cultist crimson.

'Ah, the Enlightened Sisters,' Temsa greeted them coldly. 'Of course.'

Silence reigned. Hands gripping his cane to keep from shaking, Temsa dug his rings into his palm as hard as he could. Anything to find a distraction from what seemed a rather spectacular failure on his part. It was not a word that he usually entertained, but it now filled his mind like the pealing of a bell.

Temsa looked around at his trembling soldiers, the waiting shades, and the cultists standing on the dais. No matter where his gaze moved, he saw nothing but imminent bloodshed. What troubled him deeply was that for once it might turn out to be his own blood.

'Serek Boon,' he said, trying a smile. 'Surely you'll do me the honour of enlightening me.'

'Quite the apt word,' said Sister Liria, stepping past Boon and unveiling her bald, glowing head. 'And I would have thought you smarter than that, Temsa. It is quite simple. Serek Boon here has been a brother to the Church for more than a decade. He was always to be your last mark, and your last heist. It is fortuitous that our good empress-in-waiting loathes him as much as she does.'

Serek Boon shrugged, his silks whispering. 'I have that effect on many people. What can I say?'

Temsa threw up his hands, still refusing to believe the obvious. 'That's it? You used me to cause a bit of fear and strife, but for what? To grow yourself an army?'

Liria sighed, as if she dealt with a child. 'You have such low expectations of us, Temsa.' She gestured to one of the other hooded shades as she spoke, one in a grey robe. The figure stepped forwards. 'When we have our sights set so high.'

'What riddle is this, Liria?' Temsa demanded.

There was a whisper or two traded between the two shades, and then the one in grey threw back his hood.

Temsa stamped his foot with a clang. He had been cheated, and if there was one thing in this life he hated – more than scheming half-lives, more than useless employees – it was being cheated. 'Ha! Well, if it isn't Caltro Basalt. We meet again!'

'And this time under much more favourable circumstances. For me, at least.'

'Are you enjoying this, Caltro? Enjoying playing both sides?'

The locksmith looked around the chamber. 'I have to say, it's satisfying so far.'

Temsa's reply was a coarse growl. 'I knew we'd make an Arctian of you yet.'

Serek Boon had been trying to pick his nails. A habit of life, clearly. 'This coming from the man working with both the Church and the empress-in-waiting,' he said.

'Then call us both the villains and backstabbers in this story, Boon. This is Araxes, after all,' Temsa said with a dramatic sigh. Behind his casual exterior, his mind churned, counting figures in the glowing alcoves. Swords. Spears. Tallying, checking. He thought of the open door and sweating soldiers behind him. He looked between his hulking guards, one glowing, the other red-faced with anger. Backstabbing was a coward's way. It was much more satisfying stabbing people in the front, and seeing their faces fade as the blood or vapour drained from them.

'Ani. Danib. Fetch my locksmith back for me, would you?' Temsa said, casually ringing his blade against his golden talons, as casual as a tal summoning tea with a bell.

Only the shade moved. Danib heaved up his giant sword, making all the soldiers present bristle and set their jaws, ready to fight or die. But instead of a warrior's stance, he slung his blade onto his shoulder with a clunk and strode towards the dais.

For a moment, which Temsa dragged out as long as possible, he thought the shade was playing coy. It was only when Danib nodded deeply to the sisters and turned to stare back at him that the coin dropped.

'Danib! DANIB! You dare to betray me? I am your master!' Temsa's teeth clamped so tightly he heard them crunch. He glared at Liria. 'You're making an awful habit of taking my things!'

'Danib was never yours, Tor. The coin you hide in your private vault belongs to another shade, long gone.'

Temsa whirled to face Ani, then each of his soldiers, but all of them wore the same desperate face with the word 'No' emblazoned across it. Ani shook her head, slowly, as if her neck were stiff. Judging by the ripcords of tendons tautening her skin, that was not far from the truth. Her eyes held cartloads of blame.

Again, Temsa roved the chamber, his mind working over ploys, tricks and last stands. He didn't like the sound of the latter. He forced a wide smile, tapped his cane on the floor, and tried to ignore that his world – so gleaming with promise only moments ago – was crumbling around him.

'Well, then. We shall be going, and leave you to your duplicitous ways. It's been a pleasure working with you,' Temsa said. But even as he turned, the doors to the dark chamber shut with a bang, sealing them inside. Temsa had conducted enough tortures and executions to know what that meant.

Head hung low, he took his time turning back to face the shades on the dais. A dozen emotions clamoured for his attention. Among them was hatred towards these half-lives who had conspired against him. Used him, even. There was a numbing disbelief. A frustration in his own failings, that his dreams were now dust in his head. And embarrassment, as the hot and accusatory eyes of his sellswords turned on him. Half of the soldiers were either white as marble or flushed red.

And then there was Ani.

He met her furious gaze for a brief moment. He had never seen so many types of hatred crammed into one pair of eyes. He had seen that look on her face many times before, but never aimed at him. It sent his stomach plummeting into guts that were already far too loose for comfort.

Taking a breath, forcing a wide and genial smile, Temsa looked up to the Enlightened Sisters and put his faith and future in the hands of the only thing he had ever truly trusted. Coin. 'Surely we can come to some sort of arrangement—'

The scream that followed was so inhuman, Temsa thought a savage beast had broken into the chamber. It had come from behind him, and he was in the middle of turning around when he realised what had made it.

The axe bit straight to his spine and kept going. It struck with such force and speed there was almost no pain. His throat was unnaturally cold, and all too abruptly he was falling. The world spun several times before he found himself rolling, mouth agape and leaking blood, eyes bulging. He saw Ani with a dripping axe, heaving with rage. He saw his own body, lying sprawled and spurting blood from the stump that had been his neck a few short moments ago.

He was left with the cold, glare of Ani's dark eyes. It wasn't the reflection of his murder in them that escorted him to death, but her emotionless stare.

ANI WATCHED THE BLOOD POOLING around her black boots. Temsa's head lay in his own crotch, staring up at her with shock in his eyes. There had been a moment where she still felt him looking back at her, while his mouth gasped like a fresh fish on a monger's stall. Those eyes stared through her now. To another world.

Movement. With a snarl, she twitched her stray locks aside and stared at Danib. His sword was now in his hands, but between the eye-holes in his visor, she saw a look blanker than she had ever seen. There was a pause, and then the blade rested again.

Ani didn't want to admit how glad she was about that.

She thumbed the warm blood sliding over her knuckles. She was barely tired, but still breathless. She couldn't quite remember swinging the axe, but she remembered the snap that had drove her to it. She could not have endured another word from that lying, scheming, putrid mouth. A mouth from which she had never known a kind thing to fall. And even in his last moments, Temsa had put it to work, wheedling a way to save his skin.

'My, my,' said one of the sisters. Ani didn't care which one. Caltro Basalt was staring at her with a mixture of shock and happiness. She rested her wet axe on the marble and raised her chin.

'That's saved you a job, I imagine,' Ani said.

'We have clearly misjudged you, Miss Jexebel. We thought you had little aspiration for anything except severing heads,' said the sister.

'Which you do expertly, it must be said,' said the other.

Ani snorted. 'I think you've judged me well enough. I have no aspirations for any of this. Temsa paid me well enough to fight for him, but in the end, not well enough to die for him. I'd rather leave you all to it and walk out of this tower with clean hands.'

The sisters took a step forwards, almost as one body. Caltro poked his head over their shoulders. Both ghosts wore a smile.

'And no interests in the Church, Miss Jexebel? Your axe could have plenty more work.'

Ani shook her head, sure as she had ever been, and fighting the urge to spit on their robes. Of all times, now was the time for restraint. 'A tavern is what Temsa should have stuck with, and I think that'll do just fine for me. I want a quiet life, if that's such a thing in this fucking city. I want no part of this. And you can keep your smart-mouthed locksmith for all I care.'

The pause was heavily pregnant. Ani raised her axe to hold it below its double blade, blood still dripping from its notched edges. 'Well, have we a deal? Or does my axe need to do some more work?'

At the foot of the dais, Danib tensed.

Her heart beat like a battle drum as she turned the copper edge of the axe towards them. Her eyes crept to Danib again, hoping he wouldn't move any further. She had always wondered about fighting the big monster, old Ironjaw, and how many pieces they would have to carve from each other to find a winner. Perhaps it was finally time to find out.

It felt like a week passed before Liria waved her hand. The squeak of the opening doors set Ani's boots moving, slowly, as she cautiously watched the shades in the alcoves. She tried to hold back the sigh of relief that threatened to burst from her.

Temsa's soldiers moved with her, sweating more profusely now even though their freedom had been granted. A few jogged, not trusting the Cult to keep their word. As it turned out, Ani was the last to leave, and with one last nod, she closed the doors with a bang, shutting all of Temsa's idiocy and trouble behind her. For good.

Ani Jexebel wiped her hands on her sleeve and, with a satisfied sigh, sheathed her bloody axe.

'AND NOW?' I ASKED, UNABLE to tear my eyes away from Temsa's headless corpse. The severed neck was still pumping blood, but it was a gurgle now, instead of the fountain it had sprayed earlier. I couldn't quite see his face, but the sight of it detached from his neck was pleasant enough. Enough for a gruesome scene, at least.

The rabid wolf was dead. All of his spite, his cruelty and his foul ambition had been paid for with the swing of an axe. The only taint to the satisfaction was that I hadn't been the one to swing it. It was an off sort of justice, like seeing a tree fall on a thief as he flees.

'He will be bound and presented,' Liria said softly, her eyes also fixed on Temsa.

'A present for the princess,' said Serek Boon, clapping a soft blue hand on my shoulder. 'So you're the one everyone has been talking about, eh? Those in the know, that is. You're going to make us proud.'

I immediately didn't like this fellow, with his gaudy chains, sheer silk, and permanent air of smugness and entitlement. It was a trait I found in most politicians: they made it so very easy for me to hate them. The glowing hound sitting at his heels, however, was infinitely more interesting. A phantom, I'd heard the sisters call it.

'When do we go to the Piercer?' I asked the sisters, ignoring the serek.

'Tomorrow,' said Yaridin, already guiding me off the dais. 'As for you, Caltro, tonight you rest. A final gift of the evening. We will show you to quarters, and you are free to read, to explore the Cathedral, or simply to rest, and think.'

'You spoil me,' I said. I gave one last look to Temsa's head as I trod the shadows between the columns. I could see his face now, staring up at a long-gone Ani Jexebel. It wasn't hatred in his eyes, for once, but fear, surprise, and disbelief. Perhaps even a hint of sorrow.

I wondered how being a half-life would sit with the twisted old soulstealer. In the morning, I would find out. I rubbed my cold hands together as I walked from the chamber.

CHAPTER 15
PROBLEMS

I tell you again, there is something being built beneath some of the major avenues! Look at the facts, damn you! I have reports of subsidence from a tavern and a jeweller on the Avenue of Oshirim. Others have complained of noises, or of shades moving carts of earth in the middle of the night. Why won't you investigate this matter? I demand answers!

AN EXCERPT FROM LETTERS REPEATEDLY SENT TO THE CHAMBER OF THE GRAND BUILDER IN 994

THE ARMOURED SHUTTERS SUFFOCATED EVERY room in the royal levels. They covered the peak of the Cloudpiercer in sheets of copper and iron. Arrow slits were the only way sunlight penetrated the gloom they cast. Shafts of yellow light speared the pinstripe metal and marble floors at sharp angles. Dust motes danced on the precious breezes they let in.

Royal Guard and shade soldiers in full armour stood at every doorway, every stairwell, every junction, and even in the more precious or private of rooms. They were armed to the teeth, with short spears, swords and hatchets. Shade triggermen in scale mail stood in silent formations along balconies, or waited behind covered peepholes. Not a single eye amongst them left the sky.

The Sanctuary had ranks of guards standing before it, clogging up the grand corridor like a cork in a wineskin. A rather fearsome cork at that, bristling with hooked lances and spiked shields. The empress's chambers, although empty, had a similar treatment. The guards around Sisine's chambers accounted for a good quarter of the fighters occupying the top floors of the Piercer.

There was a fetid silence about the royal chambers. They were unnaturally empty, with most of the house-shades sent to lower, less important levels. The Cloud Court remained vacant of its sereks, and those that lived in the Cloudpiercer had retreated to other towers, or those of allies. The air behind the building's armour was taut as well as stuffy. An uncomfortable silence hung between the soldiers and guards. Every cough and shuffle reverberated around the pristine marble corridors. It brought about a sense of dread, not confident readiness.

Sisine sensed it. Curse it though she might, anxiety stuck in her mind like a splinter.

The sand fell begrudgingly through the hourglasses spread about Sisine's chambers. Waiting for the hours to pass was a depressing pastime. Watching an hourglass closely enough made moments feel like they were being dragged through molasses.

Sitting still had never been one of Sisine's virtues, ever since running through these marble corridors as a child with minders and nurses scurrying behind her. She was trying it now, and finding it altogether tiresome. Her chambers had been roamed and paced to death, and as General Hasheti had strongly suggested that she not roam the balconies, one of her sitting rooms would have to suffice.

Sisine had chosen one with the shelves full of scrolls. An old hiding place before her tutors had begun to drag her from games and into adulthood. She had never liked the smell of the place, and it had only increased with the years. She didn't like it now, but it was distracting enough. Sisine drank in the musty smell with relish.

Some of the scrolls looked familiar. Their labels or cases had certain colours, or strange glyphs, that tickled her memory. Sensing another distraction, Sisine pushed herself from the opulent couch and went to the nearest shelf. She wrinkled her nose at the dust, and let her fingers walk over the familiar scrolls, remembering their titles.

Emperor Phaera's Legacy.

Ruling Houses of Araxes Years 566-760.

Notable Successions & Assassinations.

Proverbs on Ruling a Half-Dead Kingdom.

The Tenets of the Bound Dead.

Whether there were answers to her mood – perhaps even her problems – in these scrolls and parchments, she didn't care. Sisine hadn't the inclination to waste her time looking. She had been schooled in this literature a long time ago. Whatever was in her mind now was a product of the tutors and their droning. These were the scrolls of a child. A juvenile. She was above such things. She was an empress-in-waiting.

And wait she had.

Patiently so, ever since she had learnt her place in the order of Araxes at the tender age of six. *Where else is one supposed to ascend to in life when they are born only a handful of murders from the top?*

She reached for a parchment off the shelf. *The Tenets of the Bound Dead.* A simple, decorated page listing the Tenets in fancy, ancient glyphs. Sisine squinted, reading them silently. They were such simple words to define a kingdom as vast as the Arc. Perhaps the whole of the Far Reaches, in time. Certainly during her time. Perhaps then she could call herself an empress, instead of a princess.

Sisine lifted her head to the high shelves, and wondered how many scrolls would be written of her conquests; how many princesses would grow learning her name, and how she had beaten a new age into the Arc.

This time, she reached for a scroll: a fat, heavy thing encrusted in dust and ink-stains. Its title read *Ruling Houses of Araxes Years 761-877.* Jerking the handle, Sisine saw the mess of names scrawled across it in the usual tentacle-like fashion scholars used to show the ever-shifting and interconnected families that had ruled the Arc. Few reigns lasted more than a smattering of years. Nine was the longest she saw in her brief reading. Here and there, families were cut off completely with no heirs, replaced by an entirely new house. The scrawl introducing each house and the circumstances of its ascendance did not interest her. Only the names.

She remembered none. Not a single name. Sisine recalled no statues or busts of these people. Barely even a silken tapestry featuring them. It was shameful, really, that none had left a mark on Araxes even as little as a hundred years ago. It made her angry that they had merely been concerned with staying alive, rather than having the guts to seize more. Even her father conducted his wars from the safety of his Sanctuary. Sisine curled her lip contemptuously.

Before she let the scroll snap shut, she spotted a familiar name. Another Sisine, thirty-second of that royal name. Dead one hundred and fifty years now, before the Talin and Renala houses reclaimed the throne through butchery. They ended up killing each other over it. The thirty-third Sisine – and a Talin Renala, too – was just a thumb's length away and born twenty years later. She had not lasted past her second birthday.

With a sneer, she threw the scroll back on the shelf and turned to face Etane as he drifted into the room. The noise of his armour had given him away.

He looked resplendent in a silver suit of plate and fine mail, polished to a gleam. The crest of the emperor was chiselled into his breastplate, alongside a dark feather symbol. A helmet hung ready at his belt, alongside a curved knife. His mighty sword Pereceph balanced on his shoulder. It had a fresh glow to it.

The same couldn't be said of Etane himself. The old shade looked as glum and bothered as Sisine felt. The distractions of the scrolls and her future faded, and doubt came crawling back in their place. She cursed him for it.

'News?'

'None, Your Wonderfulness.'

'Nothing about Widow Horix?'

'No.'

'No word from Temsa of the attack on Boon?'

'Not a peep.'

Sisine clicked her knuckles against her palm. 'Then why the fuck are you here?'

'Checking you weren't tearing your hair out, Your Magnificence.'

Sisine folded her arms behind her back, bracelets jangling, and approached him. 'Tell me, Etane, how long have you been a shade?'

'You know how long—'

'Remind me.'

Etane sighed. He was not fond of the subject. He even moved his hand up to the white scar on the right of his head, where a Renala mace had punctured it long ago.

'One hundred and twenty-six years, Princess.'

'And of that time, how long have you spent serving the royal houses?'

'One hundred and twenty-six years. Passed down from ruler to ruler. You know this.'

Sisine smiled. 'And in all that time, somehow, despite constant rebukes from however many royals, you still think it fit to speak with such cheek. You are a house-shade, Etane, not a court jester. There is a good reason my great-grandfather banned their kind.'

Etane bowed his head, whether seeking patience or forgiveness, she didn't know. 'Your mother never minded,' he said at last.

Sisine wanted to strike him, but that seemed to do little in the way of curbing his tongue. 'Don't mention my mother to me! The woman has abandoned us, and if she ever returns from Krass or wherever she has run to, she will find a very different Araxes greeting her.'

'No word from your falcon, then?'

'In all honesty, Etane, I've given up caring. She gave up her chance at the throne, and now I'll teach her the lesson of turning her back on me. Her and father. She's just lucky she escaped my knife.' Sisine patted her hip, where hung a blade encrusted in silver flowers.

'Maybe that's why she left in the first place,' mumbled Etane as he looked around at the shelves.

'Then she is a coward as well as a fool. I have greater problems to deal with. Such as your recalcitrant, oafish ways,' snarled Sisine. 'I have half a mind to throw your coin into the Nyx when I sit upon the throne, and be done with you.'

Etane met her gaze, and held it firmly. 'Then be done with it, and I'll have my freedom at last. It's been a long hundred and twenty-six years, Princess, and if I'm being honest now, I think I've earned it. So by all means, be done with me. And when the next schemer comes to claim you, the same way you are aiming for your father, I hope you regret not having me there at your side.' He drummed his gauntlets along Pereceph's blade.

'You dally with treason, shade.'

'Says the princess plotting to kill her emperor.'

Sisine was about to give him a stern lecture on the validity of forced abdication in Arctian royalty when a noise of armour came crashing through the chambers. All discussion was thrown aside. Etane placed himself between the princess and the doorway, his sword balanced across his arm and ready to stab.

'State your business!' he yelled, making the soldier skid he stopped so hard.

'A message for the empress-in-waiting, sir.' The man waggled a fine piece of parchment, littered with scrawl.

'From whom?' Etane asked, snatching it away.

'From Serek Boon.'

Sisine's hand stopped in mid-air as she reached for the message. Then she snatched it, half ripping it, and eagerly devoured every word. Then again, disbelieving it.

'OUT!' she screeched, sending the soldier sprinting.

Etane waited until the papyrus was a crumpled ball in her hands. 'Temsa?' he asked.

'He has failed me,' she said, in a voice so strangled by anger – and, though she wouldn't admit it, worry – that it came out as a whisper.

'Failed!'

'What does Boon want?'

'To hold court!' she shrieked. 'He tells me the sereks will be gathering come midday. *Tells* me! He goes on to say ambassadors of the Church would like to attend, as they have news. Not in two decades have they been allowed inside the Piercer, and this dead bastard thinks he can change the rules!' Her anger became a shrill cry, and she ripped the papyrus ball to shreds. 'That eagle-legged fuck Temsa has ruined me! How could he fail me now?'

Etane thumbed his wrinkled chin, waiting for the tantrum to end. 'Weren't you going to kill Temsa anyway? Show the city you'd caught the big bad wolf?'

'That's the point now, isn't it, you idiot shade? Now Boon can play hero all he wants. Why else summon the Cloud Court? He has stolen my plan.'

Etane had the sort of look that was normally followed by the words, 'I told you so.' Sisine cut him off before he had a chance to speak.

'Don't you fucking dare!'

She needed to pace. Then she needed to throw something across the room. Preferably at Etane.

A sealed Sanctuary. Horix stealing the locksmith. The confounded flying machine. Sisine's problems had already mounted tenfold. Now that Temsa was possibly dead and with Boon lording it over her, those problems had begun to tower over her. Sisine bared her teeth.

'Fine! We forbid the rest of the sereks to enter the Piercer! Special circumstances. Kill Boon there and then. I'll do it myself!' she spat.

'Boon will suspect that. He'll refuse.'

'Then we send a messenger to Temsa's tavern. Perhaps he escaped.'

'Fine. I'll send a runner.'

'We ignore Boon!'

'He'll just gather them elsewhere, and he'll say you're losing it. Denounce you.'

'We have the word of the emperor behind us, curse it! The Piercer is in danger!'

'So you'll hide like your father?'

Sisine lashed out at him then, hurling a scroll into his face. Etane leaned casually to the side and let it smash against the shelves behind him.

'No!' she yelled. 'I refuse.'

'Then you know what you need to do. Unless Farazar comes out of that Sanctuary to stop this, it's your blood against Boon's weight.'

Sisine scowled at the shade, stepping closer once more so she could stare at the vapours of his face, and the vicious scar across his bald skull. They barely stirred. He kept his usual blank expression, one many decades practised. 'You once belonged to the Cult, Etane. I have never forgotten that. Nor will I. You would not be serving their interests over mine, would you?'

The shade actually managed to look offended, though his tone was dry. 'No, Princess. I would not be. Not in the slightest. My best interests have always been for this family. Whoever rules it. Last time I checked, that is not the Cult.'

'Hmph,' was all Sisine had to say on the matter. Trust was not earned or built in Araxes, never mind the royal reaches of the Cloudpiercer; trust was stamped out. Trust was a weakness. Something for betrayal to work with, an open door for a thief. Confidence in oneself, coin, and power; that was what was earned and built.

Sisine shook herself, trying to forget her anxiety, and waved Etane ahead. 'Go. Prepare the guards and the Court. I want every serek checked! Every weapon confiscated. As much as a thick thread or a sharp ring, and you throw it out the nearest window. My house, my rules!' she said, breathing hard. 'And fetch Rebene, so he may answer for his uselessness.'

'As you wish, Your Worshipfulness.'

Another scroll chased him from the room.

———————◆———————

THE MOTH-EATEN CURTAIN TWITCHED as Nilith lifted its corner. Little had changed. Another phalanx of soldiers was tramping past. Its officers' voices were harsh against the hush of the streets. A handful of ghosts scurried before them, arms full of boxes and bundles. Two beggars baked in the sun that poured down between the towers, their cracked lips muttering secrets with their eyes closed.

The soldiers' heavy footsteps receded, and calm was restored. Though that was the wrong word. Calm implied peace, and there was nothing peaceful in this district. Just the marching of soldiers and a teeth-grinding, finger-tapping tension in the air. It was as if the sky had grown heavier, the air thicker. Nilith's heart hadn't stopped beating a quick-march though she'd done nothing but lie sprawled in an old shop since dawn.

She let the curtain fall, and rubbed the dust from her nose. 'Never seen this many soldiers on the streets.'

'W—what?' Heles croaked. She had been half-asleep in a pile of discarded cloaks.

'The soldiers. That's the third patrol I've seen this morning. Something's happened.'

There was a rustle as Heles changed position. 'Scrutinisers? Proctors?'

'None so far.'

'Any more red-robed ones? Cult?'

'No, and don't remind me of them. These are the emperor's soldiers. And what they're doing this far out I have no idea.'

'What?' A glowing head poked out from behind a mess of papyrus packaging in the far corner.

'You even think of attracting attention, Farazar…' Nilith didn't have any threat to back it up, but she waggled her finger anyway. After all this time on the road, she'd run out of threats to throw at him.

He mimed something foul. After almost two days of insults, both muttered and vocal, it seemed he had either accepted Nilith's plan or was biding his time. Nilith assumed the latter, just to be sure. She had already lost him once. Twice – especially here in the city – was not an option.

She took a deep breath through her nose, and immediately regretted it. The body in the other corner still reeked in the enclosed space. The old tailor's shop in which they were hiding had been abandoned some time ago; maybe left behind when profits moved elsewhere. They were still a day away from the Core Districts, and even though the buildings were growing steadily taller, there was a grime and tarnish here that would not have been tolerated in the inner districts.

On the walls of the streets, graffiti jostled with soot and dubious stains. Hiding behind the newer stone pillars and between alleys, older buildings of wood and adobe hid. These too looked half-ruined, as if they were still in the Sprawls, as if this had been a small hamlet once, a neighbour to a growing city. But Araxes had swallowed it up, crushed it, and moved on. It made Nilith sad, but somehow all the more determined. The city had not just one plague, but many, and they were all rooted in the profits of death.

The silence grew into something uncomfortable, and again Nilith lifted the edge of the curtain. The window had been smashed a long time ago, but jagged shards still clung to the sill. She checked on Anoish, tethered in the shadow of the building. He was still there, arse in the sand and eyes closed. The city had not finished spooking him, but somehow he knew the importance of what Nilith was doing, and persevered like the rest of them.

One of the beggars had keeled over, and the other was looking at him hungrily. Keeping his hands down by his side, he began to scrape a length of wood on the wall, sharpening it to a point. Nilith shook her head. Peering right let her glimpse Araxes' core; the tall crown of spires and pyramids that dwarfed the rest of the city, all gathered around the mighty Piercer. Little smoke and dust obscured the sky today, and the blue between the buildings and cobwebs of high-roads was purer than she remembered it.

Nilith gazed up at the Cloudpiercer, shading her eyes from the sun's glare and feeling a crunch in her neck as she took in its height. She hadn't looked at it for some time, instead focusing on the ground and the tiresome job of keeping her feet moving across it. It was then she saw something glinting at the Piercer's peak. Metal.

She turned to Heles. One eye stared back at her. The scrutiniser was taking her role of protector very seriously. Nilith beckoned and slowly, with much grunting, Heles extricated herself from the mouldy cloaks.

'What is it?' she murmured.

'Look at the Piercer.'

Heles took a moment to squint. 'Armour.'

'Something's wrong.' Nilith squirmed in the dust, teeth clenched. 'Deeply wrong.'

'The empress-in-waiting? Has she cracked the Sanctuary?'

'I don't know.'

While Heles kept watch, Nilith moved past her and laid a hand on the bundle beneath the window. There was a weak squawk, and Bezel reared his head from his nest of patchwork cloth. He blinked blearily.

'How are you feeling?'

'Like shit left out in the sun,' said the falcon.

'Your wound?'

Bezel clacked his beak. 'It's fine.'

'Let me look at it.'

Gingerly, Nilith reached past his razor beak and helped him extend and lift his wing. The dappled feathers of his underside, usually the colour of milk, were dark with dried blood. The wound in his side was now bereft of arrowhead, but still looked wet, but there was no pus. The only rot Nilith could smell was from Farazar's stinking body.

'Fucking sight, isn't it?' said Bezel.

'Not the healthiest thing I've ever seen,' Nilith said, grimacing. 'But you'll live.'

'Of course I'll live.'

Nilith templed her fingers, vapour against skin. 'Take it you don't feel like flying around?'

'Oh, sure. I'll just do it one-winged.' The falcon narrowed his dark eyes.

'Something's happening in the Core Districts,' she said.

Bezel lifted his head. 'What?'

Nilith kept her voice to a whisper, lest Farazar start yammering again. 'No idea. Soldiers keep coming and going. Armour's on the Piercer.'

Bezel did not look that bothered. 'I'm sure I'll find out soon,' he said with a groan.

'How so?'

He fixed her with a serious look. 'She'll summon me soon enough. You know that. Especially if she cracks the Sanctuary. Your ruse will be up, and there'll be no lies I can tell her to convince her otherwise.'

Nilith had thought of it many times. When she was either creeping through the streets at night or holing up in tailor shops, what else was there to do but worry? And she had a great many of those stored up. 'How does the summoning work? What can we do?' she asked.

'Nothing. The bell is rung a certain amount of times. Clever fucking Nyxites messed with the bond between a coin and a shade, worked the spell so it could drag a shade to it. Strangebound by name. Strangebound by fucking nature.'

'I'm sorry you've had to have her as a master.'

'I will say one thing: she kept me busy, when she remembered me. I did something of use for a change, instead of lurking on windowsills like a molester. Or having to deal with seagulls. Those birds are all shitting mad. And not to be crass, Majesty, but I miss… y'know.' He bowed his head towards his breast. 'Nobody's ever clasped their hands for the cock of a falcon. Ox, horse maybe. Shit, on most days you can't even see it.'

Perhaps it was that jester's glint in his eye, but Nilith didn't try very hard to stifle her laughter. 'Let us hope she forgets you again, at least for a while.'

'And if not?'

'If she summons you before this is done, I want you to give her a message for me. I may not get the chance.'

'And what is that?'

'Tell her I'm sorry, but she will understand once I am done.'

Bezel was incredulous. 'Really? Sorry for what, exactly? Fuck all?'

Nilith sighed. 'On this arsehole of a journey, I've come to realise that Sisine isn't my daughter. Flesh and blood, perhaps, but she is a daughter of Araxes. Of the Talin Renala house, not mine or my father's name. I could have stood against it, fought as hard as I'm fighting now, but I didn't. I am sorry for failing her. My punishment was losing her, and her heart turning cold against me. I don't expect that to change after this is all done, but at least she will know the truth, not just Farazar's lies. Tell her that.'

Bezel clacked his beak. 'Are you doing all this for her?'

'No. I do this for everyone.'

In the corner, the ghost piped up. 'You do this for yourself. Selfish cu—'

Nilith had let her whisper creep in volume. 'You shut your face, Farazar. You are the reason Sisine is like she is.'

The ghost sneered. 'Nature over nurture, wife dearest, and in that you're half to blame. Face it, Nilith, you've spent so long clinging to the old Krass princess that you did not notice you became an Arctian empress. Look at the lengths to which you've gone to get what you want. Not unlike any other tor or tal or serek or daughter in Araxes.'

Nilith turned back to Bezel, ignoring the emperor's snide words, even though they sounded far too true for her liking. 'Will you tell Sisine that?'

Bezel narrowed his eyes. 'And what of our bargain?'

'I will give you your death, Bezel, as promised.'

'Then yes, I will tell her.' The falcon clacked his beak. 'But know that I will not suffer any torture from her, if it comes to that. I owe her no allegiance.'

'Thank you.' Nilith bowed her head, understanding, but not able to ignore the motherly role of a protector. She got to her feet. 'We need to get moving.'

'Now?' Heles whispered.

'There clearly isn't any time to waste.' She looked down at Bezel. 'With whatever's going on, we shouldn't linger.'

Farazar hadn't given up. 'What's going on?'

Nilith reached for the sword she had left in the corner – the one that had dropped from the sky – and swung it at him. Part of her wasn't entirely concerned where she aimed. Part of her wanted to cut him in half, and be done with it. Go back to Krass and the white-capped mountains. It was all she had wanted, in truth, and she ached for that day to come.

Fortunately for the ghost, and for her, it slashed through the papyrus packaging and scratched a white line across his belly, but nothing more. He howled all the same, and she had to jab him again to keep him quiet. *'Careful,'* said a voice in her head, just a whisper, but Nilith knew it wasn't her conscience. She looked down at the sword, balancing its blade on her finger. She wiped some of the mist from its mottled blade with her thumb.

'You really think the middle of the day is the best time for smuggling him through the city?' Heles remarked over Farazar's groaning. Before, she would have looked uncomfortable, still trying to shrug off her loyalty to the crown and Code. But she had heard Farazar's mouth, and Nilith's plans, and she had chosen her side.

Nilith looked around at the collection of rags and torn clothing around them, then up at the wall, where more rotted on spindles. Even the curtains were looking attractive.

'We gag him. Bind him. Bundle him up. Bury him beneath a load of fabric and strap him to Anoish. We're already in rags. We'll look like travelling traders and a trusty steed,' Nilith said. She paused, going over the words she had spewed out without much thought. She nodded. They didn't sound half bad.

Heles shrugged. 'It might even cover up some of the smell.'

The emperor was already up and examining the new groove in his vapours, still glowing white. He looked up as the two women advanced on him, mouldy cloaks held like shields.

'How dare you!'

A SHORT WHILE LATER, TWO humble traders plied the streets with a horse, heading north into the city's gleaming core. Shuffling and heads bowed, their eyes were sharp, looking up and down the quiet streets at every junction. Their wares were piled atop their steed, looking mouldy, bleached or ragged. In some cases, all three.

Had anyone looked closely, they might have seen the shape of a sword beneath one of the women's cloaks. Looking closer, they might have seen some of the piled cloths jiggle every now and again between the horse's trotting. And if they had cocked an ear to the bundles, they might just have heard a muffled stream of cursing coming from somewhere within.

CHAPTER 16
CONTEMPT OF COURT

Upon trying to track down the smiths who
worked on Emperor Farazar's Sanctuary,
you will swiftly discover not a trace of them
has been recorded since the Sanctuary was
completed. Farazar most likely had them
destroyed once they were done, shade and all.
The vaultsmiths, the engineers, even the damn
shades that carried the bricks. All disappeared.

FROM A NOTEBOOK WRITTEN BY
EMPRESS NILITH, FOUND IN 1001

IT WAS ALL TOO SIMILAR. Disturbingly so.

I had expected more from the Cult. Some gold trim, perhaps. Marble rather than bare, cold rock smeared in dirt. Even a few more candles would have been nice. In the end, their halls of binding were no different from Temsa's sordid basements. It put a deeper chill in my vapours, and even the feeling of my half-coin under my grey robe did nothing to assuage my feeling of unease. The only reason I didn't look away was my desire to watch the binding. I had never seen the accursed process this empire revolved around.

I stood upon a bench behind a wall of scarlet cultists. They formed a line around a well of brick and wood in the floor. Judging by the inky tidemarks on its sides, it looked shallow to me. The pipes that hung over its far edge dripped rather than flowed.

Yaridin and Liria stood before the Nyxwell like the pillars of a blood-smeared doorway. On the earthen floor in front of them was the body of Boran Temsa, still clad in all his finery. At the sisters' command, red-robed binders came forward to strip the body. They were swift, practical, and there was little respect for the man. I was glad for it. *Let Temsa be treated how he treated countless others.* Hundreds. Thousands, even.

After his clothes and jewellery, there came a clang as they put aside his golden foot, its metal still covered with blood. The naked corpse was dragged to the edge of the Nyxwell, and with a casual nod from the sisters, pushed into the black waters.

There was a hiss as the body met the waters. The dark hall went silent as the binders and sisters waited. Half the crowd began to stamp their feet, unbidden by any order or timing, yet still in unison.

The moments stretched. The rest of the cultists joined in until the seconds were deep, echoing beats that filled the caverns and made my vapours tremble.

It was then that a blue hand burst from the oily surface of the Nyxwell. The binders, wearing copper-core gloves, dragged him forth, bringing the ghost of Boran Temsa back from that wailing cavern, his head firmly clenched under one arm.

I was torn whether it would have been better leaving him there, to witness what he had contributed to, or to live as the half-life he had always despised. It was no choice of mine. I was just there to watch a punishment unfold. It delighted me, in all honesty. More so than sending Kech to the void. Kech may have been a murderer, but Temsa had given him the knife. I was just jealous that many here had most likely been wronged by Temsa, and that this ceremony was not only for me. I wanted this moment all to myself. I wanted to stand over him, greeting him to his half-life with a grin.

It was comforting to see him retching and flailing, as I had done. He stared around with glowing white eyes, still dripping with black Nyxwater. There must have been fifty shades and living in that hall, and despite standing behind half of them, those searing eyes found me amongst the crowd. And how they stared. I smiled down at him while Temsa mouthed unformed words and made sounds akin to a drowning goat. Here was my justice. Here was my moment of glory. I raised my half-coin to him, dangling from my clenched fists, and let it catch the sparse light.

He raised his spare hand to point at me, slumping on his side instead. His disembodied head pulled an animalistic face, and even though his voice was not formed yet, through sheer force of will and stubbornness, he yelled at me.

'YOU!'

All eyes followed Temsa's pointing hand, landing on me. I crossed my arms.

Temsa's gaze was broken as the binders dragged him into the shadows, and half the crowd filtered away with him, like spectators following the condemned to the gallows. I was left standing there like a rock at low tide, the sisters my only company.

They both turned to me. 'Content, Caltro Basalt? Both your murderers have met their ends, and yet you don't seem pleased.'

Their knack for reading my mind prickled me. 'Somewhat.'

Liria took a step towards me. 'We have given you what you wanted.'

'You have,' I admitted.

'Now we have proven ourselves, it is down to you,' said Yaridin.

'Steel yourself, Caltro. We will all have justice soon.'

I nodded, feeling weight descend on my shoulders once again, as I had without my half-coin. Somehow, I felt trapped again. Not by binding, but by promises to gods, to the Cult. Once again, I found myself wishing Pointy was by my side. My surrogate conscience. I wondered what he would tell me now.

I was already tumbling down a pit. I decided I might as well keep falling. I pasted a smile upon my face as I looked up, and nodded to the sisters.

'Lead the way.'

HE HAD SOME NERVE, THIS Boon. Swaggering this way and that across the high-road as if he had built it with his own hands, which I highly doubted. He walked with the Enlightened Sisters at the head of our column. I could see his jaw yapping, but the wind brought me no words. Liria and Yaridin didn't appear to be in the most conversational of moods today.

I could at least distract myself from Boon's pompousness by looking around. It was hard, with the ranks of armoured ghosts around me, but I had never been on a high-road before, and I was determined to make the most of it.

Between the dead soldiers, clad in either red or polished gold, the narrow road was edged with thick stone blocks. They rose and fell like a row of teeth, and between them, I could look down into the streets, or over the multitude of rooftops spread below us. Several other high-roads brushed them, or used them as columns: the rich, literally treading on the heads of the poor to cross the streets.

Below, I saw how empty the thoroughfares were. I remembered being pressed and harried down there. Now, I would have had to first find a crowd, and then jump into it. Nobody besides soldiers or black-clad scrutinisers stood or moved in groups larger than a handful. Everybody hurried, the living most of all, what scant few there were amongst the smattering of ghosts. Any armoured carriages that plied the dusty flagstones moved at full gallop, daring anybody to get in their path.

The towers above us seemed a little closer, but not by much. I was craning my neck to stare at them when I realised our high-road had reached one.

I heard Boon's call over the clanking of armour and the ruffle of the breeze. 'Serek Moreph! A pleasure to see you well.'

'What is all this about, Boon?' bellowed a rotund man, so surrounded by spears and dark grey armour he looked like a fern. 'I was happier behind my walls. And you've brought an army with you. And the Cult of Sesh, I see.'

'It is a joyous day, Moreph. You will see shortly.'

With his neck-fat jiggling over his necklaces of gold and silver, Moreph made an effort to see past the guards and cultists. I met his eyes, but he didn't see me beneath my hood.

'Fine! But after you, Boon,' he said.

'I know the etiquette, Serek.'

The Cult and Boon's guards moved past the tower and onto the next high-road. Moreph's guards waited for us to pass before joining the parade to the Piercer. They kept a good distance, however.

The same happened at the next junction. A woman covered in a gown of peacock feathers remarked on the Cult before waving Boon and Moreph forwards to the Piercer.

I had never seen the almighty tower so close before. The crown of Araxes. The spire to end all spires. It boggled the mind, it was so tall. Standing at its feet, staring up at the violently sloping walls, I became convinced it didn't have a top, and kept going into the heavens. It was true that you could build anything with an endless workforce of the dead, but the Piercer had me wondering if the gods had a hand in its construction.

It was pointless counting the windows or balconies. Far enough up, they became specks that blurred into one. I could see the ages in the building, though. Decades, centuries even, and the ambitions of all the kings and queens that had sat atop it were written into the tower in the colour and fineness of its stone. At its base, where a mighty pyramid gave the Piercer stability, great arches reached up for our high-road. One rose so high it swallowed it, and the thoroughfare disappeared inside. The flagstone courtyards below us would have been thriving on any other day, I imagined. Great statues of rulers and heroes stood in alcoves around its majestic walls, keeping guard. Here and there, where someone of history had fallen out of favour, their head was missing, leaving an alabaster stump.

I would have entered that way, had I made my meeting with Etane and the empress-in-waiting. Had Kech not seen it worth a coin or two to murder me. I was now weeks late, but finally I was entering the Cloudpiercer, and meeting those who had called me here in the first place. After all I'd been through, I didn't know whether to curse them for summoning me, or my greed for accepting.

My eyes adjusted slowly from the bright sunlight to the gloom of a vast interior. A long hall greeted us, along with phalanxes of Royal Guards, living and ghost alike. Their spears were lowered, and a steel corridor escorted us inwards. Behind our welcomers were thick square columns painted with glyphs and stick-legged figures acting out events old and forgotten. I tried to read their stories as we walked onwards. Whale-oil lamps hung in clusters where the drawings stopped.

The boots of the soldiers and guards around us became a deafening, rolling thunder. It felt as if we were marching to battle, not a court. Not that I had ever done such a thing, of course. I'm not a complete idiot.

We came to a wide-open circle where other long halls met us, and other sereks and guards waited around a vast column reaching up into a marble and gold dome. Shafts of sunlight fell through great slits high up in the walls.

Each serek looked as pompous as the next. The thief in me eyed their gold and silver baubles: nose rings and earrings, bracelets, necklaces, circlets, tiaras and diadems. Their kaleidoscopic silks and velvets reminded me of birds flaunting their feathers when challenged. My eyes found their guards next, and they were just another display of wealth and pride. The sea of armour sparkled silver, gold, copper and sapphire. Forests of spears belonged to ghost and living alike. Some were dressed with plumes or bristles. Others wore animal heads covered in gold leaf. Mercenaries jostled with army veterans. There were darker skinned folk from the deeper south, and pale ones from my sort of climate. No doubt there were a few Krass sellswords in that crowd of ghost, flesh and metal. My countrymen and women are famed far and wide for our brawn and ability with a blade.

A somewhat familiar ghost stood tall beside an abutment of stone that seemed to grow from the marble floor. A grizzled man with a punctured skull, heavily armoured in silver and steel. There was a dark feather etched into his breastplate. He had a rather large sword laid flat across a stone lectern. Royal guards stood four deep between us and the giant column, spears bristling. It was then I noticed doors set into it. Ghosts stood by to open them.

'You know the rules, Sereks!' yelled the ghost at the lectern. 'Trust me. Today they will be strongly enforced. Ah, Serek Boon.'

'Yes, Etane?' said Boon, not bothering to bow.

Etane. Here he was. The empress-in-waiting's right-hand ghost. The man who had sent the invitation to my doorstep. He lifted his chin, staring down at the red-robed crowd around me with an emotion I couldn't fathom. In any case, it wasn't full of trust. Once again, I wasn't recognised.

'You dare to ignore the emperor's decree and bring the Cult of Sesh into this royal house.'

'I do it in the best interests of the emperor. This is not the Cult you think you remember, Etane. This is a Church. One that has been greatly supportive and charitable in this time of tumult. You should know, after all. Were you not a member yourself, once?'

Etane held up his hand. 'This isn't your Cloud Court, Serek. A handful of the Cult may attend, but they carry no weapons, understand?'

'Etane—'

'That is final.'

I saw Liria and Yaridin lean closer together, sharing a whisper behind their hoods before they turned and chose their lucky few. I was brought forwards, along with four ghosts escorting another in a grey robe that had been bundled and tied up. The figure was carried past me and onwards through the ranks of soldiers. Danib came too, armoured as always, though not before leaving his greatsword with his fellow cultists. I was glad I hadn't crossed his path until now. Not up close, anyway. I wondered if he was still sore from me impaling him.

'As for the rest of you,' Etane continued. 'No house-guards. No weapons. No arguments.'

But the sereks did argue, and at length as each approached the soldiers and waiting ghosts. They stood as far apart from each other as possible, trading wary looks in between bickering about etiquette. They were stripped of anything remotely sharp, despite barely allowing the ghosts' hands to come near them.

After a lengthy process, the doors were pulled aside, and platforms with gold railings were revealed. They were expansive, and had copper-thread ropes at each corner. They sat in tall shafts slightly wider than themselves.

In groups of twenty or thirty, the sereks and their unarmed retinues entered. The concertina doors were shut behind them, but not before I saw the platform lift up. Ropes whispered, and I wondered at how many ghosts must be stationed below or above, working the great contraptions.

It took some time for the lift to reach the top of the tower and descend again. The sisters, Boon, their ghosts and I were shown to one of our own, where Royal Guards promptly followed us in. They stood around us in a square, swords half-drawn and ready, eyes narrow and glowing through their helms. I heard the low growl of Danib, standing behind me. It sounded like it was for me.

Liria and Yaridin stayed silent through the journey, watching the ghosts about them with mild interest. Boon cycled through a variety of pretentious postures and rehearsed words in quiet mutters. I tried to count the levels as we rose up. I lost count around seventy-something. The progress was smooth, if a little slow.

Finally we reached the upper reaches of the Piercer, and I found myself feeling odd. My vapours seemed ever so slightly lighter. Less dense. I was preoccupied with it until the doors were wrenched open again, and we stepped out into a corridor of marble and silver etching. If I'd thought the previous rooms opulent, I was sorely mistaken.

Although darker than I had expected, the peak of the Piercer was practically all marble and precious metals. Any plain sandstone that dared show its face was polished or painted or studded with gems. Peeking down adjoining corridors showed me windows covered with metal sheets, and rows of archers staring patiently through bright slits. Watching for Horix, no doubt. I wondered where the old bag was, and whether she had survived the Cult. The sisters had said nothing on the matter since the day I'd reclaimed my half-coin.

The corridor led us to a mighty hall with a colossal sloping ceiling of glass. Metal slats covered a good portion, but they looked makeshift, and light still flooded in. It made the stone glow yellow and the sereks' jewels and silks sparkle. They sat high above the great stretch of polished floor in tall-backed chairs, on three tiers backed by stained-glass windows. Four columns interrupted the huge space, holding the roof high above us. The towers of minor nobles could have fitted into that space with room to spare.

The Cloud Court rustled with stilted conversation. A hush fell as our entourage was led to the space between the columns. From there the sereks stared down at us, equal parts curious and fearful. Many pointed at the giant ghost behind me. The last time the Cult were in the Piercer, an emperor had died. No wonder they were all so bloody tense.

I waited with folded arms, not liking the scrutiny but thankful for my hooded robe. I could see myself starting to like this garb, and wondered why I'd always favoured coats instead of cloaks. I huffed, uncomfortable at how easy it was to forget the dead gods' words, and remember I was here to stop the Cult. I wouldn't go so far as to use 'like' or 'trust' in a sentence involving the Cult, but it certainly wasn't hatred I felt towards them, or fear.

I wondered if this was the moment I was supposed to stop. There were ten of the Cult, however. Only ten, and none looked like the Strange Ranks. There was only me. Surely not even Danib was fit to take on all of them and enact some sort of flood. The Royal Guards still surrounded us. They had multiplied in number and faced us with a ring of sharp spears. I was more prisoner than guest, but that was how Araxes worked.

On the opposite side of the Court from which we had entered, I saw a glittering entourage of royalty and soldiers approaching. Etane was at their head, his sword balanced by his side. Behind him, at the centre of the heavily armed group, dressed in pure white silk and with a crest of swan feathers and gold filigree, came Sisine Talin Renala the Thirty-Seventh. My would-have-been employer.

She was strikingly alluring, with the carved features of a royal line and skin a shade darker than most of Araxes' citizens. Her face wore a practiced look of disdain. Her lips had been painted a bold turquoise, and black paint underlined her golden eyes. Though her gaze roamed the tiers of sereks, it kept returning to Boon and the rest of us. Each time, disdain briefly turned to hatred.

With practised manoeuvres, the soldiers fanned out to merge with the Royal Guards, and expanded the circle to a ring around the nearest column. Sisine came to a halt twenty paces away, with soldiers crouched at her feet, spears raised and ready. Etane stood by her side, and rested the point of his sword on the floor. The metal chimed in the silence, emitting a faint grey mist. I was immediately drawn to the blade.

Another man was ushered forwards to stand with them. He wore formal black and grey attire, with official-looking medals pinned to his breast and intricate tattoos spread across his neck and hands. He was sweating profusely from his receded hairline. He stood to one side and waited with clasped hands.

'Speak,' said Sisine in a clear yet taut voice. She stared straight at Boon.

The serek stepped ahead of the sisters and bowed deeply. 'I see your patience is short, Your Majesty.'

'I do not take kindly to being summoned, Serek Boon. You have called this Court together. I have done you the favour of indulging you. Speak, and tell us all what is so important. I will decide what I do and do not have the patience for.'

Boon turned to his fellow sereks, arms wide and palms open. I saw the dark blue scabs of burning on them, still etched in vapour. 'I am delighted, first of all, to see you able to gather here once again. These have been dire weeks for Araxes. We have lost many tors and tals to this brutal and unknown threat, but I am even more delighted to tell you that the time of fear is finally over.'

The serek waited for the murmurs to spread and for the suspense to build. I rolled my eyes. Showmen were just that: for show.

'Our empress-in-waiting and glorious Emperor Farazar, in their wisdom, have allowed the Chamber of the Code to work with the Church of Sesh in order to make our city safer than before. Chamberlain Rebene here…' said Boon, pointing to the nervous man busy sweating a puddle on the marble.

'Y—yes, Serek?' he said, fidgeting with his hands.

'He and his scrutinisers have been fighting a losing battle for centuries. We are all aware of that. It is what gave rise to such danger in the first instance.'

Rebene somehow managed to look personally responsible.

Boon continued. 'But with the Church's help, we have managed to put an end to this campaign of violence. Last evening, my tower became the target of the infamous murderer that has brought havoc to this city. Who should come to my aid in my hour of need but the Church of Sesh? They managed to succeed where all others have failed, and were personally responsible for catching and punishing this murderer, this man responsible for every butchered tor, tal, magistrate and serek over the past weeks.'

The bundle of robes was thrust forwards at the same time as the cords on it were loosed. It slumped to a heap, wriggling awkwardly. I heard a muffled voice from within.

Boon dragged the wrappings back and a blue glow poured across the stone, turning slightly green in the sunlight. 'I present to the Cloud Court Tor Boran Temsa.'

I had seen few sights as pitiful as this one, and yet I still found it hard to feel sorry for the man.

Curled over a missing leg and his own severed head, the naked ghost of Boran Temsa slouched on the floor. A stump of a neck remained where Ani had beheaded him. Gone was the eagle claw of gold and copper. A scarred and twisted thigh remained, now drawn in faint cyan vapour instead of flesh. The mumbling was coming from Temsa as he struggled to make his fingers grab his own goggle-eyed head. I saw its lips twitch on every other word. He was a fresh shade, and barely functional yet. I knew that feeling too well.

I met Temsa's white eyes as he manhandled his head under his arm. It might have been separate from his body, but the mind in that skull was still sharp, and clearly boiling with rage. He looked half mad.

I tried to gauge Sisine's reaction. All I saw was a swallow in her slender throat. Her eyes remained unblinking, her regal pose uninterrupted. There was a slight tremble in the great crest of feathers, if I looked closely.

The empress-in-waiting stepped forwards, her guards shifting with her. She looked down at the glowing figure before her, and the disdain deepened.

'This is the man?' she asked. I knew full well she was sure it was.

Temsa mouthed something, but it was lost in the susurrus of conversation between the sereks.

Boon bowed again. 'The very same. A soulstealer, murderer, blackmailer, forger and thief. He was behind the deaths of Askeu, Yeera, Merlec, Kanus, Urma, Busk, Kheyu-Nebra, Ghoor, Finel, and countless others. The man was betrayed at the end by one of his mercenaries. Hence…' Boon gestured at the head in the crook of Temsa's elbow. It looked like it didn't want to stay in place.

'Justice has been served,' replied Sisine, half the volume gone from her voice.

'That it has, Majesty.' I saw Boon's wink as he held out a half-coin for all to witness. 'And as such, we present to you a gift to mark the occasion!'

A soldier took it for him, and passed it to Etane. The empress-in-waiting sighed as she grabbed it, turning it over and over in her hands. Her reply took some time to come.

'I recognise and acknowledge the Chamber for its work in bringing this man to justice. The emperor will be pleased. Will that be all?' Sisine asked. Nearby, Rebene wiped sweat from his forehead.

Boon deflated a little, clearly feeling his moment had been trodden on. 'Perhaps it would be proper to recognise the *Church* for what they have done, Highness?'

Many murmurs of agreement came from high above. Sisine met them with a scowl.

'A small effort, really, to repay the debt the Cult owes to this city,' she said. 'You are lucky I even tolerate your presence in this building,

Sisters.'

Liria and Yaridin both stepped forwards, flanking Boon.

'We admit the mistakes of our predecessors, Your Highness, and beg forgiveness for them. We seek nothing more than to heal this city,' said Liria.

Yaridin chirped up. 'More than simply bringing one murderer to his knees.'

'To that end, the Church of Sesh offers another gift to the empress-in-waiting.'

I had been too busy staring at Temsa, and had almost zoned out when cold and vaporous hands ushered me forwards.

Me.

Boon looked befuddled. 'We do?'

Sisine's golden gaze turned on me and I endured the full weight of her anger. I noticed other looks, too; from the sereks above; from every soldier around us. Even this chamberlain fellow stared. Etane watched me with narrowed eyes. It was an unusual and altogether disturbing feeling for a thief.

'Another gift, Boon?' asked the empress-in-waiting.

'I... It appears so, Your Highness.' The serek was looking questioningly at the sisters. They ignored him, and spoke anyway.

'A man waylaid by Temsa several weeks ago after stepping off a ship from Krass. A man of great importance to you, we understand,' said Yaridin.

Sisine examined me, from my shining neck wound to my simple grey robe. No doubt the ample belly that hid behind it. I pulled back my hood to bare my face. If they wanted to look, then fine; they could look. Let them stare at the greatest locksmith in the Reaches. I said this over and over in my mind as I felt the weight of all the attention. I remembered it being a hot, prickly feeling in life. In death it was just as prickly, but colder.

'OUT!' shrieked Sisine.

Silence and inaction answered her.

'I said get OUT! All of you! Every serek, every soldier!'

The soldiers began to file from the hall in lines. In the tiers above, others forcefully ushered the sereks from their seats and benches. There was a fair amount of grumbling and shouts, but it was hard to argue with a wall of spears, no matter how powerful your name was.

'You stay,' Sisine said to me and the members of the Cult by my side. Her guards crept closer, and I stared down at a spear blade, banded with copper, wiggling near my throat. The sisters didn't move. Only Boon protested, but Sisine ignored him. I saw in her then a darker bitterness than I had seen in Horix, perhaps even Temsa. There was a cold calculation behind those piercing eyes. I could only imagine what manner of employer she would have been. Perhaps my throat was always destined for a knife in this city. Perhaps everybody's was, eventually, the longer they stayed in Araxes. If it wasn't one of steel, it was one of betrayal and rancour. One that cut the soul instead of the flesh.

When the sereks had filed from the hall, and unseen doors had been locked, Sisine waltzed up and down her line of remaining soldiers. Ghosts, every single one of them, glowing through gold helms. Thirty still stood around her and Etane and his smoking blade. I doubted I could even lift his sword, never mind swing it with any accuracy. He was still looking at me.

'It's some game you're playing, Boon. Giving me the locksmith, for dead gods' sake. What do you hope to achieve from this?'

'It was not... I...' He flashed a fierce look to Liria, then Yaridin. They still only had eyes for the empress-in-waiting.

Liria stepped forwards, bringing her throat barely an inch from Sisine's row of spears. She clasped her hands at her waist. 'Serek Boon is a member of our Church, your Highness, but he is not a leader of it. We are, and as such, we lead it in the direction of peace, unity and prosperity. Ambition is a dangerous thing in this city, as I'm sure you are aware, but it can also be powerful. Altering. Dangerous. We have watched enough emperors and empresses of Araxes sit on the throne, and we know who displays the right kind of ambition. We see it in you, Your Majesty. You are one who does not hide herself away, but stands here, facing your problems. Allow us to remove one more for you.'

The blade sprang from her sleeve, just above her wrist. It was barely the length of a writing reed and double the width, made of a burnished copper. With a darting strike, it pierced Boon's blue cheek and kept going until it exited through his ear, causing him to convulse. With a screech and a crackle of white light, his vapours lost themselves. He trickled away, fading in the sunlight. His rich silks and ornaments fell to the floor, ownerless.

The guards closed up without a word uttered, shield meeting shield with a succession of confrontational bangs, spears forcing the sisters back. I realised my mouth was hanging agape and promptly shut it.

Liria allowed two of the guards to wrench the spring-blade from her wrist and force her to her knees. Danib grunted, but the sister held up a hand.

'Boon was of the dangerous kind, Your Highness,' she said, incredibly calmly. I would have been needing to piss had I been alive. 'He wanted the throne for himself. He thought we could promise it to him. Instead, we put our faith in somebody else. You, Highness. A better heir to the throne than Boon would have ever made. Or your mother, wherever she may be. The Cult of Seshh wants you to be remembered for a thousand years. To make Araxes, and the Arc, the greatest kingdom in the Reaches. An empire in its own right.'

Sisine weighed every word; I could see it in her eyes. The silence was long and awkward, weighed with danger. The sisters had played a gamble, leaving themselves completely at the mercy of the empress-in-waiting, and she looked far from the merciful sort. She could have clicked her fingers and had us all put to death. Except me, that is, and that took some of the chill out of the situation.

It appeared we shared the same conclusion, Sisine and I. Slaying the sisters now would be like cutting the head off a snake that had ninety-nine more heads. It would also be costly taking Danib down. I had seen her eyes creeping to the big ghost more than once. Just like Etane's.

'Why?' It was all Sisine said, in a tone colder and flatter than a slab of marble.

Yaridin answered. 'The city is sick. We need a ruler who can heal it. Boon would never have been that. You might.'

'*Might*?'

'With our help. And that is why we offer you Caltro Basalt.'

I did not like the sound of myself as something to be offered up, like a morsel of meat or cheese on a platter. I decided I wanted a say in all of this. 'I would have come sooner, but a certain somebody delayed me.' At my feet, Temsa just made an empty sound. 'The Cult were kind enough to free me from Widow Horix and bring me here.'

Sisine was looking at me as if I had laid a turd on her marble floor. 'And you'd just give him up?' she snapped. '*Him*? The locksmith everybody has been fighting over?'

I raised a hand, though I liked the compliment. 'Erm. I came here of my own free—'

Liria cut across me. 'Yes.'

'We would,' affirmed Yaridin.

'And what of this Tal Horix?'

'Dead,' Liria responded quickly. 'The last we saw of her, her flying machine was crashing into the desert, aflame.'

'You are either idiots, liars…' Sisine paused, apparently hating her next words. 'Or telling the truth.'

I heard Etane mutter something, but the princess shushed him.

Liria spread her arms. 'Despite the Code, the city and the court are not likely to accept a shade as emperor. Your mother is gone. Your father inept. Who else is there?'

A far-off shout answered her. It was barely discernible, more a noise than words, but it was loud enough to make every soul present look about.

'Etane…' Sisine began.

More shouts now, from the corridors behind us. I heard a multitude of boots sprinting across stone. Metal clangs sounded. Orders began to beat out the pace of the activity. I heard a distant, 'Loose!' come once, followed by the applause of loosed bowstrings. A great thud of a ballista, too. Royal Guards began to flood into the Court chamber once again. I saw sereks gathered outside in the corridor, flapping their hands and silken sleeves, raucous in their complaints. Sisine stayed where she was, though she let Etane step close to her, sword held like a spear.

'It's her, Majesty!' bellowed a heavily-armoured ghost amongst Sisine's guards.

No sooner had the words left his mouth than a dark shadow passed across the hall. I barely had time to look up at the sky before the Vengeance came into view, her envelope bristling with arrows and out of control. The sound of her hull colliding with the glass was ear-splitting: a deep boom that would have shamed a thunderstorm, combined with a rending shatter. As diamond shards of glass rained down, the flying machine kept going, her momentum driving her past the columns and into the sereks' seats. Chairs flew apart in splinters. Marble broke and fell in wagon-sized chunks. I clapped my hands to my ears as the *Vengeance* collided with one of the great pillars with an almighty crack.

Reeling, the craft came spinning towards us. Her envelope was in tatters now, encrusted with glass shards and leaking something that made the air ripple behind it.

Even in that moment of panic, even as I sprinted out of the way, I caught a glimpse of her through the shattered glass window. Horix, clinging on for dear life in the cockpit of her great creation, a mask of blood and madness on her face. Her grin was terrifying.

With another deafening bang, the *Vengeance* met the marble, crushing several Royal Guard to bent steel and crimson paste. One man practically exploded out of his armour. Sparks flew, and just as the craft was beginning to slow, fire bloomed over our heads. It was inexplicable: one moment the blue sky was full of shattered glass and dust. The next, a yellow firestorm billowed into the upper reaches of the hall. The remaining windows exploded with the burst of heat. Whatever was made of wood caught light immediately. The envelope of the *Vengeance* fell in smoking tatters alongside shards and cinders. As quickly as it had bloomed, the firestorm sputtered out, leaving smoke and dust to descend.

I had found my place on the floor, curled up in a ball several feet away from where the crumpled nose of the airship had come to rest. A wall was propping up my right shoulder. Abhorred by my almost-crushing, I sprang up and stumbled over the rubble to be clear of the infernal machine.

I was not the only one whose head whirled. Royal Guards tottered this way and that, picking up lost pieces of armour and broken spears, their turquoise cloaks painted white in the dust. Several bodies lay in pools of blood, impaled by enormous glass shards. A few guards were trying to form up into lines, but were too busy falling against each other. Even the soldiers pouring out of the *Vengeance* staggered this way and that.

Soldiers.

What few had escaped the guard's blades or death in the crash now set about painting the marble with more blood. Horix screeched over the tumult, bleating something about time and how it was nigh. I kept out of sight of the old witch, hunkering down behind a chunk of marble. Liria and Yaridin were standing firm with Danib in the centre of the hall. The big shade had found a sword and half a spear and was twirling them both.

In a few very short moments, the hall descended into a madness of which I had never seen the like. I didn't know where to look; whether to move or stay still; whether to holler for help or huddle down further and wait.

'Sisine!' shrieked the old widow.

The empress-in-waiting was standing behind a phalanx of guards near the back of the hall. There was blood on her brow and smeared across her white silk gown, and half her swan feathers had been torn away. There was a black gash across one cheek. 'Widow Horix!' she yelled.

The fighting found a lull as lines were drawn: Sisine on one side, Horix on the other, the Cult in the middle, and me somehow stuck in between all of them.

Wonderful, I sighed. *Just wonderful.*

CHAPTER 17
THE SANCTUARY

Took a woman aboard yesterday. Ageing, grey of
hair. Had an ex-soldier or three with her. Wise,
considering she's bound for Araxes. One a big
chap by the name of Kalim, or Kalid. Strange
thing was, she wanted to be on the ship before
anyone else and get off after everybody had
disembarked. That went for my sailors, too. Maybe
some strange tradition these Arctians have, but
fuck, they paid me enough. I was happy to oblige.

FROM A LETTER TO THE WIFE OF IRIN SVISGAR,
SKOL CAPTAIN, WRITTEN IN THE YEAR 986

HOW I ENDED UP IN Horix's arms was my own fault.
Haunting had sprung to mind easily enough, but I'd forgotten about the copper lining the breastplate of the nearby soldier. He had been too busy menacing an enemy with his spear to notice me running at him.

Across the smashed and smoking Cloud Court, a muted thud and fizz could be heard as I bounced off him and landed in the rubble. Very dignified indeed. I hadn't been trying to flee; simply to hide until all the blood had been spilt and somebody needed me to open a door. Or I could slip out unnoticed. I was still deciding.

All eyes were on me as the soldier scooped me up in a stranglehold and dragged me to Horix. There was copper in his armour all right. It was sizzling against my shoulders and enough to make me wriggle.

'Ha!' Horix barked. Her throat sounded as if she'd swallowed a bag of nails. 'The locksmith is mine!'

'You're supposed to be dead, Tal Horix!' Sisine yelled, visibly trembling with rage. She levelled a finger at the sisters in accusation. I could see in Sisine's face she had expected this day to go a completely different way. As had I. The old bat had done it again. She refused to die. I was almost impressed.

Horix smiled wickedly at the sisters. If I wasn't mistaken, there was a scowl on their faces. Temsa wriggled in the grasp of one of their shades, his head still under one arm, blinking owlishly. Horix saw him, and smirked with contempt.

'The Cult tried their best, my dear Sisine, but they made the mistake of not finishing the job. That is not the first time that has occurred.'

'How dare you…' It took a moment for the princess to compose herself. Etane was trying to whisper in her ear again, seeming urgent now, but she swatted him away. 'You will address me as Empress-in-Waiting, or Your Highness! Who do you think you are?!'

'Ahh,' Horix sighed, looking about the ruin she had made of the Court. She swaggered this way and that, taking in every inch of broken marble and crushed glass. She raised her hands to the shattered roof. 'Many years have I waited to stand in this hall again. Many years, it has been, and not much has changed. There was blood on the floor last time I was here, too.'

There was a fiendish glimmer in the widow's eyes, as if she were a witch seeing a curse take hold. I saw the sisters exchange disturbed glances.

'Who are you, curse it?' Sisine yelled again, red-faced and blood a-boil. It seemed she and I were the only ones who hadn't figured it out yet.

Horix played offended, though I could see the grin hiding beneath. She shook her head, standing as tall as her crooked frame allowed. 'I'm disappointed, Sisine. You should listen to Etane. Why, don't you recognise your own grandmother? Shame on you. It has only been… what? Some twenty years?'

Sisine's shaking stopped.

Etane ceased his pawing, rolling his eyes.

The sisters raised their chins.

My mouth fell open a fraction, maybe two, and struggled to rise back up. *The old bat used to be an empress.* The depth of her patience was highly impressive, in a dark and insidious way. The smoking ruins of Sisine's Cloud Court took on a profounder meaning.

The widow's torn black skirts, wet with blood, dragged across the rubble as she swaggered forwards, painting ugly, random smears behind her. She took six paces, and stamped her foot.

'HERE!' Horix cawed. 'Here is where your father – my fuckwit of a son – decided to make his name. Butchered my husband Milizan in front of his throne, with the Cult looking on, all agape and useless. A fair claim, if not a necessary one. Milizan was losing his mind to the ideals of Sesh.' She spat the name like a grape seed. 'But the male Talin Renalas have always been lacking in the department of the mind, and my own son Farazar saw fit to banish me, didn't he? To the very edges of the Far Reaches, where sand is a thing of dream, and ice dominates all. He banished me! The very mother who raised him on her own teat, instead of some wheedling wet-nurse! I should have struck my son over the head and let his body crumple over his father's, and dragged them both to the Grand Nyxwell myself. He was a snivelling brat then, and as an emperor, waging war from his tower, he is no different! My son hides even now, does he not? Even though he must have sensed my arrival in his precious Sanctuary. You ask who I am, Granddaughter? You, who would follow in his footsteps?' Horix curled her lip. 'I have watched you for years. You are undeserving. You are unworthy. You're a snivelling quim if ever I saw one!'

I fought not to whistle. I felt the sting in that and I had been a bystander. A non-consenting one, but still. The room bristled. Sisine began to shake again, her shock overcome by rage.

Horix beat her chest. 'I am Hirana Ash Renala, widow of Emperor Milizan Talin Renala the Fifteenth, and I have come to claim what is rightfully mine!' she yelled.

I preferred Horix. It was less of a mouthful.

To Sisine's credit, she didn't let her grandmother steal the light for long. She waded through the rubble, arms wide and fists clenched. 'Your time is long past, old hag! My father no doubt saw the wickedness in you and decided to save the kingdom from it! It is *my* time to rule! *My* birthright! *My* future, not yours!'

Horix—Hirana was laughing. I saw a new side of this woman, no longer the widow I had known. It was as if I had always known her in shadow, and she had just stepped into a sunbeam. It didn't make her glow, or gleam, but highlighted just how deep the crags and scars were. I had fought for my freedom for barely a month. Here was a woman who had fought for twenty years to stand here, and have her day in the sun.

'Is that so?' she asked.

Before I knew it, she was marching back to me. Hirana pawed at my half-coin with her talon-like fingers, managing to pry it away from me despite my avid struggling and foul-mouthed protests. She held it up for all to see, dangling on its broken chain. I could have murdered her right there and then, just for how fleeting she had made my freedom. She took my coin as I had taken it from her. The soldier held me tight, even waggling a knife in my face.

'I own the locksmith now!' Hirana shouted.

Fuck it. I shot a desperate look to the sisters, Sisine, even Danib, but none of them moved a muscle, until Enlightened Sister Liria held up a blue hand.

'Calm, Empress Hirana.'

'Calm? This is no time for calm.' Hirana put her arm around me, and the knife to my already savaged neck. 'I'll kill him, and neither of us will have the throne,' she threatened.

'Then how will you open the Sanctuary, *Grandmother?*' Sisine said, with all the spite in the world.

Hirana pouted, veins in her crinkled old forehead throbbing as she thought. She stared about, counting, weighing, listening to the sounds of reinforcements gradually stacking up beyond the doors.

'A temporary truce, then,' she suggested, words as bitter as dirt. 'When he is of no importance any more, then we can decide.'

Charming, I thought, at the coldness of that statement. 'Any more' had such a sharp and murderous ring to it. I had been so keen to tackle the Sanctuary, I hadn't considered my worth and freedom after I had cracked it. Or if I couldn't. All I had was a thin promise from the sisters, and after their ploy, it had just gotten thinner. I wanted to gulp.

Etane leaned into Sisine's ear while Yaridin and Liria shared a long and silent stare with each other.

Hirana soon ran out of patience. 'I'm waiting! Or shall we decide here and now? With swords and spears?'

At her words, Hirana's remaining soldiers banged their spears on the ground in perfect unison. I always found it surprising that when a soldier was faced with a very slim chance of surviving, often they would not cower, but instead rise up and embrace the berserker. I had seen it with drunks, half-beaten to a pulp in an alley, or in taverns when a pickpocket is caught and chased. Extraordinary things will happen at extraordinary times, and the day you die is far from ordinary, even if it's the second time you're dying.

Sisine took some time replying. I could almost see the hatred and anger fighting to burst from her, but to her credit, she restrained herself. 'Truce,' she hissed, looking to the Cult.

'Truce,' chimed the sisters. Beside them, Danib threw down his half a spear. 'Though we stand with the empress-in-waiting.'

Without another word, the three sides knitted together into tight bundles of steel and sharp edges. Like dancers with plague, they circled around each other, remaining as far apart as possible, until they had reached the doors.

Sisine went first, still too untrusting of the Cult ghosts to have them walk anywhere near her, especially now they had picked up discarded blades. Then came Hirana, and then the Cult. With open mouths, the Royal Guard reinforcements watched the strange procession of enemies filter out of the door, one by one. I would have shared their amazement if I didn't still have a knife to my throat. Sisine ordered the guards back down the hallway as per Hirana's threats. Etane shoved those too confused to remember where their legs were. The empress-in-waiting was still in charge, at least for now.

Every now and again, a spear would touch and everybody would freeze, swapping wary glances. The tension was unbearable. Flesh and vapour prickled under armour. Like duelling crabs, we edged along the corridors and up several floors into the peak of the Cloudpiercer.

'You thought you could escape me and leave me for dead, didn't you, Caltro?' Hirana whispered in my ear. 'Tough luck.'

I had no fear of or respect for her by this point, and therefore cheek was all that remained. I remembered how much she enjoyed it. 'And you thought you could fly in here and take the throne with no trouble, *Horix*. How's that going?'

Her blade nicked my throat and pain shot across my shoulders.

'Guess you'd better open the Sanctuary and find out.'

When I could, I looked to the Cult's glowing, red-robed formation. I always found at least one of the sisters meeting my eye. They were blank as virgin papyrus, but they seemed to beg trust. I begrudgingly, or rather hopefully, gave it to them.

It took an age for the standoff to extricate itself from the crowds of Royal Guards, and climb the stairwells to the uppermost levels of the Cloudpiercer. At long last, we came to a long, empty corridor that held the Sanctuary at its end. With an intoxicating mixture of excitement and trepidation running through me, I stared at the large, ornate wooden door set deep into the sandstone, and itched to know what lay beyond. So confident was Farazar in the vault's construction that he had just a handful of guards to watch his Sanctuary. Four soldiers in full battle armour, bright gold and turquoise, stood before it. They looked somewhat perturbed to find such a varied horde gathered at their post. Their spears were low and pointed at us, and I had to credit the soldiers for how steady they held them.

My practised eyes were already looking for keyholes amidst the lacquered wood, copper and gold filigree, but I found only handles instead. It was purely ceremonial. I stared at its foreign carvings, wondering who was special enough to be emblazoned on the emperor's door.

'Move,' ordered Sisine.

The tallest of the emperor's soldiers spoke up, voice cracking. They had seen the size of Danib, blocking out most of the sunlight in the grand hallway. 'We cannot move for any order but the emperor's,' he proclaimed.

'I am the empress-in-waiting.'

'We cannot move,' the soldier repeated, evidently wishing he could.

'Allow us,' said Liria. Danib stretched his arms, to a grinding of steel plates.

'No. Etane,' Sisine said, and with a sigh, her house-shade raised his sword.

'Unavoidable, chaps,' he told them as he closed the gap between us and the Royal Guard.

'Stay back!' the soldier yelled as the ghost started to weave his giant sword in sweeping arcs. The blade looked vaguely familiar, a mix of grey steel and obsidian, and with silver on its handle. The sword must have been five feet long, but Etane made it look as weightless as a breadstick. Mist emanated from the blade, curling around the crossguards and over Etane's gauntlet, mixing with his vapours.

Etane was as spry as he was merciless. The first soldier came at him, shield up and spear flat, jabbing rapidly. Etane lunged beneath the spear thrust and brought his sword up under the shield, cutting the legs from beneath the man. He fell with a scream, painting the white marble with blood.

The next soldier leapt high, hoping to skewer Etane, but the ghost sidestepped and swung the blade behind him as the woman passed, slashing through her armoured neck.

The third guard had his spear halved, halved again, and the giant sword driven through his shield as if it were papyrus.

When only the fourth remained, he took a different approach, laying his shield and spear down and prostrating himself on the marble.

Etane tutted. 'No honour.' The huge sword came down, a thunderbolt of dark steel, and impaled the man where he lay. The sword bit into the marble with disturbing, and somewhat familiar, ease.

Wrenching it free, the ghost turned back to us, gave Danib a wry look, and sauntered back to Sisine's side.

'After you, then, Grandmother.' Sisine pointed to the door.

'Unlikely. I know your kind, snake. I birthed the reptile that spawned you. You open it. Have Caltro go in.'

I spoke up. 'Not to dampen anybody's enthusiasm, but I will need tools.'

A cloth pouch was produced from within the Cult's group and passed forwards. I was released to go and seize it, and I walked silently alone, three phalanxes of spears and shields surrounding me. The largest challenge of my life or death was in front of me, and my chances of walking away were nil. I felt a sinking feeling, one that I hadn't felt since seeing the earl's son run through by a guard's sword. It was the sense of failure, and I hadn't even seen the emperor's vault yet.

I took the pouch, pausing. I knew even without opening it. The weight was as familiar as a handshake. 'My tools?'

'Danib was kind enough to retrieve them from Temsa's tower, Caltro,' said Liria softly, making the nearby brute grunt begrudgingly.

'I thought they had been lost for good.'

'Get on with it!' yelled the widow.

My eyes returned to the door as two soldiers kicked it open. Its two halves opened with a sonorous groan, revealing a small antechamber, a solitary bench, and a gold and copper display of intricacy and design that I had never seen the like of.

I have knelt before countless doors and vaults. Keyholes, latches, bolts, levers and dials in their thousands have been broken by my fingers. There was not a design I had not studied or leafed over. In the Far Reaches, there was not a method of keeping me out besides a brick wall and no door at all. My tools were my sword and shield; time and somebody else's ingeniousness, my enemies. And yet, gazing at Farazar's Sanctuary, what little I had left of a heart sank.

It was the grandest lock I had ever laid eyes on. Just roaming over its curves and patterns made me feel like a freshpick. Gold light spilled from plated sconces set into the plain marble above the Sanctuary door, setting aglow scenes of battles and hordes of subjects prostrate before pyramids. Desert flowers unfurled across its face, wrapping around a seal of a spiked crown and a half-coin. Five holes were spread across the vault's centre in a circle, surrounded by jewels and more gold filigree. Between their points shone a fist of amber diamond.

Already, my thief's mind was going to work. My keen eyes picked out thin seams for tiny openings, likely for passing things through the door. The hinges were buried deep behind the stone and metal, both of which I judged to be at least a yard thick. Nothing had been bolted or screwed, but cast and welded with fire. There were no plates to pry free. No boxes of mechanical workings to break open.

I raced over old memories of every vault I'd ever broken. There were many, but few as worrisome as this.

'Well?' said a voice. It took me a moment to realise it was Sisine's. I felt the warm prickle of eyes again. 'Hurry up, locksmith!'

A murmur of agreement came from Hirana. Liria and Yaridin stayed silent and impassive. I walked into the antechamber to the sound of armoured feet shuffling and deep breaths being taken. Stepping around the bench, I found a large number of scrolls on the marble floor, still sealed with wax and starting to pile up.

I thought of the emperor himself, lurking behind this door. I imagined him with an ear to the metal, listening to his would-be assassins clamouring for his life. No doubt he was smug and secure in the knowledge that his Sanctuary could not be broken. That image steeled me. I adored proving others wrong. Especially the man who had locked himself up so tightly it needed me to pry him free. *Me.* The best locksmith in the Far Reaches.

Evalon Everass could go fuck herself.

I flicked open the lip of the pouch, trying to block out all the eyes peering at me. All the bated breaths. All the desire and pressure piling up at the entrance behind me. This was not about them. Nor Araxes. Nor the Reaches. This was about me and a door. It always had been, and it was now.

The gold lantern-light dimmed at the edges of my vision. Sounds heightened. I heard every sniff and impatient shuffle.

With measured movements, I pushed the scrolls aside and stood before the crest. I moved slowly, tracing my fingers across its gold surface, its patterns, its steel desert flowers. The gold was warm beneath my cold touch, and I left a gentle smear of cold mist behind on the metal and its intricate holes. They were keyholes, just as expected, belonging to keys that I had a strong suspicion were locked behind the vault's door. I probed the holes, finding their inner workings well-hidden and recessed deep behind the gold. I found another seam encircling them. I tapped the metal, I even kicked it to listen to the vibrations, and then, like glimpsing an enemy's battle plans, I realised the Sanctuary's workings. My next moments unfurled before me.

Five-key entry.

Sunken deeplocks.

Glass cylinders.

Cyclical rotating mechanism with freezing tumblers.

Encompassing master dial structure.

Shattering foul-plates.

And...

No. I should have been sweating profusely by now. I checked again, tapping here, thumping there, pressing my vapours against the metal to see where they felt cold. I stepped backwards, shivering instinctively even though I had no skin to prickle.

... and a deadlock.

I should have guessed the finest vault in the Reaches would have the finest lock known to thieves, dead or alive.

'What is it?' Hirana snapped at me.

'This vault has a deadlock.'

'So?'

'A deadlock. Don't you remember?'

'Just get on with it!' yelled the widow.

The Sanctuary was the work of not one vaultsmith, but of many. A collective genius for me to battle, and they had poured every trick they knew into it, including a deadlock. Rarer than rare, only the second I had ever encountered, yet here it was. A survivor of a simpler time, a magic before mechanisms and clockwork had taken over.

'This door will kill anyone who tries to open it without the keys,' I said in a louder voice.

Sisine huffed. 'What are you talking about, shade?'

I snapped at her over my shoulder. 'A deadlock, princess. Like I said. Half a ghost, a soul split in two, and bound into the door. It's always hungry for more, and it strips the soul out of anyone who doesn't open it right.'

'Get to work, Caltro,' said Hirana, waving her hand dismissively.

'It will kill me!'

'You don't have a choice.'

'I won't die again, just for all of your greed,' I cried out, staring at each of them.

'Then open it right, Caltro,' said Liria, impossibly calm over the hissing and cursing of granddaughter and grandmother. There was no threat in her voice, simply advice, and I took it for all it was worth. 'You are more gifted than you think.'

Fuck it, I told myself. It was a motto that had brought me this far, and I trusted in it once again.

Facing the door, letting the calm descend once more, I slid my tools from the pouch and looked at my weapons. I grasped them tightly before I began, feeling how soft their edges were against my vapours. With a series of precise movements, I snapped the tools into a long lockpick. I concentrated, closing my eyes, and held it up before me like a sword.

I started with the highest keyhole first. It was an old habit; getting the fingers working before I had to stoop and bend. As a ghost, I had nothing to warm up, only nerves to quash.

My lockpicks slid into the keyhole. I tested the tumblers. Little touches, tentative. I angled myself, driving into the door to get the measure of its absent keys. I pushed. A click came from within the metal. I bared my teeth, and pushed harder. Another click, this time permanent. Had I sweat it would already be dribbling into my eyes.

I took up another pick, working backwards against the other tumblers. Click, click, click, they went, like a blade landing blows on flesh. I had fathomed this lock now, and it fell before me within a tense half hour. With a twist, I felt the brittle glass cylinder turn. I could have roared, had there not been four more.

Before my onslaught, the next lock fell as quickly as the first. Almost as if it had wanted to be broken. It was a lie. A ruse to trip me on the third. It was a stubborn beast, armoured tumblers and all. I attacked it with miniature stabs and parries, tricking the mechanism into sticking until I could fix the rest. Five, six, seven. The tumblers were fooled, and turned into the darkness within the door with a satisfying clunk as I turned the third lock.

The fourth was a bastard, almost tripping me twice before I managed to get the feel of it. It was clever, with screwing tumblers that moved deeper with every attempt. I got the better of it in the end: a cheap shot with three picks held intricately in my cold hands. The onlookers stared on like an audience to a duel. Despite all my jiggling, cursing and imagined sweating, they were none the wiser to my struggle. It was a battle of wits where only one fighter apparently had any. For all they could see, I might as well be hammering at the door with a club. And yet the futures of all who stared hinged on me.

I let the pressure mount, using it, bending it to my will as I had always been able to. Every stare. Every tap of a foot. Every crackle of armour. I ate it all up and threw it at the fifth and final lock.

Kicking scrolls aside now, I hunkered down, raising my tools once more. My teeth were constantly bared now. A tremble had crept into my knees. This last lock postured and parried, but it was no match for my sharp picks and wrenches. I thought of the faces of Araxes that had sneered, spat or cursed me, and I put those faces on each tumbler I faced. They fell, one by one, and with a twist of my wrench, the fifth lock surrendered.

I stood up, dropping my tools at my side, and pressed my face to the door. Whispers from behind perturbed me. I didn't need noise now, but deathly silence. Only the dial remained, and its waiting deadlock.

I swore I could feel the hunger in the metal, as if I were pressed up to a cage with a wild animal within. The gold wheel under my fingers was taut, like a coiled spring. I set my shoulders and my feet square. Seizing hold of the steel flowers, I moved to turn the dial. In truth, I had no idea which way I should turn. The deeplocks' mechanisms had given me little clue to the deeper workings. The wrong way, and the deadlock might claim me. It would all be for nothing. All this time. All this struggle, and I would find myself in oblivion. Or worse, on the endless planes of the dead, howling at myself for turning right instead of left.

'Which hand does Farazar write with?' I yelled over the tense silence.

I felt a ticking beneath my hands as some despicable cog within the door turned. It was getting faster. That was not good. The deadlock was getting ready to pounce.

Hirana scoffed at me. 'What does that have to—'

'Which hand?'

Grandmother stared at granddaughter for the first time with something other than hate in their eyes. Hirana raised an eyebrow. Sisine folded her arms, eyes narrowed in thought.

'WHICH FUCKING HAND?' I bellowed.

'Left!' Sisine snapped. 'The ink is sometimes smeared on his decrees.'

I stamped my foot as I made my decision, praying to those dead gods for luck and mercy, or any other creature listening.

Clunk!

The dial jolted as its inner teeth sprang over cogs. I heard the timing cog lurch, reset. I discerned the looseness in the steel flowers; the ever so slight imbalance. Praising sloppy workmanship, I threw the dial right.

Clunk!

Once more for luck, and this time no clues came to save me. I braced myself, leaned back from the Sanctuary, and yelled a wordless noise of hope.

Clunk!

Something heavy fell to a stop within the door. *The deadlock.* I tried to drag my hands away from it, but the copper veins of the steel flowers held me fast, gluing me to the vault. I felt the metal go ice-cold. Something pulled on me, deep and hungry like an angry sea drowning a sailor. I wrenched, but still it held me tightly.

Panic set in as a ghostly face emerged from the etched kings and pyramids of old. Tendrils of dark, blue-grey vapour poured from the keyholes, swarming together until a fleshless skull grinned at me. As my hands began to sink into the metal, the skull opened its bony mouth, inches from my own, and the air rushed past me as if it inhaled.

'*Caltro!*' came a faint cry. A voice of many, entwined as one. Some I recognised. Others were strange.

Another voice whispered, so close I thought it the skull that spoke. '*It's not time.*'

'No, it fucking isn't!' I roared. I started to push, to play the deadlock at its own game. If it wanted to take me, it would have to fight me. I threw my hands into the door, feeling cold metal scrape past me. I felt the soul trapped there, and all the years it had spent hungry. I saw it now: misshapen and angry. I knew its pain, and for a moment I shared its place in the door. I haunted it. I saw the skull in a cramped darkness, its empty jaw hanging agape as I wrenched myself free.

The first thing I realised was that I was on the marble, sprawled on old scrolls and with my head propped up against the bench. In front of me, the etched steel and copper flowers were collapsing in on themselves in mechanical stutters. A metal whirring and clanking accompanied their strange death. There was a resounding boom, and the Sanctuary door parted down the middle with a puff of dust. A seam so fine I hadn't even noticed it opened up, revealing the thickness of the door. Almost two yards, just as I'd guessed. The two slabs of the door swung open gradually.

Exhausted, I remained sprawled as others crammed into the ante-chamber. The Cult hung back in the corridor. Behind me, Etane jostled with Hirana's spears as the empress-in-waiting and the widow fought to be the first into the Sanctuary. Although their eyes were hungry to see the gold and copper slabs swing open, I saw the looks they gave me. They weren't congratulatory, or thankful. More like I had soiled myself while fighting the door. I was a tool that had served its purpose. I couldn't have cared less. I just patted my vapours, happy to be whole. Only Temsa looked at me, as I had found him often doing since being hauled from the Nyx. I'd never had to make eye contact with a detached head before, and it was an experience I was immediately not fond of. He wore a permanent scowl. If he broke his stare, it was to leer at the Enlightened Sisters, or Danib.

Hirana and Sisine took their places on either side of the chamber, enclosed behind walls of spears and armour. A thin band of light had now appeared in the doorway. I could almost hear the crunching of jaws and molars as the historic moment came to pass.

Through the widening gap, I spied ornate cream and yellow marble. Gold-leaf frescoes. Silks so fine and sheer they looked like sunbeams draped over the white columns. Sloping walls coming to a golden dome. A hundred rubies and emeralds outlining the constellations. Far in the distance, I saw a bed with pure white linens lying unmade.

'Your time of reckoning has come, Father!' Sisine shrieked, voice echoing loudly. She had taken a sword from one of her soldiers and waved it above her head.

Not to be outdone by a Renala a quarter of her age, Hirana also raised her voice. 'Prepare yourself, Farazar!'

I felt the air in the chamber lessen as deep breaths were taken, and held. The Sanctuary doors yawned wide, and with a heavy thud, they came to rest. A wide gap flanked by yards of heavy gold beckoned us in. The expanse of marble was vast. I could make out the shape of the Piercer's pinnacle in the angle of the walls. Thin windows, rough and bevelled so as to be translucent, sat in deep hollows of thick stone. Dappled sunlight poured through them. But most interesting of all was that the Sanctuary was bereft of movement. No house-ghosts. No pompous emperor. Nothing.

Until a faint shuffling was heard. Spears were thrust into the doorway, ready. Hirana and Sisine stood almost side by side at the doorway, Etane between them. All their weapons were raised, but they were unnecessary. I had already spied the faint sapphire glow on the marble.

'Father!'

'Show yourself!'

An aged ghost appeared behind the doors and immediately collapsed to his knees. He was bald and sported more wrinkles than a leather wineskin, now just dark lines in his blue vapour. A simple grey linen robe hung from his shoulders to his sandaled feet, and a golden feather was emblazoned on his breast. His glow was weak, pale like twilight. I saw no wound other than the tail of a white scar running from his ear down below his collar.

The ghost spread his palms flat to the marble, mumbling unintelligible nothings into the floor – prayers or apologies, I didn't know.

Hirana and Sisine strode inwards, racing each other. They stood either side of the prostrated ghost, eager soldiers at their backs.

The widow seized the ghost by the sleeve and hauled him upright. Sisine menaced the sword close to his face. He whimpered quietly. I found vaporous hands lifting me up, and the sisters at my elbows. With them, we walked into the Sanctuary. The deep cold of Danib wafted over me from behind, and somehow, I felt safer in the shadow of that great beast.

I looked on as the ghost was interrogated.

'Who are you?'

'Where is my father?!'

The ghost was too busy trying to manage his quivering lips. He looked terrified.

'Find the emperor!' Sisine bellowed, and her soldiers began to tear the room apart. Cushion feathers rained. Shards of goblets and decanters skittered over the floor. Silver-leaf chests and mahogany closets were hacked open, and the thief in me shed a private and imaginary tear at the loot going to waste. Once more, I'd cheated locks for nothing.

That was when I noticed the small mounds of food: plates covered in dried smears and leftover morsels in varying stages of rotting. A months' worth at least. I understood now the spectators' deep breaths. There must have been a stench in the air.

'Nothing, Your Majesty!' came the holler.

Etane rested his sword on his shoulder with a clang. 'Empress-in-Waiting, I—'

'Not now, shade!' Sisine berated him. 'Speak! Who are you?'

But Etane would not be silenced. 'He is Balshep. Farazar's house-shade. He tended my family when I was but a boy.'

Showing strength I didn't know she had, Hirana lifted Balshep up off the floor, her claws around his collar now. He flinched away as she dug in with her cracked copper nails. I could have sworn I saw some crimson in those grey cheeks of hers. That old fire in her eyes had not died, but grown into a storm.

'I vaguely recall you now. Explain yourself! Where is my son?' she said.

Etane struck his sword against his pauldron one more time, and the entire room flinched at the ring of it. 'He can't speak, Hirana. Your son saw to that a long time ago with a copper knife.'

Sisine waved her sword in a dangerous pattern. 'Can he write?'
Balshep nodded vigorously.

'Of course he can,' said Etane. He removed his golden helm and
threw it across the floor. I saw the deep V on his skull, etched in white.
'Who do you think has been writing the decrees for the past two years?'

A vase smashed in a distant corner of the Sanctuary, and after its
echoes had died a deathly silence remained.

Sisine's painted lips were now the ones quivering. 'This... *this* shade
has been writing the emperor's words? Can the emperor not write them
himself?' she whispered, looking around the chamber.

Etane had the audacity to smile at the rage-filled faces staring at
him. 'Not if he's hundreds of miles away in Belish.' He withdrew as he
spoke, stepping away from the two women and choosing a spot where
a sprawling golden glyph had been set into the floor. 'I'm afraid, Your
Majesticnesses, you've been looking in the wrong place all this time.'

At their stunned silence, Etane elaborated.

'About five years ago, a year after he built it, Farazar decided he'd
had enough of his precious Sanctuary. In the depths of night, he se-
cretly fled the Piercer and the city, and ensconced himself amongst the
nobility in Belish. Having a right old time, by the sounds of it. All this
time, Balshep here has been following Farazar's orders. Passing out the
emperor's decrees, keeping the food coming and going to keep suspicions
low. All of you thought Farazar was going slowly mad, staying silent in
this Sanctuary. All the while, he's whoring himself into a naked stupor
in the south. Very clever, really. For him.'

I could have applauded in that moment. Hirana and Sisine exchanged outraged looks. Both sported veins that threatened to burst any
moment. Both had lips drawn as thin as reeds. Both had eyes that burned
like forges. All this work. All this blood and sweat, and for nothing.

Etane's sword dug into the soft metal beneath his feet with a clang.

Behind me, I heard a crunch as Danib shifted his stance.

Hirana's voice was like a whetstone on steel. 'I will hunt him down.'

'No need,' said Etane. 'Empress Nilith already has.'

'What?' hissed grandmother and granddaughter in unison. I saw the nervous twitching of their fingers.

'Your mother, Sisine – your daughter-by-marriage, Hirana – has already gone to fetch him. In fact, Nilith should be returning any day now.'

I felt my vapours shrink as the heat in the room grew. Perhaps due to the boiling of Hirana's and Sisine's blood. All I did was nod, appreciating this Nilith's balls even though I had no idea who she was.

'*What?*' asked Sisine. 'Explain yourself, half-life!'

Etane's face grew stony. 'You heard me, Princess. And I am done taking orders from you. I never belonged to you.'

'How long?' asked Sisine. There was so much venom behind those words it barely sounded like a question. 'How long have you known?'

'Since before Nilith left.'

Sisine asked her next question, even though it was obvious to all. Perhaps she needed to hear it aloud to believe it. Even I was still reeling, and I hadn't just had my entire life and purpose hollowed out in front of me. 'And why tell me only now?'

'Because that was the job your mother gave me. To keep the spoiled brat away from her father's Sanctuary for as long as possible.' Etane looked around and shrugged. 'Looks like that job's about done.'

'Guards…' breathed Sisine. The sword quivered in her grip.

The spears turned from Balshep to Etane in one landslide of a moment. Step by clanking step, Sisine's Royal Guard and soldiers began to advance on him. Danib pushed past me, as if personally offended. He held a sword in each hand now. Liria and Yaridin left me behind as they backed away towards the door. For the first time, I saw genuine worry on their faces.

Etane whipped his sword up in a salute. 'Neither of you will ever lay claim to the throne. Instead, you will soon know a different Araxes, with Empress Nilith on the throne!'

A moment passed as Sisine managed to rein in her emotions enough to give her orders.

'Kill him!' she shrieked.

With a lunge, the ghost swung his huge blade, taking the tips off the first line of spears. There was barely a halt in that swing, and I realised then it was a soulblade, or something close. Cries came as the sword swiped aside shields and found gaps in armour beneath. Within moments, the Sanctuary became the opposite of its namesake.

While Sisine's guards pressed on Etane, she and the Cult also pounced on Hirana's soldiers. The old bat shrieked with rage, taking down the nearest soldiers herself with a borrowed sword before retreating to the far wall, by a window. Naturally, I did the same, choosing a nearby corner to avoid the roil of soldiers and spatters of blood. More bodies flooded past me, reinforcements eager to defend their princess. Over the helmets and plumes I saw a long blade dancing in great arcs and jabs. Wherever it went, blood or sparks followed, and cries of anguish and dying. Above it all, the ceaseless and shrill voices of Sisine and Hirana, howling for each other's deaths.

I stared over my shoulder, realising I was not remotely considered an enemy. I had been forgotten. I could slip between the ranks, haunt my way free, and put all of this behind me… if only I'd had my coin around my neck. Instead, it was once again with Horix. *Hirana*. Old habits died hardest.

There came a mighty roar as Danib and Etane finally clashed. Soldiers both royal and Cult cleared a space for it. I couldn't see much, but I saw Danib moving faster than I had ever seen, whirling and parrying, blue vapour trailing him like a shadow. Shards of metal scattered from his twin swords every time they met Etane's sharp blade. Heavy blows rained down on the smaller shade, yet Etane met every one, equally as nimble. Their weapons became wheels of silver and sparks. Not a word was spoken between them. I watched, rapt, as their duel weaved back and forth across the marble.

When one of Danib's swords was sheared away, he used his huge fists instead, striking Etane in the ribs or face whenever he danced close enough. It staggered him enough for Danib's sword to cut gashes in Etane's gold armour. But for every blow that touched him, Etane cleaved a chunk from Danib's steel plates, baring more and more blue.

The old ghost was a masterful fighter, using Danib's own momentum against him. Every lunge became a stumble, every swing an overreach. Etane's giant sword whipped back and forth, nicking arms and legs to slow his opponent.

Danib could not be slowed. If anything, he redoubled his efforts, getting the measure of Etane's feints and dodges. The huge ghost doubled back with swings, switched directions, made false jabs, all until Etane was finally caught out. An almighty kick from Danib sent him flying into a small dining table of rainbow coloured marble. With a resounding bang, Etane broke the table's back, sending rubble skittering.

Danib was relentless, marching after the downed ghost before he could get up. Etane fought valiantly from his position on his arse, taking several more inches from Danib's blade before diving between his legs. The giant sword came swinging, biting into Danib's ribs and, unfortunately for Etane, sticking there. The brute of a ghost trapped the blade with his arm and swivelled, hauling Etane back into the table and pinning him. Danib's sword came swinging, landing a vicious blow across Etane's chest, buckling his cuirass inwards. Again, the sword raised. Etane began to kick his own blade, hammering it further into

Danib's side until the ghosts were roaring with the pain and effort. Once more, Danib's sword came down, carving a length from Etane's arm with a burst of light. His cry reached the rafters as he stared at his stump of a hand. Harder and harder Etane kicked, but Danib had gripped Pereceph by its ownerless handle. He wrenched it from his side, blue mist twirling in its wake. He raised the mighty blade aloft victoriously, but before he could strike the killing blow, Etane struck him hard in the face, once, twice, three times, denting Danib's helmet.

'For Nilith! For freedom!' roared the ghost.

Danib reeled, but all it gave Etane was an extra moment to sit up and bare a mad grin at the battle raging around him. I glimpsed in his face that most elusive of expressions; the face of a man that can look upon his work, his toil, his career of decades, and say with a smile that it was done.

Pereceph came down like an axe meeting lumber, splitting Etane from the forehead to the waist. Sparks scattered as the soulblade bit into the marble. Blue vapour swirled and crackled with white light as Etane's ghost died its second death.

My attention was dragged away by a howl to my left. Hirana was baying for blood, and with the widow's orders, her soldiers pushed outwards, leaving a small vacuum between their mistress and the fighting. The red-faced old bag was framed in the light of a window, waving a sword like a banner, eyes half-popping from her head.

I bared my teeth at her, hating all the bitterness I saw in those eyes and that craggy face. I had thought her different; bold; justified, even; but I could see now she had been consumed by it. She was no better than any another iniquitous soulstealer, willing to slit any throat that got in her way.

I began to move, barging through the soldiers as best I could until I ran along the edge of the wall. Silk drapes hid me here and there as my feet pounded the marble. My eyes remained fixed on the wretched widow. The roar of battle became a dull drone. I didn't see Hirana. I saw the Horix who had put me in a sarcophagus. The widow who had tied me to a stake and left me in the sun. Whose bargains had never meant anything. The widow who had only seen me as a means to her end.

Hirana saw me coming too late. Her sword swung over my head as I rammed my shoulder into her layers of black frill. I found a bony form beneath, and I drove it forwards. Haunting was not on my mind, and yet my sheer will pushed me under her skin. Just before her back met the glass, I saw to the core of her: that black, withered heart of hers, hanging in the darkness like a rotten chestnut. I saw her years spread behind her, every one of them spent in hate and hope of vengeance. We were all the sum of our years, but also the product of what we made of them. A life spent in hate will cripple any soul, wrap it in shadow and rot it from within. As it was with Hirana. She was beyond help.

When I wrenched myself from her twisted soul, I found my hands locked on hers, with the half-coin trapped between our fists. We heaved and pulled, each fighting to shake off the other.

'Give it up, Hirana! Give me what's owed!'

'You're mine for all time now, Caltro! That will punish you for your disrespect!'

I bared my teeth, pushing once more instead of pulling. Hirana screeched as my blue hands fused with hers, and I felt the vibration of her cry in my throat. I felt shock and surprise, but more than anything, rage. It was powerful. I pressed and pressed, dragging up all the strength I had left to fight it.

'Give! It! Back!' I yelled, half in her voice, half in mine. I shoved as hard as I could manage, while plucking the half-coin from her grasp.

It worked, but it worked too well. The half-coin and chain came free of her gnarled fingers, but the haunting spell still gripped me. Hirana's fiery soul railed against me, battering against me, and my coin fell to the marble as we toppled.

A smash of glass dragged me back into sunlight, and the shards of a broken window rained down on my head. The haunting refused to let go. I was still watching through her eyes, somehow turned around and watching my grey hands grapple madly for purchase on the slick marble. My fingers left bloody smears behind as I began to slip. A screech filled my mouth. Shouts filled my ears, terror my heart, as my feet found nothing beneath them.

Nothing but several thousand feet of air.

Although I was already dead, the fear of heights lay deep in every ground-dwelling soul. In my own panic, I started to pull away from Hirana's body, trying to get back into the Sanctuary before she tumbled into space. I flexed all my strength, wrenching my blue arm from Hirana's body. It fell just short of the coin. I strained again, feeling my vapours shudder and pain pound in my head.

My finger grazed the very lip of the copper half-moon. Even in the roar of battle, I heard its gentle chime as I fumbled it across the white, polished stone. I tensed, throwing myself further, but it felt as though somebody had me by the legs. The spell seized me, hurling me back into the widow's body. Our souls duelled for dominance. Even now, with death waiting below her, she fought me. Her spite stabbed me like needlepoints.

If I cannot win, nobody will. I heard the words echo about Hirana's skull.

So be it, I told her, and gave her what she wanted.

I poured my will into her fingers, and I plucked them one by one from the lip of stone as if she were playing a harp. Just as she lost her grip, I threw myself into a mad dive for my coin, pushing everything into one act of will. At the same time, so did she. That rage refused to let go, matching my will.

Such is the way of falling that the ground's attraction doesn't snatch a person right away. It lets you hover for a moment, just to enjoy the feeling of looking down at the grave you'll soon occupy. Hirana forewent her moment, as did I. She was too busy still pawing for the glass and the soldiers' arms now poking frantically into the hot sun. Empty air was all she grabbed. I was too busy watching my half-coin disappear from view.

'Tal Horix!' I saw Colonel Omshin screaming, his eyes wide and desperate.

A scream tore from me as the earth pulled at us. I burst from the widow's chest, or she threw me out. All I knew was the rush of falling. Even though I had little weight, I fell alongside Horix. My vapours were ragged and violent in the wind. Before me, the sandstone sprawl of Araxes loomed, thundering upwards to greet us with its immovable flagstones. I wanted to scream, even though I knew deep within I would be fin—

Copper fingernails lashed my back, scoring white lines of pain across my shoulders.

She was attacking me! Even in her final moments, plummeting to her death, Hirana groped for my throat and scratched at anything else she could grab.

I tumbled, cartwheeling over and over, kicking out at her when I could. Somehow the old bat grabbed my foot, and dug her nails into my calf. I cried out, but the rushing wind stole my voice from me. I grappled with her, and we spun like a barrel in a stream until I was atop her. As the tip of a lesser spire rushed past us, I found the time to curse the Cloudpiercer's height.

Another peak of a white marble spire flew past, and seeing the blur of windows and balconies flying past intolerably close, Hirana knew the sand in her hourglass was running short. She struggled afresh, scratching my chest and face. She berated me at the top of her lungs, determined to have the final say. Her voice was still faint over the roar of air.

'Curse you, Caltro Basalt! I will have my vengeance from the grave!' Hirana cried.

'That's if there's anything left to bind!' I bellowed. 'You should have kept your end of the bargain!'

As we rocketed past a high-road, I saw Hirana's eyes widen, and heard the scream of aggravation rip from her throat. Holding her wrists as her defences crumbled, her emotions rushed through me. Her rage and frustration, but above all, her fear. She was human, after all.

We had cheated the ground long enough. The flagstones met us at terrifying speed. I felt the almighty shock through Hirana's body before I followed, a hair of a second later. I folded into the widow's body, half haunting, half pressure. The flagstones shattered, the blood sprayed, and I felt her ribs burst through my chest.

It was over in moments. The spell of falling broke so abruptly my head spun like a top. Shuddering, twitching, I burst from Hirana's smashed body and stumbled over the stone until I fell in a heap. I heard the screams, the shouts, and saw through my blurred vision the chunks of rubble around the base of a huge tower, and people running.

I had a powerful urge to do the same. I rolled to my back, feeling the warm wet of blood mingling with my naked vapours. My ghostly body could not stop trembling.

Move, Caltro. 'Move,' I said aloud.

First the knees, then my hands, and I was up, tottering like a fresh fawn but up nonetheless. I craned my neck up at the Cloudpiercer, and almost fell. Steadying myself, I could see smoke and dust pouring from its peak. Hirana and I were not the only ones to exit the Piercer the quick way. I saw black shapes flying from all sides of the tower. I reached up a hand, as if I could pull my half-coin down, but ended up making a fist instead.

I stared down at the broken Hirana, skull cracked and spilled like a pomegranate thrown against a boulder. One leg was bent entirely the wrong way. Blood seeped from every pore, filling the shattered dent she had made in the flagstones. Her gaze was bloodshot and skewed, but still gazing upwards at the Cloudpiercer, as if longing for it.

'You should have kept up your end of the bargain,' I whispered, feeling strangely wretched, as if her dying moments had leaked into my body.

One foot forward, and then the next, and within moments, I was running, leaving Hirana in the dust. I did not know where I was running to, but I ran anyway. *If only to test my legs*, as Pointy had once told me.

CHAPTER 18
OLD ENEMIES, NEW FRIENDS

Hunt 'em!
Chase 'em!
Break 'em!
Bind 'em!

ARCHAIC AND INVENTIVE
SOULSTEALER CHANT

THE TRAIL OF SMOKE COULD be seen across Araxes. The black line, stretched by the wind, was drawn east with its origins at the peak of the Cloudpiercer.

Huddled in their borrowed garb, Nilith and Heles had not seen the strange flying machine. They had barely heard its crash, so far above them and so muffled by the huge buildings around them. The streets had come alive with talk of it only moments after. Doors were unlocked. Windows unbarred. Heads poked into the street and craned upwards. Mouths came alive with talk of a machine. Of a coup. Of sorcery.

They had waded through such talk until the boom had emanated from the mighty tower, and smoke began to pour from its top. The whispers had taken on a different tone. *A coup! Sorcery!*

The streets had emptied once more. Merchant stalls were packed away. Armoured carriages sprinted homeward. Shouts and cries were chased by the clamour of doors shutting and locking, and all too quickly, Araxes fell into a strange, haunting silence.

Before long, Nilith and Heles were practically alone again, and despite the air of fear, they were glad for it. The streets had begun to get busier closer to the Core, scrutinisers and proctors more common. But with the attack on the Piercer, every soldier standing guard had run for the Core Districts. The Cult soldiers they had seen in previous districts seemed absent here. Another blessing.

They were in Yeresh District, a prosperous corner of Araxes where the almost rich had built their modest towers. It sat at the end of the Avenue of Oshirim, before dusty narrow streets became a grand flag-stone avenue.

The towers cast few shadows in the noonday sun. Nilith baked under the mounds of fabric; their musty smell had refused to burn away in the daylight. She stared up at the buildings with their sweeping balconies and grand decorations, each trying to outdo its neighbour. Half of her had missed the tight and rich press of the Core Districts, as opposed to the wide-open desert. The other half was just glad to be there.

Nilith's heart beat a fraction faster with every turn they made, every quiet junction they came to. Street names started to sound familiar. Earlier that morning, she had even recognised a bazaar she'd not visited in years, and her heart had drummed almost out of her chest. Mostly with excitement, but worry had soured it the moment smoke started billowing from her tower.

Nilith felt her ruse crumbling, felt the sand running through the hourglass faster and faster. This journey had never seemed more like a race than it did now. She put a hand up to her collar, brushing her neck with cold vapour, and clenched her numb fist instead.

'Steady, Nilith. You'll tire yourself,' said Heles, still insisting on a whisper despite the fact they were alone.

Realising she had been storming ahead, Nilith slowed her pace, and moved to stroke Anoish on the snout. He looked tired. He grumbled deep in his throat, and she patted him.

'Good horse. Not far now,' Nilith said, more to reassure herself.

'We'll pass not too far from the Chamber of the Code. I could implore Rebene for some trusted scrutinisers—'

Nilith shook her head emphatically. 'No, Heles. Nobody in this city is to be trusted, not with the emperor's body unbound and right here.' She whacked the pile of bundles and a muted curse came from beneath. 'You think seeing the Cult standing side by side with soldiers and scrutinisers is a sign we can trust the chamberlain? Something has changed in this city since I left. The risk is too great. No, we do this alone and quietly before it's too late. Am I clear?'

'Crystal, Majesty.'

Heles nodded, moving ahead like a scout. Her bruises and cuts had mostly healed, but her wrist was still broken, and there was a limp in her right leg. Nilith's wounds, however…

The empress took advantage of the lack of attention to peel back some of her wrappings. Her good fingers felt the cold almost immediately. Wrinkling her lip, she traced her collarbone until the firmness frayed away into vapour. Nilith clenched her cursed arm beneath the cloth, still feeling nothing but a memory of a muscle. She gritted her teeth until her eyes watered.

'Getting better?' asked the falcon on the horse's back. She had forgotten Bezel was there, he had been so quiet.

Brushing an escapee tear away, she shook her head. 'Of course it's not.'

'That makes two, then,' he replied with a grunt.

Nilith traded a look with those dark eyes and found them calm. There was no frustration there, or sorrow; just calm.

'A break!' she called to Heles, and they found a shady alcove in between two stout buildings. Warehouses, by the look of their ramps and wide doors. Letting Anoish free of his bundles, she dumped Farazar and his body onto the flagstones with a thump and a curse.

'Damn you, woman. Show me a little decency, if I'm going to be part of your lunatic plot, and go down in history as some patsy. Some piece of property,' he snapped.

'I see you've had some time to think in there,' scoffed Nilith. 'And it's a little too late to be worrying about the history scrolls now, husband. You should have thought of that years ago.'

Farazar shook a damning finger at her. 'You will ruin the Talin Renala line with your arrogance! Society itself will be broken. Tors and tals up in arms!'

'Good, I say,' spat Heles, leaving phlegm in the dust to make her point. She parted her wrappings and held her face up to the hot sun, eyes closed. 'About time they changed their ways.'

'I agree with my friend here. What about this city works, Farazar?' Nilith raised her arms to the towers around her. As inwardly elated as she was to be back in the city, it only reminded her of why she had left it in the first place, and travelled over a thousand miles south to fetch this wretch of an emperor. 'Look. These are fortresses, not homes. These are not streets, but gutters. Their inhabitants are not citizens, but prisoners of a society that sees them as expendable. This is no way to live.'

'The empire will collapse!' he said in a savage growl. Somehow, after this entire journey, he still hadn't learned that aggression got him nowhere but pain. He had not listened to a damn word, nor opened his eyes to any of the downtrodden around him. He clung to his noble pride, and Nilith had come to pity him for it.

'It's collapsing as we speak, you fool. I'll be saving the empire.'

Nilith shoved him back down into the cloth pile, and he got the notion of silence.

She helped Bezel down from the horse and laid him in some of the spare cloth. His eyes were now half-closed, but he was a fast healer. The blood on his makeshift bandages was dry.

'If I were you, I would have cut out that shit-brain's tongue a long time ago,' he said.

Nilith smiled. 'You mind your tongue, bird.'

'I'm a fucking falcon. I'll say what I want.' Bezel sighed to himself. 'I was wrong about you, though,' he said. 'I thought you were just another murderer, hunting for half-coins and glory. No. You're something new. Proved this old bird wrong, didn't you?'

'You're the first of many, hopefully.'

'Good luck. You'll probably need it,' he whispered. Bezel closed his eyes, settling into sleep.

'Mm,' Nilith hummed, thinking of her dream of the beldam. She traced the string and chain around her neck, clutching the copper coin and Fen's bag of powder against her chest. 'I think we'll all need it.'

She patted Bezel's wing and got to standing, catching Farazar eying the falcon from his pile of clothes, watching him carefully. Nilith frowned.

Anoish took some water from a nearby communal trough. Something nice about the city, for once. It had its beauty and conveniences, Nilith had to admit. But so did any city, and most of them didn't see murder as a national pastime. She listened to the horse's slurping as she stared up at the Piercer between a gap in two narrow spires.

Smoke still poured from its tip, a fainter grey now. There were no flames, at least that she could see. She wondered where this supposed flying machine had come from, and which sorceress or sorcerer had a hand in it. *Prince Phylar?* Surely not. How untimely that would be, for him, at least. He would find the prized Sanctuary as empty as a bad gambler's pockets.

'How far to the Grand Nyxwell, do you reckon, Heles? It feels like an age since I was in the city.'

'As the rook flies, maybe forty, fifty miles? Through the streets, avoiding certain places… sixty.'

Nilith sighed. 'That sounds like such a small number, considering all the miles behind me, and yet such a huge number at the same time.'

'It's the last stretch. That's always the hardest part, or so they say. I haven't left the Core in more than a decade.'

Nilith looked at the scrutiniser, who was staring up at the Cloudpiercer with narrowed eyes, as if blaming it for all those years.

'What made you work for the Chamber?' she asked.

Heles snorted. 'The more important question is why did I carry on working for the Chamber?' she replied, knuckling the tattoos on her jaw and the side of her head. 'Twelve years, I've given Chamberlain Rebene and your so-called emperor. But that being said, it was my father's job before mine. I was a wayward child, no proper daughter of a scrutiniser. I refused to follow in his footsteps, though he wanted it desperately for me. He used to come home stinking of shit, or covered in blood. One time he came home half-dead and I decided that night, only ten years old, that I didn't want that life. I took to trying to keep him from working. Hiding his shoes, getting in fights. Ran my mother spare, I did, but his dedication was absolute. He punished me black and blue, but he always maintained this idea I would change. That I would come right. I proved him correct, in the end, but not before being so angry with him I started a fire in the cellars beneath our hole of a building. A child's idea; it was soaked in emotion and utterly without sense. I wanted to show him he was wrong: that I would match his view of me. The fire spread to a bucket of tar-rags, and all too quickly, I couldn't stop it.' Heles eyes were glazed with memories. 'Two houses burnt. Fifteen souls in all died that night. Two families, including mine.'

'I—' Nilith began to speak, but Heles shook her head.

'Don't do that. I've had plenty of time to torture myself with those memories. I know I was scared, stupid. Young. The past is for keeping mistakes in, and that's what I did. I dodged the soulstealers and orphanages and survived the streets until I was old enough to hold a spear and guard a door. That door was in the Low Docks, and one night I'm chasing some fuckhead thief along the piers, and I run into my father, literally speaking. Stopped my heart nearly dead to see that proud face a-glow and dark from the burns. I wouldn't have recognised him if he hadn't said my name. He was bound to some stealer boss in their warehouses.'

'What did you do?'

'First thing I did was forget about the thief. Then I went to find the foreman of the warehouse and punched him right in the nose. Dragged him to his boss, stabbed them both in their guts, and then left their bodies in the gutter. Didn't wait for the scribes and their towers of claims, as I should have, but at least I gave them the justice they deserved. As for my father, him I set free. Put him out of his misery as kind as I could. Not the way of the Code perhaps, but seeing as the rest of the city bends the Code, why shouldn't I? I took a job at the nearest Chamber office and didn't look back.'

Nilith shared Heles' bitterness. Though the details were changed, it was a story she had heard many times before. And like all the others, she tucked it away in her mind. Those stories had been like bricks of a wall to her. Once, they had built a purpose; now, they shored up her reserve.

Heles continued. 'That's what made me work for the Chamber, Majesty. I swore to serve fifteen years for the fifteen innocent people I killed. Call it guilt, if you will. It might have been that at the start. Now it is duty, and I know why my father stepped out our door every day with the black uniform on. For all the other fathers and mothers, brothers, sisters, cousins and plain old fucking neighbours who don't have a choice in life or death.' The anger got the better of her, and Heles shuddered. 'You know they say there are more dead in this city than there are living?'

'I can tell you it's true,' said Nilith. 'I've seen the city charter.'

Heles shook her head, but the empress was firm.

'I looked at the charter not long before I had this grand idea of mine. It was one of the things that pushed me over the edge. This kingdom is more dead than alive, and if it doesn't stop here, the same will eventually be true of the Scatter Isles, then Krass, and Skol, and whatever lands lie beyond.'

'And that is why I bend the Code now, and choose to help you,' said the scrutiniser, as if shoring up her own reserve, and proving to herself her decision had been the right one. 'Might I ask a question?'

Nilith nodded, and Heles leaned close, conspiratorial.

'How are you going to do it?' she muttered.

Nilith shook her head. 'What do you mean?'

'The Grand Nyxwell. You're going to just throw him in? Claim him there and then?'

'I—' Nilith had thought long and hard about that very moment. 'I'll announce myself to the Nyxites. Have them protect the body while I call for the Cloud Court and Sisine. The citizens will gather to witness the crowning, as is tradition, and after Farazar is bound, I'll have my say.'

'I have to ask: what if you run out of time?'

'Then Farazar will vanish into oblivion, and Sisine will be empress. Her father made sure she stood above the rest of the Court, gave her a share of the army, too. I am empress in marriage only. But I have time.' *Though barely.*

'Then what?'

Nilith was about to answer when she heard a gasp from behind them, previously masked by Anoish's last slurps. She whirled, hands on the sword.

Bezel was in the middle of twitching, still half-asleep but rousing quickly. Soon enough his eyes were open and wide.

'She's…' The falcon paused to shake violently. His eyes scrunched up in pain. 'She's ringing the fucking bell!' he hissed.

Nilith rushed to Bezel's side. She tried to hold his wings still, but it just hurt him more. 'How many?'

'Seven? I… agh!' The falcon's beak opened wide as he cried out. 'It's been a fucking pleasure, Nilith. If I ever see you again, you owe me big, remem—'

Bezel convulsed again, and in that moment the spell began to bite. At the same time, Farazar leapt for the falcon, placing a hand on the falcon's feathers just as he was whisked into a crackling rift in the air.

'Farazar!'

The ghost's hand was dragged into the rift, somehow keeping it open. His arm began to stretch into the flashing light, pulling his shoulder and head towards it.

With a ring, the obsidian sword was brandished high aloft. The air and dust rushing around her, Nilith swung down as hard as she could manage.

———————◆——————-

SISINE BARGED INTO HER ROOM so quickly she sent her guards flying. Apologies had not passed her lips since early childhood, and she was not about to break that streak now, exhausted and covered in blood as she was.

She stormed onwards, winding deeper and deeper into her chambers until she came to her private bedroom.

The chest flew open, splintering the foot of her bed with its metal edges. Sisine snatched up the small bell and wrapped white knuckles around it.

'Mother!' she yelled, thrashing ring after ring out of the bell. *Clang, clang, clang!* Seven, eight, nine...

With a crackle, the air before her split. A sudden wind buffeted her torn and blood-washed white silks. Feathers flew at her, and as the thrashing shape of the falcon began to form, she heard a long, drawn-out wail accompany him. It sounded like her father's voice. Bezel collapsed onto her bed-linens, still somehow wrapped up in the spell. Above him, where the air was still split, a spectral hand appeared, groping for her with blue fingers. Behind it came a face Sisine recognised. It was faint, its vapours barely holding together, and it lasted but a moment before the spell broke, and the air rejoined with a wobble.

Sisine slammed the lid of the chest, staring the falcon in the eye. He looked damaged somehow, bloodied on his side, and stiff as he pulled himself up to match her stare.

'Explain yourself, bird. Where is my mother? If you've been lying to me, I—'

'Had a spot of bother, have you, Sisine?' he croaked. He had seen the blood on her. Spots of crimson still decorated her face and gold-wrapped forearms. A strand of ebony hair hung across her eyes, and she slapped it away. 'I saw the smoke, too,' he added.

'You…' She paused to wrestle her trembling lip. 'You're in the city? *They* are in the city?'

Bezel was attempting to shuffle forwards. One wing hung at an angle. His hopping steps were slow and unsure. He spoke as he approached, and Sisine saw the contempt in the curve of his beak.

'Yes, they are.'

'Yet another fucking traitor!' snarled Sisine. 'I have had my fill of those today!'

'My, my, and it's barely past noon.'

'Where is she? Where is my bitch of a mother?' She thought of the blue face, crying out to her. *My father.* 'Were you with them?!'

'Just to the north of here, in fact. Sitting comfortably in the Low Docks, right under your nose. We were just about to have lunch, in fact.'

'You despicable creature. You dare to betray me, your master?' Sisine raised her hand to cuff him, to break his little neck, when he raised a pinion feather.

'Tut tut. I wouldn't do that. She had a message for you. One she asked me to deliver should you finally open the Sanctuary and realise how stupid you've been.'

Sisine bared her teeth. 'Speak quickly then, bird. Give me Nilith's message, and then you will find out the punishment for crossing me.'

Bezel stared at her, holding his smile. He shuffled forward, coming to a halt a mere foot from her face. Sisine saw the crusted blood under his wing. She could smell the rot on him. The bird was nothing short of worthless.

He stared deep into her burning eyes, his own as black as old tar, ringed with sickly yellow and flecks of red. 'It was long-winded and frankly a little sentimental for my tastes, so I'll condense it down into the short version for you, Princess,' he said, taking a ragged breath. 'Fuck you and your dreams. Fuck you to death.'

With a piercing screech, Bezel flew for Sisine's face, wings flared and hooked talons reaching. Sisine was already reaching for his neck, a strangled roar of rage in her throat.

CHAPTER 19
SHELTER

Nothing is certain in Araxes.
Not even death.

OLD ARCTIAN PROVERB

M Y FUCKING HAND!' FARAZAR YELLED, clutching his white, fizzing stump of a wrist. Nilith had swung so hard the sword was halfway into the flagstone. She pried it free and held it to his neck.

'Go on! Finish the job!' he yelled. 'Make your journey pointless!'

Nilith found Heles' hands on her arm, and with a grunt, she shrugged herself free. Nilith thrust the sword into her belt and began to throw blanket after blanket at Farazar.

'You shut your face, ghost. Heles, we're moving on.'

'Now?' the scrutiniser asked.

Nilith fixed her with a look, daring her to protest further. 'If my daughter didn't know Farazar was gone before, she does now. And Bezel might…' Her voice cracked on the last word, and she turned away to get Anoish ready.

'Good luck, you irascible bird,' she muttered beneath her breath, as she coiled Anoish's tether about her fist.

They walked north until the sky turned the colour of burned oranges. The smoke hung in the air, like a stain of soot on silks. The docks and factories and warehouses that had woken their furnaces that day added their smog to the haze. The sun made stark silhouettes of the buildings, making jagged teeth of the towers and spires. High-roads crisscrossed the gaps like morsels stuck between them. The last rays of the day fell in red and angry bars on the streets. The light drew out their shadows, making elongated monsters of them.

Silence had been the order of the afternoon. The two women each kept to their thoughts, timed to Anoish's brisk plodding. The streets had remained mostly vacant. Horns had blared from the Piercer shortly after noon. Battle-horns, and dozens. Any guards or soldiers left in the outer districts had sprinted north at the sound of them. The horns had sounded intermittently until sunset, receding ever northwards. That was some comfort.

Thin trails of ghosts occupied some streets, where businesses and merchants couldn't stay closed any longer. No braying and charming clatter of night markets yet, with their rainbow lanterns and mishmash of music. No rattle of armoured carriages, or tramping of soldiers jogging alongside a litter. Even the beggars were few, though that may have been the quality of the district.

Street brats there were plenty of. Alive and dead, filthy or glowing faintly, they ran in flocks through the adjoining alleyways, teasing what few shades they could find. If a basket was dropped, or a satchel slipped from a shoulder, the brats would descend, thieving whatever it was they could lay their grubby paws on. They were clearly nimble enough to dodge the street-guards and mercenaries; and with few, if any, of those around, they were having a ball. Twice, they tried to rob Nilith and Heles. The first time, the scrutiniser cuffed one around the ear. The second, Nilith showed them her sword. There was not a third attempt.

The sun surrendered itself to the earth, and the horizon turned a dusty pink. The night swooped in from the east, a blanket of darkness that smothered the colours from the sky. Once again, the horns crowed. Closer this time, nearer the Cloudpiercer again. Nilith cursed that great pillar, now speckled with lanterns. It was closer than ever before, and it dominated the skyline. Against the dusk, she could see a ragged edge to its peak, though it hurt her neck to crane up at it.

'Shelter?' Heles spoke up, surprising her.

The empress shook her head. 'No. We press on.'

With that, the matter was settled. They kept their pace and their direction, though their eyes became more watchful. Darkness swallowed the city. A few lamplighters crept out to keep it at bay with whale oil and tinder. Other ghosts hurried across their path here and there, painting the flagstones blue. Ghosts with stubborn, uncaring masters. Nothing was exchanged between passersby, not a word. Not even a polite nod. Fearful glances, maybe. Everybody was an island in Araxes, and like the volcanoes of the Scatter Isles, the results were explosive when they collided.

Only once was the rule broken, and that was by a rotund man on a shiny beetle that passed them. The insect's clip-clopping on the flagstones seemed hurried. The man held on to a floppy hat with one hand, the reins with the other. He puffed a sigh from red, sweaty lips.

'Not a good time for trade, misses. I'd head back the way you came if I were you,' he advised, half-breathless.

But they did not, and they let him go by with blank looks. Nilith tried to forget him, even as the dust from his beetle's scuttling stung her eyes.

'Something's got him rattled,' muttered the scrutiniser.

'We keep moving,' Nilith said firmly.

Another hour passed, and they spent it following a winding street that led slightly west. Nilith spent it staring down at her feet, counting paces until Heles touched her arm. It was the one the ghast had poisoned, and Nilith flinched away.

The scrutiniser pointed ahead. She'd been staring up at the lofty spires, now glittering with their own lamps and candles. A high-road stretched between two of them before winding into the city. A row of torches perched on it. Tucking Anoish behind a wooden stall, Nilith and Heles peeked out from the curve of a wall. The torches wandered slightly, held by hands rather than sconces. When the night breezes played with them, they betrayed the glint of armour and spears.

'That's not good. They're hunting for something.'

'Who do you think?' Nilith said. 'We need shelter. Until they grow bored or move on.'

Heles dutifully began to limp around, poking in alleys and testing doors. This was a populous area, and what wasn't a soaring face of a building was tightly locked. A few warning shouts followed a few shoves of a shoulder on one particular door. Heles moved on.

'This way,' she said, and they took an alley onto another street, where awnings for a large soulmarket had been left over vacant, quiet stalls and pens. It was dark here; the awnings blocked starlight instead of sunlight, and no lamplighters had bothered to come here. It added more shadow to an already murky night.

Heles pointed. 'There.'

A small shop sitting on a corner had been boarded up, and poorly so. It looked as if the owner had run out of planks before they were finished. It was their own fault for having walls that were practically all archway. Wooden stools and tables sat piled up against the boards as an extra measure.

One by one, Heles and Nilith began to stack them elsewhere. The boards were pried away easily enough, and they ducked into the darkness.

It turned out to be a coffee tavern, or so Nilith thought. The proprietor's last measure had been taking away anything of worth. She saw dark rings on the stone counters where amphoras and brewing pots had recently stood. All furniture was missing. The floor was bare of carpets. Even the tapestries had been rolled up and carted off. Despite the effort, the bitter-sweet aroma of coffee still hung in the air. In one wall was a hatch leading to the next shop, and a stomach-rumbling smell of grease and pastry wafted through it.

Once the bundle of corpse and ghost had been stowed in a corner, Anoish was led inside. The boards were balanced back in place, and what little light the soulmarket had offered was shut out.

Nilith dug in her pack for tinder. She was fresh out, but Heles found a tallow candle in a drawer, so stubby it had not been worth taking. The two of them gathered around it. Nilith placed the sword on the dusty floor, more sand than stone, and sighed as she lit the candle.

'We'll move on when this is burned out,' she said, more promising herself than telling Heles.

The scrutiniser didn't seem convinced. 'You sure?'

'It'll be better later, when they're tired of looking. One more day, and I think we'll be there.'

'These rags won't hide us long out there. You—'

'We have little choice! I refuse to waste any more time!' Nilith snapped.

Heles bowed her head, clearly swallowing words. She watched the scrutiniser in the weak, flickering flame. It threw up a pillar of dark smoke, and its light was the colour of vomit. At least there *was* light.

They stared at it in a hush for what felt like an hour. Around them, the city continued its hunt. The occasional yell of an order and a distant echo of boots came floating through the boards, but that was all.

When the candle was no more than a thumb's thickness and starting to sputter, Heles spoke up again. It was no more than a whisper, but it sounded loud after straining the ears for so long.

'I'm sorry about Bezel. Though I only knew him a short while.'

'Don't be. We don't know what's become of him,' replied Nilith, her voice tight.

'You didn't get to finish what you were saying earlier. About what will happen after you bind Farazar's shade.'

'Trying to take my mind off him won't help, Scrutiniser Heles.'

Again her head bowed respectfully. Nilith saw the whiteness of her knuckles. 'Of course not, Majesty.'

Nilith stared at the candle until its light left spots dancing in her eyes. The night was warm, and under her rags, she sweated. With a growl, she started to peel them off, throwing them aside irritably until her face and head were free. She turned her nails to more, dragging the cloth from her shoulders and arms. A faint blue gleam joined the pallid light of the candle. A cold draught fell from her. She saw Heles shiver as she struggled to hold her empress's eyes.

'Look at it,' Nilith grumbled.

Heles did, her eyes creeping down to where Nilith's collar bone and bosom were being eaten away by dark tendrils of vapour; where her whole left arm glowed, black veins etched, turning to white where puncture marks showed. Nilith lifted more cloth to show her ribs, were the skin was already beginning to blacken and crack. Sapphire light shone through beneath.

'You asked what was next, should I somehow bind that bastard of an emperor?' Nilith asked. 'I don't know, that's what. I know I will say my piece, make my decrees, and then the choice is down to the city.'

'But you will be empress.'

'A dead empress if this rot doesn't slow! Damn that ghast! Damn that fucking Consortium for its meddling!' Nilith went to dash the candle from its cradle of sand, but she stopped herself. With a sigh, she said, 'There is a reason why no ghost has ever held the throne of Araxes longer than a day. The city will not stand for it. My decrees will be close to worthless.'

'They will stand for the Code.'

'Don't give me that. You're not that naive. I will be shitting on a thousand years of the Code in one fell swoop, not to mention that by freeing the shades, I remove my only claim to authority besides a crown and a throne. This doesn't end with Farazar being thrown into the Nyx.' As she said that, Nilith felt the weight of her burden triple. It was her turn to hang her head, feeling heavier than lead, not half-ghost.

Heles sniffed. 'You're not alone, Majesty.'

'Don't call me that.'

The scrutiniser thumped her fist against her thigh. 'I said you're not alone. My being here only proves that. The dead proctor, Jym? He would have fought for such a thing, too. Every fucking shade out there wants it! If you grant freedom to them, then fuck the living! You said yourself the city is more dead than alive. Be the empress of the dead!'

Nilith shook her head, but Heles pressed on.

'I've walked these blood-stained streets, same as you. I've seen the downtrodden. The beggars. The fear in the face of every tourist caught out after sunset. The lepers slitting their wrists just for release. The Code is a poison, Nilith! A plague that eats away at vapour and blood and bone alike. I'd wager it won't just be shades that will stand for you. Take away the Code and you give them hope. Even the smallest pinch of it, to a soul that has none, is reason to fight! You shrug off the title of Majesty, but you would make every fucker in this city feel like an emperor or empress. Just for a moment.'

Nilith had been measuring Heles' words carefully. As much as she wanted them to crumble and show their nonsense, they were proud and gleaming words. Truthful, and reminiscent of the same speeches she had made to a burnished silver mirror not too many months ago. She thought she had conquered the desert, but its punishing grit was still lodged in her. Not under fingernails or in her hair, but in her mind. She had survived, rather than conquered, and the weakness it had taught her clung on. Hearing Heles' words made Nilith feel as if she had been picked up and shaken out, like a sandal full of sand. It didn't rid her of all of it, for weakness is a stubborn thing, but that burden was lighter again. Enough to nod, and slide the rags back over her freezing arm. The heat of the night had done nothing for it. She heard the whine of a breeze outside the board.

'Just for a moment,' she repeated.

Heles clenched her hands in the air, as if grasping for something intangible. She bared her teeth. 'Just for a moment, and this cursed city will change. You will be far from alone.'

'You make some fine points,' Nilith relented. With a sigh, though not one so heavy as to drag her into the dust, she got to her feet. She stretched with a grimace and sheathed the sword again. 'Besides, I think I have a good idea for a distraction.' She patted her chest, where the old leather bundle of powder hung.

Heles growled affirmatively, and helped her ready Anoish and the stinking bundle. Farazar hadn't said a word all afternoon. That could have been because of the rags they'd stuffed in his mouth, but who knew? Maybe he was contemplating his behaviour.

Laying hands to the boards, Heles and Nilith shared a look. The empress tried a smile. It was an old movement, rusty like boat-chains, but satisfying.

'After you, Your Majesty,' she said.

Heles cracked a smile of her own, and she looked just as foreign to it. 'Why, thank you.'

With that, the scrutiniser ducked out beneath a board.

The tarred burlap sack came down over her head in a black blur. The butt of a dagger followed fast behind it, and with a thud, Heles went limp.

———◆———

CHASER JOBEY'S FOUL MOOD HAD not waned in days. If anything, it had only grown fouler with every step.

Inner Araxes perturbed him. He was a desert man. Sprawls-born.

He was of the entrenched opinion that so many bodies so close together in one place was not good for sanity. Even though there seemed to be a troubling quiet in the city, he was itching to be on the open roads again, hunting fresh debtors.

Once this bitch and her shade are in a cage.

The shrouded slatherghast at his side was leading him in a straight line north, but on nothing more than a faint trail. They had travelled day and night, and the creature had only given him the occasional hiss to change direction a notch or two. The ghast could scent in ways hounds only dreamed of, but this was a city of shades. Any hound would be distracted in a butcher's shop. Jobey's arm ached savagely from keeping the creature on a short leash.

More than once, Chaser Jobey had shamefully flaunted with the idea of giving up. Of finding some unsuspecting woman and shade and passing them off as the debtors. It shocked him to be considering such ideas, after all his years of impeccable service. Not since he had been fresh to the job had similar thoughts crossed his mind. Such was the frustration this woman had caused him.

A lonely gull, still riding what was left of the day's thermals, mewed above him. Jobey flinched, throwing up his hands. His sleeve caught against a scab on his eye and he cursed quietly to himself.

He was dabbing blood from his brow when the slatherghast opened its jaws wide, and let loose a disturbing gurgle. Its claws grasped at the chill air, pointing down a curving street that split off from theirs.

Jobey tugged the leash, all buckles and leather, but the ghast refused to budge.

'That way?'

A hiss.

'Are you sure?'

The ghast strained on its leash, and that was answer enough. Jobey clicked for his horse, and the beast followed dutifully. He wished he had not abandoned his wagon, but chases through the streets of Araxes were best suited to legs, not wheels.

The creature led him on, leaving a moist trail in the dust behind it. The ripped grey cloak that Jobey had wrapped it in did little to disguise the ghast's gruesome features, but nobody had looked closely enough to worry him. It seemed there were more interesting things afoot in the city. He suspected the smoking Cloudpiercer he had seen in the afternoon had something to do with it.

Another gasp from the ghast, and Jobey followed its intent gaze to another road, split off from the first. After a few minutes, it led to a vacant space that looked like a market of some kind. A soulmarket, if Jobey wasn't mistaken. He recognised the loops for manacle chains and the pens for unsold shades. Uncouth, was what it was. Chilling, if he was honest. The Consortium didn't dirty itself with the business of death and shades. It had realised a long time ago that silver, plain old silver, was better for the soul. It didn't involve giving it up for eternal servitude, for one.

The slatherghast was growing impatient. It wriggled something awful and began to gouge furrows in the sand with its blue claws. Its tendrils poked clear of its shroud. They seemed to be pointing to a certain corner. Jobey tugged the leash hard, eliciting a choking noise from the ghast. With a growl, it relented, dribbling black spit on the stones while it waited for its master to follow its suggestion.

Jobey knew ghasts well enough to know when they had picked up the scent of their almost-kill. He narrowed his eyes, trying to blink the lamplight from them. The only light was the faint glow of stars hidden behind awnings and a day's worth of smoke. At his feet, a faint blue stained the dust, emanating from the ghast's jaws. Then he saw it: a thin yellow hair of light, escaping from the boards of a shuttered shop across the market.

His heart flinched. Lost hope flourished anew. A broad smile crept across his split and scabbed lips.

'You're mine.'

Creeping closer, keeping the ghast quiet and still as best he could, he stalked the shop. At its corner, where wooden furniture had been stacked, he heard voices. Jobey strained his ears. Two women, he guessed. His nostrils held the smell of horse and rotting body.

He caught some muffled words.

'You're not alone, Majesty...' said one of the voices.

The chaser's eyes grew wide, aching at the edges. *A majesty?* He thought back to the journey from the Sprawls, while the woman had taunted him from her cage. Her demeanour had been very regal, now that he considered it... No. *It can't be.*

The voices continued, and he listened to broken remnants of the conversation. '...empress of the dead... lepers slitting wrists... Take away the Code... give them hope!'

The slatherghast whined, stealing the rest of those words away from him, but what interesting words they had been. Jobey tied the creature to a nearby column. Its work was done. The thing snapped its jaws, and he held a finger over his lips.

He heard another whisper as he moved back to the boards. 'Just a moment...'

'Just a moment.'

Jobey began to slide a tarred sack from his belt, and a pair of shackles he'd found for this very moment. His hands shook, though not with nervousness, but pleasure. There were always three stages to every chase: the letting loose, the catch, and the delivery. The catching stage was always the most gratifying and now, he was about to capture an empress. An empress who owed the Consortium a debt. Oh, how the directors would be pleased.

He tucked himself against the boards, the sack poised in his hands. He listened to the sound of a horse's hooves, and feet shuffling across flagstones. They sounded weary, and Jobey grinned in the darkness.

Voices again. Inches away. 'After you, Your Majesty.'

A shuffle of feet. Fingernails on wood. 'Why, thank you.'

Jobey swung the bag over the woman's head, clutching her neck in the crook of his elbow. A knife appeared in the other, menacing the other woman who burst through the boards with a cry.

———◆———

'NO!' NILITH YELLED, TRYING TO tug the sword from her belt. Anoish whinnied, rearing up, kicking two planks far into the market. They clattered against awning poles, shattering the quiet of nightfall.

'It is over!' yelled the man, all dressed in black. His face was hidden in the thick darkness but his accent was clear. She spied the slatherghast tied up behind him, straining for her, not Heles. She felt the wobble in her arm as she saw its glowing jaws part.

'You let her go right now!' Nilith ordered.

Chaser Jobey wrestled Heles for a moment before he answered. He hadn't hit her hard enough, and she was already coming to. The knife was pressed against her face. 'Keep still!' he warned her. 'And not likely, madam! Keep the horse and shade. This woman's debt to the Consortium will be paid by her own titles!'

'You fucking—' Nilith stopped herself, thrown by the reply. Her tired mind caught up. *He thinks Heles is me.*

There came a resounding click of irons around wrists. 'It is none of your business! Refrain from interfering, and you may keep your life!' Jobey was reaching for the leash now, fiddling with it while he balanced the knife with two fingers. Nilith made to chase him, but the blade came back to Heles' throat quickly enough.

'Stay back, I say! This woman is the Consortium's property now!' he warned. Anoish was whinnying something awful. The horse was still trying to kick his way out of the shop. Over his noise, Nilith swore she heard the clank of armour somewhere nearby. She began to sweat.

'Go!' yelled Heles, muffled through the sack.

'Listen to your empress, madam!'

Nilith bit her lip. She heard scattered voices now, raised in urgency. 'I won't!' she hissed.

The scrutiniser was insistent. 'Do it!'

It was at that moment the slatherghast turned on its own leash, savaging it with dead fangs until the leather fell to blackened ash. Bursting from the column, it slithered straight for Nilith, leaving Jobey panicking.

'Not that one!' he cried.

Mouth gaping in horror, Nilith watched the monster come at her; glistening talons reaching, jaws glowing and wide. She would have frozen had a voice not yelled at her, so deep in her mind it echoed like a landslide.

'MOVE!'

Nilith sidestepped as the ghast leapt for her. Vaporous claws snagged the cloth of her chest as the monster sailed past. Had it eyes, she no doubt would have seen a surprised look in them. It snarled as it hit the ground. Nilith was already standing over it, sword raised and ready.

'Oh, shit!' cried a woman's voice.

All too late did Nilith hear the slap of bare feet on sand, and see the dark shape barrelling from behind the corner of the shop. A woman slammed into Nilith's side, knocking the empress straight to the ground. Her assailant cartwheeled into a heap, but not before seeing the slatherghast writhing to right itself.

'Thefuckisthat!' cried the woman. Her voice cracked, going deeper momentarily.

Nilith was on her feet in a blink, sword point facing the ghast and the pommel pressed against her ribs. With a roar rising through bared teeth, she charged it. The ghast squealed as it rose up to meet her with disturbing delight. Its claws swung at her, but not before she had driven the blade into its throat. The blue jaws flashed white as they gnashed down on the sword's metal. Something in the blade stung it, fighting back, and the ghast writhed in anguish. It was all Nilith could do to duck the thrashing claws.

Nilith felt hands around her ribs, dragging her backwards and driving her to the ground again. The sword came with her, stubbornly sticking to her palms. The slatherghast continued to writhe, snapping its jaws between retches of black blood. Its tendrils were rigid with pain. Nilith rolled away as it gnashed at her boots. The woman next to her yelped, and dragged her feet clear.

The sword found the slatherghast again, though this time its neck. The blade sheared completely through its pallid flesh and gelatine bones, and the ghast sagged to the floor in two pieces, twitching sporadically.

At a strangled cry of anger from behind her, Nilith whirled around to find Jobey disappearing behind a wooden stage. Heles was still in his grasp, struggling just enough to keep him occupied. Nilith made to start after them, but she wrestled herself back.

The woman spoke up, making her flinch. She was still in the dust, feet tucked into her chest. She was pointing at the carcass, which was leaking obsidian blood and yellow bile. 'Seriously, what the fuck was that?' she asked, breathless.

For the first time in the poor light, Nilith recognised the leathers of a cheap street-guard, and the shorn dark hair of an Arctian. She held the sword to the woman's throat before she could rise.

'Move and die,' Nilith muttered. 'You almost got me killed. Who are you?'

The guard shifted away, despite her warning. She looked itchy to run. 'Stop moving!' Nilith cried.

Before she could whack the woman with the flat of the blade, Nilith's eyes appeared to deceive her. Blue vapour pulled from the guard's body, as if her soul was fleeing too fast and forgetting her body. The ghost of a man with a cut throat appeared behind her, face scrunched up with effort, his mists still trailing behind him. With a grunt and a snap of white light, he tumbled from her form and scrambled in the sand. The guard flopped over, completely overcome by the experience.

Nilith didn't blame her. She was still trying to keep her eyes in her sockets while the ghost found his feet and started to run. She had just gathered the wherewithal to shout when somebody beat her to it. It was a man's voice, bodiless, and it was coming from her hip.

'Caltro!' he cried.

The ghost stumbled, head craned over his shoulder.

In her shock, Nilith scrambled to be rid of the sword, throwing it to the ground.

'Caltro Basalt!' the sword called again.

———◆———

DEAD WEIGHT WAS A DIFFICULT thing to cart even a few paces, never mind four streets.

Chaser Jobey threw Heles onto the bed of a wagon with a curse in a tongue she'd never heard. The smell of the tarred burlap wrapping her face was offensive, but she endured for Nilith. It would buy her some time before Jobey realised he was a fucking fool.

Heles had caught him chuntering over the loss of that foul creature she'd heard gnashing and wailing. Dying, if her ears hadn't deceived her, and for the merrier. But there had been another voice in the commotion, too, unknown. Man or woman, or both, she hadn't been able to tell. Wrestling that worry into trust had been difficult, but Heles relied on the fact the empress could handle herself.

'You thought you could outrun me, and yet here we are once again. I told you, in all my years I've never missed my mark,' the chaser was bragging. Heles heard the clinking of bridles and reins. 'And what an interesting turn of events. I must say, Your *Majesty*, you are going to make me very popular indeed.'

Heles chuckled in her sack, making Jobey pause.

'You go right ahead, Chaser Jobey. Drag me back to your Consortium. I'd like to have a look at you all before I dispense my justice.'

She hoped that had sounded haughty enough. Krass enough. The empress's accent was a strange mix of empire and foreign, but the burlap muffled Heles enough to maintain the ruse. She might have been playing a part, but justice was precisely what she wanted for these people.

'Your royal blood means nothing now. Not now it's been poisoned by my ghast.' That last word was tight. 'I wonder how long until it claims you.'

Heles was jolted about as he climbed aboard. Hands pawed at her neck, and she shrugged them away, thankful she still wore yards of cloth. He snorted. 'I shall just have to be swift then, shan't I?'

With a snicker, Jobey wrapped a rough bag of sackcloth about her head, tied her hands with twine, and pushed her flat on the wagon. Heles too hoped the journey would be a short one; she didn't fancy baking in the morning sun.

CHAPTER 20
THREADS

They say the Krass are a noble race. I don't see it.
Their cities do not stretch for the skies as ours do.
Seasons and snow mean their roads and streets are
full of muck, as well as horse and goat shit. They do
not even embrace binding as we do. In weeks, our
armies could crush them. Why is this marriage even
necessary? Must I entertain such a peasant of a wife?.

FROM A LETTER WRITTEN BY EMPEROR-IN-WAITING
FARAZAR TO EMPEROR MILIZAN IN 982

WE DARTED THROUGH THE NIGHT until the sun came up. Like rabbits running from a fox, we scampered here and there, dodging every glance of light or echoing voice. North was our average direction, back the way I had run. Patrols came and went, but we – this woman, her corpse-laden horse, her bundled ghost, my sword and I – shunned them, taking canyon-like alleys between the growing press of buildings. Though I swore they hunted me, she moved like she was the prey. All I cared about were answers. Every attempt to get them had been met with a curt hiss. Words had been few between us. Conversation nil. She had told me to run, and I had run.

Her rags had fallen away in her fight. The heat of running had made her discard more. On the edges of lantern and torchlight, or when we crouched beside her horse, I studied her face.

Wild-eyed and drawn with weariness, she had the cut of an easterner. I saw her skin was darker than an Arctian's. Her hair was raven black, and though I imagined it had spent much of its time combed and curled, it was matted around her ears and thick with sand and mud. The emerald of her eyes was caught by my glow, and I saw a quickness and cleverness to them. They never seemed to stay still. And oh, how they watched me. I was never out of her sight; her back never turned, and the sword in her hand – my sword – was always pointed in my direction. During my time as a ghost, I had grown used to my nakedness, but now, under those piercing eyes, I felt the need to cover myself whenever I got the chance.

Pointy was strangely silent, as if owing something to this new master of his. '*Come with us,*' had been his only words to me, silent and in my mind. I had seen a familiar twitch in this woman's eyes, as he had no doubt reassured her I was worth taking along. She seemed shocked to hear a voice in her head, but she had not questioned it. Not yet.

My answers took some time in coming. For another hour or two we wound north towards the Core Districts. The eastern sky was beginning to blush a powder blue. Buildings lost to the darkness of the night started to find their edges again. Much to my delight, the soldiers' horns had fallen silent for some time. Patrols had thinned to the point of vanishing. *The lateness of the hour can defeat even the most determined of hunters.*

Irritatingly, the woman took it as a sign to press on, not stop and hole up. I wondered what it was that drew her to the core, but if she feared attention, she was going the wrong way. Her logic was all wrong. When we bunched up at the edge of a wide thoroughfare fringed with palms, I took the opportunity to tell her.

'We should find some place to hide.'

'We press on,' the woman growled at me.

'They'll start searching again come dawn.'

There are some people in this world who can shrink a person with a simple look or tone. This woman levelled both at me, and despite all my posturing, I felt like a scrawny child.

'Look, I don't know who you are, or why you felt the need to interfere tonight, but you're lucky this talking sword – I can't believe I just said that – this talking sword knows you or I would have lopped your head off with it already. Understand you are not in charge here. You haven't the faintest clue what's even going on. I suggest you keep your inane suggestions to yourself or fuck off somewhere else.'

I grimaced, and consoled myself with the fact she was likely angry over losing her friend.

'Nilith…' said the sword.

'Shut up. Both of you.'

I watched Nilith stare across the street for a moment before bowing her head with a frustrated sigh. 'Move,' she ordered.

With the horse clip-clopping noisily over the flagstones, we dashed across the thoroughfare and into the next side street. We stumbled onto a pocket of penury in an otherwise soaring district. The houses here were low and poorly built, mudbrick plastered to look like granite. They leaned over drunkenly, making the going even more claustrophobic.

'*Trust her, Caltro,*' Pointy whispered to me. '*She knows what she's doing.*'

'As do I,' I muttered, hoping the sword could hear me. Treachery, was what it was. He had fallen into the lap of some madwoman and forgotten me. He hadn't seen what I had seen.

Soon enough, the dusky blues in the east began to burn orange, and the fires of dawn were stoked. With a curse, Nilith held up a fist. I almost walked straight into it. I had been too busy admiring an ugly old spire hanging above us, its sides spiked with wooden poles. Half of its plaster had fallen away over the years, leaving it piebald and sorrowful.

'Fine. We hide for now,' Nilith muttered, her words slurred with weariness. I had noticed her pace starting to fail.

I nodded. 'What a great idea. Where?'

'I don't know about you, ghost, but I could use a bed.' She pointed to where the lights of a building still burned. 'Looks like a tavern to me, wouldn't you say?'

The glyphs on the rickety sign said *The Tal's Castle*, though it was anything but. Sandwiched between two lofty lumps of granite was an establishment that looked as though it had been stitched together, not built. From cartwheels to crates, discarded bricks to sailcloth, the face of the building was a hodgepodge of materials. None of it bore any symmetry. All of it was disconcerting to look at. They'd managed to get three floors out of the detritus, and a handful of slanted windows showed a bit of lamp or ghost-light. There were bars, but no shutters.

No matter what the weather, or holiday, or catastrophic event, you can always trust in a tavern's doors staying open. I had the sudden urge to taste the sourness of beer on my tongue.

A sleepy-eyed stable boy lay slumped atop a barrel beneath the rickety sign. The lad nearly fell off his barrel as we approached. Nilith had sheathed Pointy, but any stranger in the depth of night is a worrisome sight to wake to, especially in Araxes. He blinked owlishly in my glow.

'W—what?'

'A bed,' Nilith said, fighting a yawn. 'In the stables with the horse. I don't leave my... wares.'

The boy scratched his nose. 'We got cots.'

'Good, and I don't want to be disturbed.' She tapped the blade with a fingernail. The boy nodded emphatically.

'S'a reputable place, miss,' said the boy, sniffing as he took the horse's reins. He seemed undecided whether the stench was Nilith or the big bundle on the beast's back. 'Got a bath too, if you need.'

Nilith rubbed her eyes and waited for the grubby child to fetch a key and open the stable doors, which were apparently made of driftwood and palm frond. Inside, the stables were dark, lit only by one fluttering lamp at the far end. I helped light the way as we followed the boy past half a dozen pens. Most were empty. I counted two horses, silver and black-maned, and one enormous centipede. It was curled up in a tight, spiralling ball the size of a tent. Its plates of burgundy armour rippled and rattled in its dreams.

'A silver a night for stable and bed. Food's extra. So's drink,' said the boy through a yawn. I smacked my lips habitually. Well, as best as a ghost can.

He opened a door that squeaked like a strangled mouse. Nilith took out her sword and leaned it against the driftwood walls of our allotted pen. There was straw on the floorboards, and nosebags of water and feed.

The horse, a stocky desert beast, immediately moved to investigate them.

I had never been one for horses. It had absolutely nothing to do with lacking the legs to easily mount one. Nor was it to do with somehow finding my arse in a muddy puddle after every attempt to. They were creatures of burden, and anything that suffered the whims of most humans was likely to snap at one point. With a horse, that snap is likely to lead to a similar snap of the neck.

The stable boy returned with the cot: a simple wooden frame with canvas stretched between its corners. Nilith seized it immediately and positioned it at the entrance to the pen. A barricade, with me and her horse behind it.

The boy hovered around until Nilith dug out one silver coin and one copper, and pressed them both into the boy's hand. 'Supper, if there is any left. And beer.'

I caught a different edge to her accent. 'You're Krass,' I said, once the boy had retreated inside.

'As are you. Me? I used to be. Feel more Arctian now than anything else.'

Nilith still held Pointy in a claw of a hand. The other was held tightly to her chest, as if injured. She spun the sword on its point, drilling a hole into the board.

'I don't care if this sword vouches for you. It could be slaved to you. Some sort of sorcery. Or plain mad for all I know.'

'You wouldn't be far off...'

'What is it? Deadbound?'

'I am indeed.'

'You keep quiet,' Nilith ordered Pointy. She looked up at me. 'We do this the old way, then. The Krass way.'

That was a sense I could grasp onto. I sighed, my tension lessened. 'The traditional way.'

'Questions and truthful answers until friend or foe has been decided.'

Pointy butted in. 'I must say, I could probably tell the tale—'

'Shut up, sword,' said Nilith and I, together. We swapped uneasy looks.

'You first,' she said. 'I want to hear it in your words. We'll see what the sword has to say in a moment.'

That was easy. 'What the bloody fuck was that creature you sliced up?'

Nilith crossed her arms, still favouring her left. 'A slatherghast, if you must know. A foul thing from somewhere far away. It and its master had been hunting me.'

I opened my mouth to speak, and closed it as Nilith glared. Tradition dictated she speak first, being the one to suggest it.

'Who are you?'

'I am Caltro Basalt of Taymar.' I crossed my arms to match her. 'Who are you?'

'Empress Nilith Rikehar Renala, daughter of Krass King Konin, Lady of Saraka.'

I looked to the pommel of the sword, and found a serious look on Pointy's face.

'Ahhhh.' It was the only sound I could think of making. I performed an awkward dance as I tried to decide between bowing and standing taller. 'Well… then, Empress Nilith. Milady. Your question.'

'Why are you here?'

'A long answer, but the short version is I came for work, was murdered, and through a long series of tedious events, I am here. Why do you have my sword?'

'Your sword?'

'That counts as a question, and therefore avoiding an answer.'

Pointy was slammed into the floor. 'Hmph,' he grumbled.

We paused our mutual interrogation while the boy returned with a clay bowl of stew the colour of sharkskin, and a foaming earthenware tankard of beer. I tried to lick my lips as I watched the empress reach for it, slopping some foam onto her cloth-wrapped hand. I imagined it to be my hand, feeling the cold beer against skin filled with rushing blood…

'Don't you dare.' Pointy must have seen my envy, and stopped me from pouncing. The empress was soon facing me again, bowl in her lap to cool, beer by her boot, sword still twirling in her fingers.

'It fell from the sky a few nights ago. Skewered a soulstealer's lad as he was about to call his friends. Well-timed. Lucky,' she said, idly spinning Pointy around on his tip. I wonder if he ever got nauseous. 'He was useful, so I brought him with us. It was impossibly sharp. You don't just throw away something like that, now, do you?'

'Is that another question?'

The glare I received was nothing short of murderous. This empress seemed to teeter on a blade sharper even than Pointy. I made a point not to push her. Yet, at least.

'No, you don't,' I answered her. 'Though I was made to. And in answer to your previous question, *I* dropped the sword while I was being ghostnapped by a certain Tal Horix. You may know her as Hirana Talin Renala the Somethingth. Oh yes, she's the one who smashed into the Cloudpiercer yesterday.'

The sword stopped spinning. Nilith was frozen apart from her lips. 'The flying machine,' she whispered. 'You have my attention, ghost. Hirana, you say?'

'Yes, I did, but it's my turn,' I said. The blade was slammed into the floorboard. A full third of it punctured the wood. Maybe I should have showed some respect. Though not my empress, she was the daughter of King Konin. My king. But everybody was equal when they were brandishing a sword at you.

I waved a finger at the bundle of rags on the horse's back. 'Speaking of long-lost royals, I imagine there's an emperor under those rags?'

Nilith almost spilled the stew as she rose up from the cot, sword flashing in the lantern-light. It found a resting place a few inches from my torn throat. 'You can imagine if you want.'

'Truthful answers,' I reminded her, my hands hovering by my ears. I can be a stickler for rules at the worst of times.

She snarled. 'Yes. There is. And if you're here to take him, then I've already made my decision on whether you're friend or foe.'

'Majesty. Caltro—'

'Shut up!' she snapped at the sword, waggling Pointy so much I had to lean backwards. 'How do you know that, Caltro Basalt? What's your part in this? Why were you running? And how is it you stole a woman's body?'

'I believe that's four questions…' I swallowed my words, finding less sarcastic ones. The time for tradition was over. 'All right. Because I'm the one your delightful daughter hired to break into the emperor's Sanctuary. Only I was delayed on the way. Murdered by a man called Boran Temsa. A man who, working with Sisine and the Cult of Sesh behind each other's' backs, managed to turn this city into a battlefield in just a few weeks, until he recently met his end at the sharp end of an axe. In the meantime, I have been stolen, traded back and forth between nobles and villains, locked up, beaten, and foolishly put my faith in a tal who turned out to be the mother of the nest of vipers you call royals. A viper with a flying machine and a burning desire to see your family pay for banishing her. She crashed into the tower and forced me to open the Sanctuary. After they realised Farazar was missing, a battle broke out. I tried to take my coin from Hirana, and we fell from the Cloudpiercer. So I ran. I don't know why, with my half-coin behind me.'

I would have been breathless, but all I felt was colder lips and strained eyes. Recanting my tale made it seem all the more woeful. Pointless.

Nilith pressed a thumb to her temple as though her head was spinning. 'The Cult… flying machines… and Hirana, back from the dead?'

I winced.

'And the stealing bodies thing?'

There was no use trying to hide it. 'I can inhabit bodies if I feel like it. Beasts, even. Haunt them. I was using the woman as a distraction from a patrol I ran into, shortly before colliding with you. A gift of the dead gods, supposedly, but so far all it's got me into is more trouble. The Cult of Sesh were keen to wrap me into their grand game of changing Araxes because of it. Now it seems the gods…' I faltered, holding back that section of my story for now. It always sounded like madness aloud. 'The gods wasted their time with me.'

Nilith lowered Pointy until he was hanging by her side. With a grunt, she moved past me and took the horse by the chin to bid him to lie down. With his reins free, he whinnied and started to munch the hay while Nilith took apart the pack. Layers and layers of cloth slid free, revealing a stained bundle that looked suspiciously body-sized, and a naked, wriggling ghost, busy pulling a rag from his mouth. He got up, eyes wild and hand clenched to his breast. He was puffed up with rabid anger, looking between me and Nilith as if choosing which of us to curse first. There was a doughy paunch on him, and he was a hair taller than me. I looked at the ragged gash at his throat, and he saw mine. We traded a brief glance that was something other than anger. Empathy, perhaps. In a moment, it was lost, and rage swooped in to fill the vacuum.

Emperor Farazar pointed a handless stump at me. 'You… You eastern filth! You're a fucking *liar*! No man can break into my Sanctuary!'

'I'm no man, Emperor of the Arc. I'm a ghost,' I replied haughtily. This man was definitely no royal to me. 'And the best locksmith in the Reaches.'

'And my mother! How dare you insinuate she defied my banishment! And a flying machine? She didn't have the guts to do anything about my father, never mind have the wits to build a flying machine! If you believe this liar, wife, you have finally snapped!'

I looked to Nilith. 'Is he always like this?'

'You have no idea,' the empress replied with a roll of her eyes. 'Days, Mr Basalt. Weeks, I've endured it.'

'Look at what you've done to my city, Nilith. Madness! A battlefield! And now the Cult?'

'So you took that bit on board…' I piped up.

Nilith ignored him, keeping her gaze on me. 'When did my daughter hire you?'

'Months ago. I arrived here a few weeks back, maybe a month. I was killed my first night here.'

'And how long had the tal been in the city, building her machine, Mr Basalt?'

'Years. A decade, perhaps.'

Nilith laughed. 'And you blame me, Farazar? Did you hear that? If I hadn't acted, Sisine would have. Or your mother. What do they all have in common? You.'

With the point of the sword, Nilith steered the emperor into the corner and made him sit down. With nothing but driftwood and stone behind him, he had nowhere to run. She came back with more questions for me.

'My daughter knows about me, and what I've done?'

'Her ghost, Etane, told her, shortly after they found the Sanctuary empty. Or should I say your ghost.'

'Lies,' came a bitter hiss from the corner.

'And what of Etane?'

'I don't know. The last I saw of him, he was fighting a brute of a ghost called Danib. It didn't look like it was going well.'

'Ironjaw. I remember him from Milizan's last days,' Nilith whispered. I saw the concern in the wrinkles of her brow.

With a sigh, Nilith took me out into the stable, near to the sleeping centipede. 'And the Cult? How are they involved? I've seen their preachers and their patrols of armoured shades. What has happened while I've been gone? How have they resurfaced?'

I was torn. They had handed me over as if I was still bound, even though my half-coin had been around my neck. And yet they had welcomed me in, given me the gifts of justice. I was honest. 'They want to fix the city. Provide charity and aid. Freedom for shades. They orchestrated Temsa's rise and fall to get close to Sisine, and now they say they want to put Sisine on the throne, to start a new era. They brought me to the Cloudpiercer after taking me from Hor—Hirana, intent on me opening the Sanctuary for your daughter. They say all the right words, but...'

'What?'

I faltered. 'I...'

'Tell her about the gods,' Pointy whispered.

I shook my head. 'Just a sense.'

'I know what you mean.' Nilith blew a sigh, running a mitten of rags through her knotted hair. 'I can't believe that old bag Hirana is still alive. And here in Araxes all along.'

I held up a finger. 'Erm. She's not exactly... alive.'

'What?'

'After Hirana crashed into the Piercer, when they found nothing but a ghost in place of an emperor, she and Sisine fought. She managed to take my coin. In the commotion, I...' I bit my lip, tasting mist.

'I pushed her through a window. Hirana and I fell, and after... well.'

Nilith had a strange glint in her eyes. 'You killed my mother-in-law?'

I was already looking for the nearest door. Knowing where the exits are is half the trick to surviving. 'I... not intentionally...'

'Well, thank fuck for that.' Nilith blew a sigh of relief. 'That woman is sheer evil. The very definition of a royal Arctian. And yet you ran. I'm sure my daughter and the Cult would have been thankful. Why not stay with them? With your coin? Why run and hide?'

I had no better an answer for that now than I did standing over Hirana's splattered corpse. It didn't stop me from trying to make one. 'It seems it's what I do. I run. I've been running most of my life. I've run this far, and so far I haven't vanished in a puff of air. I can only assume the Cult have my coin, and aren't finished with me yet.'

Nilith shook her head, as if she had already galloped ahead of my weak explanations. 'They want your gift. It's clear. Their kind always want something,' she grumbled. 'Ungh! Why did they have to complicate things?'

Once more, I was ready to spill the story of the gods, but I held back as I watched Nilith start to pace. Curiosity hooked me. Had I fallen in with just another claimant to the throne? I wondered how far I'd have to run to be free of those.

'What exactly are these 'things'?' I asked. 'What do you plan to do with the emperor?'

'Farazar will be put into the Grand Nyxwell according to the Code, and I will claim the throne.'

I snorted. 'And what's your reason for killing your way to the crown, hmm? You all seem to have one. Spoiled birthright? Jealousy? Vengeance?'

'Change, Mr Basalt. Your story is one of hundreds I've heard since living in this godsforsaken city. I seek to change those stories. To bring freedom to your kind. To…' She bit her lip, and I swear I saw blood. 'To my kind.'

'Come again?'

'I like to think I can recognise the difference between a cog in the machine and the hand that turns it, Mr Basalt. You seem to be the former.'

I wondered if that was some sort of veiled insult.

'I have trusted you this far. I don't know why I feel I can trust you further, but I shall.' With that, she began to pull aside the wrappings at her neck and reveal a sight I had never beheld.

A black and ragged tear in her skin separated bone and flesh from dark, angry vapour. Her faint blue glow joined mine as she tore the rags from her arms. I saw the punctures at her wrist, glowing white like my own stab-wounds. She showed me the edges of where ghost met living, reaching across her bosom and down to her hip.

'You asked what that monster was? The slatherghast did this to me. I was told its poison slowly kills a person by turning them into a ghost. It certainly seems to be true. This has only been a few days. All I feel is cold, and a hollowness spreading through me.' She pointed to the bite marks in her wrist, her tone low and wistful. I knew that pain, although I envied the graduation of her transition to the grave. She hadn't tumbled into it, as I had, but was slowly slipping. It was a poor comfort to her, I knew, but a richness I wished I had been gifted. I might have taken that over my haunting, just to spend my last days living in all the ways I would miss as a ghost. The first sips of beer. Grease rolling over fingers. A lucky bedding. Or a cheap one, in my case.

I didn't share the same worry she did, and so I scowled. 'I'm sorry,' I offered awkwardly. 'A half-life isn't so bad, all things considered. Better to have half the loot than none of it, my old master used to say.' Those optimistic words tasted far too sweet in my pessimistic mouth.

I got the sense I hadn't provided the supportive words she might have been seeking. Nilith waved her hand dismissively and wrapped herself back up. 'All I care about is time, and a clear path to the Grand Nyxwell.'

'And freeing the ghosts,' I reminded her.

'Abolishing the Code, Mr Basalt. To be exact,' she corrected me.

'Lofty aspirations, Empress.'

'They are the only aspirations that matter. And now, perhaps they matter even more.' A glazed look came over her eyes. They were glassy in the dim lantern-light. 'I don't trust the Cult any more than my husband, or no doubt his mother, did. I saw their manipulation of Emperor Milizan with my own eyes, before Farazar murdered him. They are a pox on what the dead gods stood for.'

I cocked my head.

Nilith went on, working herself up until she was hunched, a bow bending before pressure. 'They worship a god of chaos, not the true concept of *ma'at*. Balance, Mr Basalt, in Arctian. Charity? Aid? I highly doubt it. If they're involved, putting Sisine on the throne is most likely the next step on their ladder.'

'A flood,' I blurted, seeing whether the word sparked anything in her, testing the gods' warnings.

'A flood? What flood?'

I tested her trust some more. 'Since I came out of the Nyx, I have been... *visited*.'

'Visited?'

'Visited. By dead things, claiming to be dead gods. There was a dead man called Horush, then a cat called Basht. Then a cow. Haphor. And a shade all green. Oshirim himself.'

Nilith was cocking her head at me now. I could hear the absurdity of it, and although it felt good to get it off my chest, I could see myself sliding into the same category as the supposedly mad sword.

Pointy spoke up, deciding to break his silence. 'He has, Empress. I saw Oshirim with my own eyes.'

Nilith raised an eyebrow.

'They have repeatedly warned me of the Cult. Say they want to flood Araxes. The Arc. Maybe the whole Reaches. Yet when I was with the Enlightened Sisters, I saw no sign of any such plans. They seemed genuine, devoted to this idea of a new Araxes. To your idea.'

'You trust them?' Nilith looked at me, shocked.

'I…' I stammered.

'Caltro, surely not,' Pointy admonished me.

'It's not that I trust them. Every opinion is against them, but they speak of freedom and justice just like you do, Nilith. They used me to open the Sanctuary, of that I'm sure, but they have my half-coin and haven't killed me yet. The dead gods keep saying I need to use this gift to stop them. Begging me, even, and yet I see no malice in the Cult's plans. Fuck. I thought after getting my freedom existence would be simpler, but I'm even more wrapped up in Araxes' games than I was before,' I sighed. 'In truth, I have no idea what I'm supposed to do now.'

Nilith reached out to put a hand on my shoulder. It was her left, the dead one, now wrapped in cloth. 'Me neither. Not day to day, at least, and somehow I've scraped through. I just kept moving. I find if a person has enough will, enough determination, a path opens up for them. Who knows? Perhaps the dead gods wanted you to run into me. Do you believe in luck?'

I shook my head. *Luck is a scapegoat for the unfortunate and a trinket for the untalented and noble-born.* 'I make my own.'

Even as I said it, my thoughts betrayed me. Yet again my half-coin was once again out of my hands. My fight for freedom was far from finished. Maybe the gods did have a path planned out for me, and I was following it unknowingly.

'Luck has seen me through the desert, Caltro. Given me allies when I needed them most.' Nilith mumbled, green eyes faraway and vacant. 'I was with someone, a scrutiniser, but she was taken before you arrived. A bargeman. Nomads. A strangebound falcon, too, wherever he is now. And now you, turning up out of the shadows. I've learnt not to turn my nose up at company, but suit yourself if you wish to carry on running. Though, I could use the help...' She took a moment to unclench her jaw.

I studied her, every twitch of her eyes, every shift of her lips. 'You're really going to free all the ghosts in the Arc? You'd take that step? You, a royal with a dead emperor penned up and all the wealth of the Reaches in your grasp?'

I felt the determination in Nilith's eyes pressing into me as she stepped closer. 'Every last one. You, the sword. All of you. The Code is a poison and a plague and I can stand no part of it in this city any more. Balance will reign again, Mr Basalt. Neither the Cult nor my daughter will get their hands on the throne. Then this flood of theirs – if such a thing exists – will be no more. You and the gods can rest easy.'

Those might have been the truest words I had yet heard spoken in Araxes. I paused to think. There was no trace of duplicitousness in her. No squeeze in that hand on my shoulder. No subtle movements of the sword lest I refuse.

She saw my hesitation. 'Make your mind up, Caltro Basalt. Stay or go.'

'Will it get me my coin back?'

Nilith withdrew her hand, and led the way back to the pen. 'If I pull this off, locksmith, you can forget about your half-coin.'

I thumbed my chin. The decision seemed far too easy, almost as if it had already been made for me. Once again, I considered luck and fate, and the weaving of its complex threads.

A person can live all their life seeing a tapestry woven behind them. See themselves as the product of chance meetings, steered by nothing but the frantic flutter of a butterfly's wings. I had always refused the notion. Believing such things took the reins from my hands. It was like trusting bolting horses to lead your wagon in the right direction. No, I preferred to steer, and trust to my own choices, even if I chose the wrong direction. I'd had little choice of late, and so I made my decision right there and then, and steered.

I followed Nilith, heading for the pen. Once again, my finger poked the air. 'Don't suppose this means I get my sword back, does it?'

'No.'

BARE AND GLOWING FEET WHISPERED across the white, glasslike marble. Crimson cloth and shade-light stained it a deep purple. The chambers were so quiet that even their ghostly movements seemed loud.

Creaking doors led to vacant chambers, all opulent and pointless. Studies with blank scrolls on their shelves. Bedrooms themed by colour; here a violently yellow room, there a blue room with fish painted around the walls. Dressing rooms that bore tables laden with jewellery. Lounges with furniture of oryx horn, ivory, and a plethora of silk cushions. And all of them empty.

The Enlightened Sisters continued their search.

Not a squeak had been heard from Sisine in hours. Not since she had stormed from the ruined Sanctuary in the aftermath of the battle. Her last words had been a challenge to the Church to find her mother. To prove their worth, as it were. It struck an uneasy truce between them and the Royal Guard. For the first time in two decades, brothers and sisters walked freely through the Cloudpiercer.

'Majesty?' called Liria, her voice echoing through the honeycomb chambers of marble.

A wheeze.

Both sisters heard it, surging towards another bedroom. Another door led on from that, hanging ever so slightly ajar. Liria placed her hand upon its edge and pushed.

A bloody scene appeared before them. The bedroom was doused in it. Where it hadn't been left to pool, it was drawn across the pristine floor in great arcs. Crimson hand prints showed here and there, like the grotesque painting of an infant. The sisters' eyes followed them from the marble to the snowy linen sheets of a great bed. They had been dragged to the floor and were now a patchwork of dirty and clean. Chestnut feathers were strewn across that pile, and at the centre of their explosion lay two bodies. One was a falcon, blood-soaked and with its neck twisted at a horrific angle. The other was a princess.

Sisine lay crooked, almost horizontal, with her head propped up by a bundle of cloth clamped to her bloody neck. It had been white once, Liria imagined, but now it was as red as her own robes. Stretching out from the cloth's corners, raw, wet gashes stretched across Sisine's throat. Her bottom lip had been torn in two, and her nose carved down the middle. One eye had been completely gouged out, and not cleanly. Rake-marks of talons crisscrossed her bloody socket like a scribe's mistake. The skin that had gone untouched had a hint of grey in its Arctian tan.

Sisine's other eye glared at the sisters. She drew a breath, and it rasped through her throat. She tried to speak but some of her letters had been stolen from her. Blood sprang afresh from her split lip.

'My mother,' came the ragged hiss, barely audible.

Liria knelt at the empress-in-waiting's side. She did not touch her; she merely looked. 'We have all available bodies and souls looking for her. If Empress Nilith has made it to the city, we will find her.'

'I will be empress.' Something caught in her windpipe, and she dribbled more blood. 'I will be empress.'

Liria looked to her sister, who wore a sorrowful face. 'May I, Your Majesty?' she asked, and after some more glaring, Sisine's hand peeled away from the rags.

'Fucking cursed bird.' Sisine tried feebly to lash out at the falcon's limp corpse, but instead her fingers flopped on the sheets, scoring three red marks.

Liria peeled the rag away, making the princess hiss. Beneath it, she saw how much skin and flesh the talons had torn away. No wonder she lay in a pool of her own blood.

'All this deception will be over shortly, Your Majesty,' Liria whispered, leaning closer. 'No more games.'

Sisine closed her eye, gurgling something.

Liria nodded, dabbing her neck and jaw where the blood still seeped. 'Araxes will have its new empress, we promise you that.' She tended her lip now, and as Sisine croaked in pain, Liria put a comforting hand behind her head.

She whispered gently in her ear. 'Though it will not be you.'

The rag clamped over Sisine's mouth. Feeble hands clawed at her, dragging back her hood. Liria pressed harder, pinching the nose. One eye fixed her with a fierce, wide stare throughout the struggle. At last, when that struggle finally waned, all the air had gone from her; the eye rolled up into her skull, and Liria let the body fall limp to the sheets.

'How bold of you, Enlightened Sisters,' croaked a voice, small and muffled. Liria and Yaridin stood tall, staring down at the falcon. With a series of cracking noises, his head turned back to its normal angle. 'How bold indeed.'

The Enlightened Sisters shared a look.

CHAPTER 21
THE GRAND NYXWELL

What a sight the Grand Nyxwell is, Melia!
Oh, how it gleams! Oh, how its river runs fast
and strong, like no other fountain of Nyxwater
in the Reaches. It bleeds magnificence, exudes
power, and not to mention royalty! You can
almost feel the souls of every emperor and
empress that has passed through here. Oh, if
only the queues weren't so detestable.

FROM A LETTER FOUND ON A DEAD TOURIST

THE BRIGHT DAY PASSED US by as though somebody had spun the sun's wheel far too vigorously at dawn. Dare to yawn, or drift into a daydream, and an hour would shoot by. The streets had found their pace again, and it was a brisk one. Everybody hurried, keen to make up for lost days of cowering. Where uneasy silence had reigned for far too long, the citizens seemed to be making an effort to balance it out. My ears shook with the noise of heavy carriages, hooves, crowing merchants, and all sorts of curses and threats one used when negotiating the busiest of streets. Even parrots squawked raucously from the edges of awnings and pennant poles.

The roiling crowds were a hiding place of sorts. Our rags blended effortlessly with the kaleidoscope of fabrics and colours that filled the thoroughfares. Having a horse gave us some right of way without drawing too much attention. Anoish was not alone in the press of bodies and ghosts. Carriage-teams rattled down the centre of the streets. Stick-legged insects tapped their way ponderously through the crowds.

Before dawn had even risen, Araxes' furnaces had flared like Scatter Isle volcanoes. Smoke belched into the sky from the High and Low Docks, filling the air with a film of filth. I half-heartedly rubbed my thumb across the sky, like trying to smear soot from a window. Nothing changed.

Armour and blades were everywhere we looked. Whether they were guards of rich folk, street-guards, or Cult and royal soldiers, we did our best to avoid them. Sticking to the thickest threads of crowd. Pulling rags over faces. Even haggling with a few merchants whenever gazers became too curious. These were our tactics.

The hunt was clearly not over. I knew edginess when I saw it. In the guards I could practically feel it washing over my vapours. Their eyes moved too quickly. They spoke behind their hands. Every now and again a shriek would come as women or shades were plucked from the crowds and shaken down. We bowed our heads, and took different streets.

The miles fell away beneath our feet agonisingly slowly. While the sun raced overhead, it took us half an afternoon to cross two districts. Here and there I saw places I had already run past in my spiralling, nonsensical fleeing from the Cloudpiercer. Re-treading old ground is not comforting. I find it's usually because you've forgotten or regret something. Or previously failed. I didn't bother to decide which I was.

In our efforts to evade the hungry eyes, we found new places, too. Nilith was preoccupied with staying upright, but I spent the walk gazing up at the city. High-roads stretched between spires, sometimes at violent angles. Some were so old they were beginning to bow. I heard laughter, and on a corner saw two tiny ghosts frolicking behind a pen of dour-faced guards. I caught glimpses of them between spear-shafts and chainmail. They wore frocks of yellow, throwing about a beetle made of fur and stuffing. Older shades stood behind them, deep in conversation. Important and hushed conversation, that was for sure. What made me sick were the white lines in the ghost girls' forearms, where they had been bled before they'd seen their tenth birthday. Nilith was right: the Code was a poison.

I had to admire this determination of hers. The ghast's bite was beginning to rob her sleep. A handful of hours, maybe more, she had tossed and turned on the cot while Pointy and I traded stories of what had happened since his impromptu exit from the *Vengeance*. He hadn't shared in my elation at Hirana's death, even calling it murder. He hadn't judged, but he had grown silent since.

In fact, barely a word had been shared all day. Such was the pressure of traversing the busy streets and staying inconspicuous. Nilith no doubt had her pains and worries to attend to, as I had my own. The sensation of my coin around my neck had been a brief one, but I already missed it. It was as if I had left a part of me in the Piercer. I sensed its faint pull, as subtle as a hair out of place, and longed for it.

As for what the sisters planned to do with it, I still had no clue. I was still whole… well, for the most part. I decided that if they truly wanted justice and freedom for all shades, they would show their faces when the empress dumped her husband in the Nyxwell, and they would be smiling. Perhaps they were just keeping my coin safe for me. It felt like a child's reasoning, but it was the only one I found comforting. I'd had more than my fill of betrayal.

When the afternoon slid from early to late, and then later still, we reached the bright splash of colour that was the Royal Markets. The bustle here was fierce; a deafening battleground of barging and hollering. The days of hiding meant spoiled wares. Spoil meant sales. Sales meant madness. It was simple economics.

Gangs of ghosts and people besieged the stalls. In one poor fruit stall's case, they overran it completely. I saw the crowd erupt into a thrashing mass of limbs and flying oranges. Nobody else seemed remotely bothered by the kerfuffle, and they continued braying like branded donkeys.

I found distraction in the sights and sounds: slabs of pink meat and ugly sea creatures in tanks; arrays of fruits that would make rainbows hang their heads; cloths and silks from every corner of the Reaches; jewellery that glittered as if it was still molten; armour and blades for all nefarious deeds; household contraptions, full of spring and clockwork; extravagant furniture, the kind that Busk would have snapped up; perfumes, spices and powders piled in earthenware bowls; dyed cats and dogs and birds slumped in palm-wood cages; and, of course, shades in shackles and queues. All of them could be found under the vast, sail-like awnings of the Royal Markets. I looked up, fancying the red-tiled rooftops to be the bulwarks of a mighty ship. If I half-closed my eyes, I could imagine a sway in the earth beneath me.

'Caltro.' Nilith's voice was croaky from lack of use.

She nudged me, digging a dent in my rags. I followed the direction of her pointing finger, and saw one of the reasons the markets were so densely crowded: they were a partly captive audience.

Where a street led out of the bustle, a string of royal soldiers were spread across the road. Black-clad scrutinisers moved between them, halting anyone carting more than a satchel. Quite a queue had built up. I looked left, to another street, and found it similarly blocked.

'Roadblocks.'

'And we're still half a dozen miles away.' Nilith grunted. 'This way.'

She led the horse and me to the eastern side of the markets, where a wider road connected with the Avenue of Oshirim. A wall of guards occupied it. The crowds were too thick here to halt all of them, but the soldiers and scrutinisers were doing a good job of trying.

'Talk,' I said as we walked. Stopping now would have been suspicious. We continued on at a tentative pace. A soldier standing in a doorway was already watching us. I hoped he was just admiring the horse.

'What?'

'Guilty people prefer silence. They're concentrating too hard. Act like it's beneath you.'

Nilith pulled her rags back, showing me a sweaty face covered in stray hair. She had darkened her skin with soot that morning, but it was starting to wipe clean. 'Talk about *what?*'

'Anything. Just talk normally,' I hissed. 'Remind me: when did you leave Krass?'

'Erm.' She hesitated as a scrutiniser appeared in our path, two dozen feet away 'Well,' she sighed. 'It must have been twenty years ago now.'

'Did you come by ship?'

'Of course…?'

I kept talking, acting interested. 'What was its name?'

'One of my father's ships. The… The…' Nilith snapped her fingers. 'The *Bromar*.'

I chuckled loudly. 'I remember that story.'

'The Hero of Holdergrist? I had a nurse that would tell it to me almost every night. Of course, I asked for it. I always wanted to be Bromar, and face the Winds of Treachery to climb to the dragon's nest.'

'I always likened myself more to Bromar's brother.'

Nilith looked genuinely confused. 'Kennig? That coward?'

'Not everyone who runs is a coward. Sometimes it takes a clever man to know when it's time to tuck tail. Kennig knew the dragon would be trouble and had enough sense to stay in the inn. Bromar went up the Dolkfang, and ended up dying alongside his prey.'

'A heroic ending.'

'I prefer a comfortable living—'

'Halt!'

A scrutiniser's gloved hand blocked our way. I saw Nilith's lips tighten as she turned.

The man was a short, rat-like fellow, wrapped up in black leather and a mask of silver mail. This rogue had carved the shape of bones into his. I knew his type immediately: the sort that lacked weight in the body department, so they sought other types of authority instead. It always seemed to be the short, balding ones.

The man's eyes roved over our moth-bitten rags and dusty horse. 'State your business, in the name of the emperor and the Code.'

'Cloth merchants from the Sprawls,' I said, and he seemed surprised to hear me talk. 'Been a terrible day for trade.'

'Which district you from?'

'Far District,' Nilith added.

The scrutiniser stepped close to me, looking at my neck, visible over my makeshift smock, and the cut of my face. He held up a silver coin to me, matching my face with the one etched in its metal. He grunted. 'You don't look like a Sprawler.'

'I'm not. I'm from Krass.'

The man turned on Nilith with a scowl. 'You let your shade speak freely?'

I could see the empress trying to stay cordial. 'Why not? He's free.'

The scrutiniser spat. 'Then you need to put a white feather on him, or else he might get snapped up. People are desperate at the moment.' He moved closer to the horse, sniffed and then seemed to gag. 'Go on. Away with you. I can see why you haven't sold anything. Bloody reeks!'

The soldiers at his back seemed to agree, and they cleared a path for us to move on. We did so, not quickly, but certainly not dawdling.

'And here I was thinking the smell wasn't that bad,' whispered Nilith, sniffing deeply.

'It's the ghost part of you, I'm afraid. Enjoy the spices and perfumes while you can.' Nilith nodded, and I quickly added, 'But it comes in handy. Rotting bodies, for instance. No more gutter-stink.'

The empress gave one more sniff, close to the horses, and came away with her eyes rolling. 'True,' she said. 'Do you miss Krass? Saraka, was it?'

'Taymar, and every day,' I said. 'But mostly because I wish I'd never left its shores.'

'Why did you take the job?'

I had asked myself the same question on many a dark night, and it was a deceptively simple one, which made it all the more infuriating. 'Your ghost Etane wrote a letter to me. It made no mention of the Sanctuary, just an offer from the Cloudpiercer. What locksmith wouldn't jump at the chance? Even with all I knew about Araxes, I was sure a royal writ would see me right. But my captain had made a deal with Temsa, and his men were waiting for us after sunset.'

Nilith hummed. 'Sisine would have killed you in any case, once she was done with you. She has little stomach for ghosts.'

'I had thought of that. It's why I wish I'd never set foot on the Arc in the first place.'

'You'd trade what you have now – even your haunting – for life?'

The hope in her eyes was plain. The answer would be hers, as well as mine. Soon she and I would be the same. Experience is always sought after by the unknowing. Fear lessened by knowledge.

I thought hard. I did wish for life, but only because I felt I had been robbed of it. Had I been offered a choice on that dark night, a choice between haunting and death or to get back on the ship, I don't know what I would have chosen.

'If I had my freedom as well as my gifts, then I might not. In truth, it makes lockpicking a lot more interesting. That, and I did fall from the top of the Cloudpiercer without a scratch. That's somewhat... useful?'

Nilith stuck out her chin. I didn't know whether I had lessened or confirmed her fears. 'Farazar has complained the entire way. Then again, he complained for most of his life, too. It is the unknown that puts the fear in death. How much will it hurt? What is it like? You would think a city full of ghosts would assuage some of that terror of the afterlife, but it doesn't.'

'At least you get a dignified slide into it, Empress,' I whispered. 'No knives or grinning soulstealers or dingy binding halls for you.'

'Small consolation, but it helps.'

'Better than being a deadbound sword,' a voice reminded us both, muttering from Nilith's belt.

The empress was silent for a time as we avoided the Avenue and took a side-road north, and then: 'Tell me of Krass. Tell me what I've missed spending my time in this sand-clogged, festering arsehole of a country.'

I had to smile. *Nobody swears like a Krassman, except for a Krasswoman.*

———————◆———————

WE TALKED TO MAKE THE flagstones pass quicker. We talked to keep up our ruse under the soldiers' eyes. We talked of home and the Arc and all the miles in between. We talked of the deserts, and all the trials Nilith had been through with a woman named Krona. We talked of my tribulations; of Busk and Widow Horix, and of Temsa's mad rise to power. Mostly, I believe we talked because we sensed it could be our last chance for something as simple as conversation.

'...when I began to occupy myself with the scrolls of the Arctian dead gods, I saw they were hardly different from Odun, and our Krass pantheon. Maybe they are cousins of our gods. Brothers or sisters, even, but they were real. Or are, if your stories are to be believed. They believed in balance above all else.'

I remembered that word. '*Ma'at.*'

'You listen well.'

'I've locksmith's ears.'

'I saw the difference in what the Arc had been and what it had become. Call it Sesh or the idiocy of man, the world has changed for the worse since their absence. Look at Krass, how it doesn't meddle with murder or slavery as the Arctians do. That's why I've kept going. Why I'm here now, and although my daughter knows I'm coming and the Cult stand with her, what else can I do now but keep walking?' Nilith asked with a shaky breath. She showed me a copper coin on a thong about her neck, hanging next to a pouch of leather. 'That's why I've carried this the entire way. Just for Farazar. Tell me, why do you keep going?'

I shrugged. 'At first I wanted justice, plain and simple. I wanted somebody to pay for my murder. I turned to the wrong people to give me that, and after bad choices and lucky escapes, I realised it was down to me and me alone to get my freedom. And I did, for a short time. Now I have to get it back, so I'll start all over again. Fortunately, I also have a locksmith's patience. As for why I didn't just throw my coin in the Nyx... I don't want to go back to that cold, screaming place beneath the earth where the souls wait.'

Nilith shuddered. 'I have dreamed of such a place, the last few nights. When I can sleep, that is.'

'Oblivion would be no better. I'm not done with my half-life yet. It's either carry on or shove a copper blade in my eye and let them win. Call it stubbornness. Pettiness. I call it my right to freedom. If that lies in the same direction as your batshit plan, then fine.' Maybe you're right. Maybe this is what the gods wanted from me: to run into you.'

'Who knows what the dead gods want. It matters not. You want your freedom.' Nilith put another hand on me and smiled. It was a tired, limp thing, but a smile nonetheless. It did a good job of hiding the doubt behind her eyes. 'And freedom, Caltro Basalt, is what you shall have.'

Our paces measured out the silence as we negotiated a throng of traders clamouring in front of a warehouse. They looked agitated by something. Empty barrels lay on their sides about the group. Grey-robed Nyxites waved their hands at the doorway, shaking their heads.

'What's going on here?' I asked quietly.

'The Nyx,' Nilith replied. 'I've seen dry wells all over the south. Mobs outside warehouses like this one. There's a shortage.'

We traded looks, knowing what that meant for the emperor's body.

'A question,' I said. 'Would you count yourself a murderer?'

Nilith cleared her throat, evidently challenged. 'We all take action in search of what we think is greater. The question is whether those actions outweigh that greatness. I've taken lives on this journey, or caused others to lose theirs.' She took a moment, recalling faces and names. 'Many lives... but will it be worth their sacrifice? I think so. All I can do is believe that. Was Temsa murdered? Or was he killed for something better? Would you kill a child if it meant the end of death? Think on that, Caltro.'

'Your daughter stands in your way. Your child. Would you kill her to save the Reaches?'

'I...' Nilith flapped her mouth, wordless. It took her several paces to whisper, 'If I had to. If I must.'

My reply was interrupted by a fight breaking out between two of the crowd. Punches began to swing, and with them came street-guards. Red-robed cultists appeared from within, holding short spears and with mail on their breasts. I narrowed my gaze as they broke up the fight, standing respectfully by while a scrutiniser came to berate the pair.

'Caltro.' Nilith's voice called me onwards, leading to a northward detour. 'Night's coming.'

And it was. Over what felt like a mile, the sun's glare sank and died and dusk came to hang over us. It brought stars with it, but the city's smokestacks blurred them and stole their light. No moon dared to show its face. It seemed to have no wish to watch the empress's victory.

Our talk died the closer we crept to the Nyxwell, as did our pace. As the bustle of the streets faded after sunset, patrols of soldiers eagerly took up the mantle. More than once did ranks rush down adjoining streets with torches blazing or lanterns dancing on poles. We did our best to stay clear of them. When a group came thundering past, we were almost menaced with spears before a drunkard called the soldiers "a bunch of noisy cunts" and was immediately beaten for his opinion. We managed to slink away in the confusion, and meld into a crowd on a busier street.

Had I been alive, I knew my heart would have been in my mouth, and I could sense Nilith's was. Neither of us spoke of the situation. It hung over us like a black and slowly closing umbrella. Our eyes were glued ahead. In my peripheries, against the bruise of dusk, I half-recognised the flanks and peaks of spires, though they seemed turned around.

'What's your plan?' I asked Nilith once, but she just shook her head. She was set on marching on, putting the final few miles behind us. In some way I could imagine what this final stretch meant to her.

I guessed it midnight when we found ourselves alone and glimpsing the hornlike structure of the Grand Nyxwell. Between two towers and over the rooftops, we saw it. I heard Nilith gasp. She tugged Anoish's reins. Wary, I followed, wondering where all the people had got to. The lamps were lit but only stragglers shared the flagstones with us.

To the smart trot of the horse's hooves, we aimed for the Nyxwell. Lost and found it was between the buildings, over and over until we found a street pointing straight for it.

Pointy spoke up. 'Where are the guards? If your daughter knows—'

'Silence!' Nilith ordered.

Farazar had sensed the tension and started to thrash in his prison of rags. I could just about hear him, like a madman shouting into a pillow. Anoish whinnied nervously.

'Calm, now,' Nilith whispered even as she led him on to the well. It sounded as though she were talking to herself. She laid a hand upon the pommel of the sword, as if she muffled Pointy. The empress threw me a glance, and in it I saw worry and determination wrestling. She pressed on.

For all our hurry, it was with ponderous steps that we came to the edge of the Nyxwell's grand plaza. A vast wash of grey stone, descending in slanting steps to a great hollow in the earth. I gazed once more at the tusks of stone that rose up and over the Nyxwell. Clumps of lanterns dyed them a sulphurous yellow. It gave them an aged, bestial look.

Aside from a few wanderers and shuffling beggars, robed figures stood upon the dais at its centre. Half a dozen at most. The plaza was so quiet I swore I could hear the chattering of their voices. It was hard, though, over the heavy breathing of Nilith by my side.

She pointed. 'Soldiers.'

She was right. Where scores of streets and alleys ringed the plaza, every so often I saw the gleam of metal and the glow of shades. I strained my weak eyes, and saw ranks of shields. They were motionless. Waiting.

Nilith shuffled backwards to the horse and began to unwrap the cloth binding Farazar and his body. The body came first. I saw the dark stains in its wrapping, and wondered morbidly what forty days of desert and travel did to a corpse. I was glad I'd been spared that.

Farazar came next, and with a sword an inch from his lips, he swallowed whatever words he had nocked to his vocal chords like triggerbow bolts. He was guided forcibly off the horse and made to stand next to me. He looked at me as if to complain, but my eyes met his with a resounding, 'Fuck off' written into them. The emperor looked to the Nyxwell, and I saw the bobbing of his ruined throat; the old habit of a lost body. Like Nilith, he knew his final moments were upon him.

The empress was busy draping herself over the corpse. 'Caltro. You'll lead the horse. Farazar, you'll walk next to it. I will be right here, ready to chop something else off you if you think of opening your mouth.'

Farazar's voice was cold even for a ghost. 'Your threats are hollower now than ever before. This is how your great and epic conquest ends, I see? No great battle. No fanfare and trumpets. Just sneaking in the dead of night. And you call yourself an empress?'

Nilith patted him roughly on the cheek as she dragged rags over her. 'You're about to be immortal and free soon enough, husband dear.

If I were you, I'd decide how I'd want to live that life. You've already lost a hand. How about a leg?' She flicked the sword blade, making it ring as it slipped out of view. I could see its dark point hovering near Farazar's knee.

I shrugged at him. 'Take it from me, Emperor. When you're dead, it's better to hurry up and realise it.'

'Do not dare talk to me, liar.'

'My pleasure.'

I tugged on the reins, and the horse begrudgingly obeyed me. Every clop of his hooves seemed to echo dreadfully. I could almost feel the scores of eyes levelling on us: two shades and a laden horse. I concocted lies in my head. A pilgrimage of two free shades, perhaps. Would-be Nyxites. Or just plain lost.

Facing dead ahead, I watched for movement at the corners of my vision. I could see spear blades now, copses of them tucked into streets. Around some ranks, the stone glowed. It was my turn to feel like gulping. The runner in me placed a hand on Anoish, feeling the fast thump of his heart. *Just in case*, I told myself.

'Keep going,' whispered Nilith.

The hoofsteps were getting louder. Perhaps it was the silence around us deepening. I looked around for others in the plaza and found none. It was as if we were rowing a lake of stone, the shores of which were made of shields and spears.

Down the first step, then the second. I had just started to think luck was on our side when I heard the clank of the soldiers beginning to move. One column began to pour into the plaza from behind us. A torrent of steel and glowing vapour. Two more columns came from both left and right. They were unmistakably aimed at us.

'Fuck!' swore Nilith. 'Run for it!'

Before I could react, the horse jolted forwards. Anoish's hooves battered the stone. The march of the columns became an all-out sprint. Their silence became a rising roar of voices and clanging armour.

All I felt was terror, primarily at being left alone. I raced after the horse's tail with every scrap of strength I had. To my dismay and shock, I found Farazar sliding alongside me, as if bound to Anoish with an invisible rope. He was already yelling at the top of his mist-filled lungs.

'Save your emperor! Save your emperor! Stop the mad empress!'

I swung a punch for him, but a jolt from the horse rippled through him and he shifted out of my reach.

'Nilith!' I yelled, knowing she would do nothing but carry on.

More soldiers were pouring into the plaza now. Streams of them reached inwards towards the Nyxwell, like the tentacles of some great sea monster closing in on a ship.

My eyes raced back and forth, measuring, analysing. They had no cavalry. No carriages. No chariots. Just legs and the weight of armour. Nilith had a head start. As for me, I was being left behind.

I lunged for Farazar, hooking both arms around his legs and bending all my concentration on grasping him. I felt my vapours begin to meld with his, and held the haunting there, like an anchor.

'Unhand me, peasant! Get him off me! Save your emperor!' he bellowed in a constant stream of words, like a man suddenly allowed to speak after a decade of silence. I clung on.

Ahead, more soldiers were attempting to head us off. Anoish galloped for all he was worth. As I bounced around, I reconsidered my opinion on horses. The flagstones raced by, scraping the rags from my legs. I caught a brief glimpse of Nilith on her steed: she sat astride the corpse, one hand clutched to it and the other raising a sword to the faint stars. I could have sworn I heard an old Krass battlecry over the buffeting of wind and stone and the howling of a cowardly emperor.

The tusks of the Grand Nyxwell towered over us now. I could hear the shouting of the Nyxites, calling, 'Calm! Calm!' More of them had gathered in the commotion. In the lantern-light, their robes had taken on a red hue.

Anoish's halt had zero grace. He practically tumbled to a stop, whinnying horribly as he crashed into the stairs that led to the dais. I was thrown free of Farazar, slamming into a block of stone. Nilith and the corpse skidded across the flagstones. In a blink, she was already hauling it over her shoulder, roaring at the effort. I scrambled to help her, but not before Farazar leapt on her. His blue fists were a blur as he pummelled her head and face.

With a flash, he fell away with a cry, a white scar lanced across his chest. I pushed him from the steps, and didn't stop to watch him tumble.

'Don't stop!' I yelled over the thunder of voices and galloping feet. I drove my scant weight into the corpse. Nilith's face was a mask of strain, but she kept on, driving her legs up and up to where the Nyxites flapped their hands. A wind abruptly whipped at us, as if the very weather sought to foil Nilith's efforts.

Nilith roared as she barged her way onto the dais. 'I am Empress Nilith, and I present my claim to the throne! And I—'

Farazar hollered from below. 'I am your emperor! Kill her!'

Guards advanced with short swords. With her free hand, Nilith lashed about with Pointy, sending one guard spinning and turning another into a bleeding heap.

'—have had—'

I pushed as many Nyxites out of the way as I could in our dumb rush forwards to the edge, where the Nyx waited far below us.

'—ENOUGH!'

With a bellow like that of a dying beast, Nilith pushed the emperor's corpse off her shoulders and pitched it over the edge of the dais. I threw myself to Nilith's side to watch it cartwheel end over end, down, down into—

Thud.

The only thing wet about that landing was the squelch the body made as it struck the riverbed. The ink-black, dry riverbed.

'NO!' Nilith cried, long and hard and with a tell-tale sob at the end. I simply stared at the bundle of cloth, my lip curled and my brow furrowed deeply in confusion, as the soldiers descended on us with copper clubs and nets.

CHAPTER 22
ONLY BUSINESS

Here lies Gawperal.
He told you he was sick.

FROM AN INSCRIPTION ON AN ANCIENT
ARCTIAN TOMB

IF THERE WAS ONE UPSIDE to being dragged to uncertainty with her head in a sack and her hands tied, Heles thought, it was the chance for a lie down.

The sacking smelled like old cheese, but at least it masked the rot of the gutters sweating in the sunlight. Heles knew how they could reek.

Chaser Jobey had remained silent enough, cursing now and again at passersby running to and fro – panicked, by the sounds of it, as if there was some ruckus befalling the city. Heles swore she heard mobs chanting in distant streets, their cries soft, loud, then soft again as the mouths of streets passed her by.

At least the great slavering creature was no longer with them. Heles had not seen nor heard it with them on the journey, and it was excuse enough for Jobey's silence. The scrutiniser had relaxed thanks to its absence, watching through her rough sacking as the glow of torches passed them by, then the lightening of dawn, and now the shadows of spires and taller buildings as they took street after street.

Just as Heles was imagining herself in the Outsprawls, Jobey's wagon and horses came to a lurching halt. Through the stench of the sack, Heles could smell the tacky, earthy waft of grain. Through the brown fibres of her blindfold, she glimpsed rounded towers reaching high into the sky, and Jobey jumping off the wagon to the dust. The jolt in the carriage confirmed it.

'Overseer,' Heles heard him say. 'I'm pleased to say I've delivered the woman as promised.'

There came a tut. 'What of the horse and shade?'

A sigh. 'Vanished, I'm afraid to say. They were taken by authorities.' A lie, on Jobey's part.

'The debt was two shades and a horse, Chaser,' said the overseer, a woman by the sounds of her voice, and a stern one at that. Heles was glad, if not a little worried about what was to come.

'I understand that, Overseer, but this was the best I could accomplish. Believe me, this catch is worth far more than the debt you speak of. Far, far more. Allow me to present her to the directors, and I promise you won't be disappointed.'

The overseer laughed, a harsh striking of steel on flint. 'Ha! And for what? For a measly river debt owed to those morons at Kal Duat? No.'

'You have to trust me.'

'You have not ear—'

'This will be of the greatest benefit to the Consortium.' Here, Heles heard Jobey pause, and swallow. 'And to you, Overseer. I assure you.'

Heles had been offered many a bribe in her years, and she knew this wait. This arbitrary wait while the morals crumbled enough.

'Bring her in. But I swear, Chaser, you better be on the silver.'

'Where has the trust gone in this organisation?'

'Proof is in the proof, as the directors say.'

Heles was dragged to the edge of the wagon by her foot, and casually dropped onto the dust. She wheezed from the impact, but Jobey had no reason to allow her to recover. Heles was dragged a short distance; rope was looped about her foot, pulled too tight for comfort, and a horse was smacked on the arse, or so the whinny and clip-clopping of hooves told her. Heles soon found herself being yanked forwards, first over sand and fine pebble, and then over smooth, cool sandstone. Cold shadow fell over her, and she felt the ground descend beneath her in ramp after ramp. Torchlight was scant. Her back began to ache, sore and grazed from the dragging.

'Can't I take this off yet?' Heles called to Jobey. 'And can't I walk like a dignified woman?'

The chaser's voice had taken on a reverent tone. 'I urge you to pipe down, Empress. We're drawing near.'

Heles smiled beneath the sackcloth. The ruse was still intact. Jobey was still a moron.

'How very dare you,' she said in a high-pitched voice. 'I thought a man of business would have more respect.'

It was enough to make Jobey haul her to her feet, so she could be dragged along by the horse upright instead of on her backside. Heles took the opportunity to stretch out her aching muscles beneath her swathe of rags, feeling tendons and sockets pop with the strain.

'You will behave. I may not have my ghast any more, but you have a triggerbow beneath your chin,' Jobey warned. The butt of something solid prodded Heles' jaw, making her bite her tongue. 'I will not hesitate to pull it in the presence of the directors, should you get any ideas of escape or rebellion.'

Heles nodded under her sack, too busy massaging her sore backside to really pay attention. She just wanted to get this over with, and return to the Core.

'How long?' she sighed.

'We're here.'

Heles sensed a brush of warmth as she passed under the glow of a skylight. As far as she could tell from behind the sackcloth, the rest of the musty room was dark, lacking torchlight, and full of the murmuring of urgent voices.

The slither of armour and the unhitching of the horse informed Heles they had been admitted into the darkness of the room. Heles saw the starkness of tall pillars around her, bereft of light.

'Who enters?'

'Chaser Jobey, my lords. With a grand transaction for your perusal!' Jobey's voice echoed around the vacuous space.

Heles wanted to scoff, but she bit her lip.

'Overseer?'

The woman's voice came from behind Heles. 'I recommend him, Directors.'

'Enter.'

Heles was tugged further into the darkness, coming to a rest somewhere she wagered was in the centre of the crown of pillars about her.

'Speak,' croaked an old voice, coming from above them.

Chaser Jobey took a deep breath before speaking. 'I present to you a thrilling opportunity, Directors. One that has eluded this Consortium for quite some time.'

Another voice, chime-like and young, called out, 'And that is?'

'Royal backing.'

'Our Consortium has survived for centuries without such luxuries. Why should we accept it now? We do not need such favours, Chaser…?'

'Jobey,' he answered, and Heles heard the gulp in his voice, as if his moment of glory had just been spat on from on high. 'But believe me, Directors, when I say I see what this city is becoming. Riots brim at the doorways and gates of Nyxwells. Chaos reigns in the Core Districts. Preachers of the Cult of Sesh stand on every street corner. No doubt you have heard of smoke pouring from the Cloudpiercer's summit? Yes? This city is becoming wild, Directors. Unpredictable, which does not bode well for profit. Instead, in such uncertain times, we need assurances. Allies.'

The silence was far from damning. It was thoughtful, ponderous. Heles was almost impressed by the man's speech, even though she despised him.

'Who have you brought us, Chaser Jobey?' called a woman's voice.

'Who, indeed? Directors!' Heles heard the shudder in his throat as Jobey took a breath. She wagered he had been waiting for this moment for some time.

'I present to you, Directors, Empress Nilith Renala. The body she was dragging was none other than the emperor himself. She meant to take the throne, and now, she is our debtor!'

Jobey tugged away Heles' sacking, revealing her dark raven hair, and in the faint light of the chamber, the black, swirling tattoos that wandered across her neck, jaw and bruised cheeks. Even though she wore nothing but road-filth, dried scabs and rags, the markings were telltale.

As Heles' eyes made sense of the dark chamber, she saw ten obscured figures, maybe more, wrapped in silks or rich cotton. They sat atop high pillars and tall-backed thrones, like gaudy crows upon perches. As she remembered to bare a smile and play her part, Heles wondered how on earth they ever got down from those lofty chairs.

The rest of the chamber was stark, grand only in the size of its columns and domed roof. A lone, yet wide shaft of sunlight eked through a glazed skylight far above. Heles jutted her face and neck into its light, for what little warmth it gave her.

'It seems you have brought us a scrutiniser, Chaser Jobey, not an empress.' Now the tone was damning, and coldly so. Heles' eyes were still having trouble focusing on the directors.

'No, I... the slatherghast—'

The chaser's hands seized her, dragging aside Heles' ill-fitting rags until her shoulders were bare. There, the tattoos swirled around her collarbone, accusatory.

She felt the stiffening of Jobey's grip on her halter rope, and the yanking at her collar.

Jobey had been so eager to show off his prize, he had forgotten to check its worth by peeking under the rags to see her arm made of skin and flesh, not blue, cold vapour. Heles stared at him, eyes full of derision and a smug look on her face.

'You are correct, Directors of the Consortium. I am in fact Scrutiniser Heles.'

The crows in their perches squawked loudly over one another.

'Time wasted is profit wasted, Jobey!'

'Take her away. Dispose of her.'

'And the chaser, too!'

Unseen in the darkness between the pillars, soldiers clad in sea-green mail and hoods appeared, tridents in their fists. They encircled them in moments.

'Wait!' Jobey cried, robes flailing.

'I think you'll want to hear what I have to say,' called Heles, voice husky but loud enough to stall the directors. 'You're fond of bargains, I wager? I have one for you!'

Fingers clicked, and in the darkness, blue flame sputtered, lighting the porcelain bowl of a pipe. The glow lit a face of broken veins and narrowed eyes. Tentacles of white smoke reached out from the darkness until they seemed to wither in the sunlight.

'Speak,' said the smoker, enunciating the word so hard it sounded as if he spat loose pipeweed.

Heles shrugged Jobey off, hissing. She jabbed a thumb at him as she looked up at the dark shapes and shrouded faces above. 'This man here may be a piece of worthless shit, but at least he's right about one thing. The city is changing. You will need help to survive it.'

The crows cackled.

'We have weathered the whims of Araxes for centuries,' said one.

'Our ways protect us. Silver buys many resources half-coins cannot.'

'Now we are stronger and more profitable than ever!'

Heles nodded while they finished congratulating themselves. She knew the thirst rich men and women had; the thirst to be richer still. Wealth was a never-ending mountain, littered with the bodies of fools craving a summit. 'And yet you could be more profitable still, couldn't you?'

Looks were traded between the crown of pillars. 'Speak!' came the order.

'Empress Nilith has killed the emperor, and she goes to claim the throne as we speak. She might have already pulled it off for all I know.'

'We care little for the games the royals play,' said the one with the pipe, voice thick with smoke.

'You might if one had it in their mind to abolish the Code.'

Heles let that hook dangle, just as she'd planned behind the sackcloth. She might have been quick with a blade, given more punches than she'd taken, but the scrutiniser was at her most dangerous when left to think and plot.

'You trade in silver, correct?' Heles asked.

One of the directors scoffed. 'And have for a thousand years,' she replied.

'Then imagine a city that relied on silver instead of copper.'

The director with the pipe took too eager a drag and spluttered smoke for some time. When silence was restored, doubts began to rain.

'Nonsense!'

'Lies!'

'Why would a royal do such a thing?'

'No noble would stand for it! Nor the Nyxites!'

'Neither would the Chamber of the Code!'

'They might,' Heles yelled over their squawking, 'if somebody powerful stood with her at the Grand Nyxwell when she scraps a thousand years of soultrading. Somebody like this Consortium.'

There was no answer, just the fidgeting of silk and ringed fingers.

'When the city sees a better life, they will take it. All they need is to glimpse it for long enough,' Heles breathed. 'You and I both know this city is rotten. How much longer can you go on surviving off its corpse? I know I'm tired of it. Dog tired. Aren't you?'

She was finished. Her argument had been made. Egos were stroked; her words were spent. Heles let their echoes die and waited for some time to see if her gamble would pay off.

Cinders fell as the director tapped out his pipe. They showered a soldier, but the man didn't shift an inch. Some switch or lever was pulled, and with a rattling of chains and cogs, the director's pillar began to lower. The mechanism moved at an infuriatingly leisurely pace, and by the time the director came waddling through the trident points and into the light, Heles was close to tapping her foot.

Bronze silks washed about him. Gold chains hung around his neck, some reaching to his waist. They sported jewels and gems, just like his fingers. The man's hair was a thin stripe across a bald head, as if a wagon had run a tarred wheel across his skull. His cheeks were pudgy, much like the rest of him, and his movements were sluggish, and yet there was a fierce gaze in his eyes. Warrior-like. Bloodlust.

Heles stood tall as the director approached, soldiers flowing around him.

'And your bargain?' he asked of her.

'Stand with the empress, and as payment for her debt, you can help her build a new Araxes. I may not be Empress Nilith, but I'll speak for her, even if she doesn't want me to,' said Heles, matching his avid stare.

'Too costly.'

'Too afraid of a risk, Director?'

'What do you gain from this? Loyalty has a price.'

'Peace,' Heles spat the word. 'And some fucking quiet.'

After a brief glance around the hall to each of his fellow directors, the man took a sharp breath. 'We will hold your soul as assurance, should you be tricking us. You'll spend the rest of your days in Kal Duat.'

Heles swallowed the lump in her throat, wondering how much she trusted Nilith. How much she was willing to sacrifice for a faint dream of a different world. In the end, she thrust out a hand for him to shake.

'You'll see,' she whispered.

CHAPTER 23
FROM BEYOND THE GRAVE

Worshippers of the old ways are like woodlice.
You see one, two, perhaps a dozen, and assume
they are all that infest your abode. But prise
up a floorboard and you will soon discover the
writhing masses hiding beneath your feet.

FROM 'ON THE ORIGIN OF GODS' BY WRITER
GEER BURJALI, WHO MYSTERIOUSLY VANISHED
AFTER ITS PUBLICATION

RIP. DRIP. DRIP. IT FILLED the dark smoke of my dreams: a constant dripping and trickling of water over bare stone, where no moss dared to grow.

I heard it then, as the dullness faded: the shuffling of countless feet. The rising moan of the disillusioned dead. A voice cried out behind me, and a cold waft rushed passed me.

No...

Blue shapes appeared in the grey smog, barging me aside as they ran. Towards what, I did not know, but my legs moved unbidden along with them. Soon enough I was rushing through crowds, like one clueless beast amongst the herd, fleeing an unseen predator flitting through the grass. I looked behind me, but saw nothing but the faint blue outlines of other ghosts, mouths open and crying out.

I refused to be here again. Trapped beneath the earth for eternity. Surrounded by the moaning dead.

Five points of white light glowed above me, and I charged for them, feeling cheated. A hill rose up beneath me, and despite my ghostly form, the effort drained me. Inky water spilled down the slope's craggy, obsidian surface. I was soon crawling on hands and knees, spitting curses at the lights whenever I found a moment. The other ghosts had flowed around the hill, leaving me alone. A blue river coursed below me.

'It's hopeless!' I yelled to the stars. 'Fucking hopeless!'

The stars began to flicker, as if they burned too hot.

'I tried to help! I fought hard! Killed! And for what? This fucking place!'

One star fizzled out, closely followed by a second. I took a stand on a rock, feeling the rivulets of freezing water pushing against my feet. Their flow was increasing. I heard the pounding of a waterfall somewhere in the darkness.

'Who knows what the gods want, eh? I certainly have no idea, but I know it's not my best interests!'

A third star was extinguished.

'Maybe the Cult was right!' I roared. 'You hear me, Oshirim? Maybe you did get too greedy, and betray your kind!'

A fourth.

'Maybe you deserve this flood!'

Caltro... a voice boomed above me, thunder to the storm I heard growing. The smoke above me cleared, revealing the impending fangs of colossal stalactites.

The final star burned yellow, then orange, then as it flickered to red, the blackness claimed it, and the endless cavern fell dark. Even the glowing river of dead below me died away, leaving me alone, a blue candle against the night.

With a shockwave that threw me to my backside, a roiling wave of scarlet light tore through the darkness. The dark was dragged back like a black cloth from a table, sucked into a single point of absolute nothing. It sat between the dead stars, now grey husks against this new backdrop of fire and light. When all but the last of the dark had been consumed, the vortex collapsed in on itself until it glowed a fierce crimson. There came a searing heat as its great eye turned on me.

The water cascaded around me. I shielded my eyes, only to see a towering wave of black water spilling down the cliff above me. I could do nothing but hold my breath through old habit, and curse the dead gods for giving me such a calamitous thing as hope.

DRIPPING FILLED MY EARS AGAIN. An incessant patter of water on bare stone. There was a ringing of chains, too, and in the darkness of my closed eyes I wondered how this endless cavern could become any direr. I wanted to curl into a ball, burst into light and blink out like a star.

'Caltro,' called a woman's voice. This voice did not shake the skies like thunder. In fact, it was rather hoarse, and close by.

I tensed, feeling no trickle of ice-water beneath my ribs, lying as I was on the stone. There was no waterfall. No storm. Only dripping.

The chains rattled again. 'Caltro!'

My eyes cracked open to find, not slick black rock, but dusty, straw-covered sandstone. My hands glowed in front of my face, and I found thin, copper-core manacles around my wrists. Weakly, I pulled at them, and heard my own chains rattle in their fixings. It was not over.

'Thank fuck,' I breathed.

I heard the voice again. 'They must have hit him harder than I thought.'

'Fucking buffoon hasn't realised he's a prisoner yet.' Another woman's voice this time, and that stoked me into action.

'Oh, I have,' I replied to whoever had insulted me, and with much dizziness and difficulty, I propped myself up onto my elbows to look around.

The chamber was a simple circle of sandstone with a heavily barred door, and I knew instantly it was a prison cell. The roof was distant and the walls devoid of windows. There was only a skylight, set high in the stone wall. What meagre sunlight it let in bounced from carefully arranged polished blocks of stone, making it zigzag around the chamber. It showed me the faces of my cellmates, all of whom stared at me. It was quite the gathering.

Empress Nilith sat cross-legged, arms splayed by a chain and a yoke. One hand was blood-stained and clenched. The other hung limp and glowed blue. She still wore her rags, as I did. The slatherghast's poison was spreading; I saw the black veins creeping up her neck, reaching for her ears.

Beside her was Farazar, trying to murder me with his gaze alone. He too sat on the floor, his arms and hands wrapped up in lengths of chain.

At his side, I recognised Pointy, dangling point-first from a single piece of rope. He swung ever so gently, like a failing pendulum.

Directly below him, lying in the soulblade's shadow, was a small creature. It took me a moment to register it was a falcon, and a dishevelled one at that. The bird looked half dead, with feathers all out of place and bloody gashes on his speckled breast. His neck was cocked at an uncomfortable angle, but there was a glint in his yellow eyes that told me a soul lay within him. *A strangebound.*

To my right were three ghosts, and though I recognised them, it didn't temper my shock to see them here, chained to the wall like me. The closest was the ghost of Boran Temsa, his head propped up on one knee. Next to him, surprisingly, was Sisine, empress-in-waiting, with a great gash across her neck and her face covered in claw marks and a gloomy scowl. I saw now why the falcon's claws were caked in blood. It appeared I had missed much since my fall from the Cloudpiercer.

Last, but far from least, was a ghost with a misshapen face and skull, bent arms, and broken legs. Her ribcage was a shallow grave, and she seemed… *flatter*, somehow. And oh, how Hirana glared at me, her killer.

'Well, what a delightful party this has turned out to be.'

Any further words and questions I had in mind were drowned out by a burst of shouting from all sides. It seemed they had been waiting for me to wake up.

'You despicable murdering half-life, Caltro Basalt!' Hirana screeched, words still difficult after her recent binding.

'All that work! How was I supposed to know the Nyxwell was dry?'

'I'm glad!'

'I will kill you over and over for your treachery, falcon!' *That answers that question.*

'Like I told you before I cut your throat: fuck you.'

'You conniving bitch of a mother! Living under my nose for so many years after I banished you?'

'I don't know why I even got involved with any of this!'

'Murderer!'

'Happy now, Mother?'

'Traitor!'

Their shouting dried up as they realised I was silently shaking my head at them all. I felt like I was trapped in a wagon with a bickering family and screaming children. I did not care about them, not even the talking falcon; I was just elated to not be under the earth, away from the jaws of water and fire. I couldn't deny that the nightmare, if I could call it that, had shaken me. *A black flood...* I would have dwelled on it longer had the old widow not challenged me.

'What are you so smug about, locksmith?' Hirana snapped.

'Happy to be half alive, and not in some dark cavern,' I said, immediately recognising the flinch in hers, Temsa's and Sisine's faces. I knew they had seen it, too. Even the falcon nodded soberly at me. 'You know what I'm talking about. The so-called afterlife. The great lie.'

Hirana was far from happy about my survival. 'Unimportant. You murdered me, you foul creature!'

'You should have given me my half-coin.' I was hardly in the mood to argue with the woman, especially now she had no flesh about her, and was finally on my level.

Temsa interjected on his own behalf. 'You should have left well enough alone, old bag,' he hissed, setting off the argument once more. It was strange seeing his lips move, and hearing breath and voice coming from his dismembered head. His spare arm gesticulated on his behalf.

'You're one to talk, Boran Temsa!'

'So you're Boran Temsa,' Nilith muttered. 'I expected you to be taller.'

The soulstealer's face darkened as the empress continued.

'This is nobody's fault but Farazar's!' cried Nilith. 'You're all blind to it. We're all here because of his ineptitude.'

Sisine spoke up. 'I want answers, Mother! Father!'

Nilith raised her chin, staring at Sisine's wounds. I could see the marks of tears down her soiled face. Perhaps it was at the death of her daughter, or perhaps because of failure. 'Seeing as we're all gathered here together, why the fuck not?'

Sisine stabbed the ground with a blue finger. 'How long has the Sanctuary lain empty?'

'Four or five years,' Nilith answered. 'Annoying, isn't it? Thinking that he outwitted us?'

I swore Sisine was turning a shade of purple. I busied myself by looking for a stiff bit of straw.

'And how long have you known?' asked the empress-in-waiting.

'A year, perhaps.'

'And all the while you've let him ruin this empire, driving it to chaos?'

'Pardon me, but I didn't see you marching across the Duneplains and Long Sands to fetch him. And it's strange how such chaos should erupt the moment I leave the city, daughter.'

'That is *their* fault,' Sisine hissed at Temsa and her grandmother.

'I strongly recall being summoned to the Piercer for a conversation all about chaos, Princess,' said Temsa. 'You got what you wanted. And what you deserve for all your scheming and double-crossing.'

'Rich, coming from a cultist like you.'

'Cultist…?' Temsa's head spluttered. 'They approached me. Betrayed me in the end like everyone else!'

'You're the one who let them into the Core Districts once more, Sisine. But it is moot. Farazar brought this upon himself the day he banished me. Isn't that right, son of mine? You two simply got in the way,' Hirana growled, still staring at me. I evaded those white eyes. She constantly shuffled around, as if loathing the feeling of vapour instead of skin.

Farazar scoffed. 'And gladly so, I say. Your cunning and ambition know no bounds, Sisine. And you, Mother. Apparently not even the sky can hold you, it seems. I should have had you killed like Father.'

'You could have tried.'

'Where is Etane, daughter?' Nilith asked.

Sisine narrowed her eyes. 'You do not call me that. You have no right. I raised myself.'

I saw Nilith flinch as that insult nicked a nerve. I'd found my piece of straw, and while I watched the bickering, I shuffled closer to the wall, clasped the lock, and began to waggle the straw in the simple lock.

'And Etane is beyond the grave. Danib Ironjaw saw to that. Etane Talin proved himself a traitor in his last moments, though I bet you already knew that, seeing as he was your shade all along.'

'Somebody had to keep an eye on you. I see I was wise to do so, what with the riots, tals and tors murdered en masse, and a Nyxwater shortage, of all things. How did you manage that? You want the throne, Sisine, but you're not fit to sit upon it. None of you are.'

'I'll fucking second that,' said the foul-mouthed falcon, much to my surprise.

Hirana rattled her chains. 'And you are, Nilith? What has all this been for? Just so you can claim the throne for yourself?'

'And what is that sorcery, making you half-alive, half-shade?' Temsa demanded.

'A long story, is what it is, but it makes me more alive than any of you. Alive enough to take the throne and change Araxes for good.'

'She plans to set them free,' Farazar growled. 'Every half-life.'

Laughter erupted from Temsa and Hirana. Sisine just boiled, as if her entire future had just been reduced to cinders before her. Nilith sat straighter, enduring their mockery like a cliff endures the sea, though I could see in her eyes a weakness. A tiredness come from fighting too long, too hard, and for it all to come to naught in a sandstone cell.

'Madness!' cried Sisine.

'Everything seems like madness when attempted for the first time, daughter,' Nilith whispered.

Hirana was outraged. Her smashed face contorted with rage. 'This is what you get for marrying a foreigner, Farazar!'

'You would have murdered me anyway, Mother!'

'*He's* the murderer!' Hirana yelled at me.

Silence fell as eyes turned on me. I answered it with a simple *click* of the lock. My manacle sprung free.

'You're all murderers,' I said calmly, though I wanted to shout it in every one of their faces. I didn't know whether it was the stress, the haunting, or the soldiers' clubs, but I felt broken. Tired. 'Every one of us. Even me, and I came to this city a thief, yes, but not a taker of lives. This city's changed me, just like it's changed and warped and corrupted all of you. You play this great game of yours even if it kills you, and yet you all lose in the end. Whether it's the knife, indenturement, banishment, or just simply forgetting what it's like to have a soul. Or humanity. You lose. None of you are innocent.'

'*Thanks*,' said Pointy in my head.

I met every one of their scowls even as I tackled the second lock.

'With the exception of the sword. He didn't really have a choice. The talking falcon I don't know.'

'He's guilty all right,' muttered Sisine.

'You are far, far from innocent. You can blame each other all you want, but look where it's got you. Dead and in the dirt. You all play along because it gives you an excuse to be cruel and to do as you please. You breed hate and fear. Celebrate callousness. Life has become worthless, not a miracle or magic, and nobody has given even a moment in the last thousand years to think whether things could or should change. None except this woman.'

They took a moment to stare at each other as I gestured to Nilith. The empress kept her eyes on me as I broke open the second manacle and got to standing. It felt strangely good to look down on them all.

Sisine tried to spit at me, but forgot her ghostly form. By the way she shook, I wagered she was far from happy with it. 'I refuse to be lectured by a Krass thief who has never owned a soul in his life!' The words, although malformed by her fresh binding, were damning enough.

I threw up my hands in exasperation and pointed at Hirana, Sisine and Temsa. 'As far as I'm concerned, you all got what was coming to you. Killed. Chained up. Captured by…' I looked around, confused by the sunlight all of a sudden. 'Who's in charge?'

As if they'd had ears pressed up against the door, waiting for the perfect dramatic moment, the locks slid in their brackets, and in swept Enlightened Sisters Yaridin and Liria. Gone were the monkish crimson robes, replaced instead by red cloaks. They wore dark steel breastplates etched with glyphs, kilts of mail, and greaves. Swords hid under the scarlet folds; I saw the tips of their scabbards. The sisters' bald heads were bare, their glow bright and their eyes shining. They did not look victorious, or magnanimous, but outraged.

'Liria and Yaridin, if I'm not mistaken,' muttered Nilith. 'It's been some time.'

Farazar growled. 'The very same.'

'Release them,' the sisters chorused, pointing to Nilith and me, though they quickly realised I'd already shed my manacles. I held my hands up as if they had a triggerbow trained on me. I had assumed my use to the Cult was over now that the Sanctuary was open, haunting or not. Three ghosts in robes scuttled past them and quickly saw to Nilith's yoke and chains.

'We see no lock can keep you for long, Caltro,' said Liria, her face softening slightly.

'None ever has,' I replied.

Farazar seemed far from pleased to be left locked up, especially by the Cult. 'Release me, Sisters! I am your emperor!' he yelled.

'You are no emperor, Farazar,' Yaridin told him, looking down on him like a child might look at a bug before squashing it. 'You have not been for some time. If you ever were.'

'Outrageous!'

'Filthy cultists,' said Sisine. 'They have been behind all this. I know it.'

'Played us both,' Temsa muttered. He seemed subdued, almost defeated in that moment. Perhaps my words had finally got into that disembodied skull of his. I found it ironic how much they hated each other, yet were bonded by their hatred of the Cult. It could have been useful, had they ever had the wits to put their minds together.

'Correct, Tor, Empress-in-Waiting. A starving person will do much for a morsel, and you two were hungry indeed.'

The ghosts came with red robes and draped them over both Nilith's shoulders and mine.

'Careful now, Caltro. Showing your true colours.' Hirana narrowed her skewed eyes at me as the sisters and Nilith left the room.

I ignored her, looking to Pointy instead. His pommel stone wore a deep frown. 'My sword?' I called after them.

The sisters eyed me from the corridor, measuring me, assessing my intent. They nodded as one, and I reached for Pointy, turning him against his own rope. The threads split at the merest touch of his metal, and the falcon on the floor breathed a sigh of relief.

'Thank fuck for that,' he said, closing his eyes.

The heavy door closed with a bang and a crunch of bolts behind us, and we found ourselves in a corridor that had a faint and constant rumble to it. The sunlight was gone, replaced by the familiar ghostly glow of lanterns filled with fluttering insects. The other ghosts withdrew to the ends of the corridor, while Liria and Yaridin stayed with us. Nilith stood apart from us, shoulders heavy with burden, but eyes sharp and awake with suspicion.

'Our sincerest apologies, Empress. Our brothers and sisters were too eager in their attempts to make sure you were safe. You were not meant to be treated so harshly. You are our esteemed guests, and as Mr Basalt can testify, we treat our guests with the utmost respect.'

I shrugged, unable to deny them but eager to get to the point. 'Where is my half-coin?'

Neither of the sisters looked at me as they spoke. 'All in good time, Caltro.'

'Wait—'

'Three questions, Sisters,' Nilith said, holding up three glowing fingers. The rest of her arm stayed hidden under her robe.

'Ask away, Empress. Though we—'

'Where are we?'

'Beneath the Avenue of Oshirim, in Katra Rassan. That rumbling you can hear is the streets above.'

'The Cathedral On Its Head. Farazar always suspected…' whispered

Nilith, understanding the Arctian. 'Where is Farazar's body?'

'Safe, below us in a sealed chamber that only we have the key to.'

'And where is my horse?'

'Also safe, above in our stables. Quite the animal. Extraordinarily protective.'

I wondered how many ghosts had been kicked across the plaza before the Cult had managed to subdue Anoish.

Nilith cleared her throat and began to walk away, down the corridor. 'You may show me to both, and then you may escort me to the Grand Nyxwell to claim Farazar's body,' she said. 'Interfere and face the consequences.'

'*Have I mentioned how much I admire her?*' Pointy commented in my head.

The sisters had not moved. 'We plan to do nothing of the sort.'

'Do you not? Whose soldiers and ghosts apprehended us at the Nyxwell?'

'Sisine's forces. Unaware of the… shift, shall we say, in power.'

Nilith stopped. 'Whose power?'

The sisters smiled. 'Won't you walk with us, Empress?'

Nilith was far from convinced. She put a hand to her hip, as if reaching for a sword handle, but realised she was unarmed. Her fists clenched in any case.

'We know your time is short. Please. A small amount of your time might be worthwhile.'

'On one condition.'

'Yes, Empress?'

'I know the old ways of healing with Nyxwater and the touch of a ghost. I witnessed it first-hand in Abatwe. I want you to heal the falcon.'

Liria and Yaridin shared a look. 'Empress,' they said. 'We found the falcon Bezel beside the body of your daughter. He was the one who—'

'I'm very aware of what he did,' Nilith said, a crack in her voice. 'Heal him. He's had enough pain.'

Yaridin raised a hand to one of the nearby ghosts while Liria led us forwards, into a stairwell and through a network of ever-burrowing tunnels and steps. The Katra Rassan seemed to be a hive of busyness that day. At junctions in the corridors, teams of shades and hand-carts passed us by, their loads covered in scarlet tarpaulins. Every chamber I glimpsed was host to some sort of activity or another, filled from wall to door with ghosts and red-robed living. Nilith stared about, as baffled as I was by the hustle and bustle, and curious how large the Cathedral was. Her gaze did not stop roving.

Liria stayed silent until she brought us to a wider corridor with an open end. Another rumble filled my ears, though this was not from above, but below. It grew louder as we approached the twisted iron railings of a wooden walkway, and became a dull roar as we emerged. Gusts of air disturbed my vapours, made my robes flap around my legs. Sunlight from above cast veils of spiralling dust motes. Below us was a glowing sea of ghosts and red cloth. They were stacked on every level of the Cathedral's deep pit. Crowds of cultists flowed like purple rivers around ramps and stairwells and walkways, cascading down each level like waterfalls. Many simply waited, shuffling about as they conversed. Many others still worked away at their frantic errands. I leaned out over the iron railing, and felt dizzy staring into their depths.

'Welcome, Empress, to the Church of Sesh,' Sister Liria said softly, barely audible over the roar of the crowds.

Nilith began to chuckle, softly at first, then a loud laugh that echoed through the giant rafters of the Cathedral's roof. 'All this time we've been fighting amongst ourselves, and you've been building your own empire under our noses. You were right, Caltro. This has all been for naught.'

'On the contrary, Empress. This has all been for peace. This is all for you.'

'Lies.'

'We see Caltro hasn't told you of our intentions.'

I crossed my arms.

'Oh, he has. He told me it was the Cult that orchestrated much of this chaos. That it is Sisine you plan to put on the throne. Not me.'

Liria sighed, placing her hands on the railing as Nilith had. She followed her gaze down into the crowds. 'We are not so different, you and the Cult. Though we have alternate methods, we strive for the same result.'

'And that is?'

'Peace, justice, and freedom for all. We too believe the empire sick, and its poison is indenturement. The Code. The Tenets. We recognise the system is broken, Empress, and people like Temsa, Hirana, and, with respect, your daughter, are content to keep it broken. We want to heal it, as you do.'

'But you worship chaos.'

'We worship the god of death. Of change. Chaos is but Sesh's tool.' Liria turned to face the empress, and Nilith met her gaze. 'We tried many years ago, when you were but fresh to the Arc, barely Emperor-in-Waiting Farazar's wife. We had hoped to breed the idea of freedom in Milizan, but your husband thwarted us, drove us out. For two decades, we have watched Farazar drive the empire into decline, waiting for an opportunity not for revenge, but for change.

'The Church of Sesh trades in information, and after gathering all our knowledge together, we knew another ruler was needed. We originally chose you, Empress. According to our spies, you have never been the Arctian that Farazar expected, riling against every Code and Tenet that stood in your way. We had planned to help you ascend to the throne, but when you disappeared, Empress, our plans changed.

Like the rest of the city, we believed you had fled back to Krass, finally tired of your inept husband. We knew your ambitious daughter would make a move on his Sanctuary, and that she longed to make a name for herself. We assumed, perhaps wrongly, that her ambition could be used for good. And so, through Etane, we introduced her to the only person in Araxes with ambition enough to match hers: Boss Boran Temsa. He had not only the ambition, but the means. As with many other soulstealers, such as Berrix the Pale, or Astarti, we have been watching Temsa for years. We placed Danib with him when he began to show promise, and a thirst for climbing Araxes' ladder. We used that thirst, providing him tors and tals with private vaults, showing Sisine that with enough uproar, she could draw Farazar from his Sanctuary and emerge the saviour of the city. She took our example to heart, and the pressure in the city rose to boiling point. We knew Sisine and Temsa would clash eventually, becoming rivals instead of partners. Such minds can never work well with others. By creating a villain in Temsa, we were able to deliver him to Sisine as a gift, giving her a scapegoat she could use to play the hero she longed to be, and patching the rift Farazar put between the city and the Cult.'

Liria paused and I found myself nodding appreciatively. Nilith was content to listen. I could almost hear the cogs of her sharp mind working.

'For all our years of careful planning, we did not account for several rogue factors,' Liria continued, holding up three glowing fingers of her own. 'A vengeful grandmother every Arctian thought banished or dead. The Reaches' finest locksmith, murdered his first night in Araxes...'

Both women looked at me and I find myself trying to suck in my gut.

'And you, Nilith Rikehar. A wife who would kill her husband and drag his body hundreds of miles home.' Liria sighed thoughtfully. 'You've fought hard, haven't you, Empress?'

Nilith couldn't help but agree, or so her slumping shoulders and weary blink told me. 'The question remains: who will ascend to the throne?'

There was a tense pause until Liria broke it. 'Who would you choose? A rampant soulstealer, thirsty for power and blood, still trying to prove his young self right? A cruel old woman, too consumed with vengeance to remember trust and loyalty? A daughter so full of hate she would ruin an empire just to appear its saviour? Or a woman who would cross a desert twice with the emperor's body, fighting to heal the corruption of a city that's not even hers?'

I knew which I'd choose. I could see why these sisters called themselves enlightened. They made a damn fine argument.

Whether tongue-tied, tired or simply waiting for the answer, Nilith stared at the sisters long and hard.

'We would choose the latter,' answered Yaridin, emerging from the mouth of the corridor to stare down into the masses. 'You are Farazar's rightful killer. The city will not accept any claim but yours, especially given the fact any other candidates are now dead and bound. We can help you take the throne, and you will be free to make the changes you have fought to make.'

Perhaps their ears had been pressed to the door after all.

Liria stepped closer, conspiratorial. 'We know what you intend to do with your authority, Empress. To bring freedom to shades. It has been a dream of the Church's for an age, and we would gladly stand beside you upon the dais of the Grand Nyxwell.'

'You forget this.' Nilith held up her left fist, shrugging the robe and rags along her arm and casting sapphire light across the balcony's iron and wood. With her fingers, she dragged away her ragged collar, where blue vapour had now claimed most of the skin of her chest. It was now clawing its way up her neck, the brown of her skin turning to ash and charcoal where life crossed into death.

'And you forget this,' said Liria, reaching for Nilith's other hand; sand, blood, chipped nails and all. Nilith shrugged away, but got the sister's meaning. 'Though there is no cure we can offer you, the slatherghast's poison hasn't claimed you yet. There is still time.'

'Half alive is better than half dead. Is that it?' Nilith spat.

Yaridin conceded with a nod. 'In the eyes of the City of Countless Souls, yes.'

'So, I'm your last choice.'

'No.' Liria shook her head resolutely. 'You are our last hope. The city teeters on the edge of ruin. The Nyx has all but dried up. Order has been abandoned. Justice is a long-lost memory. The time is short for it to be saved. It will require sacrifice, but worthy sacrifice.'

The words fell heavy between us. I would have bowed under such responsibility, but Nilith straightened, looking down her nose at the sisters as if spectacles balanced on its tip. It was the most imperious I'd ever seen the woman, and I saw the empress in her rise to the challenge.

'And here I was expecting to have to fight my way out of a Cult of Sesh dungeon,' she said.

'We prefer *Church* of Sesh, Empress, and we would rather be an ally than an enemy,' Yaridin said, wearing that thin sisters' smile. Cold and empty, but a smile nonetheless.

'Will you let us help you achieve what you want?' asked Liria, staring deep into Nilith's emerald eyes, searching them eagerly.

It took the empress some time to answer, her gaze locked on the sisters'. 'I will,' Nilith said at last.

'*But the gods, Caltro. The flood...*' Pointy reminded me, deep in the recesses of my mind as if he feared the sisters would hear him even within my skull. Perhaps he was right; Liria turned to look at me, beckoning as Yaridin led Nilith along the walkway. A series of zigzags in and out of the earthen walls brought us to a set of stairs leading to a long, drawn out platform. Suspended by a series of golden chains, it thrust out into space, almost to the centre of the great pit that was the Cathedral On Its Head. The sheer breadth of space between the flimsy wooden cladding of the platform and the glowing depths dizzied me, and I had fallen from the tip of the greatest spire known to humanity.

'Farazar will fucking love this,' Nilith said, adopting a weary smile. 'What now?' she asked.

For once, the sisters held their tongues and simply gestured to the empty platform. Nilith took a step forward, realised I hadn't moved, and waved a hand for me to follow. I wanted to gulp. I stayed where I was, unable to help craning my neck to peer over the edges of the walkway, like a morbid urge to run your finger along the knife, just to test its edge…

'Caltro.' Nilith beckoned to me again, and I did as I was told.

I followed closely behind her, nervous, and unavoidably mindful of the last royal I had teetered on the edge of a great height with.

Nilith strode out before me, as if this was the very least of the challenges she had faced in the Arc's deserts. I wondered if they would make my tribulations as pale as sun-bleached papyrus. I had no choice but to join her at the strict, bare edge of the platform, where we leaned over to feel the cold draughts of air swirling up the jumbled tiers of Katra Rassan.

Before we had realised their presence, Liria and Yaridin called out from behind us as one. I almost tumbled over in shock.

'Presenting the new ruler absolute of the Arctian Empire, Empress Nilith Rikehar Renala!'

The roar that filled the Cathedral was so thunderous I half expected the rafters and sunlight to come crashing down. Swathes of ghosts fell to their knees, like fields of corn bending before the oncoming storm. Those wearing breastplates or bearing shields beat their swords against their metal, giving an avid heartbeat to the massed crowds of dead. As they swayed and bellowed, they became one great beast, hungry for action.

'Finally, we shall have our freedom! Sesh be praised!' the sisters chorused, their words echoing around the chamber and bringing the voices to deafening levels.

I watched as Nilith raised her hands to the crowds, drinking in their praise and cheers like a warlord atop a conquered castle. I watched her wide eyes flit about the masses, watching them bow and punch the air with their fists. Perhaps not the victorious moment she had imagined, deep beneath the earth with the fanatics of the Cult, but she had earned it.

As the roaring continued unabated, Liria and Yaridin led us back to the shadow of the walkway.

'Tomorrow, Nilith, you will stand at the Grand Nyxwell. The Church will make sure of it!' said the sisters, shouting over the noise.

'The last stores of Nyxwater are being prepared to refill the well.'

'Chamberlain Rebene has already been informed of your return.'

'The Chamber of the Code stands with you.'

'As do the shade soldiers Sisine put upon the streets.'

'And the brothers and sisters of the Cult are at your disposal.'

Nilith bowed her head.

'For now, you may rest,' added Yaridin. Ghosts appeared unbidden from a nearby archway of sandstone, red as their robes. 'Our brothers and sisters will lead the way.'

As the ghosts gathered about her, Nilith cast me a look over her shoulder. 'Maybe it's time to stop running,' she called to me, with a grim nod. No sooner had the ghosts appeared than they vanished into the warren of Katra Rassan, and I was left alone with the sisters, one hovering at each of my shoulders.

'I would listen to her, brother,' breathed Liria, standing so close her cold vapour mingled with mine.

'Three times you have run from us now.'

'We would find it hard to accept a fourth.'

'What was I supposed to do? You bargained with me like a pawn when you wanted the Sanctuary open. Where is my half-coin?' I asked, not moving, not turning, just staring at some grimy spot on the iron railings under my glowing hand.

The words had barely escaped my mouth before I found it dangling beside my cheek, on a clean chain of silver and copper thread. The faint lanterns about us gave it a greenish hue. I snatched it away, praying for the metal not to burn me, but all I felt was its faint weight, and the dull cold sitting in my palm. Relief flowed through me like a breeze.

'So what now?' I asked them, turning to challenge their blank expressions. 'What do you need of me?'

Liria looked somewhat offended. 'Nothing. You are free to do as you wish, Caltro, as any of our brothers and sisters are. You may leave Araxes if you please. We will even have a ship prepared.'

Now there were some enchanting words I had longed to hear.

'However, we hope you will stay. Join us at the Grand Nyxwell. Be a part of our... *revolution*,' said Yaridin, words soft and sticky like cold honey.

'Stand with us and the empress tomorrow, and watch justice come to the City of Countless Souls.'

I looked between them. The pieces had been swept from the board. Only they and the empress remained. For all intents and purposes, they had finally won. Royal backing. No challengers. Freedom in sight. And yet I couldn't help but rack my brains to figure their angle, their cut, their play.

I jabbed a thumb over my shoulder. 'You convinced Nilith easily enough. But I have no stake in the Arc. My fight's over now. I'd quite like to go home.'

'*You promised, Caltro.*'

'You would not stand with your brothers and sisters?' Liria stated, making it sound accusatory. Once again, she spoke my thoughts before I could. 'Do you not trust us?'

'It's not that I don't trust you—'

'We have given the empress what she wants. What the city wants.' Yaridin stepped closer, eyes narrow, appearing hurt. 'Have we not given you the same kindness? Given you justice?' She tapped the half-coin in my palm. 'Your freedom?'

'You have, but—' I daren't even think of the gods' warnings, in case the sisters saw into my mind.

Liria spoke in my ear. 'We would make you a king amongst the dead, Caltro Basalt.'

That stumped me. 'I… what do you mean, a king?'

'*A king? You? Really?*' Pointy piped up. I covered his face with my hand. '*Lies.*'

'We told you before, Caltro. A new era is coming, and its dawn is tomorrow.' Liria smiled. 'If you must be shown, then we will show you. Perhaps once you see, you will finally trust us, and stand with your brothers and sisters at the Nyxwell.'

Before I knew it, the Enlightened Sisters were guiding me along the walkway unusually forcibly. Their mail jingled furiously with their hurried pace. They marched me to a lift, one with thick cogs intruding on every wall, and with the shuffling of some levers, the cogs began to turn, dropping down into a black shaft.

Not a word was said during our jittering descent. Pointy was quiet for the most part, despite several overbearing coughing noises and muttered warnings about rabbit holes. I busied myself thumbing the face of my half-coin, trying and failing to feel the ridges of a glyph that was not my name. If I ever made it out of the Cult's shadow, I would carve *Caltro* across it.

When the archway of a corridor rose up to greet us, a yank of the lever stopped us dead, and we began to wind through knotted stairwells and halls propped up by thick, cubic pillars.

Beyond and below those halls, we came to an iron-plated door adorned with glyphs I had never seen before. This door had no locks, but simply weight and heavy bars to keep it closed. The sisters pressed their hands against twin lines of glyphs, and the bars began to recede of their own accord. I got the feeling this wasn't going to be the most bizarre portion of the day.

Old hinges whined as the room beyond was revealed. From what I could see, the room was a bare box of polished stone tiles. I felt a draught of heat against my vapours, as if the trapped air was desperate to escape. The tails of my borrowed robe billowed.

'We must leave your sword here,' said Yaridin, fingers already around Pointy's handle. Though I flinched away, she relieved me of him and hung him from two pins in the wall.

'Why?' My nervousness was growing.

'Come,' Liria said, her hand pressed into the small of my back. The word 'cell' flitted through my mind. I cursed myself for not being my usual charming self. I blamed my nightmare.

The only feature in the room was a circular stone construction, the height of my waist. Radiant coals lay atop it, trapped beneath a slab of seamless granite and yet somehow still burning. A dusting of black sand had been cast across the slab. The whole lump of stone looked half forge, half altar.

'The age of the living is over, Caltro,' said the sisters in unison. 'The age of the dead is beginning.'

The door had swung closed. I couldn't feel the soulblade in my mind any more. Black smoke began to eke from the coals, dripping down the side of the altar-forge.

Liria spoke alone, voice rising in pitch as though she were being squeezed. 'Nilith's ascent to the throne is just the spark to a flame that will change this world once more.'

Now Yaridin. 'We will usher in a new peace. A new empire. One united under the master who gave us our half-lives.'

Black sand began to pour out of unseen holes in the granite slab, swirling in breezes I couldn't feel. The smoke began to rise, filling the air about us. The coals flared once, spitting flame, and then darkened to a ruby glow. For the first time since being dead, I felt a warmth in me, and not one of a scorching sun.

'Prepare yourself, Caltro.'

'It is not every day you meet a god.'

How I fought not to correct them. Instead, I stared into the pile of sand before me, writhing as though worms duelled beneath the black grains.

Just as I was about to ask what this mystical pile was, the sand built itself into a tower, a crude model of the Cloudpiercer. Before it reached the tip, the sand fell apart.

If a snake could speak, and was choking as it breathed, it would sound like the voice that filled the silence. 'Caltro Bassssssalt,' it said, its hissing echoing through the smoke.

'Sesh, I presume. We have met before,' I replied, wishing I could see the look on the sisters' faces.

A grinning wolf appeared in the sand, rolling back and forth across the granite slab as if it shook its head at me. 'You doubt me,' came a great exhale. The wolf collapsed into itself, and two robed and hooded sisters rose from the sand instead. Where their eyes should be, the sand glowed hot, as if lava flowed within it. 'Doubt my children.'

'I do,' I said. I felt my lips quivering, as if Sesh were trying to drag the words out of me.

The sand became restless, thrashing back and forth, drawing faces I didn't recognise. 'Liessss, you've been told. Countlesss lies.'

'I've been told so many that every word is starting to sound like a lie at the moment. Enough. I was brought here to be shown the truth. Let's see it.'

I heard the sisters' slight gasp at my bluntness to their living, breathing, smouldering deity. Waves ran across the sand pile, crackling with sparks.

'Backbone. Excellent. Sssomething many of my children lack. But they were correct. You will do well amongssst us. Give me your hand, thief.'

Black sand reached up, belching smoke as a palm and fingers formed. I wrinkled my lip. Self-preservation might have been my religion, but curiosity had always been my ruler. It was too late to change that now. The final question of the flood had to be answered.

I thrust out my hand, and the god of chaos took it willingly. Black grit swarmed over my blue vapours like the tentacles of an octopus, drawing me down and to my knees.

SUNLIGHT FLOODED THE SMOG-FILLED room. I stumbled onto my knees, feeling the dry warmth of stone beneath me. White sand scattered around my glowing toes, unhurried and playful. I blinked in the brightness, making out a plaza of stone stretching out into the distance, where tall spires were wrapped in smoke and lacked detail. Shadows swung across the bleached stone, tracing the shapes of dark claws. I raised my head to see tusks towering above me. Where they breached the earth, I saw a queenlike figure standing upon a dais, and she was translucent and turquoise in the sun's glare, raising a half-moon of copper to an endless crowd of dead.

As I staggered to my feet, feeling the world slip beneath me, I called out, hearing nothing but an echo amongst the buildings. In a blink, the queen had turned to me. Her hand reached over the dust and stone to take mine, and I felt the sun's light grow brighter.

I stood with her upon the dais of marble, and looked out over the faceless multitudes. Outlines, they were, and nothing more, sketches of flowing blue, but they raised their hands to me all the same, and cheered with undrawn mouths. I felt the weight of metal on my forehead, and saw the glint of gold at the corner of my eyes. Lifting my gaze, I saw the queen with a crown upon her head, taller than a spear.

Again, I heard the voices of the dead, watched the crowd prostrate themselves before me. I looked over them, a lord in an empire that wasn't my own. And as I looked beyond the glow of the crowds, where the sun turned the flagstones to light, I saw the bodies filling every inch of stone across the plaza, and the lone red star hanging in the pale sky.

———◆———

HEAT SEARED MY HAND, WRENCHING me from the sunlight and back to the smoggy room. The altar-forge before me was still belching smoke.

'Ssstand with usss, ssssaviour.'

The sand writhed back and forth, forming the mandibles of an insect, then the pointy ears of a jackal, before collapsing. To the breath of a prolonged whisper, the sand drained away into the granite slab, and the lava-glow of the coals faded.

I looked up to find Liria and Yaridin standing over me. With a scuffing of sand, I got to my feet and brushed my robes free. They spoke in turn, voices almost singsong.

'Our secrets have been laid bare, Caltro.'

'Your decision?'

'Stand with your brothers and sisters? Reap the rewards of the new era?'

'Or fade back to Krass? Forgotten?'

I shifted towards the doorway and they trailed me, waiting, watching me like a wolf watches a rabbit hole. They must have assumed me dazed, or humbled.

The door was shut behind me and the bars retreated back into the stone arch at their own idle pace. Keeping my silence, I took Pointy from the wall and slid him back into my rags.

'Caltro?'

'Thank you for showing me the truth,' I whispered, facing away from the ghosts that hovered behind me. 'Tomorrow, Sisters.'

'Tomorrow, brother.'

And there I left the sisters, alone in the dark, tiled corridor. I left them there to stare at each other, and share a smile between themselves.

———◆———

YARIDIN SIGHED AS SHE WATCHED the locksmith disappear around a corner. She sounded weary. 'Do you think he trusts us now, Sister?'

Liria did nothing so perceptible as nod. 'If anything is true of Caltro Basalt, it is that he is incapable of making decisions for himself. He is a magpie hungry for silver, and we have just shown him gold. He will join us, if only for the convenience.'

'And if not...' Yaridin mused. With the clink and thud of chainmail and steel-plated boots, Danib lumbered into view, his new greatsword Pereceph leaning casually against his shoulder as if it were no more dangerous or heavy than an umbrella. The vapour snaking from between the plates of the shade's battle-armour had a heavy mix of white amongst the blue. One arm hung limply, and he seemed to list towards his left side. The duel with Etane had cost him.

'Caltro's is not the only soulblade in the city,' said Yaridin.

'Then we proceed.'

Yaridin extended a hand, and Liria took it, vapours entwining. 'Indeed we do, Sister.'

'Let us take the city, Brother Danib.'

Danib growled like a storm on the horizon.

CHAPTER 24
A NIGHT OF A THOUSAND KNIVES

Dunewyrms, though fearsome, are supposedly
poor imitations of their ancestors. The
nomads still trade tales of dunedragons,
creatures so large they could swallow entire
caravans in one ravenous gulp. These beasts
had hides like mountain slopes, could spit fire,
and the beating of their wings was known
to blow sandstorms across the plains. Even
today, many nomads believe that storms come
from the last dragons beating their wings.
How confident are we in our learning and the
reach of our Empire, that we can know with
absolute certainty these are merely stories, and
that wild and ancient powers don't still lurk on
the borders of our knowledge?.

FROM 'THE YOUTH OF MAN'
BY ESPER DRAK

CHAMBERLAIN REBENE PICKED A CRUMB from the corner of his eye while he tested the limits of his lungs. Once he'd crammed as much breath as he could into his ribcage, Rebene let his head loll against the back of his chair, and exhaled.

As the air left him, he deflated into his cushions, sagging like a squeezed wineskin. It felt as if the weeks of collar-tugging and sweating, of heart palpitations, of yelling and screaming – both at him and by him – were, for now, behind him. There might have been a Nyx drought, a smoking Cloudpiercer, and a city on the verge of collapse, but they were tomorrow's problems. At that moment, tomorrow was a year away.

Rebene picked at the unravelled message once again, flicking it with a finger to turn its papyrus to face him. He had read the glyphs ten times since it had been delivered, not by Etane, as he would have expected, but by a speechless cultist in a faded rose robe. The shade had left quickly, leaving behind a single scroll.

Nilith is claiming the throne on the morrow.

The chamberlain chuckled to himself loudly. It sounded odd in the emptiness of his vaulted hall. Unpractised. Perhaps it had been too long since anything but worry and anger had come out of his mouth. It was good to laugh again, and what a joke it was. Rebene scanned the glyphs once more, making sure.

Empress Nilith had returned to Araxes, and with none other than Emperor Farazar in tow, dead and glowing and ready to be bound.

As he breathed another sigh, Rebene wished he hadn't tucked tail and fled the moment the roof had caved in. He wished he could have been there to see the cheated looks on Sisine and old Empress Hirana's faces when they found the Sanctuary empty as a beggar's purse. It must have been such a joyous moment, but Rebene had only his imagination to entertain him. Even so, it brought a wide grin to his face. Sisine deserved to be cheated so.

Rebene had always liked the empress. Admired her, even. Though their paths had crossed little, Rebene had always noticed an unnecessary kindness in her. Even though it might only be the bid of a good day, it was foreign enough to Araxes, and always appreciated. But oh, how she had proven herself to be as cunning as any Arctian. It was the last move he would have expected from her, and that was why it was brilliant.

Rebene reached for the scroll, rolling it back and forth across the desk in different directions, furling and unfurling it. Hope was a fickle beast. It had been so long since he'd dared to feel it, he didn't recognise its touch at first. *What a day tomorrow will be.*

'Scribe!' barked the chamberlain. He listened to the echoes bounce about the room as he waited, stifling a yawn.

'Useless woman,' Rebene said to himself, drumming his fingers on his desktop. 'Scribe! Get in here! It's late, and I wish to go home.' To the chamberlain, it felt as though sleep was an old habit, long shrugged off and stamped out. Tiredness already clawed at him.

'SCRIBE!'

Rebene arose from the cushions and stalked around the expansive breadth of his desk. The throbbing in his head – the one that had at long last begun to die away – resurged.

'Come tomorrow, I will find myself a new assistant! One that doesn't fall asleep at their post, or fail me in every way, shape and f—'

Rebene's tirade sputtered out as one half of the tall oak doors creaked open. In its gap stood his scribe. The chamberlain didn't think it possible, but the woman's glazed-over eyes had become even more distant. The scribe seemed to look through Rebene, rather than at him.

Useless.

'Finally! Dead gods, woman. I want you to dispatch a note to all magistrates, scrutinisers and proctors that they are to assemble in the Grand Nyxwell,' he said, pacing back and forth. 'The new empress will need our support. Let us show this city the Chamber of the Code isn't dead yet, and is far from the toothless wolf they believe it to be. And find me Heles, damn it! Boran Temsa is dead and bound; what could she possibly be—Are you listening to me, woman?'

Hands upon hips, Rebene stared at the scribe, trying to find so much as a reflection in her glassy gaze. As he stared, a drip of bright blood pooled in the corner of her mouth, hovered as it swelled, and then dribbled down her chin. Two drips pattered on the flagstones and spread like blossoming roses.

Without so much as a gurgle, the scribe's glazed eyes rolled up, and she pitched forwards into the chamberlain's office. A black-clad shade stood behind her, his glow wrapped up in leather and ashen mail. He wore no expression, and all he held in his hand was a curved and bloody knife. Behind him, matching shades stood over corpses of guards and proctors. Rebene could hear screams echoing along the corridors. The chamberlain began to sweat profusely.

'Guards! Scrutinisers! Anyone!' called Rebene, retreating as fast as his long robes and flimsy golden sandals would allow. He stumbled once, only to scramble upright and flee for his desk, where a sword lay wedged in a compartment.

'What is the meaning of this?' screeched Rebene as he ran, all hope demolished, all humour trampled. He could almost see his bright future catch light at its edges, and begin to burn, blacken, and curl into ash. 'Who are you? I don't understand! Temsa is dead!'

As he fled, Rebene looked back at the impassive blue face behind him, not chasing him, just keeping pace. The shade's knife left a trail of blood-drops. Other half-lives now stood at the door, waiting. Watching.

Chamberlain Rebene reached his desk with ragged breaths. He sprawled across it, half-mounting it in his desperate attempt to escape. He grabbed the scroll in his panic, but no sooner had his sweat-slick fingers grasped its cylinder did he feel the blade puncture his shoulder. Then his ribs. Again and again.

Retching with pain, Rebene slumped across the mahogany of his desk, watching his own blood pool around him, dying his cream silken robes a dark crimson. He could hear it dripping on the stone.

As the lights of his chamber were snuffed, Rebene gasped his last breaths and ran a shaking thumb across the glyphs of the scroll, staining them with blood.

———————◆———————

'TO HAVE ENDANGERED OUR FAMILY in such a way! Our proud name! This bank! I... I can't even look at you!'

Russun Fenec bowed his head to his father, cheeks afire. He furiously thumbed the sleeve of his gold and grey silk robes, annoyed at how easily the fabric slipped over itself. He wanted to slip away just as easily, away from his father's furious face.

The death of Temsa had been a relief to many, Russun imagined, but to none more so than him. The sharp and heavy blade that had dangled over his sons, his wife, and his own head, had been removed. He was not ashamed to say he had wept at the news of the empress' return, and the capture and binding of Tor Boran Temsa.

However, it seemed even in death, Temsa was intent on cursing Russun. Punishment for trespassing against the Code and his father. Unfair punishment, so Russun thought.

'I had no choice, Father. I have told you again and again.'

'You should have spoken to me! The Chamber would have—'

'Temsa bade me not to speak a word. He would have killed Bilzar and Helin! And Haria! What then?!'

'How dare you interrupt me!' Tor Fenec bellowed, spittle flying from his lips. His temper ran so hot, his face had gone beyond crimson and was now a shade of beetroot.

Russun threw up his hands, bursting from the chair to pace around the room, trying to calm himself with walking.

'Once the empress takes the throne, normality will resume. As will investigations. The Chamber will want to know how Temsa climbed so high. Why we Weighed him. Do you know how many of his half-coins we have stacked in our vaults? How many investments built upon them? Don't you see, boy? This will ruin us!'

'Don't call me boy!' Russun Fenec snapped. 'I'm well aware how many bloody coins we have in the vaults. I'm the sigil, after all! I forged the transfers!'

Tor Fenec was unused to hearing his son shout back. He took a controlled breath, pressed his fingertips to the desk, and spread them out, cage-like. He narrowed his sage-coloured eyes at Russun and chewed his lip and moustache for some time until he reached his decision.

'I will not stand to see Fenec's Coinery soiled by soulstealing barbarians like Boran Temsa. Or fools like you, putting your peasant wife and bastard children ahead of this proud name. I gave you a tower, a career, hoping you would prove yourself. But I have been proved wrong,' Fenec growled. In his pause, his face grew blank, impassive. Devoid of any emotion. This was not family any more, but business. Such was the casual savagery of the banking district. Even sons and daughters could become debtors. As the saying went in Oshirim District: copper was thicker than blood.

'You will take the blame for this travesty. You broke the Code;

an errant sigil, blackmailed by a soulstealer. I trust the Chamber will have mercy on you,' said Fenec, the only hint of emotion a stumble in his voice. He bowed his head. 'You have no idea what you've done to this family.'

Russun ripped the sleeves of his robe. 'No. If anything, I've saved *my* family. That's all that matters to me now.'

Leaving his father to swipe a fist at a nearby stack of half-coins and scrolls, Russun kicked his way out of the office door and strode across the mirror-like marble. His reflection was dark with the lack of lanterns. Four sleepy sigils still toiled atop their tall towers, heads bowed, or wiping dribble from their lips at the noise. Four accompanying guards came to attention.

A purple-faced Tor Fenec appeared at his doorway. 'Don't you walk away from me, Russun Fenec!' he screamed, jolting the other sigils violently awake.

Before he reached the grand steps to the ground floor, Russun turned, opened his bare arms wide, and gave his father an ambivalent wave. His face was thunder, but he stayed silent.

'Don't you dare—'

A mighty crash cut rudely through Fenec's shout. Glass and splinters and stone dust filled the lower level as two battering rams breached the doors. Before Russun could take a breath, dozens of shades in russet armour and crimson cloaks flowed through the wreckage. Short swords and short spears in hand, they fell upon the ranks of house-guards struggling to form up. As dozens became a hundred, it took mere moments for the shades to mount the stairs.

With a scream, the sigil was enveloped like a rock in a stormy high tide. As blades pierced him, cut ribbons from him, before he was lost in the silent, murderous crowd, Russun held his father's gaze. Even then, his father was a coward, backing into his office in jittering increments, half-frozen from shock.

My family is safe… Russun told himself over and over, as the cold, vaporous feet trampled his corpse, and he descended into a world of black water.

ANI JEXEBEL SLAMMED HER PALM on the pitted wood of the bar-top, making several nearby patrons jump and then shuffle away, stools squeaking.

Starsson appeared from somewhere behind the bar with a fresh tankard of a beer that was vaguely green, and had a head on it like a snowcap. His pale face was smeared with black grease.

'This'll help drown them sorrows, Boss. Aged volcale, from the Bladehorn back home in Skol. Proper northern beer.'

'S'all fucked, Starsson,' Ani grumbled, slowly grinding her studded knuckle into the sticky wood. 'It's not sorrow. Temsa got what he deserved. Fell from the tower he built with his own hands. You didn't see how close he came to madness. I did him a favour, in truth.'

'So you said, Boss.'

Ani looked up at the smudged mirror, and at the smattering of patrons that occupied the Rusty Slab tavern. Two dozen were scattered across the tables, some in clumps, others drinking alone. A single bard with an arghul in a far corner did his best to lighten the mood with scraping ditties and old favourites, but it turned out to be too heavy to lift.

Ani didn't blame them. Cultists had been seen on the streets throughout the day, proclaiming the return of Empress Nilith and a great gathering at the Grand Nyxwell on the morrow. The city had begun to peer out of its doors and shutters, but the locks were still in place.

The great murderer Temsa had been brought to justice, the empress had returned, but the Nyxwater shortage remained. And according to the hushed whispers and beggar-talk, that shortage had dwindled to a complete lack. Riots had been seen roaming the sprawls. A Nyxwell had been destroyed. The City of Countless Souls still tiptoed along a cliff-edge.

Ani felt it constantly, like prickly hairs stuck in her collar. She had barely let go of her axe since leaving Boon's tower. Even now, the hand that wasn't wrapped around her beer was strangling the axe handle.

'S'all fucked,' she said, swilling the volcale around. Rarely had she been a drinker. A woman like her had too many enemies to dally with drunkenness. 'And now the Cult have Temsa. And Caltro. And Sisine and that bitch Horix by the looks of it.' The Cloudpiercer had smoked for almost a day now. Talk of a flying machine had spread like house fires. 'Something's got to snap, Starsson,' she sighed. 'This Nyx drought...'

The nearby patrons grumbled at her words. A sharp look from Ani sent them shuffling even further, right to a table by the wall.

'I wish I could swing an axe through Araxes and put it out of its misery like I did the boss. The old boss. Not the tor he pretended to be. The noble he desperately wanted to be,' Ani said, slamming her hand down again. She cursed Temsa for changing. *Scratching a living is better than slaving in death.* 'He was wrong. Our kind can claim all the coins we want; we'll still never be noble. It's in the breed and bearing. Like they can smell their own blood. You can pretend all you want, but you become a husk. "Better to be born noble, or not at all." That's what I've heard them say. That's the fucking wall they've built, and they've built it strong and high. No ladder, tunnel, ram or army's going to break it any time soon.'

Starsson watched her angry eyes flit about, looking for something to break or squish. He too had poured himself a mug of volcale. A lime-green moustache of foam clung to his thin lip. He bared his blackened teeth as he gasped.

'Ah, that's the shit. Right there,' he sighed. 'And you ain't wrong. Thousand years and nothing's changed yet.'

'"If it works for the rich, then it must work for all," Temsa once told me, just after he took me on as a sellsword.'

Starsson was staring down into his mug. 'You miss the north, Boss?' he asked, raising his green beer.

Ani thought back to the windswept beaches and black, rocky crags of her youth; to fighting fellow children with sticks, and always winning. 'It was simpler. And stop calling me that. I'm not the boss.'

'Well, who the fuck else is?' Starsson said. He was right: almost every surviving sellsword fled Boon and Ghoor's towers the first moment they could. Ani was left with the old-timers, like Starsson, and a handful of soldiers too lazy to find another job.

The barman was scratching at the octopus tattoo that covered his neck. Some sort of red rash had broken out. He beckoned, drawing her closer. 'Come 'ere. You've got Temsa's half-coins. Shades. His tavern. Noble or not, boss of nobody, maybe, but Jexebel, you ain't scratchin' no fucking living.'

She looked at her green beer, letting its sulphurous whiff tickle her nose. 'We got Low Docks captains that owe us favours,' she suggested.

'What you thinkin'?'

'I'm thinking we get the fuck out of Araxes while we still can.'

'North?'

Ani drained her tankard, and with a thump, she put her boots to the boards and got to standing. There was a slight wobble, but she stayed upright, and showed off a rare grin. Starsson matched it with his tar-black teeth.

'We go to the Scatter Isles. My home. We visit Fenec's Coinery in the morning, get that sigil Russun to sell all Temsa's coins. Then we all take what we can carry and board the first ship to Harras.' Ani sighed, deep and long, patting her axe. It would be hard to lay it down, but then again, it would make a fine ornament to hang above her tavern's bar. 'Peace and fucking quiet. At long last.'

Ani had expected Starsson's grin to widen, and for him to crack his usual woodpecker laugh that could cut through the chatter of even the busiest night. Instead, his face fell. Ani tensed, realising the bard had stopped scraping at his arghul, that all the chatter had died to complete silence.

'Starsson?'

A whisper of, 'Fuck,' was his only reply.

Ani slowly turned, scanning the room. Every one of the drinkers had turned to face them, even the eavesdroppers from before. Half were shades, hooded and cloaked, giving the pipe-smoke haze a bluer tinge. The rest were living. Every one of them held something metal and sharp in their hands, and they stared at Ani with soulless, piercing eyes. She spied the tell-tale red beneath their cloaks and rags.

Ani Jexebel's shoulders sagged, and she looked up at the somehow beer-spattered ceiling in utter exasperation. 'Of course. It couldn't be that bloody simple, could it?'

Before any of the cultists could think about leaving their seats, Ani burst into action. She tore the axe from her belt and drove it into the nearest table and chairs. The furniture fell to matchsticks, cascading across the tavern's hall. While the splinters were still falling, Ani swung again, taking apart another table and the two cultists that were struggling to escape her blade. The first man it caught was cleaved in two. The next lost an arm and collapsed to the floor, screeching as he hosed the stone with his blood.

Ani spun in ever-changing circles, sweeping legs and forming a clearing of destruction about her. Stools and chairs exploded either side of her. The cultists swarmed, but even lucky cuts across her bare arms failed to slow her. If anything, it goaded the blood-crazed beast within her.

Starsson had hauled a triggerbow from under the bar and was busy blasting any cultist that attempted to vault his bar. When his bolts ran out, he smashed a flagon and began to hack and slash at anybody that moved.

No sooner had Ani lopped the head from the bard than more shades flooded into the bar. No disguises masked these shades; they wore their armour and robes openly. Ani welcomed them in, picking up a short sword to swing alongside her axe. The handle was slick with blood, misted with vapour, and its blade was notched like a row of teeth, but she still grinned.

'Come on, then!'

Starsson was mid-shout when Ani realised why the shades were not charging. With a concussive thwack, the barman reeled backwards, a bolt half buried in his forehead.

More triggerbows appeared, resting calmly in gloves and gauntlets. Ani shook her head, despising them. Bows had always been the tools of assassins and cowards.

'Where is he? Where is that bastard Danib? Bring out the mute traitor!' Ani cried, raising her bloody weapons to the roof while corpses moaned about her and blue vapour traced her legs.

And there he was: the great armoured ghost of Danib Ironjaw, ducking under the arch of the tavern's hall, the horns of his helmet drawing sparks against the granite. There was a fainter glow in those white eyes tonight. Ani could see it even through her throbbing, blood-filled vision. He walked stiffly and with a limp.

'Etane must have given you a run for your silver, I see,' Ani challenged him. 'And a new sword.'

Danib drew the greatsword from its scabbard and held it calmly upright before him in a salute. He stared at her from either side of its thick blade, emanating white mist.

'A soulblade, you say?' Ani said. 'And I see your masters have no interest in keeping our bargain?'

Danib shook his head with a crunch of steel.

'I should have known.' Ani chuckled drily. 'What else would I expect from a traitorous cult like yours?'

Danib grunted.

'Church? Fuck you. That word has no meaning in this world,' Ani spat. She smacked the short sword against her breastplate, spraying droplets of crimson. She smeared it across her face, like an old Scatter Isle pirate.

'Come on then, Danib! You've always wanted to test me and my axe. I know it! Seen it in your eyes, I have. Tonight you finally can, half-life!'

Danib started forwards, but somewhere in the crowd of robed shades, a blue hand alighted on his vambrace as gently as a feather, and he halted mid-stride.

'No,' sighed a voice Ani recognised.

'Come on!' Ani roared, beginning to charge. 'Fuck the Cult!'

The first bolt hit her in the sternum, punching through the metal and kicking the wind from her, but not the momentum. The second bit through the flesh of her arm. Her axe tumbled from her grip, clattering on the floor with the ringing of a bell. Ani hurtled on as the bows continued to fire. Bolt by bolt, they slowed her, until Ani fell to her knees, a score of arrows protruding from her chest, thighs, arms and neck. And despite it all, she grinned through a mouthful of blood as Danib moved forward, sword held high. Her laugh was a bubbling wheeze.

'Like I told Temsa not too long before he died: it's treacherous at the top of the mountain.'

'Put her out of her misery, Danib,' ordered the sister, still hidden in the ranks of shades. Ani's vision was beginning to mist at the edges. 'Leave her body and shade here to rot.'

Ani Jexebel looked up at the great shade of Danib and watched him raise his sword over her head, its point shining as if bejewelled. For just a moment, she watched the flickering in the shade's glowing eyes. With a snort, she spat blood at him.

'You'll meet your match one day. Don't you wor—'

Danib brought the blade down with all the force of a landslide, piercing Ani's skull and driving the soulblade to the floorboards beneath.

———◆———

'GENERAL HASHETI!' CAME THE CRY, hollering down the corridors of frescoes and shiny marble.

Hasheti turned, finding a Royal Guard running towards him at full pelt. The man would have clattered into the wall had he not managed a skilful skid across the polished floor.

'Reports!' he gasped. 'From all over the city!'

'Reports of what, man? Tell me.' Hasheti replaced his plumed helmet and reached for his spear.

The soldier, even between deep breaths, took the time to look prickled at the fact a shade was giving him orders. Hasheti was used to it, and prodded him in the breastplate.

'Chamber's been attacked! Scrutinisers murdered in the streets, one by one! Chamber of Military Might, too. They say Lord-General Truph has been slain in his bed, stabbed so many times there wasn't a drop of blood left in him. Sereks with small armies of house-guards. A bank...' His breath escaped him again, and the guard leaned against a column.

Other shade soldiers had heard the news and begun to gather around the general and the guard. Left with no orders and no princess to protect, they'd been sequestered halfway up the Cloudpiercer in empty chambers, abandoned by some living serek who fled to Belish, or somewhere Hasheti had never been.

'Any word of the empress-in-waiting?'

'None. Wager is the Cult have her.'

'Fuck,' Hasheti cursed. 'I knew this mission would be trouble.'

'The empress will claim the throne tomorrow. Grand Nyxwell. Rumour is Sisine will be ther—'

Thunk!

The triggerbow bolt protruding from his chest distracted him. It happened so abruptly, it took a moment for him to register he had been shot. By the time he had grasped the black fletching, he was already sliding down the wall, heart stopped.

The soldiers bristled, quickly falling into formation. Hasheti stood at their centre shield high and spear forwards. He stamped his foot, and it was echoed by his soldiers. The phalanx grew by the moment as more soldiers ran to join them.

From beyond the light of the lanterns, an empty and open hand emerged, followed by a woman in smart plate and mail. Her head was enveloped in a hood, and a red cloak trailed behind her. At her side she grasped a sack made of some dead animal. The head of a dog or wolf was still attached to the hide, lolling in Hasheti's direction and staring at him with glassy eyes. Beyond Liria, Hasheti could see other shapes waiting there, and the dull glint of steel and arrowheads.

'Good evening, Soldier-General Hasheti,' said the shade, in a voice as soft as velvet.

'State your name and business!'

The woman held out the hide sack. It looked heavy, swollen. 'Enlightened Sister Liria, and my business is with you, and the question of your allegiance,' Liria replied.

Hasheti shook his head. 'That is not in question, cultist. Our master is Sisine Talin Renala.' He stamped his foot once more, and his soldiers shook the corridor.

The shade smiled. 'Is that so?' she asked.

Seizing the bottom of the hide sack, Liria shook it out, casting a pile of half-coins across the marble.

'Now you are your own masters.'

Hasheti could feel the draw to his coin, somewhere amongst the pile; the slip of copper he had not seen or touched in years. Behind him, the soldiers began to whisper. Some crept forwards, breaking formation.

'What is it you want?'

'Your allegiance,' Liria said with a shrug. 'But through choice. Stand with the Church of Sesh tomorrow at the Grand Nyxwell. Watch the dawn of a new era.'

With a pretend clearing of his throat, Hasheti threw down his shield and spear. They clanged against the marble, breaking the silence. Then he removed his helmet, and after looking at his lack of a reflection in the polished steel, he cast it aside.

CHAPTER 25
A SPARK

A weaker mind is broken by struggle and
misfortune. Greater minds triumph over them.

FROM THE GREAT PHILOSOPHER MENEM

POET ONCE SAID THERE IS such a thing as too much thinking; that a constant search for better answers can dim even the brightest of ideas.

Caltro Basalt looked as though he had done far too much thinking. He had spent the night doing nothing but, after all, and as unusual as it was for him, he had done it in almost complete silence.

There had been the few odd words. 'Stop staring at me,' and, 'Nothing. Just trust me,' whenever Pointy questioned what Caltro had seen in the small, smoky room. Whatever decision he was striving to reach, it seemed a torturous one. He had roamed around the sparse room beneath the earth, switching between bed, chair, pacing, even the floor, and back again. A cycle as repetitive as the stories he was no doubt weaving in that blue skull of his.

It was odd for a sword to pray, but Pointy felt like doing it anyway, and hoped to the dead gods Caltro was choosing the right path. He had been forced to flit between so many in his desperate search for freedom.

Through it all, the strange phantom dog the Cult had apparently gifted him hung by his side. It was a long-legged, lean thing, with a sharp snout and ears like Araxes spires. A white scar traced its entire body, from under its white eyes to its swishing tail. Gods knew why, but the thing had an affinity for the locksmith. It lay down when he did. Paced when he did. Even buried its blue nose in its paws when Caltro tried for the fiftieth time to rip out his vaporous hair.

Pointy was forced to watch the whole evening and morning on his side, laid flat on a wooden lockbox. It was strange how accustomed to that view of the world he had become over the years.

'Caltro…' Pointy spoke up after perhaps an hour or two of idly looking around the room, watching the locksmith try to sweat. 'You're running out of time. What are you going to do? Surely you're not going to help the Cult? Nilith has the—'

'Quiet, Pointy. I told you: trust me.'

The phantom dog looked at the sword with the same judging look as Caltro did, and Pointy held his tongue. For a while, at least.

'Don't I get a say in all of this? Or do I just have to hang off your hip the entire time?'

Caltro covered his face with his hands, and the phantom whined as it covered its head with a paw.

Bang, went the door, and Pointy knew the chance for talking some sense into him was over. Normally, Caltro would challenge every gods damned word. His lack of rebuttal was ominous.

An armoured Enlightened Sister Liria entered the room alone, but Pointy caught a glimpse of the thick, steel-plated legs of Danib lurking outside. The blade of a familiar-looking greatsword hung below his hip. Pointy scowled as deeply as he could.

'I trust you are rested, brother?' said Liria cheerily.

'As much as a ghost can be.'

'"Ghost." How Krass of you,' the sister tittered.

Caltro raised his chin, lips tight. '"Shade" is too soft a term for the way we are treated,' he replied, and Liria nodded appreciatively.

'I am pleased to hear that, brother. Come, time is short. Farazar's ghost wanes. However.' Liria held up a finger before moving to lift Pointy from the trunk, one hand on his blade, one on the handle. Pointy concentrated hard. It was tougher than usual, as if Liria felt him touching her mind, but he managed to make her flinch enough to slice a white line into her palm.

'Agh,' she hissed, placing Pointy on the bed. 'A sharp sword indeed,

Caltro.'

'Isn't he just?' replied the locksmith, eying Pointy with what the sword assumed to be distaste.

'We have one last gift for you.'

'You spoil me, Sister.'

Liria produced some spindly lockpicks from her robe.

'My tools.'

'The ones we could recover. Care to try your hand at the lockbox?'

Caltro seemed to stifle a chuckle. Pointy wondered how the shade always managed to have levity in these situations. He was incorrigible.

'You don't want to know what happened the last time I tackled a lockbox,' he said.

Pointy dreaded to think.

Within a few short moments, the locksmith proved his worth and heaved the trunk open until the lid stayed upright. 'Erm. Pretty?'

Pointy strained to see from the bed. The phantom dog was blocking half the view, playing at panting.

'Copper core for ease of wear and bound with steel so it does not harm your vapours. Made by the finest Church smiths. Did you know Sesh is also the god of the forge?' explained Liria.

Caltro lifted up a pauldron of hammered steel and intricate scale mail, and finally Pointy understood what the fuss was over. 'I did not,' said Caltro. 'However, I am not usually one for armour.'

Liria began to strap pieces onto the locksmith as she spoke. 'You are not usually one for standing beside an empress as she claims her throne, but you shall today. As will we all. There.'

Caltro examined himself, pulling at hinges and flexing as if he were expecting to do some gymnastics. 'All right,' he said. 'Thank you once again, Sister.'

'As we told you, Caltro, there are many benefits to being a dutiful member of the Church of Sesh.' Liria was already leading him to the door, and so far Caltro seemed content to leave both the sword and the phantom on the bed. Until the last moment, when he shrugged away from Liria's guiding hand, and grabbed Pointy's handle.

'Almost forgot,' he said with a roll of his eyes.

Pointy caught Liria's stare once the sword hung from the locksmith's belt. It was intent, examining every fleck of mica in Pointy's obsidian pommel. He kept his scowl. If there was anything an inanimate object with a soul trapped inside it was good at, it was winning staring contests, and Liria quickly lost as they weaved through the corridors.

NILITH PACED. PACING WAS GOOD for the soul. Good for the heart. Good for the mind, or so she'd been told by her daughter. This was a good thing, seeing as each one of hers was in disarray. Then again, considering how Sisine had turned out, perhaps pacing was not all that beneficial.

Nilith stopped in the middle of the small square of flagstones she had found, trapped between two levels high up the Cathedral. She had lost count of the wagons and supplies she had seen ferried past her. There had been an endless stream of ghosts, living, beetles, horses, centipedes, donkeys, each piled high with bundles. And soldiers, thousands of them, every one of them a ghost, and each bearing a sword and spear. It seemed every single one of the souls that had crammed the tiers of the Katra Rassan had now vacated above ground, leaving the Cathedral spookily empty, and devoid of sound. It made Nilith uncomfortable, much like the void of the desert nights, dreading the galloping of hooves.

She wished Etane were there. The old ghost had always managed to either goad her or scold her onto the right path – that, or make her realise she was already on it. In the evening, she had spared a single and private tear for her old house-shade, her coracle within the tumultuous rapids of the Talin Renala household. She had cursed the name of Danib Ironjaw, too.

Removing her borrowed scimitar from its sheath, Nilith swung it around to test the stretch of her old ceremonial armour, delivered sometime in the night by the cultists. It had been a decade since she had last worn it, maybe longer. It was a little looser in some places after her time in the desert, but it was fine steel and gold, studded with shards of turquoise and aquamarine. It made Nilith stand a fraction straighter, and feel the empress she had to play today.

She swung again, and there was a jolt at her throat. She dug under her breastplate to adjust the pouch of Old Fen's powder. Like the copper coin that hung next to it, both had become charms of luck. Nilith closed her eyes as she held them, feeling the cold, ragged edges of her body, and took a deep breath to keep from shuddering. The ghast's poison was barely hidden by her collar. It had also begun to spread down her stomach, bringing pains as the living parts died before turning to vapour.

A jangling of chains distracted her, telling her the last inhabitants of Katra Rassan were due to leave. Nilith turned around to find Sisters Liria and Yaridin, Caltro, and the horned monster of Danib standing with a group of prisoners. A flutter of wings told her the Cult had kept their promise of healing Bezel, but she hadn't yet asked them to release the falcon. Not yet. Nilith met his golden eyes, and though they were narrowed, she could see he understood.

Sisine stood there, between Hirana and Temsa. Iron collars were clasped around their necks – or arms, in Temsa's case – and their chains held by a group of heavily armoured Cult soldiers that stood behind them. Amongst them was Farazar, wearing the stormiest expression of them all.

'Is this how you would have the city see their empress-in-waiting, Mother? Or the Cloud Court? Chained and bound! How dare you?'

Liria approached Nilith before she could answer. In the ghost's hand, she held three half-coins. Nilith recognised their glyphs immediately.

'For when you decide what to do with them,' Liria advised in a quiet voice. 'If I may?' The sister held out a short cloak and draped it over the empress' left arm, where blue vapour curled from between the joints in her armour and frosted the gold. 'Are you ready, Empress?'

Nilith looked at her scowling daughter, knowing that Sisine would only hate her more from here on in. Hirana was just as outraged, but as far as Nilith was concerned, the Cult should have left her on the flagstones.

What hopes she'd had of Sisine coming around to her way of thinking had been dashed the moment she'd awoken to find her dead daughter staring back at her from across the cell. Quite unable to form words, except somehow she managed to form enough to curse her. Nilith's months away had gilded Sisine's demeanour towards her and romanticised their relationship. Now, seeing father and daughter beside each other, matching furrows on their brows, Nilith knew she would always be an outsider. It cut like a dagger to the heart to see it so plainly, but it was unavoidable. It felt like failure to her.

'Ready, Empress?' Liria said again.

'I am,' answered Nilith, nodding resolutely. She took her place at the head of the group, near where Caltro stood. The locksmith gave her a wry smile, but otherwise faced forwards and stayed silent.

'I didn't take you for the armour-wearing sort,' Nilith whispered to Caltro.

He flexed his ash-grey gauntlets. 'When you can't beat them...'

'Join them,' she sighed.

'Am I the only one who hasn't lost his mind?' said a metallic voice between them.

'And what would you have us do?' Caltro snapped at the sword on his hip.

Liria and Yaridin flanked them, silent, their eyes wide and eager. They seemed enlivened. Taking the lead, the sisters guided them up a series of wide ramps that emerged within a grand warehouse on what Nilith assumed to be street level. A swathe of soldiers and beasts and wagons awaited them.

'There is a whole district between here and the Grand Nyxwell,' she said.

'A parade is customary, Empress. There are those who do not believe such a saviour has appeared in their direst hours. They need to see it with their own eyes,' Liria replied. 'And do you not deserve to be welcomed as a victor, after all you've fought for?'

Liria gestured behind Nilith, and the empress turned to find Anoish standing behind her, dwarfed between two horned scarabs bearing pairs of riders. He had been groomed from snout to tail, and was bedecked with gold and turquoise ribbons. A skirt of mail hung from his sides, and a gold, spiked shaffron placed over his proud nose. His dark, chestnut eyes stared at her with part-excitement, part-blame for his costume. Nilith thought he looked regal for a desert horse.

'You deserve none of this, Mother!' Sisine cried.

'Hear, hear,' Farazar joined in.

Danib threatened both of them with the tip of his greatsword.

'You stay back, beast. You didn't scare me in the time of my father, and you don't scare me now,' argued Farazar.

Danib growled at that, making vapour puff from the vents of his horned helmet like the hot breath of a beast. Farazar shrank away.

Weak as Nilith was, mounting the horse took several tries, but with Caltro's help, she managed it. It felt satisfying to be astride the horse again. Anoish seemed to feel it, too, prancing this way and that, his hooves clopping on the floorboards.

With the clanking of chains, the doors of the warehouse were opened, and bright sunlight spilled across the dusty floor. Nilith could see palm trees and sandstone pillars, etched with weathered faces of past emperors and empresses.

A horn was blasted somewhere amidst the throng of glowing soldiers, and with a rumble of feet and hooves and armour, the entourage formed up to leave.

The procession gathered momentum within moments. Shouts ricocheted down the Avenue of Oshirim, bringing crowds from the towers and grand houses that lined the wide street. With the Cult soldiers forming a blade of shields and spears, they cut through the growing crowds swiftly, leaving Nilith to look about at the Arctians as she rode at the front of the procession. Caltro rode alongside on a horse, looking rather uneasy. The sisters rode behind them in an open carriage, shielded from the sun by cotton umbrellas. The ghost prisoners were kept in a similar carriage that tailed theirs.

'Nyxwater! Nyxwater!' came the shouts from the crowd, over and over, no matter how many cheers or yells of, 'Empress!' and no matter how much richer the avenue around them grew.

'I wish I could tell them that by the end of today, they won't need to worry about Nyxwater,' Nilith muttered to the ghost by her side.

Caltro didn't deign to reply, merely looking around, eyeing up the living who brayed for water.

'You're quiet today, locksmith.'

The ghost turned his white eyes upon her. 'Is it me, or has everything been said? Doing, not talking, is what today needs,' he replied sternly, as if trying to convince himself of the same truth.

Nilith remained silent for the remainder of the journey, too busy drinking in the moments she had dreamed of for months, perhaps years, if she was truthful. It was too easy to be swept up in the adoration, the power of it all, if she let herself fall for it. *Freedom. Justice.* Nilith kept the words spinning around and around her head, even when swathes of the crowd fell to their knees as she passed, as if she were a dead god risen, and when lotus and rose petals fell like snow on Krass steppes.

Before long, Nilith spied the black tips of the Grand Nyxwell's tusks over the smaller high-roads and more modest buildings. Her heart, stubbornly clinging on despite the flesh about it turning to cold mist, began to thud, reverberating around what was left of her body. Nilith forced herself to count every beat, less some cruel twist of luck make it fail before she had claimed Farazar's throne. She clutched the grey cloak about her left arm, ensuring it hadn't slipped.

Their progress slowed as the crowds squeezed into the half-dozen Spoke Avenues that met at the Grand Nyxwell. Looking over the heads of the masses, almost equal parts glowing and living, Nilith could see the avenues congested for miles, until distance and heat haze stole their number from view. A large quota of wagons parked along the sides of the streets complicated issues greatly, but Cult soldiers stood around them, even used them as parapets from which to watch the crowds.

Once inside the plaza, Nilith gazed out over the knight statues kneeling before the Grand Nyxwell, swords in hand and heads bowed. It took another hour, perhaps longer, for the ghost soldiers to part the crowds enough to make a path to the Nyxwell's dais. The cries of, 'Nyx-water!' became almost constant. Here and there, she spotted handcarts carrying slumped corpses, or the familiar sight of bloodied sacks tugged by ropes. Some were hopefuls, eager to bind their dead in the same well and water a royal had been bound in. The rest were desperate, and looked as though they had been dragging their unbound for almost as many miles as Nilith had, just to find a Nyxwell that wasn't dry. Fights broke out here and there beyond the ever-moving halo of cheering and bowing bodies. Red-cloaked soldiers spread amongst the crowds to put them out like forest fires.

Around the Nyxwell, intersecting rings of house-guards protected Araxes' richest – those who had apparently survived Temsa's cull. Nilith looked down upon tors, tals, sereks, celebrities and war heroes, and every one of them looked back with burning envy. The soldiers raised their shields higher as they descended the tiers of the Grand Nyxwell, and Nilith was glad for it. Her heart was climbing up her throat. The tension was a bowstring at full stretch.

A cheer began to course through the countless masses, rising and falling as it reached different hemispheres of the great stone plaza. Nilith felt her breathing become short, as if their voices stole the breath from the air.

In the vacuum between the crowds and the dais, grey-robed Nyxites waited behind ranks and ranks of dead soldiers. They watched Nilith avidly, bowing timidly as she dismounted Anoish and began to tread the stairs. Caltro walked behind her, with Liria and Yaridin seeing to the ghosts and the body of the emperor, which, Nilith was pleased to see, had been rewrapped.

Nine... eight... seven... Nilith counted down as she climbed, as if she had been counting since Belish. 'Six...' she muttered aloud as she stumbled, her left leg shaking. 'Not now,' she hissed to herself.

To her surprise, Caltro was there, keeping her upright and dignified. His face was expressionless, eyes somewhat glazed over, as if he walked through a dream he'd had before,

Up they climbed, until they stood on the platform they'd graced not two days before. Nilith was as breathless as she had been then. She stared out across the Nyxwell, and the masses stretching to a man-made horizon of spires and towers. The crowd must have been a million strong, perhaps a million more in the streets. *And half that number dead*, she thought.

Swallowing the choking beat of her heart, Nilith stood tall and strode to the edge of the platform. Below her, a pool of black water awaited a body. The vibrations from the feet of the crowd rippled lazily across its oily surface.

Nilith turned to find the platform crowded with the Cult and the chained ghosts. Before her, two Nyxites waited with the body of Farazar. They were busy cutting open the fresh wrappings. She caught Farazar peering past Danib's shoulder to ogle his own corpse. Judging by the foul look on his face, he immediately regretted it. Nilith watched as they peeled back the cloth to show a corpse twisted and warped by rot and the elements. Most of its features had collapsed, showing the white skeleton in places. Portions had dried like old meat, desiccated and speckled with sand. Other parts were black and slick with putrid liquid, and the tails of maggots could be seen waving about. Farazar's face was what held her gaze: a gawping mask of shock, visible even in death and decay.

The Nyxites had iron stomachs, and without blinking, they positioned themselves at the edge of the platform, at Nilith's feet, ready to surrender the corpse to the Nyx.

If she thought Farazar had finally accepted his fate, Nilith was wrong. He began to rage against his chains, yelling, 'I am the emperor! She is a murderer! I am the emperor!' over and over. He caused so much fuss, Danib had to squeeze his head between his arm and his chest to silence him.

As the cheering died and whispers spread between the crowds, the Enlightened Sisters came close, speaking in turn.

'It is time, Empress.'

'Take your place amongst history.'

'Do what you set out to do all those months ago.'

'Free the empire,' Liria urged.

With a deep breath, Nilith turned to face the droves waiting on her. Save for the rustling of chatter here and there, and the occasional shouting, the crowds were eerily silent.

In all the time spent fighting the desert, she had prepared speech after speech for this very moment. Now, a million eyes were turned upon her, heavy with expectation, every rehearsal had faded from memory. All she had to do was convince them to reverse a thousand years of history.

'Arctians!' Nilith bellowed, as loudly as her hoarse throat would allow. 'I am Empress Nilith Rikehar Renala, daughter of Krass King Konin, Lady of Saraka, wife of once-Emperor Farazar Talin Renala the Eighteenth, and in accordance with Emperor Phylar's decree, I am here to stake my claim on the throne of the Arctian Empire.'

While the nobles clapped their hands in mock appreciation, the crowds beyond merely rumbled with ambiguous noises. Nilith clasped her cloak tight, making sure no vapour would betray her.

'Traditionally, the emperors or empresses that have stood before me have proclaimed wealth and prosperity for all. I have always thought them liars!' Nilith proclaimed, garnering more of a response, albeit a shout for, 'Nyxwater!'

'Precisely!' Nilith yelled, feeling her momentum growing. 'Emperor Farazar did nothing but continue this royal trend. And what has he done for you but hide in his Sanctuary, and let this proud city sink under the weight of murder and poor rule? You cry "Nyxwater" because Farazar, and scores of others over the centuries, have done nothing but perpetuate a society that feeds upon itself. A society that breeds monsters like Boran Temsa, who would see this city on its knees for their profit. Like many that stand before you today!'

There came the shouts and cheers of approval. The scapegoat for the city's angst had been named. Danib thrust Temsa forward to show him to the crowd, and boos and jeers joined in the noise. They spread through the crowd like a spark through a dry field. Through it all, Nilith stared at the nobles around the Nyxwell, much to their glowering.

'Ingrates!' yelled Temsa, receiving more hatred from the crowd. Half of that audience must have been murderers themselves, yet a mob will never fret about turning on its own.

From the corner of her vision, Nilith caught Caltro staring at her, waiting on her words like every other citizen of the City of Countless Souls. She took the fierce look in his white eyes for one of encouragement.

'I wish for change, as I know many of you do! I want a city that does not need to suffer shortages of Nyxwater!'

A roar of voices rose, like a hurricane approaching shore.

'Or grain, or shelter! A city that protects its neighbours, instead of murdering them in their sleep!'

Applause joined the shouts, like fat drops of rain on a palm-frond roof.

'A city not constrained by the rules of a despot from a thousand years ago!'

Thousands of fists punched the air in agreement. Nilith ripped the copper coin and chain from her neck and held it high. Her boot hovered over Farazar's corpse, ready to push.

'A city without binding and indenturement!' she roared.

Nilith's spell over the masses broke like a stained-glass window before a boulder. Those nearest the Grand Nyxwell fell still first, and their confusion spread out in waves. Some who were not without their wits saw sense, and began to chant in favour. Ghosts, in their hundreds, took up the chant. A brawl broke out.

'No!' barked a nearby serek.

'That is treason!' yelled another.

Hot tears spring to Nilith's eyes. Tears of anger and disbelief. The entire city was comprised of fools, still reaching for fire with hands covered in burns. Plainly before them, they could see the evil that plagued their lives, and yet were content to let it stay. Even willingly invite it in. Not in all her days and nights enduring the sands had she dared to imagine this.

A shout ripped from her throat, echoing across the plaza like a battle-horn.

'I am Empress Nilith Rikehar Renala, first of that name, and my first decree is—'

It was then that Caltro seized her. Nobody was more surprised than Nilith, suddenly grappling with a ghost who was desperately trying to pull her arm off.

No.

Not my arm.

With a flapping of red fabric and the twang of a strap, her cloak ripped free, along with a gauntlet. As Nilith wrenched backwards, she bared her ghostly hand to the sunlight for all the crowd to see.

———◆———

'CALTRO! WHAT ARE YOU DOING?' Pointy's panicked shout filled my head, momentarily deafening me as I ripped Nilith's gauntlet free.

The gasp that sprinted through the masses was almost comical. What was far from comical was the reaction. Half the crowd were stunned silent. The other looked revolted. It was no surprise the latter half still had a beating heart in their chests. Scattered fighting broke out as opinions clashed.

'What is that?' came the complaints, multitudinous in their outcry.
'Is she dead or alive?'

'A dead queen!'

'No shade can sit on the throne!

'Caltro!' yelled the sword, cutting through the tumult of voices.

Ignoring him, I turned with a victorious grin stretched across my face, facing the Enlightened Sisters. Behind them, the chained ghosts struggled against their captors.

'A revolution requires a revolt. Your plan has been laid bare, Sisters!' I crowed, much to the confusion of every face in my vicinity. Even the Nyxites had the cheek to look shocked.

Nilith shoved me, sending me sprawling across the white marble. 'You stupid fuck, Caltro Basalt! Look what you've done!'

'They plan to turn the dead against the living. A massacre, Nilith. They showed me!' I yelled, trying to figure out why Liria and Yaridin still wore their infernal smirks, and why Danib hadn't reduced me to smoke. 'I figured it out. With the Code abolished, ghosts have no masters to fear. What's the result? An uprising, led by the Cult. Look! Where are the scrutinisers? The Chamber? Have you even noticed Chamberlain Rebene isn't even here? Where are your Royal Guard? All they needed from you was a crowd.'

'Dead gods, Caltro, you're right,' Pointy breathed.

I levelled a finger at the sisters. 'I know I'm right! So were the dead gods! They thought they could pull the wool over my eyes, but not me. That is the flood they want to unleash on the world. A flood of dead!'

It was as if scales fell from Nilith's eyes as she looked through the crowd. The only soldiers that stood near the dais were made of vapour. When her gaze fell upon the corpse of Farazar, I could have strangled her. I saw my own stubbornness staring back at me.

'It has to be done. To save our humanity!' she yelled.

'No!' I lunged for her once more, but her gold fist swatted me away. 'Stop, Nilith! It's not worth it.'

With a snarl, Nilith broke the copper coin in half with brute strength. I dove for her legs, bringing her to her knees. With a barrage of savage kicks, she fought me off, managing to jam one half of the coin into the corpse's disjointed mouth. With a shriek, she threw her shoulder behind Farazar's body and pushed it over the precipice. I barged Nilith as it tumbled, driving the wind from the empress with my armoured shoulder. I saw the copper half-coin burst from her hand, and I dove after it as if it were my own.

The tips of my fingers grazed its metal. I snatched it like it was the edge of a cliff I was about to topple over. In truth, that wasn't far from my situation. My body was sliding after me. My hips had already slipped over the marble edge. And yet, even as I began to topple, I still had time to watch the desiccated, rotting corpse swallowed by the Nyx. Before his grinning face was consumed by the black water, I saw the flash of copper between Farazar's ashen teeth. No sooner had it vanished than I noticed the burning deep within my palm, as the copper half-coin seared my vapours.

It was then that something grabbed my legs.

CHAPTER 26
THE BATTLE OF ARAXES

Of all the epic poems told of the deeds of
men, many forget the story of Calabar, who
purportedly stood alone against a thousand
men with a single soulblade. Few details
survive the two hundred years that have
passed, but they speak of smoke surrounding
him like a tornado, billowing from his blade.

FROM 'A REACH HISTORY' BY GAERVIN JUBB

THE FIRST THING I NOTICED was the vengeful snarling of Nilith, and her sharp fingers digging at my armour in her rage. 'Everything I've worked for!' she was screaming. The rest was wordless.

Danib dragged me away from her and threw me to the side, and the second thing I noticed was the laughing. The uproar had reached fever pitch as the masses witnessed the debacle upon the dais, and yet the musical notes of the sisters' laughter somehow cut their way straight to my soul.

It was Liria and Yaridin, baring wide smiles. 'Caltro Basalt. The wise, all-seeing Emperor Caltro Basalt, first of his name,' Liria called.

I stared down at the half-moon in my hand, watching my vapours spit and sizzle around it, and realised what I had done.

Yaridin clapped her hands silently. 'How far you've come, Caltro. You arrived in this city a thief and now you stand as emperor.'

I struggled to my feet, watching Nilith seethe. 'No. I... I've stopped your flood. The Code still stands.'

Sister Liria stepped forwards. 'Wisdom was never your strong point, was it, Brother Caltro? You were correct about the crowd, but the Code does not matter to us. It is the Tenets we trust in. Gods-given by almighty Sesh. No man or shade can change them, not even the emperor.'

Nilith stopped struggling. I swore I heard screams somewhere amongst the sea of yelling people. I chanced a look over my shoulder. There was a commotion on the far side of the plaza. I could see its ripples sweeping outwards, like those of a rock cast in a lake. I heard the anxious whinnying of a nearby horse.

'*What is it, Caltro?*' Pointy asked, sounding nervous.

Yaridin spoke loudly over the roar. 'We care nothing for the throne.'

'We care nothing for charity!' cried Liria.

I looked out, to the closest the buildings came to the Nyxwell. There was something spanning the avenue. Wagons. Barrels. A wall. I could tell not, but the crowds scattered in their thousands trying to escape it. I felt a deep unsettling within my chest.

'You snakes! It was too good to be true! What are you doing?' Nilith demanded.

'We told you, Nilith. A sacrifice is demanded to build the new world!' yelled the sisters as one.

It was a slaughter. The Cult of Sesh had made a trap of the plaza. A death trap, and their prey numbered in the millions. Panic overtook the crowd. Shoving and screaming, they surged from avenue to avenue in clumps of thousands. Straining my dull eyes, I could see the walls of barrels and wagons blockading the streets. Ghosts in red armour that had roamed through the dense crowds began to hack, stab and slash at anything made of flesh and blood. Every direction I looked in, I saw phalanxes of cultists going about their bloody work. Even living soldiers turned against their own kind. Riders on tall beetles paraded through the chaos, spearing stragglers. Even around the Nyxwell, Cult and royal soldiers that had stood guard about clusters of nobles turned their spears on their charges, bringing the murder close at hand. I saw Anoish barge his way through a shield wall, fleeing the madness.

I peered at the streets again and saw cultists attacking the barrels with hatchets, cracking staves. As murky Nyxwater cascaded onto the plaza, drenching those that had already fallen to the Cult's blades. I realised then what all the preparation had been for. Grey vapour began to curl from the waters as if they boiled around the dead.

'*Don't just stand there!*' Pointy howled, and I flinched instinctively. A triggerbow bolt clattered from the black stone tusk behind me. More bolts began to fly at the platform from a troop of house-guards. Some pudgy serek, far too slow on the uptake, seeking to make his name out of the bewilderment, even though his own house-guards were at that moment being overrun by Cult soldiers.

'Caltro!' yelled the empress.

I dove to the stone near Nilith, whose saucer eyes were still trying to make sense of the chaos that had descended upon the plaza. We were at the eye of the battlefield, and everywhere I looked, fighting and murder reigned. More insects, spiders and centipedes were barreling through the crowds on the eastern side. A fire had broken out in the north. Smoke was now sweeping across the plaza, darkening the skies.

'I...' I began, but the empress shook her head so avidly I thought she was having a seizure.

'After. If there's going to be an after!' Nilith hissed at me.

'Witness Sesh's glory firsthand!' Liria and Yaridin were screeching over the roar of the dying and the terrified.

Nilith hauled me upright with her ghost hand, our vapours mingling. 'I don't know about you, *Emperor*,' she shouted in my ear, 'but I've had about enough of those fucking sisters!'

'Pair of cunts, if you ask me. And I've come to strongly despise the colour red,' I said, baring my teeth at the sisters, and the monster that stood beside them. Dread swamped me. I had come to the Grand Nyxwell expecting to leave it fighting. I had wrestled with this inevitability every hour of the night, and still no escape had presented itself. It had taken me until dawn to realise it was the price of my freedom. And yet even now I glanced over my shoulder, considering the pit of Nyxwater below me. But alas; the runner had finally run out of places to run. 'Fuck it,' I said to myself, resolving to have a strong word with the next dead god that showed his face.

'Caltro!' Pointy bellowed at me aloud. Quickly stowing Farazar's coin beneath my armour, I seized the soulblade from my belt.

'What?!' I yelled, staring at the sisters and their damnable smiles.

'I never told you my other name,' said the sword.

Danib rolled his shoulders, and I heard the crunch of armour over the roar of the massacre.

'I remember! Absia!'

'No! I once went by another name: Yer'a Ankou.'

The great monster stepped forward, and the entire platform shuddered. With a ring, Nilith drew her scimitar, a great curve of silver and copper.

'This really isn't the time for a fucking conversation!' I held him up, yelling at his pommel stone. I expected to see wide eyes, but instead I saw a calm face, almost smug. I tried to move my arm, but I was frozen.

Danib unsheathed his huge sword, raising it high for a smiting blow.

'Pointy!'

'Do you know what it means, Caltro?'

I would have screamed at him had grey vapours not flowed down my arm, spiralling around my vambraces. His obsidian blade took on my blue hue.

Danib's horned shadow fell across me, his burning eyes focused solely on mine.

Pointy's whisper of an answer was deafening. '*Invincible.*'

Unbidden, my arm flicked upwards. I cried out in a mix of confusion and terror. The impact was enough to flatten me to my knees. I prised open my eyes, and found two crossed blades before me, edges glowing white hot and vapours reeling against each other.

'*Pereceph,*' Pointy growled. '*My sister.*'

I swear I heard a voice in the furious sizzling of the blades.

With a roar, Danib came at me, but Nilith distracted him with a blow to his gauntlet. The beast bellowed, reaching for her, but the empress was nimble. This wasn't her first fight.

Pointy drove me at Danib, spinning a figure of eight before me that left a spiral of blue smoke. Danib met us with a mighty sweep of the greatsword. Sparks flew as our blades crashed. Our vapours roiled from the impact. Pointy was arcing through the air before I could stop him. Danib's greave tore like silver foil, and he responded with a bellow that would have made a dunewyrm quail. But before I or the sword could react, the monster's boot came swinging for my ribs, and I was launched into the air.

Somersaulting over the marble sweep of the Nyxwell and the writhing mass, I crashed to a heap against a step. Had I breath, it would have been driven from me. My only injury was a crushed pauldron, seeking to pierce my shoulder. I ripped it free as I stumbled to my feet.

I was welcomed to the battlefield by a warhammer swinging at my face, a red-robed cultist grinning at the other end of it. Once again, my sword arm sprang into action, shearing through the stone hammerhead as if it was papyrus. Swing interrupted, the cultist pitched forwards. I held Pointy at my hip, and the ghost skewered himself on the blade like a gruesome kebab before exploding into blue vapour.

'How am I doing this?' I cried out.

If I listened carefully, I could hear Pointy cackling. 'You're not, Caltro. I am. I told you you were in excellent hands!'

'Who are you?!'

'This is why you should have spoken your mind.'

'Leave the lesson for later!'

I heard a screech upon the dais, and saw Nilith clutch her side as Danib's blade drew an arc of blood in its wake. Her scimitar had already lost its point, and as I watched, the great ghost cleaved the rest of it away. Pereceph came slicing, and with a cry, Nilith tumbled from the lip of the marble into the black waters below. Danib saw me amongst the phalanxes of house-guards, amid the dead and battling. He levelled Pereceph at me and began to march along the dais towards the steps.

'Fuck,' I said aloud, involuntarily ducking as a spear jabbed for my face. My parrying strike caught the Cult soldier in the sternum, and he crumpled to the ground in a pool of blue smoke.

'We have to face him, Caltro.'

'We.' I said, looking between the chaotic masses to see Nilith spluttering as she hauled herself from the side of the Nyxwell pool. I sprinted for her, Pointy's mind and mine joined together. Trust. It was the ingredient this disastrous concoction of an existence had been missing all along. The dead gods. Pointy. Even myself.

I hacked through the pillars of iron and stone surrounding the pool, and the thick bars between them. I felt the thunder in the ground as Danib increased his pace. 'Hurry, Nilith!' I yelled.

Her armour had tried its best to drown her, but she burst through the opening I'd made for her, spitting foul Nyxwater. Another cultist ran at us, sword high like a banner, but before Pointy could halve him, Nilith was already battering him with her gold and copper fists until he was a moaning wreck on the stone. His sword was wrenched from his grasp and swiftly driven through his head.

'Now I'm fucking angry!' Nilith rasped at me, seething from every pore.

Danib was cleaving a path through any that stood in his way, on purpose or accidentally. Ghosts deliquesced in clouds and shredded pieces of armour. Screaming bodies flew in great arcs across the plaza, or collided with the black tusks of the Nyxwell. All the while, Danib's white eyes burned for us.

'He's had Kalid. He's had Etane. Now he wants you and me.'

'I think it's mostly you,' Nilith snapped.

As two dead soldiers fell in heaps at our feet, Nilith and I swiftly parted as Pereceph came crashing down between us. Pointy scored a cut across Danib's shoulder before the ghost swung around with incredible speed, shearing a whisker of vapour from my head. Pointy had me rolling in a ball to avoid the vicious strikes that chased me across the stone. Sparks and chips of sandstone flew in all directions under the giant soulblade's bite.

Nilith's sword cut in like the sting of a hornet, finding gaps with the copper in her blade, making the beast roar. Every time he spun to catch her, Pointy would cut in, cutting his thick steel armour to pieces wherever possible. One, maybe two, we scored, before Danib would jab or parry, and send me running for cover. That's all I brought to the fight; dodging and diving.

Sparks showered me every time the two soulblades came together. I could almost feel their ghosts fighting through the touch of the blades. A sibling rivalry at its fiercest, each of them matching the other.

With a twist of my grip that made my vambraces squeal, Pointy forced Danib's sword away and brought the blade up to cut deep under his armpit. At the same moment, Nilith drove her sword deep into his thigh with a war cry.

The monster roared once more, but a gauntlet sent Nilith spinning into the stone edge of the Nyxwell with a crunch of rubble. Before I could move, Danib hooked Pointy under his arm and jabbed at my defenceless midriff. Pereceph made a mockery of my armour and sliced into my ribs, drawing a cry from me. It was like fire and ice searing my vapour all at once. I yanked the sword from Danib's grip, shearing more steel from him, and cutting a chunk through his arm.

I reeled away, trying to manoeuvre around the roiling masses and whirling weapons to reach Nilith. I saw the Enlightened Sisters standing at the edge of the dais, arms raised and hands clasped as they watched their slaughter unfold. Behind them, the ghosts of Farazar and the empress-in-waiting were struggling through the swarms of Cult soldiers on the marble steps. They were trying to reach Nilith, half a broken sword and a sharp wooden stake clutched in their manacled hands. Bezel, Temsa, and Hirana were dragged along with them. They watched us, rapt before our fight with the great Danib. I wondered briefly who they were hoping would die.

Fucking royals, I couldn't help but think, as I fended off blow after blow. A mighty clang dulled the roar of fighting as Pointy met Pereceph once more above my head. Light burst. Hot metal hissed. The bell-toll that ran through the blades stunned me. Once again, Pointy dragged my tiring soul back as Danib pressed me again and again.

Everywhere I moved or dodged, Danib was upon me. My arms were shaking through striving to keep up with the ghost's speed and ferocity. Though I quailed, he only seemed to grow stronger, taller.

'*Caltro...*' came Pointy's strained whisper. '*I can't...*'

Between wild, windmilling swings of the soulblade, I scrabbled backwards, slipping through the muck and black water trickling over the stone. My gaze flitted about in desperation, catching another glimpse of the three chained ghosts. Temsa was now pulling in his own direction, as was the falcon, trying to escape this madness. Hirana was damning everybody present at the top of her lungs, and Sisine was raising her shattered blade, a spear's thrust away from the the prone Nilith. Farazar was fighting against her now, intent on beating his daughter to the kill. Even in death, half-naked and glowing bright, I saw all their venom and rage and vengeance living on, refusing to die with their flesh. In their own ways, each had almost brought the city to its knees. Together, they would have conquered the Reaches.

Together.

It was then I saw the threads connecting us, pulling me towards them even now. The web fate had weaved between us. Even as I riled against the notion, I saw the perfection of destiny's plan.

'We can't do this alone!' I snapped.

Throwing myself out of Danib's reach, I wrenched the rest of my armour from my limbs, casting it away to clang on the stone beneath me, until I stood naked and glowing brightly against the smoke and gathering darkness, soulblade in hand. The sun was now a pale disc behind the black smog that had begun to belch from the Grand Nyxwell.

'What are you doing?' Pointy screeched at me, trying to force me to move. Pereceph was descending in an obsidian blur.

'What I'm supposed to do!' I yelled. *Or so I hope.* There was no more time for thought.

I dove to the side, rolled and began to run. I pelted towards the three ghosts, watching with every lunging step how Sisine's blade rose higher, and higher.

Enraged by my fleeing, the great ghost let loose a roar from behind me that silenced the battlefield momentarily. Danib Ironjaw was far from finished with me. He sloshed after me through the Nyxwater and corpses, covered in stone-dust and blood. Blue vapour streamed from his helmet. White smoke rushed along the crossguard of the sword and down onto his wrist like a waterfall.

I ran for all my dead backside was worth.

'Stay back, Caltro!' Temsa's decapitated head bellowed at me, seeing me now charging at him through the melee, a mad look in my white eyes. I cut his chains as I barrelled into him, loosing the falcon into the dark skies. I tensed every strand of my vapour to breaking as I pushed my soul into Temsa's, dominating his will, wrapping it into mine. Within a blink, I had claimed him, keeping my form and Pointy entwined with my hand. Our glow burned like a bonfire. Temsa's anger filled me like ice water flooding lungs. I felt my face contort into a mask of rage.

And still I ran, aiming at Hirana.

As her copper chain links shattered at the kiss of my blade, I came at her with a twisted grin, half Temsa's, half mine. I collided with her face-first, driving myself into her cold vapours. She buckled before me, weak as a cotton strand. With a roar building in my chest, I drank in all her hate and venom. Like hot wine, it swirled within me.

Farazar never saw me coming. The manacle exploded from his stump of a wrist as I threw myself at him, fusing him into my band of twisted souls before he could even yelp. A murderous fire ran threw my swirling vapours.

One final leap drove me into the empress-in-waiting. Sisine never saw me coming until it was too late. I threw myself at her with my arms spread-eagled, enveloping her ghost. She fought me hard, but I fed her screech of rage into my roar. Nilith's eyes burst open to find me standing over her for a fraction of a moment, arms spread, a blade in each hand, bellowing to the heavens with every inch of my lungs.

The thunder of footsteps fell heavy behind me, and I poured all the raging emotion within me into Pointy. Still roaring, I threw my body into a crouch, swords arcing backwards just as Danib lunged to grapple me. Pointy pierced the collar of his giant breastplate, driving through his thick neck to the other side.

Danib's momentum impaled him almost to the crossguard. I snarled with Temsa's ferocity and Sisine's hatred, and curled my lip with Farazar's contempt. With Hirana's callous twist, I dragged the soulblade through the remainder of Danib Ironjaw's neck. Cobalt vapour trailed behind the sword.

The words fell from me, unbidden.

'For Kalid!'

'For your betrayal!'

For a moment, the ghost held his shape, sword raised high, poised to fall upon me. Those white eyes glared at me with such ferocity I thought for a horrifying moment the monster would never die. And then the spell of binding caught up with him, and the giant deliquesced into a thick cloud of blue vapour, rapidly fading to grey. His armour clattered to the Nyxwater, hollow, and yet the horned helmet still managed to match my stare with its black eyes. Pereceph fell like a keystone, cutting a wedge from the stone as it met the ground.

I convulsed as the ghosts fought me, but I wrestled them under control. I bared my teeth as emotion flooded me, along with the over-powering desire to kill everything around me, even Nilith. I tensed my sword hand, keeping Pointy by my side, and focused their murderous desires on the Cult of Sesh.

'We have to end this!' I yelled over the tumult, staring long and hard at Liria and Yaridin. Danib's death had either escaped them, or they did not care. They were chanting to the music of battle, calling out for their god to rise.

'Sesh. Sesh. Sesh! Sesh!'

Heaving Pereceph from the stone, Nilith followed my gaze to the dais. 'Cut the head from the snake!' she said.

Our soulblades spinning in blurs, Nilith and I advanced across the bloody stone. For every step we took towards the sisters, a rank of Cult soldiers swarmed towards us.

Nilith and Pereceph on the right, Pointy and I on the left, we divided and conquered with brutal efficiency. Nothing could stand in the way of the razor-edged swords. Rows of shields were cleaved in two. Sword blades and axeheads were reduced to shards.

With Pointy's skill and the ferocity of the ghosts within me, I felt like an unbound ghost tethered to his body, content to be taken along for the bloody ride. My arms swung in intricate patterns an artist couldn't conceive. Clouds of blue smoke burst with every slice. Scarlet cloth scattered in ribbons. Whenever the living came against us, blood rained down. White burns adorned my naked vapours, but my rage eclipsed all pain.

Nilith was a dirty fighter, wasting no time on the finesse Pointy – or Invincible – displayed. If he was an artist of death, Nilith was a worker slaving away with a sledgehammer. I had no complaints. It left the same amount of blood in her trail as mine.

Body by body, soul by soul, we fought our way to the steps of the dais. We had no allies but each other. Even the nobles around us were too busy fighting their own battles. Between parries and blocks, I watched, but it gave me no pleasure to see the rich murdered like the poor, as much as I had expected it to. This massacre was a horror, powerful or peasant, dead or alive. The Cult had brought about their flood all right: a flood of chaos and murder.

And Nyxwater.

The oily water was rising, now spilling down the Nyxwell's amphitheatre steps. It blackened the white stone wherever it touched. Nilith and I sloshed through a rising pool of it as we battled our way free of the press and wail of bodies.

Snarling, growing more irate by the moment, I pushed ahead, carving a path that Nilith could keep open long enough to trail me. Through it all, my head swivelled about like a paranoid owl's, aching to spot an open stretch of stone. Transfixed by the sight of a swarm of naked souls pouring through a barricade, I stumbled and fell over a corpse at my feet. My coin came dangerously close to touching the water, and I leapt back.

But the water was not for me. It was for the bodies around me. I saw them beginning to smoke where the Nyxwater lapped them. Some were already disappearing, slipping beneath the waters as if they had fallen into a deep trench in the stone. Between the roiling masses fighting and dying, I glimpsed red-robed shades drenched in black splotches, busy dragging bodies out of their piles and spreading them through the wash of Nyxwater. I couldn't help but imagine the hordes of bodies finding themselves adrift in that bleak cavern they called afterlife, flooded with dark waters…

Clang!

Pointy rose up before my face. The offender's sword split on Pointy's blade, and its pieces scored cuts across my cheeks. I barely flinched, too busy gawping with the realisation of what the Cult's sacrifice was for. Not for vengeance or some sadistic justice, but for Sesh. The dead gods' words rushed back to me.

The flood must not claim the world.

Don't let the river burst.

Life will become death.

I saw five stars blink out in the black firmament.

'The harbinger of change,' I breathed.

'What?' Pointy yelled, manoeuvring me to skewer a charging soldier. I impaled him and his comrade on the same thrust.

'This way!'

I let the ghosts within drive me, like holding the reins of mad horses. Nilith tried to keep up, bleeding in a dozen places, and currently grappling with a shade in heavy battle armour. His mace was digging into her scalp. Pointy cut through his arms in one swipe, sending him to the Nyxwater with a squeal and splash.

'They're not sparking a revolt. They're flooding the afterlife! Bursting the Nyx's banks. It'll flood the earth with every ghost that's ever died. No living thing will survive it, and Sesh will rule over an empire of the dead,' I cried, hearing the souls within me rail at the notion. Ghostly fingers tried to pry their way out of my vapours.

'Treason!' Sisine's voice sprang from me, and I forced them into silence.

Nilith looked around, witnessing the same pandemonium I did. Tens of thousands were now pitched in a desperate losing battle against the ranks of cultists that continued to stream through the barricades. We had both seen the swollen tiers of the Katra Rassan. Who knew how many more cultists and cathedrals on their heads lay under the districts, and the Sprawls? In the brief moments our eyes met between our sword dances, the word 'hopeless' lay between us. And all the while, barrel after barrel was hacked open and spilled upon the plaza.

'I didn't survive the desert just to die at the Grand Nyxwell!' Nilith snarled.

'It's already starting to happen!' yelled Pointy.

In pockets of stillness between the murderous fighting, where corpse piles slowly melted into the Nyx, I saw groping hands and glowing fingers reaching from the sloshing waters. Hellish in their grasping, soul by soul they began to crawl through the corpses. Wherever the injured lay, ghostly hands reached for throats, rocks, daggers. A thousand years trapped in an endless, godless cavern tended to make a soul irritable. Murderous.

I looked back to the Nyxwell, where the river was now bubbling like an overheated pot. Where the smoke gathered thickest, veins of lightning and fire ran through the darkness. I saw more hands and gurning faces at the edges of the overflowing well.

The old religious types say the apocalypse will come with the sound of trumpets and horns. When I heard the mournful blares over the battle noise, I hung my head, and cursed myself for doubting them.

'Look!' Nilith wrenched me around by the shoulders.

To the west, a wall of barrels exploded in fountains of splinters and Nyxwater. Through it came a monster I had never seen the like of, and I immediately wished I hadn't. It was an enormous centipede, striped black and purple, with reaching, hook-like claws around its fearsome head. Mandibles lined with needle fangs dribbled green spit. A rider sat atop its neck, strapped tightly into a saddle. The huge insect reared up, legs rippling in a mesmerising fashion, and screeched at the top of its lungs. As the chilling noise filled the plaza, two more of the monsters broke through the wreckage to join the first. They too had riders atop them.

I could feel the moan of the dwindling survivors as a wind on my cheek. Nilith had turned an ashen white.

'Dunewyrms,' she breathed, voice trembling.

'*Flee, you moron!*' Temsa bellowed within my ear.

Hirana's broken hands groped for my neck. '*I will not die twice because of you, Caltro Basalt.*'

I pressed them deeper within me, feeling the strain of the haunting begin to tell. Pointy's force within me was an ally, but it didn't help that I agreed somewhat strongly with the ghosts. The only thing that kept me from running was the fact the creatures were not interested in the living, nor the fleeing, but merely anything wearing red. Cultists flew like chaff before the scythe as the monsters went to work destroying their phalanxes.

Through the smoke that had enveloped the plaza, I caught the glint of green and silver armour. Soldiers were pouring through the broken barricade. There were plumes on their ridged helmets, and glittering longswords and tridents held high. Triggermen with sacks of bolts sat atop armoured spiders, whose fangs tore at anything robed and dead. Men in robes of mail heaved against shrieking, slithering creatures on copper-link leashes. Slatherghasts, like the one Nilith had killed. They were as pale and slimy as month-old meat. They disturbed me greatly, but their shining blue claws and fangs had an unquenchable thirst for anything glowing, and they decimated the cultist ranks. More wonderful still, the citizens that had been kept at bay began to flow into the plaza alongside the mysterious soldiers, like villagers with pitchforks marching to the monster's cave.

'Who the fuck are they?' I cried, as Pointy dispatched a scarlet-painted man with a knife.

'I don't care, but they are most welcome!'

The arrival of the gold and green ranks was a glowing dawn compared to this gruesome night that had consumed us. The citizens of Araxes seemed to feel it, and the grip of chaos began to break. Even the nobles began to stand side by side, forming battalions that duelled with the endless swarms of ghosts.

I threw a glance over my shoulder, challenging the sisters. Their grins made me wish I hadn't looked. 'It's not over yet,' I cursed.

Another horn was sounded in reply, high-pitched and ululating. Glowing streaks ran across the walls of the plaza to the south as gangs of naked ghosts clumped around the towering knight statues, three with scaffolding and huge glyphs chiselled across them. Vapour pressing across the stone, the ghosts started to fade into the statues, and in their dozens. Peering through the haze of smoke, I began to see the glyphs and veins in the stone glow a deep purple, then turquoise, then white. Stone chips crumbled away. Cracks appeared where its limbs began to move. Fresh screams of terror rose from the masses.

'Are you... are you fucking kidding me?' Nilith sighed heavily, hefting a spear at a nearby ghost and turning him into a blue cloud. 'Now this?'

Though I was as shocked and gut-wrenched as her, at least I had an answer. 'The Cult's Strange Ranks! I'm not the only ghost with gifts, Nilith! It's an endgame.'

Thunder rolled with every wrenching, twisting movement that got the stone knights to their feet. Prising their stone swords from the earth, they wasted no time in swinging them through the masses like a callous artist splashing scarlet on a bleak canvas. The screams were silenced in huge numbers, replaced with great rumbles of stone and breaking bones. With every sweeping blow, the ground shook beneath us and lightning flickered overhead.

'Ever come up against this in all your decades, Pointy?' I cried, desperate.

'No,' he replied.

'Suggestions?'

'Few,' said Nilith, sagging with weariness. 'At least these swords can cut through stone. And I have this,' she said, pulling a pouch from around her neck.

'A coin-purse?' I spluttered.

We had little time to debate the issue. A roar from the flooded pit of the Nyxwell wrenched us around. A great mushroom of smoke belched from the well. I saw a great shadow without form rearing up within the billowing smog, reaching for the dais. Ghosts reared from the waters in droves, wailing at the top of their voices. Unholy shapes moved in the shadows behind them, the ghost-glow lighting only fangs and curling claws; older things that the Reaches had long forgotten. The earth slipped beneath us, making me stumble. Fell and foreign words filled the air.

I looked up, meeting Nilith's wide gaze. The determination that had burned within them since the moment I had run into her should have been sputtering out; a lantern withering under the gales of a storm, like me, even despite the anger threatening to burst out of me. Instead, I swore those eyes burned brighter. I wanted it.

'More,' I hissed.

'*Don't you dare!*' chorused the three ghosts inside me. My restraint almost failed as they revolted against me. I plucked the half-coins from my neck and stuffed them into her hand.

'What are you doing?'

'I'm sorry, Nilith,' I said, seizing her glowing arm, and throwing Pointy into the air.

'Wh—!'

The effort brought darkness to my vision, even before my vapours had melted into her. It was a duel that took every ounce of strength I had. Each soul fought me in their own way, and I found myself surrounded on all sides, lashing out like a rabid beast at them all. Even Nilith. But as I willed myself through bone and skin, through the heat of her muscles, the cold of her sweat, Nilith caved, and an inferno erupted within me. I opened my eyes, dizzy, as I reached up to pluck Pointy from the sky. His vapours flooded across Nilith's armour, and every inch of my body began to convulse. White light shone through her armour. I felt the raw power of each soul entwine, willingly or not, each a piece of clockwork clicking into place. In that moment, we became complete.

The cultists roared around us. 'SESH! SESH! SESH! SESH!'

I stared up at the burning sky. As lightning raced through the billowing black smoke, I saw a mighty figure pulling itself from the pit. Fire flowed through its limbs, like wind breathing life into charcoal. Two enormous orbs of light flared in the darkness. The earth quaked as the black tusks of the Nyxwell began to topple outwards, like a colossal yawning maw. One crashed behind me, spraying Nyxwater and screaming bodies.

The voices in my head were deafening, but I willed us towards the nearest stone knight, pouring everything into one singular drive: *to win*.

I sprinted through the mobs of ghosts, soulblades held wide and dealing death all around us with shocking ferocity. Mist fought to escape the confines of the golden armour, sketching shapes of arms and hands and roaring faces. White fire and blood streamed behind us. We were a whirlwind of rage and vengeance.

'*Caltro!*' came their cry as the stone knight noticed our approach, and raised its gigantic sword to smite us. Light rippled across its glyphs, and its rock face bent into a despicable grin.

I let their cries rip from me as my boots pounded the flooded stone. A hundred voices answered me as the sword descended. Lungs burning, I exploded from Nilith's chest, soulblades raised like javelins. Vapour streamed like a banner behind me as Temsa, Hirana and Sisine were wrenched from me one by one, propelling me like a triggerbow bolt into the knight's chest.

Stone crumbled before the two blades as they dug deep. I dug deeper, pressing through the glowing breastplate and straight to the heart of the stone monster. Countless hands battered me within the roaring darkness, but like Nilith, I hadn't come all this way to lose now. I felt my own heaviness, the roughness of my fingers, and clenched them into a fist.

White light seared through the air, burning the Cult ghosts from the knight's body. Blue smoke poured from its cracks like volcanic vents. I alone was left inside the crushing, cold stone, dizzy at my height above the writhing masses, but I was its master. I couldn't help but cheer. My voice was the roar of a landslide.

I saw the darkness of the Nyxwell rear above me. Fire burned in the heavens. Thunder rolled, and lightning showed me a great beast towering against the storm, still yet to take solid shape. It was enough to chill me. Gigantic, twisting horns pierced the sky. Great wolf-fangs gleamed. Nails like lances tested the choked air. Its forge-like eyes seethed with anger as they looked down upon me, as if I were but a worm.

'Caltro!' came the tiny shout beneath me. With another rumbling cry, I slid the huge Pereceph from my chest with my oversized hands and drove the stone knight at the Nyxwell. I stumbled, fell, but forced the stone upright, over and over. Sesh rose above me still. A great, booming laughter dwarfed the thunder, and stunned all about me to a horrified silence. I alone moved, and my enormous feet cracked the flagstones beneath me as I ran.

'It is over, little thief,' came a voice that made every pebble in my body rattle.

'You're right about that!' I cried as I vaulted over the rubble, sword raised like a dagger in my fist, its glimmering point aimed for Sesh's calf.

Pereceph slammed into the god's brimstone skin. Fire and black smoke erupted from the wound. Lava dribbled, and still I drove the sword deeper. Light scorched his veins, soaring up his leg and across his chest. His roar made the very ground dance. I could feel the soul in the sword screaming as her blade melted. With a twist, Pereceph came free, broken to the hilt and smoking. Above me, Sesh was still bellowing, reeling from the pain. Wings of fire and lightning rippled across the dark clouds.

'Again, Caltro!' came a voice from my chest. Pointy was yelling at me over the maelstrom. 'Strike him again!'

'Didn't you see what happened to your sister?' I shouted, drawing him free. He looked like a nail in my stone fist. I stared at the resolute face on his pommel stone.

'You still have one soulblade left!'

Horror ran through me like an assassin's dagger. 'No! You'll be destroyed!'

'Stand back!' Nilith came wading across the shaking, flooded stone behind me. She had a knife in her hand, that infernal pouch in the other. That determined fire was back in her wide eyes, unable to tear away from the sight of a god.

'There's no time!' Pointy pleaded. I refused to listen. I felt him tugging at my arm, but I wrenched him back. Fire spat upon my stone, starting to work its way through the glowing glyphs. Pain racked me.

'I'm the only weapon that can hurt him! Even you can't haunt a god!' yelled the sword. I hated him for being right. The darkness was returning to my vision. I was spent.

'I won't. I can't!'

'STAND BACK!' Nilith shrieked, throwing the pouch into the bubbling fire that still poured from Sesh. 'For Old Fen!'

Just make sure they remember me. That was all I ever wanted, in truth,' Pointy whispered in my head. In the flash of fire and lightning, I swore I saw him wink. *'To be remembered.'*

The right thing can be an evil thing when it doesn't align with what you want.

With a last roar, I threw my weight behind his blade, and thrust him high into Sesh's leg, dragging him down through the charred, smoking flesh. White light began to pierce through holes in the god's midriff, chest, and shoulders as Pointy's soul flooded him. Flame poured from the eyes of the god of chaos.

Before the explosion ripped through me, before my hand was torn from Pointy's handle, I heard his battlecry echoing and echoing through the dark and empty cavern of my mind. I knew not what he shouted, but I knew Sesh heard it also. One of the last sights I glimpsed was the god grasping at his curling horns, as if deafened.

A sledgehammer struck me in the chest as the world was consumed with fire. I fell apart as I flew, stone crumbling to rubble. I was jolted from the haunting violently as I hit the water, and skidded through the corpses. Heat scorched my back, and I felt the pull of the dark Nyx beneath me.

CHAPTER 27
A SECOND DAWN

ET UP,' SPOKE AN ECHO in my head.

I could smell burning crumbs from the bakers across the pockmarked street, hear the clatter of cleaning in the cathouse above. The linens refused to give me up, and I willingly let them hold me as rays of red sunlight poked through my window, warming my cheeks, nursing my hangover and the dream of battle and murder I'd been trapped in.

'A new day awaits,' said the voice, familiar in some way.

'I know,' came my mumble.

'Harbinger of change.'

I jolted upright and awake, immediately blinded by the hot sun poking through dark clouds. Rashes of sunset were breaking through patches of smoke. I clenched my fists, feeling nothing but cold. No skin. No hot breath against covers. Only vapour.

'Ah, the emperor wakes!' somebody beside me said.

I tried opening my eyes again, finding a woman's corpse facing me with a bulging, glassy stare. I recoiled quickly, finding blackened sandstone and rubble around me. Puddles of Nyxwater steamed in the sunlight, leaving behind rings of charcoal smear.

'Emperor…'

Two filthy half-coins dangled in front of my face, on two different chains. 'Yours, aren't they?'

My blurry vision cleared enough to find a soot-covered, blood-soaked Nilith staring back at me. Her armour had been stripped away, leaving a simple tunic beneath. Half her jaw had been claimed by vapour, giving her a ghostly leer. Most of her other arm, too. Those emerald eyes seemed to glow a little more dully now, but there was a grim and stubborn smile on her face.

I reached up to take the coins, but realised I still gripped something in my hand. I looked down, finding a broken sword, molten almost to the silver crossguard. Only a thin shard of the obsidian and copper-veined blade, no longer than my hand, had survived daring to strike a god. The handle was split down its centre, as was the pommel, where the black stone was spiderwebbed with cracks.

My face scrunched up, but I had no tears to give.

Instead I took the coins in my other hand. One felt cold and heavy, the other stung me like a hot coal, but I had survived enough pain in the last few weeks to ignore it. I saw Nilith swallow hard, but I said nothing.

I lifted my head and arched my back, moving as far away from my corpse mattress as possible. I stumbled to my knees, then one foot, feeling weak, thin as gossamer, but whole.

'We survived,' I breathed, hardly believing it.

'But at what cost, Caltro?'

I looked around me. The Grand Nyxwell was a ruin. Its jet tusks lay in pieces like the points of a fallen star. The well was no more than its crater, an ugly mess of broken marble, half-drowned in a pool of Nyxwater. Around it lay the detritus of war: ownerless weapons, split armour, and the thousands of dead that the Nyx had yet to claim. Tors, farmers, sereks and soldiers lay alongside each other in death, gold mingling with sackcloth, and as my gaze roamed outwards into the plaza, I saw they were far from alone. Fields of dead stretched out between us and the hazy, smoke-wrapped buildings. Scattered survivors, living and ghost, moved slowly amongst them, plodding with heads down, their tunics or silks ripped and torn. Nobody seemed to know what to do with their survival, and I didn't blame them.

The hot air was still, but not silent. In the far reaches of the plaza, in the Spoke Avenues, I could hear the battle for the city was not over, but I had no desire to go fight it. I left that to the ranks of silver-green soldiers, and the spiders and wyrms still growling and roaring.

There came a flapping, and the talking falcon landed on a corpse next to me. By the curve of his beak, I wagered he was no more impressed by the scene than I was.

'Only stubborn stragglers left, Nilith,' he said, eyeing me up and down. There was blood on his beak.

I interjected. 'The rest of the Cult?'

Nilith nodded, gaze now distant, ignoring the falcon. 'Half of them put their weapons down the moment Sesh collapsed back into the Nyx. The rest fought on, enraged, but the soldiers and survivors retaliated and fought them back into the Avenues. Most have scattered to the wind.'

'The Enlightened Sisters?'

Nilith's eyes narrowed. 'Dead, or so I assume. They stood upon the dais until the bitter end, so I can only hope the explosion caught them.'

I dreaded to think of those two scuttling back to the Katra Rassan, burying their heads for another day. 'What was in that fucking pouch of yours?' I asked.

'Science, a man once called it.'

'Well, it was almost the second death of me.' I swayed, dizzy.

'Is nobody going to talk about the fact a dead god just rose from the Grand Nyxwell, shortly before you two killed him?' asked the falcon, golden eyes narrowed. 'Or was I hallucinating?'

Nilith and I looked at each other for a moment.

'No,' I spoke for us. 'I'd rather not. It's done now. I'm tired of gods. If I ever have to see hide or hair of one again, it will be far too soon.' I sighed. 'What of the others? Sisine? Hirana? Temsa?' All I could see was Farazar, hunched over on a nearby rock, unable to tear his eyes off the death around him.

'With the explosion, and with Sesh crumbling to the ground, dozens of souls were caught in his path.' Nilith showed me three more half-coins in her bloody palm, turned stained and grey. 'I never got to speak to my daughter again,' she said, her voice hollow. 'I had hoped she would have understood.'

'She will,' I said. 'In the afterlife.' It was the only comfort I could give her.

Nilith wiped her bloody nose. 'Hirana is also gone. Temsa somehow survived, like the cockroach he is. He'll get what's coming to him.'

'What's next then, besides gutting the Cult's cathedral?' asked the falcon. It was a heavy and cumbersome question, one I certainly had no answer for. I was still too preoccupied with merely standing up.

'That is the great question, isn't it, Bezel?' she sighed. 'Almost as great as how you did it, Caltro?'

'Did what?'

'How you brought us all together at the last minute. How you made a monster out of all that rage and anger and fear. How did you do it?'

I smiled, looking up at the sky once more. 'You're the one who told me of fate, Nilith. You should know better than I do. Dead gods' will or luck, every one of us, villain or hero, came together here at the final hour. That was by some design, not an accident. I should know. I've spent my entire life working out the designs of smarter minds.'

Nilith opened her mouth to question me, but closed it as she saw a throng of soldiers making their way across the battlefield. Survivors reached out to touch their shields and cloak-hems, but they were poked aside with long poles just as firmly as the corpses underfoot. I could see two figures at the centre of their formation, and what looked like a horse. One was a woman in black cloth, hobbling. The other was a noble-looking man, swaddled in armour so fine and intricate it somehow looked fit enough attire for a ballroom. His hair was an oily stripe across his bald, tanned skull.

I recognised the woman somehow, but I didn't know how. There was a keen, ever-roaming look in her eye that guards and people of the law tended to have. It made the thief in me wary.

'Empress!' called the woman, and the soldiers parted either side of us.

'By the dead fucking gods. Heles!' Nilith embraced the woman warmly, if stiffly, given the number of wounds and bruises both of them sported. I was not far behind them, with white lines crisscrossing my naked, glowing body.

Heles. I knew that name.

Nilith pushed past the soldiers to the horse, Anoish. The poor beast was missing one ear, was criss-crossed with lacerations, and was limping sorely, but like his mistress, there was a glint in this chestnut eyes that was long for the grave. Nilith pressed her forehead to the horse's nose for the briefest of moments.

'This is your doing?' The empress was breathless, as if she abruptly recognised the armour around her. Heles didn't reply, transfixed by the patch of vapour around Nilith's throat and jaw.

'Somewhat,' replied the woman. 'When Jobey took me instead of you, I thought I'd see if I could make you some allies.'

'What? So who are you?' Nilith asked of the noble. She seemed agitated, and almost crumpled to her knees when another man appeared between the soldiers, covered in silks and gold chains.

'No!' Nilith began to cry, but both men raised their hands.

The noble introduced himself with a stiff bow, barely more than a nod. He too was held rapt by the glowing jawbone and black flesh around Nilith's cheek. 'Director Raspanar, if you please. I represent the Consortium, and I might be able to offer an explanation. After Chaser Jobey brought Scrutiniser Heles to us, mistaking her for you, she informed us of your intentions to bring change to Araxes. A change that we were most interested in helping you to achieve. The Consortium voted in favour of standing by you, but as we arrived to do precisely that, we saw the massacre underway. We are businessmen, Empress, and though the cost has been great,' Raspanar paused to look around at the wreckage of the plaza, 'we wager the reward to be most profitable.'

Nilith had not taken her eyes off Jobey. 'And my so-called debt?'

'Forgotten, in exchange for your favour. As is Scrutiniser Heles', who wagered her life against your success here today. The Consortium are not the threat you believe we are. We can be of great use to you, Empress, and it appears you need our help now more than ever. That is, if such chaos has not deterred your thirst for the throne?'

Nilith raised her chin. 'I have every intention of ruling, Director. I've fought for this city thus far. I refuse to abandon it now. Even if there is little of it left to rule,' she said. 'But I'm afraid you're not speaking to the ruler of this empire.'

Raspanar looked immediately flustered. 'What?'

'This *here* is the Emperor,' Nilith sighed, pointing a shaky hand at me, still taking a knee in the dirt. 'After all, it's he who holds Farazar's half-coin. He's the one that saved Araxes. Hell, maybe even the Reaches. I was the one who trusted the Cult.'

'We all trusted them,' I ground out the words. 'That's what they do. They use trust as a weapon, preying on desperation and desire until they're right behind you with a knife.'

I felt all eyes turn on me, even those of the stoic Consortium soldiers. All I did was cradle the emperor's coin in my hand, letting it burn against my vapours and send white sparks shooting across my fingers. With much effort, I stood upon my weak legs.

How the fuck did I get here? I asked myself, but found no answer in my head. The silence pained me. I wished for Pointy's voice. My surrogate conscience.

From thief to emperor. My parents, dead gods rest them, might have been proud of me, even if this was the most sordid, sprawling empire on earth. And now a broken-hearted one, its soul poisoned. Once more, my gaze wandered over the plaza, lit with a copper hue by the sun slipping between the western buildings. Above us, amidst the last wisps of smoke and ash in the east, powder-blue sky clung on to the last moments of daylight. Brushstrokes of high cloud turned to fire, like funeral pyres for the dying sun. The countless spires and towers were visible now. I had almost forgotten how many poked at the sky, and how far they stretched into the burning horizon. It would be a feat to count them, never mind rule them. Even the notion of such responsibility began to crush me with the weight of the Cloudpiercer.

In the short time we had stood there, the injured and the lost had already begun to gather about us. Their hollow eyes looked for a saviour. Or answers. Even somebody to blame.

I was a son of the Krass steppes, a healer's son. I was a thief, a locksmith, probably the finest in the known world. I had survived death, played the game of Araxes and won, been begged by the god of gods, and of late, even become a hero to some. And yet, I could be no emperor. My fight had not been for the throne, but for justice and freedom, and I had those.

'Trust me,' I said, holding the half-coin up to the sunlight to stare at it, wondering, just like everybody present, how exactly it had ended up in my hands. I sighed. 'I'd do a horrible job. Instead of a city of ghosts and murderers, you'd likely have a city of drunkards and thieves.'

Nilith cracked a half-dead smile. 'You can always count on a Krass-man to tell you exactly what he's thinking. Your sharp tongue has brought your this far, Caltro Basalt. May it keep you safe a little longer.'

With that, I handed Nilith her coin, and washed my glowing hands of it. I looked around at the battered Heles, the squinting, suspicious Raspanar, and the soldiers flanking us.

'Speaking of drunkards,' I asked, 'is it me, or does anybody else fancy a cold beer?'

TWO DAYS HAD PASSED SINCE the Battle of Araxes. Though the city survived, it had been wounded, almost mortally so. It had curled in upon itself like a dying hound. The streets remained empty but for Consortium soldiers, workers, and corpse piles. Towers stayed sealed. Doors remained firmly locked and barred. Trade ships lingered in the bay of the Troublesome Sea, unwilling to dock amidst such rumours of madness. Even the parrots and rooks and pigeons seemed subdued. They must have felt it, too, the same as every soul left in the city: the scent of death still hung heavy in the air. No matter how fast the workers tried to clear the bodies away and surrender them to the shattered Grand Nyxwell, with every passing day the sun beat down it grew fouler, and fouler.

Fifty thousand so far. Still climbing, they said. And still no ghosts arose from the dead.

With Sesh destroyed, Araxes had no argument over Nilith's banishment of the Code. The Nyx had begun to flow once more, but to everybody's abject surprise, in the opposite direction. It remained the river of the afterlife, it seemed, but without the power of binding. Not a soulmarket had opened its doors since the battle, and not a soul had been bound. The Nyxites had disbanded seemingly overnight once they realised the hold of copper over a corpse had crumbled. Word had it thousands of ghosts were gathering at Nyxwells across the city to drown their coins and claim the afterlife. As despicable as it sounded, the Cult's flood of chaos had helped turn Araxes against the Nyx. Even Farazar, offered banishment or the afterlife by Nilith, had chosen the new afterlife. The promise of duat that had been missing for a thousand years. Only Boran Temsa was not given such a choice. Nilith had decided the Cloudpiercer dungeons were the best place for him; a private cell where he could spend the years in darkened silence, lacking sleep, sensation and forever cold, just like all the ghosts he'd bound and traded over the years. He had been far from happy with that sentence. I'd taken some pleasure in watching his rage melt to horror as Nilith had swung the cell door shut. It was a fitting end for the scourge of Araxes.

It appeared the Cult's flood had spread further across the city than just the Grand Nyxwell. I was told the Chamber had been practically destroyed. Half the Nyxite warehouses, too. Even a dozen banks of Oshirim District. Soulstealer gangs in the Outsprawls had been crushed. Even the Consortium had been attacked, on some level. But no more. The surviving cultists had been chased as far as the Duneplains. The Katra Rassan had been broken open and filled with boiling oil and rubble by a vengeful army of citizens. A torrent of red clothes had filled the skies and gutters on the first day, as every scrap of the despicable colour had been ousted by noble and urchin alike. The pyres of charred cloth still smoked here and there amongst the streets. I had watched it all from the balconies and broken windows of the Cloudpiercer.

Two days had passed, and still I had not left the tower, ruined and strewn with corpses as it was. Instead, I had roamed its endless floors and its many vacant rooms. I played thief for myself, for the first time since arriving in Araxes, plucking at abandoned lockboxes and drawers in my boredom and uselessness. This new future of the Arctian Empire had no use for me, despite how many times Nilith tried to tell me otherwise.

Two days, and the new Empress Nilith had not yet slept. Perhaps it was the slatherghast's poison finally claiming her, or perhaps this was what a dutiful ruler looked like, and it was so unusual as to be foreign to me. In either case, plans, scrolls, maps and books had been ferried back and forth from the empress' rooms. Survivors of this Chamber and that came running. Even scrutinisers and proctors that had survived the Cult's knives came to join the new empress' cause. Within a day, Nilith had built herself a new court and galvanised it into turning the city around. I would have been impressed if it hadn't exhausted me just watching it from doorways.

Rumours of our feats had spread through the survivors, district by district. Talk of Nilith, at least. The city was afire with tales of the warrior empress. The dead queen. The Code-breaker. The saviour of Araxes. I was glad. Immensely so. I could have felt spurned and demanded my glory, but I now knew my worth. I didn't need hushed whispers and low bows, and gladly left that to Nilith and Heles. Even the looks I received from some of the survivors, those who had seen me on the battlefield, were too much for a thief like me. I have always belonged in the shadows, wearing a hood rather than a medal.

So it was that I had taken to hiding in the Cloud Court, away from gossip of ghosts breaking through stone knights, and the man who had finally killed Danib Ironjaw.

I stared at the turquoise throne with my head cocked, eyeing how it changed colour depending where the sun fell. I was surprised it had survived the crash of the *Vengeance*, still lying in pieces up against the walls of the court.

I reached out a finger and ran it across the glassy stone, feeling nothing and making no sound. The dust spiralled behind my touch, wafting in the soft breezes coming through the broken ceiling.

It took me another hour to lift a foot onto its pedestal and climb its short steps. It was firm, but numb to my vapours. I rested my backside against its cold surface and sat back with my arms stretched, looking out over the broken marble and shattered columns.

'Terrible view,' I said aloud. 'Wouldn't you agree?'

Two days, and I had yet to place Pointy down, never mind let go of him. Hope still clung on within me. I lifted up the tortured blade as I spoke, staring into its warped metal and longing for an answer. None came, and once again the angst welled up inside me, with no way of getting it out besides roaring at the skies. I had tried that. It wasn't effective.

I shuffled around, trying to find a good position, but it was useless.

'Good luck, Nilith. Your arse is going to need it,' I sighed. I pushed myself up, catching the stone with the broken sword as I left the throne. Even as a shard, the blade still managed to score a scratch in the turquoise. I half-turned to leave promptly, but caught myself as I saw the glyphs of names sprawling along stone. An idea blossomed.

I reached out with the blade again, and made another cut, and another, etching simple runes into the stone. Krass by name, crass by nature, perhaps, but how often do you get to carve your name into a throne? Especially one as glorious and spectacularly uncomfortable as this one.

The door thudded as it opened, spilling sunlight through the shadows, and I saw Heles framed in its arch. She had my phantom dog by her side, rescued from the Cathedral On Its Head before it was destroyed. I stood up, brushing down my smock of grey and gold.

'Empress wants to see you. It's time to decide what to do with the ghosts.' Heles looked suspicious as I approached, eying the blade in my hand. 'What have you been doing?' she asked.

'Nothing,' I said, running my vapours over the phantom's blue ears.

'Regretting your decision already, Caltro?'

'Like I said. It's not my throne, *Chamberlain.*'

'Correct. It's not.'

I pushed past her, moving to the grand windows that had been barred and barricaded against errant flying machines.

Little had changed since I last looked. Even from high up in the Cloudpiercer, I could feel the city longing to relax. To let go. *As do I.*

'Tell her I'll be right along, Heles.'

'As you wish, *Majesty.*'

Heles stalked off, the sharp folds of her Chamber uniform snapping as she walked. I narrowed my eyes, and clutched my half-coin around my neck.

———————◆———————

DEATH WAS A DEPLORABLE SENSATION. No heart beat within her chest. No breath, wheezing in and out. No heat on her skin from the sunlight that bathed her. No skin to speak of at all.

The slatherghast's poison had finally claimed her.

The wind toyed with her vapours as Nilith stared out over Araxes, her vision blurring at the edges. The city's noises were few and dull. Just the occasional call of a rook or the racing flutter of a flock of doves. Nilith had never heard Araxes so quiet, even at night. She shivered in the cold. *Always cold.* Part of her longed for the baking heat of the Duneplains on her back one last time.

The falcon by her side cleared his throat. 'They're here.'

Nilith bowed her head, pressing it to the cold stone.

'I suppose I can't put it off any longer, can I?'

'I don't think you can,' Bezel replied. 'And to be honest, I wish you wouldn't. I'm not the only ghost awaiting your judgement.'

Nilith straightened, looking out over the city's spires. 'You killed my daughter, Bezel. By all rights I should have you kept in a box for another hundred years as punishment.'

'You aren't the type of—'

'Aren't I?' Nilith felt her glowing eyes flash bright as she stared down at the falcon. A fierce moment passed between them. 'However, she said, voice sharp but level. 'We are here now, and whatever steps were taken to get here were taken exactly as they should have been. I would not change the past to look over a different future now. As much as the mother in me screams to throttle you, I will give you your freedom as I promised, Bezel. Your death. If you still want it?'

From under her turquoise robes, she produced the slender silver bell. Its etched feathers caught the afternoon sun. The falcon fluttered his wings. He lowered his head to the stone and closed his eyes.

'I will never forget your kindness.'

Nilith rested a hand on his feathers. 'Nor I yours, Bezel.'

The falcon shrugged his bony shoulders and clacked his beak. 'Who knows? Why be so fucking hasty? The afterlife isn't going anywhere, thanks to you. Maybe I'll give those dead gods a chance to stock up on wine and whores before I arrive.'

Nilith grinned.

'Empress,' said a voice. Heles stood behind them.

'No rest for the dead,' Nilith whispered before sweeping from the balcony and into the shadow of her chambers. Bezel followed, swooping down from the railing onto a nearby set of antelope horns.

'Chamberlain. Have the banks surrendered their half-coins yet?' Nilith enquired.

'Most. Not all. I have scrutinisers seeing to the rest of them. Flimzi seems to think the battle didn't happen.'

'Fool. Explain it to him again, would you?' Nilith moved about the copse of tables she'd spread her maps over. She was momentarily mesmerised by the scrawls of ink.

'Everything all right, Nilith?' asked Heles.

The empress took some time to nod. 'There is so much to do...' she muttered.

'You should know better than anyone that saving an empire isn't supposed to be easy,' Heles answered, flicking a crumb from a nearby scroll.

Nilith had to smile at that. 'I should, shouldn't I?' she said, unclenching her fists. 'Where's Caltro? I want to talk about his ceremony. It's time the citizens of this city knew who saved them.'

Heles waved a hand at the ceiling, in the general direction of the Cloud Court. 'Said he'd be along shortly.'

'Not good enough. I haven't the time to be waiting on that locksmith.' In no time at all, Nilith swept from the room, vapours and silks trailing. The scimitar at her hip jangled in its ivory scabbard. Bezel flapped alongside them.

They ascended to the chambers beneath the Cloud Court, and up again to the mighty golden door of the hall itself. With a creak, the doors surrendered to Nilith's push, and they entered the sunlit wreckage of the hall. The shafts fell across piles of rubble and the burnt shell of Hirana's flying machine. The turquoise throne glowed with its own light, sea-green under sun, deep sapphire in shadow.

'Where is he? Caltro!' Nilith called to the silent hall. Only the wind replied, murmuring across the jagged glass of the smashed skylights. The falcon flitted between the remaining columns, looking for the ghost.

'Where is that damn locksmith?' she asked of Heles, but the scrutiniser had no answer, merely shrugging.

'No sign of him!'

They poked around the rubble, but no glow presented itself. Nilith checked behind the throne with an irritated growl, and it was then she noticed the scrap of papyrus lying on the seat of the throne, and the fresh powder of turquoise glass at its feet. There above it, the names,

'Caltro Basalt' and, 'Absia' had been carved in the stone in Krass runes. Like it or not, the smile began to spread across her face.

Nilith snatched up the papyrus, ripping its fold open. More runes awaited her.

We make our own luck.

Nilith held the note in her hand, and with some concentration, crumpled it in a blue fist. Heles came closer, concerned.

'What is it? What has he done?'

'Nothing, Heles. Caltro has simply done what he's wanted to all along. He's gone home.'

'But what about the—'

'It'll be fine,' Nilith interrupted. She threw the papyrus to the ground and put her heel upon it. When she raised her head, the smile had grown into a grin. 'He'll be just fine.'

———————◆———————

A MOONLESS NIGHT AND EMPTY streets made the going easy, swift. The phantom by my side was true to his name, and silent. I saw soldiers at most junctures, but they were more interested in helping with the corpse piles than to notice me flitting though the dark alleys. Though the robe covered most of me, I tensed to keep my glow to a faint shine. I could do nothing about the whining from inside the big sack I carried, but I had no choice in that matter. The city was wary of any ghost that skulked about, and rightly so.

The shard of Pointy sat at my side. Invincible, I'd taken to calling him. It had a more fitting ring for a god-killing blade, dead or not.

As I crept between the bluffs of mighty warehouses and grain silos,

I saw fallen bodies here and there between the gutters. Though I had seen more than enough in my time in Araxes, I couldn't help but stare at their twisted postures and gaunt faces.

I hunkered down behind a barrel as a set of Consortium soldiers came tramping past. As I waited there, listening to the rhythm of their boots, I put my hand on something soft. I recoiled to find a corpse beside me, grinning with a dislodged jaw. I wrinkled my lip, and as I pulled away, its foggy eyes swivelled in their shallow sockets to look at me. The contents of my sack began to growl.

'I should have known I hadn't seen the last of you,' I said with a sigh.

The corpse had no words for me. I stood and scurried on, darting down another side street towards the docks. Always towards the docks. It had taken me several hours to get this far, and I was only just glimpsing the black blanket of the sea between the canyon streets.

Every corpse in my path began to turn their head or dead gaze to face me as I passed them. The fresher ones, those still with lips the rats hadn't got to yet, whispered at me.

'Caltro.'

'Thank you,' one called, its eyes glowing green for the briefest of moments. 'You did as we asked.'

A black cat, half its skin missing and bearing grey ribs on one side, scampered across my path. 'You saved us,' it hissed.

'And you better remember it,' I whispered back, though I wondered how many puppet strings they had pulled besides my own. How much manoeuvring had they done behind the scenes of this catastrophic play?

I ran faster still. I longed to put this city, its gods, and its corpses behind me. Dead though I was, I was Krass, and that was where I belonged. A land I knew and trusted. I had given the dead gods what they wanted; they could furnish me with peace and quiet from now on.

Yet still the eyes watched me. Still the whispers of gratitude and congratulations followed me. As I passed piles of corpses, whole choruses would wheeze my name. It was intolerable, until, as I broke out into the boardwalk, the corpses disappeared and the voices faded.

A ship lingered three piers away, three-masted and square of sail. Whale-oil lamps burnt orange through its portholes. A short queue of sailors and passengers wound around the jetty and its bollards, all eager to escape the city. I made my way to the back of it, and met the wary stares of the living waiting before me. One ghost stood among them, and that was all.

'Psst,' I called to the man in front of me, a swarthy man lacking in teeth and hair. It looked as though he had taken twice the weathering any sailor ought to have received.

'What?' He snuffled at me, wiping his grimy nose. He was immediately transfixed by the phantom.

'Where's this ship going?'

'Harras, in the Scatter.'

I smiled warmly at him. As warmly as any ghost can. 'I have a few more bags, just around the corner in my carriage. I'll give you a silver if you can help me aboard.'

The sailor thought about it for a moment. 'Four.'

'Two.' I stuck out my hand, and he sneered.

'Lead the way, then,' he said, spitting to the gutter. 'But I better not lose my place.'

'We'll be quick.' I beckoned him up the street, empty but for one lantern shining from a window. He grumbled all the way around the corner, where he soon found my hand around his throat. It was a gamble; with the Code and Tenets broken, my haunting had been in question.

I could have laughed aloud as his flesh give way before me.

When I re-joined the line, my borrowed body sweating from the duel going on within us, I flashed a gap-toothed smile at the man in front, adjusted the sack on my back, and patted the phantom between his cold ears.

For half an hour, the line shuffled forwards until it was my turn at the foot of the gangplank.

'Sailor?' asked a gruff man, perched behind a makeshift desk. He was already writing the answer down with his reed.

'No. Passenger,' I said, halting him. 'And I want a private room, if there's one left.'

The man looked me up and down, then at the glowing dog at my side. 'I—'

The pouch of silver I'd lifted from a serek's chambers convinced him, and he told me my room number in a mumble.

Fighting the old and arthritic body up the gangplank, I found my room with ease, barging the door open with my backside and settling my sack on the bed. With stiff fingers, I unfastened it, and let the phantom push its head from his temporary lodgings.

'Sorry about that, old chap. Don't think they'd quite understand you at the moment.'

The ghost hound whined at me, flicking his ears back and forth. I ruffled their faint edges for good measure, and got to my feet. As I moved to peek out the porthole, I felt a queasy rumble in my stomach. I knew the culprit of that sensation well enough. *Salt-meat stew.*

Deciding to find a place to ditch the man overboard, I went to the door. The phantom moved to follow, but I made him stay by patting him on the nose. He growled at me, but lay down.

Outside in the ship's sweaty corridors, I tried to find my bearings again, remembering which way I'd come amidships. I chose a direction, and I'd barely taken two steps before a door swung open before me, and an old, pale woman in fur-trimmed boots and a blue velvet coat bustled out of it.

'Out of my way, ugly peasant! How dare you lurk outside my door. Away with you!' she ordered me, her shrill voice and Skol accent piercing my borrowed ears.

I could have laughed right in her wrinkled face. Of all the ships leaving Araxes on this chosen evening, my old nemesis had chosen the same one.

I pulled myself aside before her lanky guard could push me out of the way, and moved on. I heard her complaints as she worked her way down the corridor away from me.

'…and I am never coming to this accursed city again! Oh! The serek's face when I opened the chest. I shall never forget the day. And with this battle… what a frightful, horrid place! I long to see the black beaches of Skol…'

I paused in the shadows along from her door, waiting for her voice to fade. I bit my lip with a snaggletooth, pondering, when my stomach gurgled again. As I brought my lockpicks from where I'd stashed them in the sailor's grimy pockets, a smile lit my face.

It was only fitting, I thought, as I swiftly broke the lock of her door, that she should arrive home as she had arrived in Araxes.

I was already shuffling my trews down before I closed the door.

THE END

Thank you for reading and treading the sands and flagstones of the
Far Reaches. Caltro and Nilith may appear in another story one day,
maybe even in another world, but for now their epic tale is done.
I hope you enjoyed it.

For all of my books, fantasy worlds, social media,
Patreon and Discord, wander over to:

www.linktr.ee/bengalley

MORE FANTASY FROM
BEN GALLEY

THE EMANESKA SERIES
The Written
Pale Kings
Dead Stars - Part One
Dead Stars - Part Two
The Written Graphic Novel

SCALUSSEN CHRONICLES
The Forever King
Heavy Lies The Crown
To Kill A God

TALES OF EMANESKA
The Iron Keys
No Fairytale

THE SCARLET STAR TRILOGY
Bloodrush
Bloodmoon
Bloodfeud

STANDALONES
The Heart of Stone
Shards

ANTHOLOGIES FEATURED IN
Lost Lore
Heroes Wanted
Lone Wolf
Inferno! 5
The Art of War Anthology

ABOUT THE AUTHOR

Ben Galley is a British author of dark and epic fantasy books who currently loiters in Vancouver, Canada. Since publishing his debut Emaneska Series, Ben has released the award-winning weird western Scarlet Star Trilogy, *The Heart of Stone*, the critically-acclaimed Chasing Graves Trilogy, and the Scalussen Chronicles.

When he isn't conjuring up strange new stories or arguing the finer points of magic systems and dragon anatomy, Ben explores the Canadian wilds, sips Scotch single malts, and snowboards very, very badly. One day he hopes to haunt an epic treehouse in the mountains.

SUGGESTED LISTENING

Below you'll find a Spotify playlist that is a tribute to the various songs that inspired, fuelled, and otherwise invigorated me during the writing of the *Chasing Graves Trilogy*. I hope you enjoy it.

Matter
ARCANE ROOTS

Drift
HANDS LIKE HOUSES

In Cold Blood
ALT-J

Silence
OUR LAST NIGHT

Everlong
FOO FIGHTERS

Monstrous Things
PICTURESQUE

Cold Cold Cold
CAGE THE ELEPHANT

Back To Me
OF MICE & MEN

Pardon Me
INCUBUS

A Light In A Darkened World
KILLSWITCH ENGAGE

Lost On You – Elk Road Remix
LP, ELK ROAD

That's Just Life
MEMPHIS MAY FIRE

Saturnz Barz (feat. Popcaan)
GORILLAS, POPCAAN

Cycling Trivialities
JOSÉ GONZÁLEZ

Broken People
LOGIC, RAG'N'BONE MAN

Set Free
KATIE GRAY

King of Wishful Thinking
GO WEST

Hurt
JOHNNY CASH

Ocean View
ONE DAY AS A LION

Chalkboard
JÓHANN JÓHANNSSON

Ingram Content Group UK Ltd.
Milton Keynes UK
UKHW012107170723
425314UK00018B/241/J